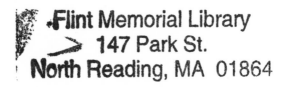

The BLACK KIDS

The

BLACK KIDS

CHRISTINA
HAMMONDS
REED

SIMON & SCHUSTER BFYR

NEW YORK   LONDON   TORONTO   SYDNEY   NEW DELHI

SIMON & SCHUSTER BFYR

An imprint of Simon & Schuster Children's Publishing Division
1230 Avenue of the Americas, New York, New York 10020

For information about special discounts for bulk purchases, please contact Simon & Schuster
Special Sales at 1-866-506-1949 or business@simonandschuster.com.
The Simon & Schuster Speakers Bureau can bring authors to your live event. For more
information or to book an event, contact the Simon & Schuster Speakers Bureau at
1-866-248-3049 or visit our website at www.simonspeakers.com.
Book design by Lucy Ruth Cummins
The text for this book was set in Adobe Garamond Pro.
Manufactured in the United States of America
First Edition
2 4 6 8 10 9 7 5 3 1
Library of Congress Cataloging-in-Publication Data
Names: Hammonds Reed, Christina, author.
Title: The black kids / Christina Hammonds Reed.
Description: First edition. | New York : Simon & Schuster Books for Young Readers, [2020] |
Audience: Ages 14 up. | Audience: Grades 10–12. |
Summary: With the Rodney King riots closing in on high school senior Ashley and her family,
the privileged bubble she has enjoyed, protecting her from the difficult realities most black people
face, begins to crumble.
Identifiers: LCCN 2019035025 (print) | LCCN 2019035026 (eBook) |
ISBN 9781534462724 (hardcover) | ISBN 9781534462748 (eBook)
Subjects: CYAC: Race relations—Fiction. | African Americans—Fiction. | Rodney King Riots,
Los Angeles, Calif., 1992—Fiction. | Family life—California—Los Angeles—Fiction. |
High schools—Fiction. | Schools—Fiction. | Los Angeles (Calif.)—
History—20th century—Fiction.
Classification: LCC PZ7.1.R4277 Bl 2020 (print) | LCC PZ7.1.R4277 (eBook) | DDC [Fic]—dc23
LC record available at https://lccn.loc.gov/2019035025
LC eBook record available at https://lccn.loc.gov/2019035026

IN LOVING
MEMORY OF
HOVER
AND
ISABELLE
AND
WILLIAM
AND
ALBERTA

BEFORE

FIRST, A MEMORY: The hillside set ablaze, the fire playing a game of hopscotch across the canyon. The air smelled like a campfire, and the sky was a palette of smudged eye shadow. A fireman, lethargic and ruddy, walked from door to door with a practiced calm, warning people there was a chance they'd have to evacuate.

"You live here?" I heard him say to my father when he opened the door.

"Yes," my father said.

"You're the owner?" he said.

"I do believe that's what my deed says," my father said.

The mailman had said the same thing when we first moved in, and my father had responded in the exact same way, but the mailman's response was much more ebullient.

"Yes! Brotherman! Moving *on up*!"

"Make sure you have a bag ready to go," the fireman said. "Just in case."

He scratched his bulbous nose and peered into our house. Then, having satisfied whatever curiosity he had, he turned and made his way down the tile steps.

My father followed after him. He walked to the side of the house where the hose was coiled snakelike, picked it up, and, with it in tow, headed toward the front of the house. There, he pressed the metal trigger. The force of the water startled him, but only a little. He hosed down our roof, spraying the shingles over and over again, so that the water dripped down like rain. My mother and I stood beside him, waiting. The neighborhood dogs barked in a chorus.

The Parker family was the first to leave the canyon, several hours after the fires began. Tim and Todd Parker, then fourteen and sixteen and already dead behind the eyes, had blown up our mailbox that first week after we moved in. Though my parents couldn't prove it, we knew. Tim and Todd followed their parents out of the house, wearing backpacks and holding a photo album and a trophy each. Their mother held what I'm pretty certain was an urn, which seemed silly to me back then, because if whoever was in there was already ash, what more could happen to them, really? This was before my grandma Opal died, before I realized the last pieces you carried of a person, no matter how small, could feel so big. Tim and Todd's father carried several paintings under his arm. Reproductions or originals, it was difficult to tell. Their black dog, Rocky, ran through Tim and Todd's legs. Mr. Parker looked over at my father and waved. I guess the possibility of losing everything had him feeling friendlier than usual.

One by one, over the course of the next two days, the rest of our neighbors packed up their suitcases and piled into their station wagons.

As the fires burned, a menagerie of animals began to trickle down the hillside. First the rabbits and squirrels, and then the coyotes began to wander down the streets, wide-eyed and emaciated. I even saw a deer.

At five years old, I found wonder in the burning, all the animals, the ash and the exodus. Two days after the fireman came by, with the air growing ever more apocalyptic, I stood next to my father, looked up, and placed my hands on my hips, surveying our prospects for survival.

"Maybe we should leave now, Daddy," I said.

"Go back inside; everything's going to be fine."

He kept muttering it to himself, as though he could save our pretty wooden house through the sheer force of repetition.

The joke goes that in Los Angeles we have four seasons—fire, flood, earthquake, and drought.

Fire season. It's part of the very nature of Los Angeles itself.

CHAPTER 1

ON THE NEWS, they keep playing the video. The cops are striking the black man with their boots and batons across the soft of his body and the hard of his skull, until I guess they felt like they'd truly broken him, and, sure enough, they had. Four of the cops who beat him are on trial right now, a trial that some say is a battle for the very soul of the city, or even the country itself. It's something I should give a shit about, but I don't—not now.

Right now, birds chirp, palm trees sway, and it's the kinda Friday where the city seems intent on being a postcard of itself. Marky Mark and the Funky Bunch are on the radio singing "Good Vibrations," and it's no Beach Boys, but it'll do. Heather and I do the running man and hump the air to the beat; this even though she's told us, in no uncertain terms, that this song is lame, and the rest of us have terrible taste in music. We're several weeks away from being done with high school, and when I think about it too hard, it terrifies me. So right now I'm trying really hard not to care about anything at all.

After we exhaust ourselves, Heather and I collapse on the old pool chairs with their broken slats. The plastic creates geometry on my skin. Heather is pudgy and sometimes doesn't shave her pits. I can see the dark of her hair in patches in the center of her pasty outstretched arms. How she manages to stay that pale given how long and how often we bake ourselves, I don't know. It's a spectacular feat of whiteness. Her lime-green toenail polish is chipped so that each nail vaguely resembles a state in the Midwest. Courtney's pool vaguely resembles a kidney.

Across from us, Kimberly and Courtney stretch their bodies out across two fat plastic donuts that are pink and tacky and rainbow sprinkled. They float into each other's orbits and back out again. Every so often they splash water at each other and shriek, "Omigod, stop it!"

Heather yells, "Jesus, get a room already."

Courtney laughs and squeezes Kimberly's boob like it's a horn.

They've ditched class two times a week for the last month. I don't ditch nearly as often as my friends do. But my parents and I are supposed to meet my crazy sister's new husband tonight, and it's gonna be a doozy of an evening, so it kinda felt like I owed it to my sanity to not be at school today.

These are the places we go—the mall, somebody's pool, or our favorite, the beach. Our parents hate Venice because it's dirty and there are too many homeless people, tourists, and boom boxes blasting, which means we love it. We flop across our boogie boards and stare into the horizon. Occasionally, a wave comes and we'll half-heartedly ride it into the sand, our knees scraping against the grain. Then we stand, recover our bikinis from our butt cheeks, and charge back into the water like Valkyries. Afterward, we eat at this place the size of my closet, where even the walls are greasy. The interior is bloodred and peeling, and a fat Italian caricature in neon announces, "PIZZA!" Just in case you couldn't tell. The previous owner, Georgi, was a skinny Italian with a villainous mustache who gave us free cookies; now the owner is a skinny Korean named Kim who does not.

After we eat, we watch the men with muscles like boulders under their skin, all of them so glazed and brown that the black men don't look so different from the white men and everything in between. Most of them lift barbells, but some of them lift and balance on top of each other, a grunting tangle of bodies in short shorts and muscle tees. Last weekend, one of the men grabbed Kimberly and lifted her up to the sky like an offering.

Afterward he tried to convince us to come back to his place, like we would be dumb enough to go just because he was blond and tan and could balance like a circus elephant.

"I've got alcohol," he said.

"Tempting, but no," Heather said.

"I wasn't talking to you anyway," he said.

"Ew, we're only seventeen," Courtney yelled when he grabbed at her.

"Then maybe you shouldn't walk around looking like that," he snapped back.

Heather kneed him in the nuts; then we took off running down the boardwalk.

"Hey, you little sluts!"

Tourists with sunscreened noses took pictures of us running, our heads thrown back with laughter. But when we were far enough away, we crossed our arms in front of our chests, and Courtney bought a muscle tee with a kitten in a bikini that said "Venice, CA" from a nearby vendor. She threw it over herself like a security blanket.

That's why we decided to go to Courtney's house today. Here, we can wear our string bikinis like highlighters, bright neon signs that introduce us as women. It's better that there's nobody around to introduce us to.

Courtney gets out of the pool and walks over to where Heather and I lie on the deck chairs. She prances like the show pony she is across the hot concrete and squishes her butt next to mine until we're both on the chair together. We're so close I can feel her heartbeat. The hairs on her body are fine and blond; she shimmers a bit.

Courtney threads her arm through mine. The water from her body feels good against my skin.

"Would you rather . . . make out with Mr. Holmes, or with Steve Ruggles?" Kimberly's stomach is already bright red. She burns easily, and once, after we went to Disneyland, she spent the whole week shedding herself like a snake.

"Both. At the same time," Heather deadpans.

Steve Ruggles is built like a Twinkie, round and a little jaundiced. He sucks at intervals along the length of his arms, giving himself little purple bruises like lipstick smears. He has always been nice to me, but he's also undeniably strange, a boy who kisses himself while we learn about the Battle of Gettysburg. Mr. Holmes is our AP physics teacher, and half his face is cut into jagged ridges like the cliffs along the ocean. The rumor is he was in a fire as a baby. Somebody else said it was a laboratory explosion. Both seem like superhero origin stories, and Mr. Holmes does kinda carry himself like somebody with a secret life. Although maybe that's just because he's different, and sometimes being different means hiding pieces of yourself away so other people's mean can't find them. Occasionally in class, I used to close one eye and see one half of him, then close the other to try to see the other half, like when you look at one of those charts at the eye doctor's. When I did that for long enough, both the scars and the good started to fade, so his face was a soft, mostly kind blur. Anyway, I think he caught me once, and so now I keep both eyes open wider than usual around him.

"Leave them alone," I say.

"I bet Mr. Holmes would be a good lay. Ugly guys try harder," Kimberly says. Kimberly acts like she knows everything about everything, even sex, which she's never had.

"So do you think I should do the entire thing or, like, leave a strip?" she says. The moles down the side of her sunburned body look like chocolate chips in strawberry ice cream.

"Leave your muff alone," Heather says.

Kimberly is getting her hoo-ha waxed for prom next week, and you'd think she was going in for open-heart surgery.

"I think a strip looks good," she says.

"Definitely." Courtney agrees with everything Kimberly says. Their moms are best friends, and they were born two weeks apart. They're more like sisters than friends. Kimberly's first name is actually Courtney, too, 'cause their moms wanted their daughters to be twinsies. For a while, we called them Courtney One and

Courtney Two, until Courtney Two had a growth spurt in sixth grade and everybody started calling her Big Courtney. That's when she started going by her middle name. Kimberly is superskinny, tall, and blond; Courtney is skinny-ish, short, and blond. Both have fake noses, and I've known them since the first day of school when we were five and Kimberly (then Courtney Two) still wet the bed.

Growing older with other people means stretching and growing and shrinking in all the right or wrong places so that sometimes you look at your friend's face and it's like a fun-house mirror reflection of what it used to be. Like, I used to have buckteeth that pushed their way into the world well before the rest of me, and a big-ass bobblehead on a superskinny body. I think I've mostly grown into myself now—though I do worry that my head might still be a tad big. That's the stuff you can see, though. It's easier to see those changes in yourself than what happens on the inside. Easier to see that stuff in other people, too.

For instance, now Courtney and Kimberly aren't into much other than themselves and boys, but Courtney used to be big into bugs. She used to collect roly-polies and ladybugs and sometimes these nasty-looking beetles. And then when we were in junior high, she got big into lepidopterology, which is all about butterflies and moths and stuff. It's a bit morbid, if you ask me, taking beautiful things and pinning them down to be admired. But that's kinda like what happens to some girls between junior high and high school, when being pretty gets in the way of being a full person.

I miss what we used to talk about then, when we'd have sleepovers, our sleeping bags like cocoons, and play Light as a

Feather, Stiff as a Board and lift each other up higher and higher still with the tips of our fingers. I used to yammer endlessly about horses, even in junior high when my friends were more into the idea of riding boys. As far as I was concerned, Jason R. was all right, but he couldn't cleanly jump a triple bar. And as far as I knew, he didn't nuzzle you as though you were the only person in the world when you fed him baby carrots. And when Jason was drenched in sweat, it definitely didn't look majestic, even if Courtney and all the rest of the eighth-grade girls begged to differ. Eventually, I took a jump too fast and fell and broke my clavicle right before graduating from eighth grade. I stopped riding then, which I think my parents secretly didn't mind too much, 'cause they were paying a buttload for lessons. I was afraid that the next time I fell, I'd break my neck. I don't remember being afraid much before that. Anyway, Jason R. tried to make out with me at a party last year, but he's not anywhere near as cute as he was in eighth grade and he smells like spit, so I politely declined.

The other day, I leaned in to Courtney and said, "Remember your butterfly collection?" She scrunched up her new nose, frowned, and said, "That was so lame. Why would you even bring that up?" As if instead of whispering about butterflies I'd told the whole school how she'd wet her sleeping bag at my house that one time in junior high.

We're cheerleaders, and that makes some people think we're stupid, but we're not. Our bodies are power—like what I feel in my thighs when I bend and throw my full weight into a back tuck, that rush of blood to my head as for a few moments I feel weightless, knees tucked into my chest, skirt flying, before gravity catches up to me. Right there, in a tumbling pass, is the light and heavy of being a girl all at once.

"'Woman is the nigger of the world,'" Heather declared one day at lunch while Kimberly and Courtney tried on each other's lip gloss. It was around the time she stopped shaving her pits. At first I thought maybe I'd heard her wrong. But I know what that word feels like in my ears, the way my heart beats faster when I hear it. Even so, I tried to rationalize it. "I'm a Jewess and you're a Negress," she used to say as a joke. For a little while in ninth grade she even called us the two "Esses." I think it was her way of trying to find the black humor in the black numbers tattooed up her *bubbe*'s forearm, the black humor in my black skin.

Courtney sighed and said, "Don't say that word with Ashley sitting right here."

"It's cool. I get what she means," I said. I'm always saying things are cool when maybe they aren't. Sometimes I have so much to say that I can't say anything at all.

The doorbell rings and it's the boys. Things were easier before them. The first boy came in sixth grade. Travis Wilson and Courtney walked around school hand in hand and even kissed at the spring formal before they broke up that summer, when she decided he was taking up too much of her time. The second boy came the next fall. Brandon Sanders wasn't so bright, but he was pretty, and Kimberly liked having him around because she was going through her awkward phase when everybody called her Big Courtney. She needed to feel pretty. To feel wanted. I think that's why she let him touch her boobs, and down below, too, which he then told the whole school about so that the boys ran around saying "Sniff my fingers" as a joke for a month straight. We became known as the "fast" girls, which meant that the other girls talked shit about us, but also wanted to be us. The third boy came for Heather. Charlie Thomas played in a band in his garage, and Heather would sit around and listen to them practice. Sometimes she would drag us along, too. Her relationship with Charlie ended when she caught him with the lead singer, Keith, and we probably should've seen that coming. Soon enough we were under attack, and there were more boys and more boys still. Boys with muscles. Boys with money. Funny boys. Skinny boys. Boys who were men and should've known better. Boys who told me how cool I was and asked if they should buy my friends red roses or pink roses or no roses at all. Boys at school dances who brushed up against my fingertips and thighs and told me how pretty I was before running off to dark corners with my blond friends.

Our boys are drunk.

Michael immediately walks over to the boom box and turns off our good vibrations. In the front yard, you can hear the hum of Courtney's gardener pushing a leaf blower across the lawn.

"This song is shit, you guys," he says, fumbling with the radio dial.

Michael is Kimberly's douche boyfriend. He's got these big, beautiful, sleepy eyes that always look like they're on the verge of winking at you. But it's not that you're in on any joke, it's that you *are* the joke. Like, if we were one of those third-grade coat hanger Styrofoam solar-system dioramas, he thinks he's the sun and Kimberly is the Earth, even though Earth isn't all that important unless you're on it. He's joined by Trevor, because Michael and Trevor are best friends who go everywhere together. Trevor is tall, with floppy hair that he lets fall into his face before he pushes it back. Michael is shorter, with tightly curled hair and muscles like a pit bull. He's on the wrestling team, but nobody much cares about the wrestlers. Michael is handsome because his face comes together in a way that people think is interesting, which is why people care about him even though his sport is full of boys in leotards bending each other into pretzels and shoving their skindogs in each other's faces.

Kimberly and Michael have been together since the end of ninth grade, before he shot up in height, so that for a while she was very tall and he was very short, but they were both beautiful, so nobody gave 'em too much shit. Kimberly has already picked out their children's names—Christy, Linda, and Naomi, after the models. And if they pop out a boy, his name will be Georgi, after the Italian who gave us free cookies. I think Kimberly mostly likes Michael because he's from New York and doesn't give a fuck, and she spends her summers there with her father. He wooed her and all the rest of us with those gruff vowels that drag out around corners and stop abruptly against consonants. Later, we found out that his real accent isn't nearly that thick and that he'd stolen those vowels from the outer boroughs. But by then it didn't matter; Kimberly was hooked. Heather says it's classic daddy issues.

We know Michael and Trevor about as well as you can know boys our age, by which I mean we laugh at their jokes and yell *ugh* when they annoy us and don't rat them out when they do truly stupid shit, like light branches on fire and set them in the middle of the road just to see how passing cars respond. Honestly, sometimes being friends with boys our age is exhausting. It feels like it's a lot of listening to a bunch of jibber jabber about everything they like and why what we like is silly. Just because sometimes our music comes wrapped in glitter doesn't mean it's empty.

Michael finally decides on Power 106. He raises his hands in the air and they become weapons, his thumb and index fingers cocked like two guns.

He drunkenly swaggers through the lyrics he doesn't know. Like I said, Michael grew up partially in New York, so he likes to pretend he's more street savvy than the rest of us, even though he grew up in Midtown and lives in Brentwood.

Trevor joins in at the chorus, "*Here is something you can't understand—how I could just kill a man! Here is something you can't understand—how I could just kill a man!*"

They yell a few more verses and then run and cannonball into the pool.

Kimberly giggles at her boyfriend, and Courtney yells, "What the fuck?" because now she's wet again.

A plane flies overhead. Trevor traces its path through the sky with his finger.

"God, I can't get wait to get out of this shithole," Trevor says. "Move somewhere with a little fucking culture."

He just got his acceptance letter from NYU three days ago, and all of a sudden now everything about Los Angeles and California sucks. He also went to India with his parents last summer and now he's oh so deep and a vegetarian. Kimberly and Michael make out across from me, which is awkward enough, but even more so after what happened last week. Normally I'd be talking, too, but the deeper she thrusts her tongue into his mouth, the more I feel like a dog with a mouthful of peanut butter.

"LA has plenty of culture," Heather says.

"Yeah? Like what?"

"I mean, maybe if you actually ventured out of the Westside . . ."

"Dude, just 'cause you've gone to a taco stand or two doesn't mean you know shit, either."

Trevor and Heather are always fighting, mostly because both can be equally insufferable. They both act like they're the only ones who watch CNN or read the newspaper and the rest of us know nothing about life just because we can't quote Sonic Youth deep cuts. Heather says the rest of us are book smart but not life smart, that we're sheltered from life's realities. But, like, I'm black. I'm not that sheltered.

"You guys want to go somewhere else?" Michael says. On his left ear are three freckles and a sunburn that gets worse by the minute.

"Venice?"

"Mars."

"The Beverly Center?"

"God, you guys are so lame sometimes."

"Shut up and shave your pits."

"Nobody's ever home at the house down the street from mine. Some Saudi prince bought it and they're doing major construction on it. They're, like, never there. And they've got a bitchin' pool."

"Why do we need to go to another pool when we're already at a pool?"

"'Cause it has a slide and a cave and shit?"

Michael lives several blocks over, and so we decide to walk. Days like this, the salt of the ocean sticks in your nostrils and on your skin. Gravel rolls underfoot. There are homes with ivy hedges like forts and homes like wacky sculptures or with windows made up of other tiny windows. Occasionally you'll see a fading home fighting against being demolished for something in Technicolor.

The boys go barefoot, their wet feet leaving sloppy prints across the concrete.

As we walk, a red double-decker tour bus pulls up alongside us and stops in front of one of the houses. The voice inside it bellows, "This is where Tom Hanks lives."

"No, he doesn't!" we say.

Several ruddy-faced tourists stick their cameras out the windows. The dude who actually lives here is an accountant to the stars, according to Courtney. Maybe even to Tom Hanks. So perhaps the tour bus driver isn't that far off after all. Heather flashes them as they pull away.

Trevor drapes his arm around my shoulder. Everyone thinks he looks a little like Jason Priestley, but I think that's being generous. Trevor's my prom date, but I'm not into him like that. Sometimes it's nice just to be near another person, to feel their warmth and the blood coursing through their veins, and to feel the both of you alive.

"Oh shiiiit, love connection." Kimberly makes kissing faces in our direction. Michael looks back at us and rolls his eyes.

"Our kids would be so hot," Trevor says. "Mixed kids are the hottest."

Then he pulls away from me and retches into Tom Hanks's accountant's petunias.

. . .

There's a hole in the construction fence where you can just raise the green tarp and enter. I pause in front of it. "Guys, maybe we shouldn't go in there."

"Are you afraid?" Kimberly says.

Yes. Breaking and entering isn't exactly something someone who looks like me should do all willy-nilly. Or at all. But I don't want to call attention to myself. Not like that.

"No," I say. "It's just that . . ."

"You don't have to come, Ash. Nobody's making you do anything," Kimberly says. She says it all sweet and shit, but we all know it's a challenge.

"Dude, I promise you it's worth it." Michael winks.

Inside, the addition to the house is a skeleton, all bones and no meat, not yet. The dust sticks to our bodies as we walk through wood and nails and concrete slabs, but also beer bottles and cigarette butts. A tractor presides over all these building blocks like a promise. The pool remains untouched, an oasis, as though the owners decided that it—and only it—was perfect, which it is.

A few dead flies float on the water's surface. Trevor bends over to scoop them up with his hand.

Courtney, Heather, Kimberly, and I hold hands and jump. There's the rush of water, the cold, the velocity of our bodies. We sink, and then back up we pop.

"Marco . . . ," Courtney yells.

"Polo . . ." Trevor belly flops in. Just like that, it's on.

We continue our call-and-response across the length of the pool. Courtney finds Heather first, and then Heather finds Kimberly. Kimberly finds Trevor, and Trevor finds Michael, until the only person left to be discovered is me. I've gotten good at being invisible. I swim under the water to the grotto. There, my friends are echoes. Dampened, they sound far away.

Inside, the walls are made of fake rock that's slightly slimy to the touch. There's a plastic opening where a light source should be, but the bulb's broken. Obscured from view, everything in the grotto feels like a secret.

"Marco!" Michael yells. He reaches his hands out and runs his fingertips across my shoulders, my face, my hair.

I don't say anything back. He splashes the water around us in mini waves.

You should know right now that I'm mostly a good person. I think.

I don't talk back to my parents, much. I would help an elderly person across the street, if there were any around. I get mostly As, with a few Bs in the subjects I don't care about. I even listen when Heather drones on about how plastic bags and aerosol hair spray make the planet hotter. All this is to say that I'm a good daughter. A good student. A good friend. A good sister. I don't have a choice.

"When you go out there in the world, you're not just you, Ashley," my grandma Opal said one summer while she braided my hair into four long strands that she embellished with yellow ribbons, "you're all of us, your family, black folks. You have to be better than those white kids around you. It's not fair, but that's the way it is."

"I'm good, Grandma," I said.

And I still am. Mostly.

"I found you . . . ," Michael whispers into the dark.

You should also know that I wasn't entirely honest about Michael. Yes, he's a douche. But he's also really funny in a New Yorky way, smart and a little overconfident, but also somehow self-deprecating and insecure, and he can be really sweet and a great listener, and he's got these beautiful curls like the ribbon on your favorite present.

Beneath the surface, he wraps his legs around mine and I wrap my arms around his shoulders until we're intertwined and our heartbeats pound in tandem. He smells like sunscreen. Water pours in sheets around us like rain. The last time we were alone together it was raining, but instead of some fancy-ass pool, the two of us were in Michael's crappy car. His lips graze my collarbone, and even though he's Kimberly's, together we're electric.

"Polo!" I yell.

Kimberly and Courtney get into an argument over the rules of Marco Polo—Kimberly thinks you can get out of the pool to avoid being tagged, but Courtney insists that's cheating, since we didn't agree upon "fish out of water" rules beforehand. To broker peace, I suggest we stop swimming and start drinking.

We pass the bottle around like a communion cup. I roll the bitter of the beer around on my tongue. I don't like beer, but we're underage, so we can't be choosy.

"What the hell?"

A crew of burly men in neon reflective vests and white hard hats enters, their faces red and sun chapped.

We scramble out of the pool and run through wood and glass and nails and trash. Pain hits my left foot, deep and searing. A piece of glass, part of a shattered beer bottle, is the culprit. The blood trickles in dark red lines down my foot.

I'm not supposed to be here. I'm supposed to be in AP physics right now, reviewing momentum and impulse. Right now, Mr. Holmes would be going into and out of focus.

"I'm calling the cops!" another hard hat yells after us.

"*Fuck tha police, fuck fuck fuck tha police.*" Trevor laughs, then punctuates it with a belch.

Across town, the trial lets out for the day. The members of the jury step out into the open air and lift their faces to the sky, glad that after a long, dark day, there's a bit of sunshine left.

No, I don't care about any of it now. But I will.

CHAPTER 2

THE SQUAD CAR pulls up alongside us as we approach Courtney's house.

"We received a complaint," the officer inside says.

"Hi, Officer . . . Bradford," Kimberly says, looking at his name tag. She puts on that voice she uses to get boys to do what she wants. Unbothered, she twirls her hair into a rope and wrings it out so the water drips onto the concrete. He watches the water as it falls.

The rest of us stand silently behind her.

"Trespassing's a serious offense." The officer isn't too much older than we are. About twenty or so, brown haired with a whisper of a jawline. Officer Bradford squeaks and then overcorrects with too much bass. We're not that close, but we're also not that far from where the Rodney King beating occurred. I wonder if this officer knows those officers. Maybe he works out with them, plays basketball or does community fund-raisers with men who laughed afterward about beating a man until they fractured his skull, damaged his kidneys, and scrambled his brains.

"I think there's been some confusion," Kimberly says. "My dad's totally friends with the owner, and he said it was okay if we used the pool while he's away."

He doesn't buy it, but Kimberly's leaned over the window and all her beauty is spilling into his car. He pulls his eyes away and looks past her at the rest of us. Grandma Opal used to say that white kids wear their youth like body armor. Bradford's eyes land on me, and he squints as though he's found the root of our hooliganism.

"You could call him if you like," Kimberly offers.

Instead, he makes us sit in a row on the curb. Michael's legs are hairy and pale next to mine. The burn above his ears is getting worse. He crosses his eyes and sticks his tongue out at me. A Mercedes speeds around the corner.

"That guy was definitely speeding," Heather says. "That's a real danger to the neighborhood, officer."

Officer Bradford ignores her.

"You've been drinking?" He sniffs the air around us.

"No," we say in chorus.

"You've been smoking?"

"No."

"Aren't you supposed to be in school?" he says.

"We're seniors."

"Truancy is against the law," he says.

It is?

"Driver's licenses and school IDs," he says. "Now."

He reaches for Michael's first.

"I don't have any ID on me." Michael shrugs. He's definitely lying, and Bradford definitely knows it.

Bradford asks Heather, and she gestures at her bikini top. "Doesn't exactly go with the outfit."

"Don't be a smart-ass." Officer Bradford points to me and reaches his hand out. "You."

My black ass is not going to risk lying to a police officer. I pass my ID and license over to him with a slight tremble in my hand. I still had braces in my school ID photo. I used alternate colors on each tooth so my smile was a rainbow.

"Oh fuck," Kimberly whispers.

"I'm calling your school," he says.

And he does.

"Everything would've been fine if Ash wasn't with us," Kimberly says, laughing, as we walk back to her place. "Otherwise we'd totally have gotten away with it.

"'Cause you're black," she says by way of explanation.

Sometimes she says "black" like it's this really funny dirty word.

"Yeah, I got it," I say.

The first time I remember one of my parents being pulled over by a cop, I was eight. The day before, my mother had brought home a brand-new convertible, white with a tan interior, like a pair of buttery leather gloves against your skin. We had a girls' day, just the two of us, and she put the top down so that the wind blew about our faces, and I reached up and out and tried to catch the sky in my fingertips. It felt a little like flying. My fingernails had been painted the pink of the inside of a seashell at the spa, same as my mother's, and the two Vietnamese spa owners had laughed and shouted across the squeaky leather chairs at each other as they pushed back our cuticles. My mother and I were laughing, our hair undone in the wind, when we saw the flashing lights in our rearview mirror. The officer was younger than my mother, with the same wispy blond goatee he must've had in high school. He looked like a bullied kid turned bully, the kind of kid who'd been too big, too poor, or too dumb and was now more than happy to pull over anybody he deemed too anything. In our case, too black.

"Why are you pulling me over?" my mother asked. Her hair looked a little crazy, and she smoothed it down quickly.

"What are you doing here?" he said.

"I live here. Just a few miles up the road." She recited the address.

"What apartment number?"

"None. It's a house. Is all this necessary?" she said.

"There's no plates on your car."

"That's because it's brand-new. I just bought it."

"License and registration, please."

She slowly and carefully reached into the glove compartment for the little folder with her new-car paperwork and insurance, announcing everything she was doing as she did it, and then she passed it over to him along with her license. He made a big show of radio-ing everything in, hand resting on his gun, which hung right by my mother's head. Instead of staring over at her, I kept staring down at my new pink nails, afraid to look up.

When the voice on the other end finally confirmed ownership, he looked disappointed, then quickly discarded us like a Christmas toy come New Year's.

"Have a good day, ma'am," he said.

"You too, officer," my mother said, smiling.

But when she went to turn the key in the ignition, her hands were trembling. She rolled up the windows and pulled the convertible top up so the car grew small and dark and our heads no longer touched the open sky.

"Asshole," she muttered.

When Lucia pulls up to Kimberly's house, I'm already waiting outside. Inside, Kimberly's mom is yelling at Kimberly, so rather than watch a preview of our own inevitable parental verbal ass whuppings, the rest of us wait on her front steps. I wave to Heather and Courtney before I make the perp walk to the car. I've hardly even opened the car door before Lucia starts yelling at me, her pretty mouth an AK-47 shooting Spanish bullets. Her nails and mouth are always red, like a gash or a rose, and she says this reminds her that she's still a woman, even when covered in somebody else's dirt. The words keep coming out in a rat-a-tat-tat until finally she pauses and sighs. "I won't always be around, *mija*."

On the radio, a grown man yells at me to go to some for-profit college: "Aren't you sick of your dead-end life? What you waiting for?"

These are the ads they play on Spanish and Black people stations— bail bonds, cheap auto insurance, ads in which grown men berate your very existence. As we drive, the surfers pack up for the day along the rocks, reedlike and tan, half-naked and black from the waist down in their wet suits, like one of those half-chocolate Pocky snacks Heather brought back from her trip to Japan.

"Change the channel," Lucia says.

Lucia is my nanny, but I don't like to call her that 'cause it feels gross. She's short—shorter than any other adult I know. Like, I was taller than she is by the time I was ten. When she cleans, she can reach only to a little bit above my head, and so sometimes it seems like she spends the day going up and down ladders to reach hidden corners, like some life-size version of the game Chutes and Ladders. Her car is matte gray with missing hubcaps, a Corolla that looks like somebody tore the secrets from its seats.

"I don't know why you always hanging with those girls when you're always telling me how terrible they are," Lucia says.

"I'm not going to tell you anything if all you do is use it against me," I say. ". . . And I never said they were terrible."

"You're lucky your parents weren't home," she says.

She's right, but also not. Once during sophomore year I ditched with Kimberly and Courtney, and the school called. Unluckily for me, on that particular day my dad just happened to be working from home and answered the phone. When I got home, he sat me down and made me calculate, down to the hour, how much they spent on my schooling to show me how much money I wasted when I didn't show up for class.

"We're not your friends' parents. You don't have some magic trust fund. This is still a sacrifice for us. We want more for you," he said.

Anyway, I'm pretty sure that nowadays my parents are far too concerned with work and analyzing what went wrong with their wayward daughter, Jo, to care about what I'm up to.

Jo is my troubled older sister. She dropped out of college and didn't tell them for a whole-ass semester. That's a lot more money than I'm wasting. Her new husband is a musician who's really a construction worker, and she's a musician who's really a secretary, and they live in a shithole somewhere on Fairfax between the Orthodox Jews and the Ethiopians. I think she's angry at all the things my parents have done to her, or haven't.

To be honest, I don't remember her ever not being at least a little bit angry. When she was in high school, she got suspended for a month because she handcuffed herself to the flagpole up front to fight apartheid.

"We got plenty of people here to handcuff yourself to a pole for," my mother said.

"Josephine helped the Resistance, and she wasn't really French," Jo sassed back.

"She didn't have to worry about college applications."

"We got to help our black brothers and sisters abroad," Jo said.

Jo is named after Josephine Baker, who helped the French Resistance during World War II but also danced around Europe naked except for a costume made of strategically placed bunches of bananas. When we were little, my sister used to tell her friends she was named after Jo March from *Little Women*; this was back before she got all into being black. Both Jos are pains in the ass, as far as I can tell.

Two weeks after Jo's twenty-first birthday, she and the construction worker wed in the Beverly Hills Courthouse and didn't even invite any of us. My mother cried for weeks that her firstborn got married in "our own backyard and didn't say a thing! Not even to her mother!"

Tonight's dinner is to be the beginning of a truce.

My mother thinks my sister is on drugs, that her husband is forcing her to be some other her. I don't think that's it, though. Some girls are given away, but some girls run.

I think Jo ran away from my parents and away from me and away from the ocean because she was afraid of drowning. When she first started teaching me to drive, she drove me up the coast to Santa Barbara and back. The car charged forth in fits and starts, German engineering under teenage toes.

I was terrified of driving both of us off a cliff, of careening out of control, but Jo just said, "Steady. Steady."

It was a quiet ride. I started to tell Jo about school, about how Heather and Kimberly were fighting that month, about how my history teacher sometimes called the Civil War the War of Northern Aggression, about how I was thinking of getting bangs but, like, half the school had bangs, so I didn't know. Jo said I needed to concentrate, not talk, so I shut up. When I started to get exhausted from all the concentrating, we pulled off the freeway and parked and walked through the rocks and down to the sand. Two girls in wet suits sat in the back of a station wagon and waxed their surfboards. Fishermen balanced on the rocks and pulled in fish that gleamed. Then they gutted them, and out the red poured.

"Poor fish," Jo said.

"You eat fish," I said.

"Yeah, but I don't kill them for fun."

We watched as the men placed them in big plastic coolers.

"See, they're going to eat them."

Jo started to build a sand castle between us. She poured water from her water bottle into the sand and started moving the earth in scoops toward the sky. When she was done, there was a moat and a bridge and two hills that were a home.

"Sometimes it feels like a piece of my brain is far off in the distance," she said, "and no matter how hard I swim, I can't quite get to it. And I'm getting so tired of swimming."

She waited for me to respond. I think I was supposed to say something, but I didn't know what.

A leathery man in neon shorts jogged by and smiled at us. We're pretty girls together, the kind that white folks assume are mixed with something else because we don't look like mammy dolls. We have heart-shaped faces and mouths and almond eyes and unassuming ancestral curves. Jo had these beautiful thick curls that cascaded down her back, but she cut it off above her ears, and my mother cried for, like, an hour over how she could do such a thing. My hair doesn't curl—it kinks—but it doesn't matter because it's relaxed anyway. I don't think my mother would cry if I cut it.

"I dropped out of school. Just for the semester," she said.

"Why would you do that?"

"I don't know. I . . . I'm going back. When I'm doing better. My counselor was the one who suggested it."

"Do Mom and Dad know?"

"They wouldn't get it. And don't tell them."

I got mad at her then, even though I knew I shouldn't.

Last year, New England was hit by Hurricane Bob, which is a pretty funny name for a hurricane. Like a sunburned white man with a beer gut and dad sneakers. Hurricane Jo is the black girl in ripped tights and Doc Martens drenching the rest of us in her feelings, and it's like we either need to batten down the hatches or be swept away.

"What do you even do all day, then?"

"Wander around campus, sleep, listen to music; I don't know," she said. She bit her lip like she does to keep from crying, and I froze. Then, just like that, the moment passed.

"Let's go," she said.

Several weeks later, she met Harrison while wandering through campus. He wasn't a student, just one of the construction guys working on the new dorms. Also, Harrison is white, but so are most of our neighbors and friends.

She took me out to drive one more time after that. As we twisted along the coast, she gushed, "He's got the most beautiful eyelashes you've ever seen, Ash. He makes me happy. So happy."

"Eyelashes?"

"Jesus, Ash." She paused and took a deep breath. "So . . . I have something big to tell you. Huge, actually."

"All right."

She's so dramatic.

"I got married . . . I mean, it just kinda happened."

"You don't just *kinda* get married, Jo. What about Mom and Dad? What about me?"

Jo and I aren't as close as we could be, but I always figured I'd be her maid of honor and tell a funny story about us as kids or whatever as I toast the marriage. Or, like, at least be there.

"Are you pregnant?" I blurted out.

"Excuse you. No," she huffed.

"Sorry. . . . Congratulations," I eked out.

"Thanks. So, like, don't tell Mom and Dad."

"What the fuck, Jo?"

We didn't talk that much for the rest of our drive after that. She took me only to the edge of Malibu and back, and we didn't stop or anything. I called her once to see if she would take me out to practice driving again, but she said, "Have Lucia do it. I'm kinda busy right now."

I probably shouldn't have asked if she was pregnant.

Jo is smart and very sad, and secretly I think it's easier for my parents that she's gone, even if nobody wants to admit it. At least fighting *about* her is easier than fighting *with* her. How do you raise a sad black girl?

Every emotion is so combustible with Jo, every feeling at full volume. I feel like I've got all these emotions just on the tip of my tongue, but it's like I'm in the doctor's office going *ahhh* and there's that sad Popsicle stick without anything sweet pressing the feelings down.

"We aren't living the blues," my dad yelled once, after Jo barricaded herself in her room to cry about nothing, far as the rest of us could tell. "Not here. Not us."

Lucia says, "Your parents don't know what she's so sad about. Sadness for them is a cause and effect, not simply a way to be."

Concrete and billboards and people waiting for the bus. Furniture stores and fast food and gas stations and thrift stores. The longer we drive, the dirtier and grayer the city gets and the browner the people get, carrying shopping bags and pushing strollers and carts across crosswalks. A man with a Moses beard rolls his wheelchair right into the street and holds up a yellow sign that says JESUS IS COMING!

Lucia slams on the brakes. *"¡Pendejo!"*

After all that business with the cop, I'm late getting home, so Lucia brought me an outfit in which to meet my sister's new husband, like I gotta dress up to see my own sister. Except she's accidentally grabbed one of Jo's dresses.

"That's Jo's dress," I say.

"But you wear it all the time," Lucia says.

"She doesn't know that," I say. "I'll just wear what I'm wearing." My foot is still in pain, and my legs are still covered in dust.

"Don't you wanna look nice?" Lucia says.

"I don't care," I say.

"Yes, you do," she says.

"Fuck Jo," I say.

"Don't say that," Lucia says. "One day your parents will leave you and you'll just have each other."

Lucia's from Guatemala and has twin sons close to my age, Umberto and Roberto, whom she visits once a year. I can't picture her tiny body carrying a single baby, much less two at once. She had to lie in bed for two months before they were born, she said. Everything hurt and got swollen, and when she pressed her fingertips into her skin, they left little indentations, like when you press into the sand before the tide comes back in; she was that full of water and baby. Even though she says they're the loves of her life, she also says, "Don't have sex, *mija*."

I wonder if she felt better leaving them, thinking that at least, even without her, they would move through the world together, tethered by their twindom.

The distance between my sister and me is fifteen songs. The first few songs are in Spanish; then there's some Madonna; then "Tears in Heaven," which is a pretty song by a racist about a baby falling out a window. Then "Under the Bridge." The Red Hot Chili Peppers went to Fairfax High School, and Heather's friend Jeannie's big sister says she sucked one of them off, which I guess makes them feel a little bit more real.

"Undadabrigdowtow is where I threw some love," Lucia wails along.

I don't think those are the lyrics.

Lucia loves music more than anybody else I know, a fact made almost tragic by her utter lack of musicality. Lucia's room is downstairs off the family room and a little bit smaller than mine. Her records are in a stack right under her nightstand, like at any time she might need to reach over in the middle of the night and listen to "Se Me Olvidó Otra Vez" or "Thriller."

After the song, the radio DJs open the lines for calls. "What do you think the verdict's gonna be, fam?"

"Fam" makes it sound like the whole city of Los Angeles is one great big dysfunctional family, and maybe it is.

"Guilty." The caller wheezes through his sentences. "Ain't nobody in their right mind wouldn't find them dudes guilty. We got that <beep> on video!"

"Not guilty," the next caller says. "The system's rigged against us. It was built that way, know what I mean?"

"We're here," Lucia says.

The buildings in my sister's new neighborhood have bars on the bottom windows, like somebody took the idea of picket fences and crafted them out of the stuff of weapons. Lucia says this is how you can tell a neighborhood is good or bad in this country: whether the fences are on the ground or on the windows.

Jo's apartment building is next to a 7-Eleven and a car repair shop and a chicken place; the air around the building smells like fried gasoline. I like the smell of gasoline. It's the smell of motion. The sidewalks have cracked and buckled in spots from some earthquake. Lucia parallel parks in front of one of them that looks like the game you play when you're a little kid—"This is the church, this is the steeple"—except the church is broken concrete and the people are the exposed roots, I guess.

For Heather's tenth birthday, all of us went down to her vacation house in La Jolla the week of the Fourth of July. We mostly spent our time running between the beach and the kitchen for meals, until the house itself was the sand beneath our feet. We boogie boarded and buried each other and built sand castles that we kicked down like little-girl Godzillas. At night we settled into the living room in our sleeping bags and held flashlights under our chins in order to better tell stories about dead people. In the morning the ground jolted underneath us, and we scrambled into the doorway together, knelt down, and held our hands over our heads and touched our elbows together so that we looked like hearts.

"It's the Big One!" Kimberly yelled.

"We're gonna die!" Courtney yelled.

"Shut the hell up!" Heather yelled. And then we started laughing because we were scared, but not that much. Still, we pressed our bodies against one another just in case. Best friends are the people you laugh with as the world around you shakes. Or at least they were then. I don't know now. Seems sometimes like growing older means the ground beneath you starts to shake and you keep trying to find the right structures to hide under, the right people to huddle with, the right roots.

Jo and I are supposed to be from the same tree, but sometimes it feels like she's off being a willow while the rest of us are sequoias.

"What you waiting for?" Lucia says. *"¡Apúrate!"*

I quickly move to the back seat and slide my arms through my dress, Jo's dress. Outside, I flagellate myself with the towel to wipe the dust off. Lucia brushes my hair the way she did when I was little, and even though I'm old enough to brush it myself, I let her.

"Come in with me."

"You couldn't pay me enough."

But my parents have for a long time. Lucia has been privy to all our history, good and bad, for years. She's been the bearer of our family secrets for most of her adult life. Lucia's the only person around whom we don't have to pretend.

"It's gonna be like *American Gladiators* in there."

"I don't need front-row seats," she says.

I step into the heels she brought for me to wear. The pain radiates through my foot.

"Shit, that hurts," I say.

"That's what happens when you ditch school, *mija*." Lucia kisses my forehead and pushes me forward down the walkway, until the distance between Jo and me is only the sound of a bell.

. . .

"That's my dress" is the first thing my sister says to me in months. Her hair is back down to her shoulders now. She's fatter than she was, but maybe that's what happy looks like.

"Whatever," I say. "You left it behind."

"I'm so happy to finally meet you, Ash." Jo's husband, Harrison, is a bear of a man, easily seven feet tall, and I suspect he might be an actual giant. I'm not sure if he means to lift me off the ground when he hugs me, but he does. As the ground beneath me drops, for a few seconds I understand everything about the two of them. If Jo was drowning, of course she would choose a man who makes her fly. In his arms, I almost don't even mind that he's called me by my nickname entirely too soon. I'll forgive him this forced familiarity because I don't want this man to ever set me back down. I close my eyes and I'm a 747, Apollo 11; I can touch the stars and the planets and all that other gaseous shit up there.

"She'll get her hair caught in the ceiling fan." I hear my mother's voice. I open my eyes and there, behind Harrison, my mother sits at what appears to be a card table covered by a tablecloth.

"Jesus, Jo, you don't even have a real table?" I say.

"Not everybody gets everything handed to them," Jo says. She totaled not one but two new BMWs in high school.

Harrison sets me back down on the ground.

"Where's Daddy?" I ask.

"He's not coming," my mother says.

"Work, apparently," Jo says, like she doesn't believe it. "You smell like chlorine."

"What happened to your hair?" My mother inspects me. She's

haughty and very tall, but also always wears exquisite sky-high heels so that, according to Grandma Opal, "Don't nobody look down on her, not ever."

"Water," I say.

"I can only handle one problem child at a time."

"Thanks a lot, Valerie," Jo says. She loves to call my mother by her name because she knows it pisses her off.

Harrison places a record on their old record player. On its cover, a beautiful lighter-skinned woman with a wispy Afro rocks a space leotard. In her hands are person-size steel chopsticks, and her long brown legs are spread and bent at angles like a spider's. She looks confident, defiant. She looks like exactly the kind of woman my sister wants to be.

"Do you like Betty Davis?" Harrison asks me, or my mother; I'm not sure.

"Is that her?" I say, picking up the album cover.

"She was married to Miles Davis. Maybe she would've been taken more seriously if she hadn't been. She kicks ass. Listen."

The music coming out of the speaker is about what you'd expect from a sexy black space lady. She growls and purrs all over funk that sounds like the past and the future all at once. It also sounds like an album you might have sex to—like *they* might have sex to, which . . . gross.

When my mother isn't looking, Harrison smacks Jo's butt, and she breaks into a grin, the biggest I've seen her smile in ages. Their bodies are easy together, like a pair of matching socks folded into each other, worn in slightly different places but made of the same stuff.

For dinner, Harrison has made some sort of chicken dish with potatoes and vegetables, which is much more delicious than anticipated, given that they don't seem to have much of a kitchen.

"This is great," I say. "Who knew you could do all this with a Crock-Pot?"

"Harrison did all the real work." Jo looks over at Harrison adoringly. "He's a great cook."

"You chopped up all the vegetables!" he says, and squeezes her shoulder. Blech.

They keep their hands on each other under the table. It's as though she has to keep touching him, and he her, or they'd be lost. My sister the sock.

"Yes. It's quite the culinary experience you've created here," my mother says. This is not a compliment. The sweat beads like pearls along her collarbone. Jo's apartment lacks air-conditioning, and the whole place is already stuffy with the weight of everything unsaid.

There's a fridge and a sink with some cupboards, but no stove. There's an archway that separates the art deco kitchen from the living room, but the living room is also a bedroom. It's a studio, but it gets a lot of light. The sunset feels warm on its walls. Nothing has been remodeled since at least the 1930s or '40s, and so there are the ghosts of would-be actresses and writers and singers and dancers, of all the people who moved back home, or moved on, or up. Jo and the construction worker have decorated it so that it looks like the inside of a genie's bottle.

Jo seems more relaxed in her skin around Harrison. Maybe it's because Harrison sees Jo—not who she used to be, not who she could be, just who she is right now in front of him. Maybe he makes her feel like that's enough.

Jo retrieves a bottle of champagne from within one of the cabinets. "In honor of our special day."

My mother purses her lips as Jo pours the champagne into mismatched glasses.

"Ashley's underage," my mother says as Jo pours for me.

"I'm pretty sure Ashley's had a drink or two by now." She continues to pour.

"Don't encourage bad behavior," my mother says.

"You know French kids don't binge drink. Because it's not a big deal there."

"Last I checked, we weren't French."

Jo sets the bottle down on the table and raises a glass that reads "Hawaii: The Aloha State."

"*Ohana!*" Harrison says, and together we clink.

"So, who are you, Ashley Bennett?" Harrison runs his tongue over the bit of chicken stuck in his crowded teeth. Jo reaches over and scrapes it off with her nail. My mother looks like she's going to vomit.

"I'm her sister . . . and her daughter." I laugh. "Um . . . I'm gonna graduate this year."

Harrison looks at me intently. His eyes are the color of dirty ocean water, refracting blue and green and brown all at once. His hair can't decide if it's red or brown. Everything on his head is indecisive. Also, he has three big red pimples on his left cheek that I know my mother will mention as soon as we're alone.

"What do you like? Who do you want to be?"

His probing seems earnest, but I don't have answers for any of it. My mother and sister look at me expectantly, like they're waiting for answers, too.

"I don't know," I mumble. "A doctor, maybe."

That answer usually gets adults off my back.

"It's okay. I didn't know at your age, either," he says.

"How old are you again, exactly?" my mother says.

"Twenty-one, same as Jo."

"A regular font of wisdom." My mother finishes her second glass of champagne.

"Have you been following the trial?" Harrison asks me.

There's only one trial to be following right now.

"Not closely," I say. I haven't really been following it at all.

"There's no way they won't convict them," Harrison says. "The evidence is right there, on video camera. That's the best thing about this new technology: It's so small that it democratizes the act of documentation. You can't just cover things up and lie to the people. Thank goodness that dude went to KTLA with it."

I nod. It's a very enthusiastic way to talk about grainy camcorder footage. The wound on my foot is starting to pulse like it's got its own heartbeat. If before it felt like a dull ache, now I'm convinced there's a chance I might have to amputate the whole thing.

"If they don't convict them, all hell's gonna break loose," Jo says. "The people are angry."

"The people?" My mother squints and somehow also raises her eyebrow practically all the way up to her scalp.

Jo ignores her and continues. "We have friends who are already planning on protesting if they don't convict those assholes. 'Cause, like, it's not just about the cops, right? It's all of it. Yes, the LAPD is racist as hell, and black and brown communities get policed differently than white ones. That's a fact. But also, the schools suck. There's no jobs. You don't give people any opportunities to make something of themselves or to see a way out of the shit they're dealing with every day. There's no hope. And when kids turn to gangs or drugs, people act all surprised. Like, what the fuck did you think was gonna happen?"

She pauses for emphasis, and I'm pretty sure she threw the "fuck" in there just to fuck with our mother. I think my mother's gonna say, "Language, Josephine!" but she doesn't. After a sufficiently dramatic length of time, Jo continues.

"You can't disenfranchise a huge portion of the population and not expect shit to go down. I mean, what they did to him is awful, but really, Rodney's just the tip of the whole goddamn iceberg."

Harrison nods enthusiastically and adoringly. The way he looks at her makes me want to gag a little bit. She's just my sister, not Che or Mother Theresa or, like, Naomi Campbell or whatever.

"Yes, Josephine." My mother sighs.

This is how we spent a good number of dinners in high school: Jo ranting about her injustice of the week, the rest of us agreeing with her and occasionally interrupting to say "Please pass the peas/salt/hot sauce." There are so many battles Jo and I don't have to fight. We're lucky black girls. My parents worked really hard to make us so. It's like Jo feels guilty for all that good fortune. *Why can't you just be lucky? Be happy? Be grateful,* they think. Harrison's a white dude, so maybe all our good luck he just thinks of as his birthright. Maybe that's why Jo can be indignant with him, why they can be indignant together, without all the business of being too grateful getting in the way.

"You know, you haven't asked to see my ring yet," Jo says to my mother.

"I didn't know there was anything to see."

Jo reaches her hand across the table. My mother looks over at the ring and takes my sister's hand in hers, bringing it in closer. It seems that right there, in that moment, the full weight of my sister comes crashing down on her head.

"It belonged to my mother," Harrison says. In the center of the ring is a big pearl from some prize oyster. It looks like Harrison dove into the depths himself to pick it out special for Jo, it fits her so perfectly. It's ornamented with a halo of tiny diamonds and sapphires that rests on a simple gold band. It doesn't look particularly expensive—at least not compared to the mass on my mother's hand—but it is elegant.

On the wall above Harrison's head, there's a simple framed photo of Harrison and Jo at the courthouse. He wears an ill-fitting blue suit, something grabbed last minute at the big and tall store. She wears a simple white minidress with long sleeves. I know that dress, like I know nearly everything beautiful in my sister's closet, but I can't remember why. I know it like I know the blue satin dress that looked like the sky and nearly showed her ass. It was ruined when she got too drunk and spilled wine on herself at my father's office Christmas party. Or the black suit with the slightly cropped shirt she wore to my grandma's funeral. My great-uncle Wally's wife, Evaline, made a fuss about how disrespectful Jo was for wearing pants and a crop top to Grandma Opal's funeral, but Grandma Opal was a sassy old bag herself—her words, not mine—so Jo looked straight at Great-Aunt Evaline and said, "Grandma thought you were boring."

"Your parents are okay with this?" My mother shakes a bit as she speaks to Harrison, a soda bottle about to blow.

"My mother is dead, and I don't much care what my father thinks," Harrison says. There's an edge to his politeness now.

This is not going to end well. I'm glad my father isn't here. Once he yelled at some guy my sister was seeing the summer after her freshman year of college just for bringing her home too late. "Nothing good happens after midnight!" he said.

"I'm an adult! We were just talking," Jo said.

"You can talk in the daytime. I didn't just fall off the turnip truck!" he said.

I swear, sometimes my parents sound like the white people in a 1950s sitcom—minus, like, the segregation, etc. I wonder what Harrison's parents and grandparents were doing then, which side they were on. Did they sign petitions or hold up signs and fight alongside us, or did they stand idly by? Or worse? I wonder if my mother's wondered the same thing, or Jo. Maybe that's what my mom really meant by "Your parents are okay with this?"

Anyway, in moments like these, I've found that it's best to provide a distraction. I take my foot out of my shoe and lift it to the card table.

"I ditched school and cut myself on a dirty beer bottle today. I should probably get a tetanus shot, right? It kinda feels like my foot could fall off."

"Get your foot off the table, Ashley," my mother says. "Now."

"It's not a real table."

"Tetanus is for nails, not beer bottles," Jo says. She seems vaguely annoyed I'm there. But she always seems vaguely annoyed at my general existence. Of course she's not grateful.

"Why were you ditching school?" my mother says.

"Senior ditch day," I lie.

"Were you drinking?"

"No. We cut through a construction site to get to Michael's house." She can tell I'm lying, but she's too mad at Jo to have any anger left for me.

"Let me see." Harrison takes his big bear hands and places them around my foot. "Once when I was a kid, I was on the roof helping my dad with this project he was working on. Anyway, I stepped on this nail, and it went clean through my Chucks. Ripped right through my foot."

For a few seconds, my mother and sister forget to antagonize each other. Both stare at Harrison, enthralled.

"Did you have to go to the emergency room?" my sister says.

"Nah, my dad said it was too expensive." He laughs.

My mother and sister look on, horrified. Mouths agape, they look like the exact same person. Two people who belong to each other.

"Got a bit of a fever and the area was kinda swollen for a month, but it healed up. No lockjaw!" He laughs again. "Dessert?"

Jo and the construction worker have started a band together. After dessert, they sit down with their guitars and sing for us. Jo's voice is raw, and Harrison's guitar is tender. Together, they're magic. They don't have a name for themselves, not yet. When they're done, Jo looks at my mother, expectant.

"That was nice."

"That's it?" Jo says.

"What? It was."

The two of them stare each other down across the room.

"Alright, whatever," Jo says. She bites her lower lip and fixes her gaze on some random spot in the corner.

"You guys are really good," I say.

She softens. "Thank you."

"Anyway, we should get going. Ashley has homework to do," my mother says.

As we head out the door, out of my mother it finally bubbles up and pops.

"Come home," she says. "Being poor isn't romantic. Not for us."

Jo looks off into the distance, then back. She bites her lip again as if she's going to cry.

"You've been very rude to my husband. In his home," Jo says quietly. From the front door, you can hear Harrison washing the dishes, humming their shared song to himself.

"Your husband?" my mother scoffs. "You're a child playing house."

Jo starts to shut the door on my mother.

"Don't you dare." My mother pushes back against her, and back and forth the door goes, Jo's bare foot versus my mother's heels. Finally, the door snags my mother's stockings and the tear runs in a ladder up and up and up. My mother stops what she's doing to look down and inspect it. Jo uses the distraction to slam the door in her face.

Honestly, I don't know why Jo just can't get it together. But also, why can't my mother just tell Jo she's good?

Sometimes I feel like I'm the door being pushed back and forth between the two of them. Why is it that they can never say the right words to each other? Why do they leave so much space between them for all the wrong ones to fall in?

"This is not what we sent you to college for!" my mother yells at the closed door.

Over the buckled sidewalks on our way back to the car, we see three black boys in a row against the white brick of the 7-Eleven, arms spread like stars, a mini constellation. Or starfish stuck to a rock.

The policemen are shorter than the boys are but thicker, two ruddy bricks in uniform. The guns at their sides are terrifying, and I'm not even being patted down.

Earlier, Officer Bradford didn't pat Courtney or Kimberly or Heather or Trevor or Michael down. Me neither, even if he did look at me longer than he did the rest.

"I ain't done nothing," the littlest black boy yells. He doesn't look much past twelve or thirteen, but maybe he's scrawny.

"We can't walk?" the middle one says. "You gon' arrest us for walking?"

The police officer presses his knee into the little boy's back, hard, and he begins to cry.

"This is what she chooses to live in," my mother says, "after everything your father and I sacrificed to make sure she didn't."

"You don't gotta do that to him," the oldest boy says. "We been doin' exactly what you say."

He turns back to talk to the officer, and the officer pushes his head into the wall.

"Should we do something?" I ask my mother. I think of the man in the video, beaten until his brain doesn't even work right. Her mind's too fixed on Jo for her to hear me. Or, rather, to actually listen.

"Like what, Ashley?" she says. "She doesn't want to come home. She wants to be a grown-up, let her be a fucking grown-up."

I think back to what my dad said that time Jo barricaded herself in her room to cry: "We aren't living the blues. Not here. Not us."

The three boys look like each other—cousins, or brothers maybe. The littlest one cries louder and louder still.

"Shut up," the cop says.

"It'll be alright, lil man," the boy's brother says.

The distance between them is just a few fingertips.

"God, did you see his pimples?" my mother says.

CHAPTER 3

T'S A WINDY night, one that makes you fear downed power lines and rotted roots. The kind of night that makes you feel as though the world itself is lifting you up and out of your skin. Every so often, the wind pushes our car gently off course, and my mother corrects it. In the distance, the ocean shimmers and seals bark.

"Ashley, I'm really proud of you."

"For what?"

"You're a good kid." She laughs. "Mostly."

"Um. Thank you."

If I'm the good kid, then Jo is the bad one. But why does it feel so shitty to be the good one? I feel like I have to be good so they don't worry about me, 'cause they've got enough to worry about. It would be nice if they worried about me, too, though. At least I'd know they cared.

Plus, Jo's not that bad. Not really.

And I'm not that good.

"So am I in trouble?" I say.

"What?"

Be here. With me. I'm here. Not her, I want to say. But it seems whiny, like a tantrum, and in several weeks I'll be a grown-ass woman.

"Are you cold?" my mother says.

Before I can even answer, she leans forward and cranks up the heat so it blows at our faces and toes in warm gusts.

"Your sister was a very difficult child, even as a baby; she'd cry and cry, and I could never figure out why she was crying or how to get her to stop. I used to drive her all around the city, talking to her in the early morning when it was just the two of us and the rest of the world was quiet. It's both very hard and very easy to talk to a baby for hours. Talking to her now . . . it's just hard."

"What was I?"

"What?"

"You always talk about Jo, but how was I? As a baby, I mean."

She pauses for a moment to think, almost like she's forgotten. Or at least it feels like that.

"You were a happy baby. Quiet . . . I left you in the back seat of the car once. I'd gone inside the house and started to unload the groceries and everything. Your sister was the one who remembered. We rushed to the car thinking you would be crying or upset or something, but when we opened the door, you smiled, and I felt like the shittiest mom ever."

"You're not shitty."

She pats me on the thigh. "I know . . ."

· · ·

My parents and grandparents have made it so that Jo and I know nothing. We know nothing of crack or gangs or poverty. We know nothing of welfare or Section 8 housing or food stamps or social workers. We know nothing of schools with metal detectors and security but no books. We know nothing of homegoings or small coffins. We know nothing of hunger. We are, according to my father, spoiled rotten little brats.

Once, Jo and I got into a really bad fight because I stole her favorite shirt, which she didn't even wear anymore, from her closet, and when she went to push me, we tussled and I bit her until I drew blood in an itty-bitty red rainbow across her palm. I still had mostly baby teeth then. She pulled her hand back in shock, examining her wound. After we'd both briefly peered down at it in awe, she used her injured hand to slap me across the face, hard.

"Stay out of my room! Stay out of my stuff!" she screamed at the top of her lungs, as though she were possessed. "It's mine!"

"You spoiled rotten little brats." My father appeared out of nowhere, as if summoned by this demon child. He dragged us by our arms down the stairs and out the house as we tried to hit each other and hollered, "She started it!"

"Where are we going?" we yelled as he stuffed us into the car, but once we got on the road, none of us said a word.

My father drove us somewhere not that far away and parked in front of a house the size of our garage. A citrus tree dropped its flesh in the front yard. A group of girls jumped rope. There was the *clack clack clack* of round barrettes, the sound of little black girls in fits of flight. I think maybe it was a dangerous neighborhood, but you wouldn't have known it at that moment.

"Seven of us in there. Me, my mother, my grandmother, my aunt Minnie, my two cousins, and your uncle Ronnie. That was the first house we lived in here, before we could afford to buy our own," he said. "I ate fast, because I had to, to make sure I got enough. I'd never even had my own room until I was done with grad school. Never had my own nothing. Shoes, socks, underwear, toys, you name it. We shared everything."

He grew quiet, and I sat there trying to understand him. It must've been summer, because I remember that, through the window, the concrete wiggled like steam rising.

"Everything?" Jo asked.

Lucia is in the kitchen chopping peppers when we get home from Jo's. As she chops, she tells my father a story.

"They kidnapped and killed all of them. The women and children, too," she says. "Usually when they do that, they burn down the village so there's nothing left, but not this time. This time they just left it empty."

My dad, Craig, was in the US Foreign Service in Honduras and speaks perfect Spanish. Now he's in international finance. He's tall and handsome, and his hair is turning into silver strands that shimmer in the right light. Before he goes to work, he slicks his curls down into a rigid wave, hair waiting to be surfed. In the company brochure, he's the lone black man in a glass boardroom, smiling, front and center. Sometimes while Lucia's making dinner, he'll join her in the kitchen, and they talk about their childhoods.

"Who did they kidnap and kill?" I want to ask, but before I can, my mother interrupts as she barges into the kitchen.

"Your daughter is a real piece of work." She slams her purse down on the counter, and Lucia and my father look up, startled.

She doesn't understand anything they're saying in the slightest, so for all she knows, she interrupted a conversation about a soccer game.

"What'd you do?" My dad looks over at me.

"I cut my foot on a beer bottle; look." I raise my foot to show him. The pain runs along my sole like a fault line.

"Not her," my mother says. "The other one."

She recounts the evening's events, but in her version we ate pig slop for dinner and Harrison was raised by wolves who let him nearly die of lockjaw, and poor sad wayward Jo is his prey. Then Jo stomped right on her own mother's foot and slammed the door in our faces before we could even say goodbye. And as we were going back to the car, we witnessed a police beating, because that's the kind of neighborhood his daughter wishes to live in these days. All of which, I suppose, isn't entirely untrue, but it's also not entirely true. We all sew a few sequins on our stories to make them shine brighter.

"I thought the slop was pretty good," I offer.

"Be quiet, Ashley," my mother says as my father pours her a glass of wine. Being the only black person in the brochure at the office is stressful. Sometimes my parents get mistaken for their own assistants, or people think they've stumbled into the wrong meetings, or their assistants think they know better than my parents do and it becomes a whole thing, even though both of them are amazing at what they do, or they wouldn't have gotten where they are to begin with. Like Grandma Opal said, "You have to be better." That's why they drink, Jo says.

"Did you do anything?" my father asks.

"About what?"

"The police and the kids."

"What should we have done?"

"You said they were little kids?"

"I don't know what they did or didn't do. And I wasn't going to jeopardize our safety to find out. We're still black. Besides, that's not the point. What if Jo and that man have kids in that neighborhood? I mean, they're probably not gonna be moving anywhere better anytime soon. And even if they move somewhere else, things are changing, but people are still ignorant. If people say or do nasty things to them or to their kids, what's he gonna do about it? Jo's a smart girl—too smart for this shit. She needs to get her ass back in school. What if people think she's her own kids' nanny?"

Lucia looks up at this and makes a face but doesn't say anything. Then she looks over at me. I've already started to nibble on the chicken going into the enchiladas. She slaps my hand out of it.

My father scratches above his eyebrow and opens his mouth as if to say something that never comes out.

"You should have been there," my mother finally says.

"I couldn't get out in time, Val. Things were too busy," my dad says.

"They always are."

My mother leaves the room, clutching her wineglass, my father at her heels. They're off to argue about Jo, which is a lot of what they do these days. Although before it was Jo, it was other stuff. Jo says they're so busy trying to be perfect for everybody else that all they have left for each other is the messy. Lucia turns to me and passes me a knife.

"You eat, you help."

They say one day when the Big One hits, all of this will just cave into the ocean, all the beauty and the rocks and the grass and the homes and the people. Our house is made of glass and wood so that you're inside and outside all at once. It's loosely modeled after a Case Study House by a very famous architect that my mother loves. Once, she took Jo and me for a Saturday drive to tour all the Case Study Houses, which are famous historical houses designed by famous architects all around the city. I think she wanted us to love those gleaming corners as much as she did, to understand how the right beam could make you feel closer to the very universe itself, but mostly Jo and I complained about how hot it was, and I had attitude all day because I was missing a birthday party for this girl I didn't even particularly like. "I don't understand why we're spending the whole day paying to look at other people's houses. It's so dumb," Jo whined. Still, we spent the day wandering through great modernist boxes, light and dark, with their big open glass windows and plywood and steel and concrete, the stuff of the houses themselves kinda like the three of us together, our parts both knowable and unknowable to one another. Eventually, Jo and I stopped sulking and started to marvel at the way all that glass in those fancy houses refracted the light in colors across our skin; and instead of being little assholes, together we chased rainbows. Anyway, if there's a Big One, we're definitely goners. On days like these, even the gusts against the glass feel as though, if they keep on hard enough, the entire house will collapse on all of us fragile in it. The roof feels like the safest place to be sometimes. Jo and I used to stand on the edge and dare each other to jump.

Courtney calls, and I climb out onto the roof for some privacy. Sometimes I see my parents as shadows at my door, listening. The roof is safer for secrets.

"Are you in a wind tunnel? Good Lord."

"Eye of a hurricane, actually."

"Are you in trouble?" she says.

"Lucia didn't tell them."

"God, I wish I had a Lucia," Courtney says. "I'm grounded, but not until after prom."

"That's not too bad, right?"

"I can't go to any of the after-parties, though."

"That totally sucks."

"Yeah, but, like, I went to them last year . . . so I guess it could be worse."

"Totally."

• • •

From my perch on the roof, I can see into my sister's room. Inside, my mother takes a book off Jo's shelves, then another and another. My father comes in, and the two of them say something to each other, come to some sort of agreement, and then he too begins to take books off Jo's shelves. Then they're not Jo's shelves at all, they're just planks of wood in need of a purpose. My mother takes down a *Purple Rain* poster. My father takes down Jo's seventh-grade photo.

"This calc homework is ridiculous. Have you finished it?" Courtney says.

"I haven't looked at it yet."

Together, my parents remove a customized trophy case with Jo's Model UN trophies. They get more and more frenetic, swept up in the act of removal as they take things off the wall and throw them on the floor. I can't tell if they're laughing or crying or both.

"So, problem eight says, 'The graph of the function *f* is show in the figure above. For how many values of *x* in the open interval $(-4, 4)$ is *f* discontinuous?' . . . like, I don't get it."

"I don't have my book out here with me."

When they tire, my parents sit down together in the middle of all the things that make up my sister's life and look at each other. There are patches of bright where the wall hasn't seen the light of day in years. The room is exposed and raw, and I'm embarrassed for them and it. Lucia appears in the doorway, and my parents look up startled, caught.

"And problem nine says . . ."

Courtney's looking for me to feed her the answers, like I've done for most of our lives. But I don't know how I'm supposed to tell her the answers when I don't have them yet myself.

"Shit. Gotta go," I tell Courtney, and start to crawl back to my room before anybody notices. I drop the phone on the roof with a thud, and it starts to slide down and off. I grab the phone and yank it up, but the damage is done.

They look out at me. My father wades through Jo's things on the floor to get to the window, which he slides open.

"You get your little ass off that roof right now, young lady."

"What are you doing?"

"We told you and Jo not to go out on that roof ever again."

Jo fell off once. We were up here together in the sun and then, like that, she fell into the bushes below and then hit the ground hard. She fractured several ribs and broke her arm and scraped her skin so hard in several places that she wasn't brown anymore but red. She spent several months in a neon-pink cast that she let me draw on with Technicolor Sharpies when I was bored. Jo fell, but I thought I saw her rise onto her tiptoes and lean forward. I thought I saw her close her eyes and lift off. But I know nothing.

In the hospital, when they were setting her arm, my father held her tenderly against his chest and sang "Isn't She Lovely" while she cried.

"Daddy, that's Stevie's absolute worst song," Jo stopped crying for a second to say.

"Girl, is you crazy?" my father said, which is how we knew he was dead serious, 'cause he very rarely uses the vernacular.

Then Jo started to laugh until the doctor yanked her arm back into place. Then she screamed into Daddy's armpit while he held her tighter against his beating heart.

"What are you doing to Jo's room?" I ask my parents.

"Jo doesn't live here anymore," my mother said.

Lucia has a stack of *People* magazines on the bed and we pore over them, imagining other people's lives as our own. Lucia loves Princess Diana, and *People* keeps speculating that she and Prince Charles might be getting divorced. Lucia's dark hair is cut exactly like Princess Diana's, and my mom's is too, so that my two mothers are each other and somebody else all at once. The idea that it's 1992 and we still have kings and queens and people born into being the heads of entire countries is weird to me, but I think my mom and Lucia both like how Diana looks good in Givenchy and happiest as she holds the brown orphans others have left to die.

"How is she?" Lucia folds laundry on the bed next to me. I place my whole head in the laundry basket. I love the smell of fresh laundry, the heat against my skin, those few moments when the clothes are like the sun instead of just another pair of faded pajamas. Lucia swats me away.

"It's been a shitty month. Her dad keeled over from a heart attack, and there's family drama. 'Diana pleaded with nearby photographers to "please, just leave us alone,"'" I read.

"Smartass. Your sister."

"Crazy," I say. "Can we talk about something else?"

"You need new friends."

"Did you know Diana's mom ran off with a wallpaper heir?"

"You're gonna miss me, you know." Lucia sighs, and when she does, I wonder if she'd rather be arguing with Umberto and Roberto back home instead. I think she's talking about when I go off to college, but later I find out that's not what she's talking about at all.

On Saturday, Lucia invites me and my parents out to dinner at her favorite place, which is this perfect Chinese hole-in-the-wall with questionable service and actual Chinese people eating there. As we slurp and my mother finishes her second glass of rice wine, she tears up and tells Lucia how grateful she is for everything she's done for us over the years and that we truly consider her part of the family.

Then Lucia awkwardly blurts out, "I have some big news."

For a second, I'm afraid she's gonna say that she has cancer, or that something terrible has happened to Umberto or Roberto, or both. I feel my stomach drop all the way down to my knees. Lucia is my best friend, even more than Heather or Courtney or all of them. I don't want to lose her. I can't.

She pauses for a second as though she's summoning up the courage to say what comes next. "I've decided to go back to Guatemala . . . for good. Now that the girls are grown . . . I . . . think it's a good time for me to go home."

My father reaches across the table and grabs Lucia's small hand in both of his.

I start right then and there to blubber loudly in the restaurant, with all those Chinese people staring at us.

"Please don't leave me." I got snot going down my face, which isn't my best look, but I don't care. Not now.

Lucia turns to me and places her forehead against mine, which is what she used to do when I was little; she would say she was taking my sad thoughts away and replacing them with her happy thoughts for me.

After that, we crack our fortune cookies open and look at Lucia, hoping hers says something like "A great adventure awaits you," but all it says is "You are beautiful," which isn't even a fortune at all.

Lucia's lived with us for thirteen of the seventeen years I've been alive. For her twenty-fifth birthday, my parents gave her a very expensive bottle of champagne, and I broke it while playing in her room. Our birthdays are only a few days apart, and so after my birthday party, I gave her two of my new dolls to replace her broken bottle. Then Lucia and I played with them together in her room until it was time for bed.

When we get home, I fiddle through Lucia's records until I find one and place it on the turntable. The record clicks and scratches as it begins.

"Are you going to nanny other kids in Guatemala?" I ask.

"I won't have to be a nanny there," she says quickly, and it's like a punch to the gut, even though I know it shouldn't be.

"What about your car?"

"Enough with the questions," she says.

"What about Umberto and Roberto? What do they think? Are they happy?"

"Of course they're happy! I'm their mother," she says, and we both grow quiet. "Let's talk about something else."

Before Lucia left Guatemala, a bunch of indigenous farmers

and student activists barricaded themselves inside the Spanish Embassy to protest the kidnapping and murder of peasants by the army. Instead of negotiating with them, the government cut off the electricity and water. While the police were trying to smoke them out, the embassy caught fire and instead of fighting the fire, they actually prevented the firefighters from attempting to put out the blaze and purposefully left the peasants and their Spanish hostages to die. The Spanish ambassador escaped through a window, and one of the demonstrators survived but was badly burned. Twenty or so men took him from his hospital room, tortured him, and shot him dead. They dumped his body on the campus of the university Lucia was attending. There, she and the others saw what was left of the demonstrator and read the sign hung around his neck: BROUGHT TO JUSTICE FOR BEING A TERRORIST.

She left school after that. Not too much later, she left the country itself.

Lucia sings "Nothing Compares 2 U" softly along with Sinead, *"I know that living with you, baby, was sometimes hard . . ."*

I want to tell her about Michael. About what happened Friday, and last week, and before. I'd told Lucia everything I'd ever done until about a month ago. Harrison makes Jo feel like she can fly. *I want that one day,* I think. Somebody whose love is like wings. I don't want to be somebody's dirty little secret. I'm not even sure I'm that much. I might be nothing at all.

Instead, I join in, and Lucia and I sing together, *"Nothing compares, nothing compares to you."*

When Lucia gets really into a song, sometimes I wonder if she's singing for a man, or for home. But sometimes a song is just a song.

A coyote ambles past the pool toward Lucia's window. It pauses, yellow-eyed and mangy, right in front of us.

I shit you not: It sits down and listens.

CHAPTER 4

THE NEXT FEW days are a blur after Lucia's announcement. After our run-in with the police officer, we don't ditch, and instead of hanging out after school, I go home to spend time with Lucia—so all the days kinda blend together. Until the day of the crickets.

When the first cricket hops past, it freezes and I freeze, and I swear, at that moment, it looks up at me like my own personal Jiminy Cricket.

"Sistas! Niggas! Whities! Jews! Crackers! Don't worry—if there's hell below, we're all gonna go."

The cricket doesn't say that; Curtis Mayfield does.

The song swells as I bend closer to look at him. I excavated the cassette, and a whole bunch of other stuff, from the rubble of Jo's room last week after my parents went to bed. My sister has weirdo taste in music—like some shit by this group called Skinny Puppy I tried listening to—but some of it's kinda good, like this. Before I can get any closer to Jiminy, a ratty Converse sneaker covered in doodles of aliens and tits steps within inches of him, scaring him off.

"Watup, Ash?"

Michael takes the headphones from my ears and puts them to his own.

"You never told me how that dinner with your sister went."

Michael is the only one I tell anything real to these days. We sit in his car and talk shit and smoke pot and tell each other secrets that we would never tell anybody else. It's easier to talk to him than to Kimberly, Courtney, and Heather sometimes. When you've known somebody too long, it's like they're talking to a version of you from years ago, even though you've updated all your software. You're the same program, except also you're not. It's a little easier around somebody who doesn't know you as well, who doesn't remember that one bad haircut from fourth grade, or the first kid you had a crush on. Somebody who doesn't feel comfortable calling your parents by their first names. Somebody who doesn't know your parents' names at all.

When our friends ditch and we don't, Michael and I hang out after school on days when Lucia's running late to pick me up. A few times he's even taken me home. Once, he asked if he could come inside and pee, but I told him I'd lied to Lucia about hanging out with Courtney, so he'd just have to hold it. I hadn't, but I wasn't sure I wanted him in my space. It felt too intimate, I guess. He'd been to my house before, but it'd be different with just the two of us alone. Well, the two of us and Lucia, anyway.

The first secret I told him was about Jo. It was the day after the second time she'd taken me to practice driving, and I could feel her secret hanging from my skin like a weight. On our way home, Jo drove while I rested my head against the passenger window. She sang along softly to this song by this old group she likes called the Hollies.

"All I need is the air that I breathe, and to love you," she sang until her breath ran out.

I had the worst thought as her breath failed her. I looked at Jo and thought, *I hate you.*

"My sister got married and I'm somehow supposed to not tell my parents. It's so fucked up, and I hate lying to them," I said to Michael.

Michael cocked his head to the side and cranked his seat up a bit. "My mother used to get really drunk in the morning, like before she would drive me to school. We crashed into my neighbor's car once. My mom told them she was distracted. Anyway, I'm pretty sure that's why she made me take driving lessons as soon as I turned fifteen—so she could stay in the house and drink and not crash. My dad knows, and he doesn't do anything about it."

Sometimes giving somebody the words in your head makes you both feel naked. Maybe that's why Michael reached for my hand and took it. That's how it started, anyway.

"Don't tell Kimberly. Please. I don't think she'd . . ."

"I won't."

I didn't. And here we are.

"The dinner was awful. They're crazy. I can't wait to go to college and get away from it all."

"Did you hear back from Stanford?"

Stanford is my dream school. My mother's sister, Carol, went there and is the current president of the Los Angeles chapter of the Black Alumni Association. Last year, she took me and my cousin

Reggie on a campus tour during the weekend of this thing called the Big Game. We hung out in a tent with a bunch of really successful middle-aged black folks in their Cardinal sweatshirts, and Auntie Carol had a little too much to drink while jamming out to the Spinners, reminiscing about the olden days and screaming "Beat Cal!" into the fog.

Before the end of the day, Reggie and I had also taken to screaming "Beat Cal!" over the sea of people and the tall trees. That kinda thing gets into you and burns in your chest like the whiskey we sipped from her red cup when Auntie Carol wasn't looking. Reggie got his acceptance letter already. Almost everybody I know has gotten theirs already, except me.

"Not yet," I say to Michael.

"You'll get in. You're smart."

"You're sweet."

"Am I?"

He places his elbows atop my shoulders, and the full weight of him rests on the weight of me.

Our school is nestled into the hills. With its manicured hedges and rose gardens and hummingbirds, it looks more like a college than a high school. The parking lot is lined with European cars, but also a handful of Civics. Those mostly belong to the teachers, though. We have courses in movie production and an award-winning Science Olympiad team. We have the children of celebrities and child celebrities. It's very peaceful, except every so often, a trio of women stands at the entrance with huge pictures of aborted fetuses. Then, for hours, three grown women yell at passing rich kids about the unborn.

Two more crickets hop past, bringing with them Kimberly, Courtney, and Heather.

"You two look awfully cozy," Heather says.

"It's Curtis Mayfield." We pull apart. Michael turns beet red.

"Didn't his dad, like, shoot him in the face?"

"You're thinking of Marvin Gaye." Heather sighs.

"She's not thinking at all." Michael wraps his arm around Kimberly and squeezes her butt. He does this to her sometimes, like he's trying to put her in her place.

But sometimes, like last night, he does shit like calling in to the radio station, even though he thinks pop is cheesy and lame, and dedicating "Emotions" by Mariah Carey to "um . . . my girlfriend, Kimberly . . . I can't wait to go to prom with you."

Kimberly recorded it onto a cassette tape that she presses into a Walkman the color of sunshine. "Listen! Isn't he the sweetest?"

"Yeah," Heather mocks, "listen."

Crickets rub their legs together to sing because they're lonely, or horny, or maybe both, like people. They do this mostly at night, though. In the day, they move quietly around and do whatever crickets do, which is why at first nobody notices them as Mr. Holmes reviews impulse and momentum for the AP exam.

"So, if impulse is the area of a force versus time graph—" he says.

"—I'm so screwed," Joanie Wang says.

Steve Ruggles looks up from making out with his arm to blurt, "Mr. Holmes, cockroach!"

Tyler Phillips leans over his desk to get a closer look, but then the thing hops and Brittany shrieks.

"Cockroaches don't hop," Tyler says, and throws his textbook at it.

You can buy crickets at a pet store to feed to snakes. In honors bio freshman year, Nathan draped the class snake across my shoulders, and I thought it would squeeze around my neck, but it stayed there looking at me, darting its tongue back and forth like a warning, or a greeting; I'm not sure which. Still, I couldn't breathe.

The next cricket passes right by me.

LaShawn Johnson leans down and scoops it up gently in his hand. Then he stands and walks toward the classroom window.

"What are you doing?"

"Crickets don't hurt nobody," LaShawn says as he opens the window and drops the cricket outside.

If it had been anybody else, Mr. Holmes would've yelled at them to sit back down, but not LaShawn.

The self-inflicted hickeys on Steve's arms run the gamut from deep red to practically purple. His pale arm is the color of a makeup palette. Steve lifts a pudgy fist to LaShawn as he passes, and LaShawn fist-bumps him right back. LaShawn can afford to be kind to a weirdo like Steve.

LaShawn and most of the other black guys who go to our school are on scholarship, usually for basketball or football. They run fast and jump high and catch and pass in the right ways. The other girls drool over the scholarship players with their brown skin and their flattops, all of them wanting to "Be Like Mike." They tell me how dreamy they think black boys are, as if this is supposed to mean something to me. Just like they tell me how cute they think Will Smith is, or how I kinda look like Janet, depending on how I wear my hair.

This last one I'm okay with. It's way better than the time I got braids in seventh grade and they called me Medusa for a week straight until I came home crying and made Lucia take them out, even though we'd driven all the way to bumfuck Rialto and it'd taken six hours and cost three hundred dollars.

"Medusa was powerful, *mija*," Lucia said. But she took them out anyway.

LaShawn's eyes are green and huge, with lashes straight out of a mascara commercial. He's built like an Oscar statuette. Allen Greenberg's dad cast him in a drug PSA, and after it aired, all anybody could talk about was how sultry LaShawn looked when he said no to crack. For a while he had his ear pierced like Jordan, with a small diamond stud, but then it got infected and he took it out. He's our school golden boy; even his skin is the color of karats. LaShawn Johnson can stop time to save a cricket.

We think that's it for crickets, until the next few come. Molly Denison gets on top of her desk, but I guess she doesn't balance quite right, 'cause the desk falls over and she goes with it. The crickets jump around her as she alternately screams "My wrist!" and "Get them off me!"

"Alright, let's go outside for now," Mr. Holmes says.

Outside, the field is green and the morning sun bears down on us. We stand the way we do for earthquake or fire drills, waiting for disaster, but it's just a bit of plague.

Molly bitches about her wrist, and Mr. Holmes sends her off to the nurse.

I place my headphones back on my ears, and the cassette picks back up where it left off. *"They say don't worry, they say don't worry."*

"What are you listening to?" I hardly see LaShawn as he approaches me. I know many things about LaShawn Johnson. I've spent a great deal of time looking at him. He's the star basketball player, and I'm a mediocre varsity cheerleader. I know that he's being heavily recruited by UCLA, Stanford, Duke, USC, Syracuse, and UNC. I know that his mama attends every game, wears wigs that look like they came from a Halloween store, and acts like a madwoman anytime he does anything. I know this and more. Other than everything I know, I don't know anything about him at all. I especially don't know why he's decided to talk to me, or why today.

I take my headphones off and hand them over to him.

"Poor Curtis," he says.

"Why?" I say. I know nothing about Curtis. LaShawn's on a first-name basis with him.

"You didn't hear about what happened? A bunch of lighting equipment fell on him and paralyzed him during a concert a couple of years ago."

"That's horrible."

"Yeah."

He grows silent. Michael stares at the two of us from across the field. Trevor sits down in the grass next to him and leans against his backpack. He picks a blade of grass and begins to chew. I wonder if Trevor knows about Michael's mother. How much of himself does Michael give to Trevor, and to Kimberly, and to me? How much do any of us give one another? Maybe Michael is jealous, but he has no right to be.

LaShawn and I are the only two black kids in AP physics. This is the most we've said to each other all semester. I'm sure the rumors are starting already about the two of us being together. It wouldn't be so bad, though, everyone thinking we're together. LaShawn is handsome and popular and girls fall all over themselves to talk to him. Not me, though. I don't fall. I make it a point to stay firmly on my feet as we speak.

When you're one of only a few black people in a class, it's almost inevitable that everyone will assume that you like one another. Like when I was in fifth grade and everybody said that Jamie Thomas and I were dating. Jamie Thomas was more interested in space than girls, and I was more interested in space than Jamie. Jamie's father was a literal rocket scientist, and Jamie went to space camp in Florida every summer. Jamie and I were both near the top of the class, and so everything we did was in competition with each other, like we were vying for the title of Best Black Kid.

"I'm going to go to the moon," Jamie would say while we were doing normal things like playing handball.

"Black people don't do that," Steve Chun said matter-of-factly. Steve Chun sucked.

"I will," Jamie said.

I asked my parents to send me to space camp so I could be an astronaut. If Jamie was going to the moon, then I would go to the goddamned moon, too.

My father said, "I'm not going to watch my baby girl blow up on national television."

Months earlier, we'd watched as the *Challenger* fell down in pieces around Cape Canaveral, and the whole nation went silent when moments before we'd been dreaming of the stars and beyond. So I suppose my timing wasn't the best. Anyway, I hated Jamie Thomas after that. I hated the assumption that we belonged together, that somehow because we were both black, we were a bonded pair. But I guess maybe in some ways we were, because when he left, I missed him more than I'd thought I would. I felt his absence as a slight ache; stupid Jamie and stupid space, we two little best black kids dreaming of flight.

Around LaShawn, crickets jump.

"Did you know that crickets are considered good luck in native folklore?" he says.

"Which natives?"

He shrugs his shoulders.

"In some places they even keep them in cages as pets."

"I know why the caged cricket sings."

It's a dumb joke, but he laughs and stretches his fingertips to the sun, ready for liftoff.

At lunch, the theater kids line up along the steps in the quad. They're loud and weird, and always singing or shouting lines from their plays at one another across the halls. The theater teacher, Mrs. Lesdoux, has frizzy red hair that reaches great heights and veins that crisscross like rivers across her pale skin. Her words are so crisp they're fried, each vowel and consonant perfectly enunciated and projected like we're at the Met instead of some rich-kid school in Los Angeles. Kimberly, Courtney, and Heather dig through Kimberly's makeup bag to primp. I don't, because the pinks that make them pretty make me grotesque.

"It's such a stupid senior prank," Heather says.

"We got out of class at least," I say.

"They're gonna kill those poor crickets for no reason," she says. Already the exterminators have begun to roam the halls like Ghostbusters, looking and spraying.

"Can I copy your calc homework?" Courtney asks me.

"I thought you did it last night."

I take out my lunch bag and start to rummage around inside. They're primping; meanwhile, I'm starving.

"I couldn't get through the rest of it. Fuck calc. I'm never going to use this shit again anyway."

"You never know . . ."

"Let's be real. Courtney's not doing jack shit with calc or anything else," Kimberly says.

"I'm not stupid! I don't test well."

"It's okay, babe, you'll marry rich," Kimberly says.

"You're a real bitch these days."

"She's not wrong," Heather says.

"Which one of us?"

"Both." Heather reaches over and grabs a forkful of the leftovers Lucia's packed me.

Kimberly's mother dressed her up like one of those creepy porcelain collectors' dolls and made her perform in pageants. We went to watch one once, at a Radisson somewhere in Pasadena, when we were in eighth grade. We piled into her mom's car and held all her dresses across our laps. The hotel ballroom was full of girls of all ages in various degrees of frippery. One girl briefly caught fire when her mother smoked too close to her Aqua Net updo and we screamed, but the girl's mom just extinguished it with her fingers like a candle. Courtney, Heather, and I sat on the hard chairs and watched as, one by one, the girls played piano or sang or twirled a baton. Kimberly sang something from *Les Misérables*, which she'd just seen on Broadway with her dad.

"He's trying to buy my love back," she complained, but she wore her Original Broadway Cast cassette down until all those Frenchies sounded like they were singing underwater.

Kimberly's voice is good enough—very technically proficient but without the fire that makes you feel like you could cry, like when Whitney in her tracksuit hit that high note in the national anthem and you felt it crawling up your spine. Even without the fire, Kimberly took second place. Heather, Courtney, and I all stood up and clapped and woo-hooed, but her mother glowered and stormed over to the judges' panel to talk to the head judge about scoring.

This was when Kimberly was still Big Courtney and the other girls were cuter and not in the middle of a growth spurt, but her mom didn't see that. Kimberly's mother is severe, thin, and long, with a general sharpness that seems to have been passed down through generations. She yelled at Kimberly for not standing up straight. She didn't get that Kimberly was trying to make herself smaller, more like the other girls, a roly-poly curling into herself to find safety. In the car on the way home, Heather grabbed Kimberly's hand and patted it while Kimberly's mother yelled, "You can't do anything right!"

All of that must do one hell of a number on a person, 'cause now Kimberly will notice your uneven eyebrows, the pimple you're hiding with your bangs, and whether you've gained a few pounds. Sometimes I feel like I'm on *Star Search* when I walk past her and she sucks in her breath and clicks her tongue, and in my head I hear, *Two and a half stars!*

"Whatever. Did you hear LaShawn got into Stanford?" Kimberly says.

I feel a twinge of jealousy, even though I know I shouldn't. My life has been easier than LaShawn's . . . I think. Probably. He works hard, but I do too. I wonder why he didn't mention it while we were talking earlier.

"God, I wish I were poor," Courtney says.

"You don't go to class," Heather says.

"Or do your own homework," I say.

"Or play a sport," Heather says.

"Seriously. You've got it made, Ash," Kimberly says.

"She's not poor," Courtney says. Courtney's going to a good school because both her parents went there and have donated a lot of money to it, so nobody looks too carefully at the fact that she got less than 1000 on her SATs.

"No, but she *is* black," Kimberly says, and laughs.

Heather looks at me and rolls her eyes.

Across the quad, I gaze over at the black kids, all twelve of them, mostly athletes. There's an easiness to the way they interact with one another, a familiarity. They bring one another in for elaborate handshakes and greet each other with "What's up, my nigga?" But only when the teachers aren't around.

The first week of high school, before they found me out, they would smile at me like we shared a secret and say, "What's up, lil mama?"

I would smile politely and reply, "Hi!" and continue down the hall.

In gym that first week, as Ms. Boone explained flag football, Tarrell and Julia somehow got to joking about eating off-brand cereal and government cheese. They started laughing, and I was teamed up with them, so I did too.

"You know ain't none of these white kids had that shit." Tarrell playfully punched my arm and snorted, "Girl, I know you know what I'm talking about!"

I didn't, but it was nice feeling like I belonged, so I laughed even harder.

After school, I found myself in front of a mirror practicing: "Nigga, please." "Ay, you know I ain't tryna hear that." "I'm finna . . ." But out of my mouth the words sounded clumsy and awkward and nonnative, like when my mother speaks Spanish to Lucia.

Fat Albert, whose real name I honestly don't know, stands up on the tables and announces, "This little nigga just got into Stanford!"

LaShawn reaches up on his tiptoes and tries to wrap his hand around Fat Albert's mouth. "Man, shut up."

But he's laughing.

As if in celebration for LaShawn Johnson himself, with a great flourish, Mrs. Lesdoux raises her wrists to the theater kids. "Nowww beeeeginn!"

"A weekend in the country / We're invited? / What a horrible plot!"

The song is from a Sondheim play, which I know mostly because of the banners around campus inviting us to their spring play, *A Little Night Music*.

"'Fuck me gently with a chain saw,'" Heather says.

I think the song is actually pretty funny.

"Make it stop," Courtney says.

Mark Grossman, who is a known asshole, throws an open water bottle in the theater kids' general direction. Luke Scott and Anuj Patel join him. They, too, are known assholes.

"Go, Tisha!" Fat Albert yells. Tisha is a person in miniature, no more than five feet tall, with Coke-bottle glasses and a Coke-can build.

The theater kids awkwardly bob up and down to the music as they sing.

"This is the longest song ever," Kimberly says.

Then something magical happens. One of the basketball players grabs one of the track stars and they start to waltz, which, for some unknown reason, we were forced to learn in PE in ninth grade between volleyball and badminton in the curriculum. LaShawn twirls Candace, this Amazonian Nigerian girl, and they sweep across the quad to join them. Lil Ray Ray has a flattop half as tall as he is. Mildred is six feet tall and has an old white lady's name. Together they dance, with her in the lead. The black kids waltz as the theater kids sing Sondheim, and nobody throws any more water bottles at all.

Mrs. Lesdoux looks confused, but even she begins to laugh.

After the song finishes, the bell rings, and everybody walks through the dying crickets back to class.

Michael pulls up next to me as I head toward AP econ. "What were you and LaShawn talking about earlier?"

"Why do you care?"

"Don't be like that." He puts his hand on my shoulder. I pull away.

"I'd, um, like to dedicate this song to my girlfriend, Kimberly. . . . I can't wait to go to prom with you," I mock.

"Whatever." He walks down the hallway and gets swept up with the crowd.

A month ago, he kidnapped me. He tied a kerchief around my eyes while I was standing at my locker and threw me over his shoulder like a sack of potatoes. He carried me through the parking lot like that. It's a good thing he wasn't a stranger, because nobody did anything to stop him.

Most of the other kids have BMWs or Jags or Mercedes, but Michael has a shit-green Nova that smells like pot and cigarettes. It's so old it has an eight-track player. The only music to listen to is some shitty Bruce Springsteen that the previous owner left, which Michael loves. His car drives like you're touching the ground with your very hands themselves, every bump and pothole a shock through the body. Blindfolded, it was like being on Space Mountain.

As soon as we got to our destination, I knew where we were because of the salt and waves, the faint smell of sewage, and the bright lights shining like spotlights all around. I could tell that much even through the handkerchief around my eyes.

"Wanna smoke?"

"Okay, I guess," I said.

"You have to keep the handkerchief on," he said.

He reached across me and grabbed a joint from his glove compartment. As he did so, his arm brushed against my chest. I could smell his funky-ass wrestling clothes in the back seat of his car, feel the slight tear in the leather under my fingertips, hear him breathing deeper and deeper still, until for a second, he stopped.

"Are you trying to get frisky with me?"

He put the joint in my mouth. "Inhale."

I couldn't see anything, but I knew where we were by heart. As we walked the boardwalk, I could feel its rot underfoot. I think, to throw me off, he took me through the arcade. The arcade is full of painted wood in primary colors and the beeps and boops of mirth. It's sensory overload, even while blindfolded. If I reached out my hands, I would touch small children riding small horses in a small circle. Arcades are like nightmares or dreams, depending on what kind of trip you're on. Skee-Ball is my favorite, because in my hands the wooden balls feel like planets.

He led me by my waist toward the Ferris wheel. A ditzy-sounding operator took his money and helped me into the car. It bucked in the wind, and I braced myself against his body.

"Why are we here?" I asked.

He took the handkerchief from my eyes. "Stop asking questions. It's a surprise."

Across from us, a tourist family in a yellow car took a picture. The father's hat went flying into the waves, and they all started to laugh.

On our second rotation back down to earth, there stood Trevor and Kimberly, struggling against the wind like sailors with a banner that read, ASHLEY, WILL YOU GO TO PROM WITH ME?

Trevor held a bouquet of yellow roses. I knew Kimberly had picked them out because she randomly thinks red roses are tacky, just like she randomly thinks weed is tacky but coke's okay.

"Wait, what? Are you asking *me* to prom?"

"No. Trevor is. Shit. I told that dumbass *I* should hold the sign and *he* should come up with you."

Michael pressed his thigh against me and curled his pinkie around mine.

"He thinks you're cool," he whispered. "Say yes."

So I'm going to prom with Trevor.

After school, I sit and wait for Lucia by the front steps, where the freshmen wait to be picked up. I know how to drive, but after Jo totaled two cars in high school, I guess my parents have decided not to let me have a car yet, though everyone else I know has one. Even if I did have a car, my Wednesdays belong to Lucia, though my friends give me shit for it. Every Wednesday after school, we go to Western Union and then get ice cream at the Thrifty's across the street. I'd rather do that than go with Kimberly to get her muff waxed, anyway.

I feel a presence behind me and think, *Michael!* But it's not. Lana Haskins is skinny and tall with fragile limbs like the branches on a freshly planted tree. She got kicked out of school a few months ago for drinking vodka out of a water bottle, but then her parents caused a ruckus and contributed to the new library upgrade, and the school quietly let her back in. Lana always looks hungry, like she could devour the world and it wouldn't be enough.

"They acquitted the officers in the Rodney King thing." She sits down on the steps next to Monica Thompson, whose whole being is like a smudged charcoal drawing. She's wearing all black everything, with dark hair that looks dipped in ink. Her roots are Benedict Arnold, though—a downright treasonous light brown.

"Whoa, that's crazy," Monica says to Lana. I can't tell if she's stoned or just doesn't have anything else to say. Monica's half-Asian, and as her tiny mother pulls up, she honks several times at her from behind the wheel of their huge car.

"I'm coming, Ma!" she yells in the direction of the car. "Jesus Christ. Later," she says to Lana.

Lana looks over at me as though deciding whether to engage, and to my utter surprise, she does.

"Did you hear about the Rodney King verdict?"

Lana's never said a word to me before today, but she never talks to anyone, as far as I can tell.

"Only as much as I heard you tell Monica," I say. "That sucks."

"Yeah," she says, "Totally. Shit's about to go down."

I shrug. She takes out a cigarette and lights it. She spreads her legs and drags on it slowly, like she's in a Calvin Klein commercial or something. We're not supposed to smoke on campus, but Lana doesn't seem to care about any of that. If the rules don't apply to you, why bother?

LaShawn walks past with two girls and waves over at me.

"Want one?" Lana says, and reaches out to me.

A cricket hops past. But I think maybe this time it's not a cricket at all.

CHAPTER 5

LUCIA AND I stand in line at Western Union behind a balding Russian man with really long ear hair like my old piano teacher. Save for the television in the corner, it's quiet, eerily so, and I try to keep my feet perfectly still so my sneakers won't squeak on the linoleum. Sometimes when I have to pee really badly or when I can't make a sound, I pretend that I'm a runaway slave and I have to be very still, or else I'll be discovered. It's fucked up, but it works. Usually this place is a swirl of tongues and transactions, like waiting at the airport, but without any of the excitement of going somewhere. There's always some baby fussing while some mom screams "Get down from there" at some kid, which sounds pretty much the same in any language. Today, it's just me, Lucia, and the bald man.

Together, we watch as a crowd pulls a white man from his truck and begins to beat the shit out of him. His long blond hair swings from side to side as he staggers, disoriented, with each blow. In a different world, he'd be a lead guitarist rocking out, not a broken construction worker tumbling. A man flashes gang signs at the helicopters hovering above. They're not even ten miles away, but it might as well be a whole different country. There are my fancy school and my fancy neighborhood, and then there's this. The television flickers in fragments across the Russian's head as he shakes it. He turns to look at me angrily.

"See?" he says.

Lucia places her body between the two of us.

"No hablar con el," she says.

The man returns to the screen.

Lucia speaks to me in Spanish when she doesn't want white people to easily understand what we're talking about. She taught me when I was younger, and then as soon as we got the chance to study languages in school, I chose Spanish. And anyway, it's LA; if you even half pay attention to the city around you, you'll learn it by osmosis. It's not like it's a secret language, but it's easier for her and easy enough for me. I'm sure to everyone looking at us we're an odd pair, a lanky black teenager and a tiny Guatemalan, always together. Lucia's favorite cashier is Jose. If he's working, everything goes smoothly, and they joke and laugh in Spanish about how he's going to marry her.

When she's done, she kisses her fingertips and places them on the envelope before sliding it across the counter, where Jose converts it to a textbook for Umberto, guitar lessons for Roberto.

Today, Jose isn't in a joking mood.

"El mundo en que vivimos." Jose sighs. His eyes are fixed on the television screen, where the news shows images of a man slamming a slab of concrete down on the truck driver's head.

"Sí," Lucia says.

Jose's hair is the dark of an oil slick at night. He's younger than Lucia, and Mexican, not Guatemalan. He lives with his cousin and *abuelita* in a small house in Highland Park with three bedrooms and a bathroom, and if you climb up on his roof, you can see the city on a clear day. He sounded like a real estate agent when he told this to Lucia.

"I'm going to own my own business," he said last week, a declaration of intent.

"Doing what?" she said.

He wants to own one of those places downtown where they sell *cobijas* San Marcos and clothing and key chains and Coca-Cola in glass bottles.

The San Marcos blankets are super plush and have different designs on them like cute kittens and majestic lions and Strawberry Shortcake and the Dodgers. A few weeks ago, Lucia took me downtown and had me pick one out. The air downtown is always the color of a nasty loogie, but I like the buildings because they've got character. Which is why I also love the blankets.

The one I chose had a white tiger on it, lounging like a queen.

"You take it with you when you go to college," Lucia said, and it was like she was preparing us both for goodbye.

"I wish I could take you with me to college," I joked, and we laughed, but then I felt kinda bad 'cause it made it seem like Lucia was my personal servant.

When I was younger and had a nightmare, I would walk downstairs to Lucia's room and crawl into bed with her, and she would tell me stories about her boys, and her country, and the handsome but very bad man-devil she divorced before she ran to the

United States. He did unforgivable things, she said, for what he thought were the right reasons. She used to think so too, until she didn't. And so he became the villain in my bedtime stories. "Tell me about Arturo, who lives in the house by the bridge," I'd say.

Jose is not like Arturo, I say to Lucia. Jose is a good man.

"What's a good man?" Lucia sighs. "They're all good, until they're not."

But I see the way she looks at Jose, like maybe she'd like to sell *cobijas* and clothing and knickknacks and Coke in glass bottles with him. Like maybe she could sit up on his roof, cuddle up in a blanket, and watch the fireworks over Dodger Stadium. I can see her dreaming up their life together and deciding maybe they could be good. I wonder if she's going to tell him today that she's leaving soon.

Although I try not to watch, my gaze finds its way back to the television screen. The truck driver lies on the ground in a halo of his own blood and hair. Nobody goes to help him. The police are nowhere to be found. Some man walks up, takes the wallet right from the truck driver's pocket, and runs off. Finally, the truck driver gets to his knees, and another man comes up almost out of nowhere and appears to kick him in the head. I feel myself wince.

"Go out with me?" Jose says. It's the first time he's said it for real and not just as a joke.

On the television, the man drags himself into his truck and tries to drive away. The people at the intersection continue to throw anger at passing cars. From up above it looks like somewhere I've driven through a thousand times, but also somewhere I've never been. I bet my dad would know where it is.

"Okay," Lucia says softly to Jose, and I look over at her because she's going home to Guatemala and what's the point of even going on a date when you're gonna leave, but maybe that bloodied truck driver made her forget, or maybe he reminded her why she left. Or maybe being around Jose makes her think she might want to stick around a little bit longer.

Jose completes the rest of the transaction in silence.

On our way home, as we cross the street, Lucia reaches for my hand like she used to when I was little, and even though I haven't done so in a long time, I hold it.

By the time we get home, the city is burning. The buildings are stripped bare, and people yank the guts through their skeletons.

Lucia hands me a small envelope.

"The Katzes said it was accidentally delivered to them, and they kept forgetting to bring it over."

"You open it," I say. My heart feels like it's going to fall right out my chest and splat right on the kitchen floor.

"It's your future, *mija*."

The envelope says my future has been wait-listed.

I want to cry. I'm in at other schools—really good schools, even—but Stanford is the school I want. Close to home, but far enough away to be some other me. Somewhere I can briefly stop being a sister and a daughter, but only an hour's flight away in case Jo needs me. I don't know for what, exactly; maybe in case her broken brain delivers a rough uppercut and she needs me to pull her up, squirt some water in her mouth, ice her bruises, and tell her to keep fighting. I need to be somewhere I can still feel the ocean, my ocean, in my hair and skin. I'm convinced Stanford is the only place I'll thrive. I want to throw up. I want to disappear. I want to crawl into a hole with embarrassment. I feel all of these things and burn up in their atmosphere as I hurtle down.

Lucia pats me on the thigh. "Everything'll work out alright."

Instead of crying, I watch.

Up goes a shoe store.

Up goes a laundromat.

Up goes a TV repair store.

Up goes a mattress store.

Up goes a liquor store.

All of it goes up.

My mother calls me from her car phone. "It's going to be a while. I'm going to try to take the 101 to the 405 and see if that's better. I'm afraid to get on the 10."

My father calls me from his car phone. "I'm okay. I'll get there when I get there. It's bad. Really bad. Stay home, okay? Promise you won't try to go out with your friends. Not tonight."

"I promise."

I call Jo from our living room. The phone rings and rings, and I'm afraid she's not there, but she is.

"Are you okay?" I ask.

"Of course I'm not. It's so wrong. I'm so tired of this shit. They had the goddamn evidence right in front of their faces. It was right there, Ashley! I mean, they don't fucking see us even when they're looking right at us." Usually when Jo goes on about one of her causes, it feels so far away—like she's angry because she knows she should be and not because she actually feels that shit in her kidneys. But this . . . this feels different. Even I feel it somewhere in my innards, pulsing.

"You should come home," I say, "until everything's blown over."

"I'm not leaving Harrison here alone," she says. Stupid Harrison. Just because he maybe survived tetanus doesn't mean he can save her from everything else.

"Just bring him here with you!"

"I'm not subjecting him to Mom again after what happened at dinner."

"Is it him you're really concerned about, or you?" I say.

She doesn't respond.

"Jo . . . don't do anything stupid, please?" I think of her handcuffed to her high school flagpole, fighting for brown people halfway across the world. She spent her suspension calling our local congressperson. Jo's the kind of person who would accidentally find herself in the middle of somebody else's riot.

"Dude. What the hell, Ash?"

The phone clicks, and then my sister's gone.

CHAPTER 6

LAST NIGHT, A Guatemalan immigrant was attacked by the crowd. They launched a car stereo at his head, stripped off his clothes, and spray-painted his whole body black, including his privates. Then they doused him in gas. A black preacher threw his body over the man and raised a Bible at the crowd like he was performing a group exorcism and yelled, "Kill him, and you have to kill me, too." In many of the worst-hit areas, the police are nowhere to be found.

My mother shakes her head in disbelief. She stands, lips slightly parted, her tongue waiting for words that won't come. The heart of the violence is around Normandie and Florence. Without the police, there's nobody's around to stanch the bleeding. Even so, all throughout the body of the city there is trauma, all of us slowly going into shock.

"Josephine needs to bring her stubborn ass here," my mother mutters. My mother calls my sister by her full name only when she's pissed or scared, or both.

When the news finally cuts to commercial, my mother takes a

VHS tape and shoves it into the machine's mouth. The sun isn't even up yet and we're going to exercise damn near a full hour before it's time to get ready for school, which she used to do with Jo every morning for as long as I can remember. Then Jo went off to college, and my mother started aggressively waking me up to join her, whether I wanted to or not.

When my mother turns to look at me, I think she's gonna say something about the riots, or, like, maybe that I should stay home from school today. According to the news, lots of schools in the hardest-hit parts of LA have shut down as a result of the riots.

Instead, my mother says, "Don't you think it's time to throw that shirt away?"

I'm wearing the same thing I wore to bed, an extra-long, bleach-stained "Where's the Beef" T-shirt, courtesy of Jo's emptied closet, and sleep shorts with dancing penguins. My mother is in a leotard that's tighter than I'm comfortable with. It's lavender, cut high up her hips, and she wears a pair of teal bicycle shorts under it that match her faded terry cloth headband. I can't be bothered to wear exercise clothes when the sun itself isn't even up, much less color-coordinate in my own home. Besides, I just got my heart broken by a university. I feel the weight of my failure with every beat. I stayed up all night thinking about what I did wrong, whether my personal statement wasn't personal enough, whether I should've done extra extracurriculars, about that one B I got in PE freshman year, all because I suck at stupid badminton. Who the hell plays badminton in real life? I don't think I even got three consecutive hours of sleep. I've read that people actually die of broken hearts. I really shouldn't be exercising under these conditions.

I decide that I'm definitely gonna ask my mom if I can stay home from school today when we're done and she's got that post-exercise high when, even though you're dripping in sweat and sore, you got the endorphins swirling around you and making you feel like just because you moved for a few minutes you can do anything. Like give your child twenty dollars.

We fast-forward through the weird courtroom sketch about piracy and throw ourselves right into the diner dance floor 1950s nostalgia rendered in flashes of neon. Richard Simmons is perfect. His voice is high, his 'fro slightly receding, his shorts receded. His tan thighs are smooth as silk and his sneakers bright as bleach. He's flanked by a lady in deep purple who looks a little like a California Raisin and a brunette in pants that are trying to eat her whole.

My mother and I begin to dip and writhe sensually with Richard to "Fever."

It definitely feels inappropriate to writhe sensually with one's mother.

"You got that fever!" Richard purrs.

"You got that fever, Ashley?" My mother laughs and squeezes her butt cheeks along with everyone onscreen.

"I got something," I huff.

"You're being ridiculous," my father yells from the kitchen.

"Let me see you sizzle," Richard says.

My father is on the phone arguing with my uncle Ronnie while we exercise. Uncle Ronnie is my father's balding older brother who likes to give him shit about where we live and how we talk and most other things about us. I think he's afraid my dad thinks he's better than him, or maybe he's afraid that he actually is. Ronnie refuses to give up his hair because it used to be his pride and joy—long, inky spirals that he wore in two braids throughout the 1960s and '70s, until the early '80s hit. When the economy got fucked, so did Uncle Ronnie's hair. Now his hairline's receded so his forehead looks like low tide. It does seem a bit unfair that one brother should have so much and the other not even so much as his hair, but I guess that's just the way it is. They're arguing over my grandmother's store, which is in the hood, which is on fire. Not the store itself, though; not yet.

My grandmother is long dead and the business should be too, but Uncle Ronnie has kept it alive by the skin of his teeth, as my dad says. Repairing vacuums isn't as lucrative as it once was, not that my grandma Shirley ever made all that much to begin with. Now when things break, sometimes it's easier to just buy another one. Still, Shirley's Vacuum Repair Spot stays. Uncle Ronnie sells vacuum accessories, repairs broken vacuums, and refurbishes discarded vacuums to be sold. Also, inside the store a woman named Guadalupe sells homemade tamales for a dollar each. The tamales do better than the vacuum stuff, even if technically Uncle Ronnie doesn't have a food permit.

"You gotta adapt with the times," Ronnie always says.

"Just come here." My father puts the phone on speaker as he prepares his morning coffee.

"I'm not leaving Mama's store," Ronnie says.

"Dammit, Ronnie." My father says this often when he's on the phone with my uncle.

"Hug yourself!" Richard Simmons says.

"Is that *Sweatin' to the Oldies?*" Ronnie says, and my dad quickly takes him off speakerphone.

"Tell him to bring Morgan here, at least," my mother shouts as she crunches her elbow to her knee.

My cousin Morgan and I should be close because we're the same age and grew up less than twenty miles from each other, but there are palm trees and freeways and brotherly beefs between us, so we're not. When my grandmother died, she didn't leave a will, and so Uncle Ronnie and my dad decided that Ronnie should take care of the store and stay in her old house with his family, which is where he'd been staying all along. The house is mint-colored with a large front window and a small front porch, perfect for watching the world go by. There's a lemon tree in front that drops its fruit in the front yard. Uncle Ronnie's neighbors steal the lemons, which he doesn't mind, because what's he gonna do with that many lemons, anyway? Sometimes passing kids will take them to pelt each other with, and when they do, the street is covered in lemon splats. When we were little, Morgan and her sister Tanya liked to throw them at Jo and me. Lemons hurt when they hit you; not like softballs, but definitely more than Nerf balls. Once Morgan hit me in the head with one and actually knocked me off my feet.

The video comes to an end and we get to my favorite part, where the success stories dance off into the sunset. My favorite is a man named Michael Hebranko who somehow lost 780 pounds sweating to the oldies, which is like making six and a half of me disappear. I saw him on *Oprah*, and it made me cry. I couldn't imagine all that hunger just weighing on your heart for years.

We land once more on the news. The Baldwin Hills Crenshaw

Plaza was hit. The rioters didn't burn down the mall or anything, just did a bit of light looting. Baldwin Hills is where our parents used to take us to sit on Black Santa, even though the first year we did it, I guess it was a bit of culture shock, because my mom said five-year-old Jo threw a huge tantrum and insisted he wasn't the real Santa. It was important to our mother that we sit on and demand things from a jolly black stranger, instead of a jolly white stranger.

These things matter, she said, even if you don't know it yet.

It seemed a little silly when I was little, but now I think she was right. If all the heroes in our stories are white, what does that make us? I'm glad we left out cookies and dairy-free eggnog for a fat black old man, even if he was imaginary. The face of our joy had gray whiskers as nappy as the hair atop my head and blasted *James Brown Sings Christmas Songs* and the *Jackson 5 Christmas Album*. I like that, for the brief window he was real, Santa looked like what I'd imagine my grandpa to look like, if I'd still had one.

I wonder if my cousin Morgan took pictures with Black Santa, or if these things don't matter as much when you're surrounded by black people as they do when you're surrounded by white people. In any case, Santa's definitely safe. It's April. Morgan, however, is not.

"What'd he say?" My mother walks over to my father now that we've cooled down.

"He said maybe."

"You hear that, Ashley? Your cousin's coming. Maybe."

"Hey, can I stay home from school today?"

She pauses briefly to consider it. Too briefly. Before she can continue, I try to make my case.

"Since Morgan's coming . . ."

"No."

So much for that.

"But I can take you to school today, if you want," she says. "It's been a while . . . we could drive through McDonald's for breakfast! You used to love doing that."

"Mom, I have to get into my prom dress in, like, three days."

"Right. It was just a thought . . ." She pats me on the shoulder, then turns and heads up the stairs.

On television, the brunette reporter chases down passing looters. Her hair's lightly flipped, and she wears a white mock turtleneck under a denim shirt tucked into denim jeans, like she went through her wardrobe and decided that only denim on denim was appropriate to wear in a riot. She catches up to a Latino man in a thin white tank top, with a handlebar mustache and socks leaping up to touch the bottoms of his baggy basketball shorts. Her voice is shrill as she jogs besides him, mic in hand.

"What did you get?" she asks.

"Shoes," he says.

"Where do you live?"

"Right here."

"Why did you do this?"

"I don't know. Because it's free."

"Don't you know that it's wrong?"

The looter shrugs and runs away, the shoes boxes practically spilling from his arms.

Outside, the Parker boys hold real guns; hunting rifles, I think. It's early, but they sit on their lawns in the fresh morning dew, taking breaths like little bombs. Their lawn chairs sag in ratty squares beneath them.

I told you earlier that Tim and Todd Parker blew up our mailbox when we first moved into our house. We weren't sure if they did it because we're black or because they're delinquents, but it's probably both. They're almost thirty now, with faces that drip straight into their necks, and they still haven't moved out. My mother says one or possibly both of them are simple, but simple don't excuse racist.

"Nobody's coming here, boys," my next-door neighbor, Mr. Katz, yells across at them as he picks up his morning paper. Last night, after the protests grew violent near the Parker Center, rioters made their way over to City Hall and then threw bricks through the windows of the *Los Angeles Times* building, and even trashed some of the offices. Still, somehow we got today's paper.

The Katzes are like the Jewish Barbie and Ken, perfectly tan and thin with muscles that lightly ripple through their surfaces. I think Mr. and Mrs. Katz are in their early thirties, but they could be as old as early forties. They're so tan I can't quite tell. Mr. Katz has the easy confidence of a man for whom nearly everything has been easy. If he says nothing is coming, nothing's coming. Except his paper.

"Gotta stay vigilant just in case," one Parker boy says as though he's now a little unsure of it himself.

"Yeah. Just in case," the simple one says.

The Parkers are mostly friendly to us these days, but sometimes they're not. They seem to go through neighborly phases depending on what's going on in the news, like they're on some sort of racist swing being pushed closer, then away, then closer. The

Olympics and Flo-Jo, closer. The Rainbow Coalition, away. The Central Park Five? Way away. When my parents confronted the Parkers about the mailbox, my mother said that Mrs. Parker had responded, "My boys would never do a thing like that. We're very tolerant people."

Fuck being tolerated.

Mr. Katz shakes his head at the Parkers. He's wearing flannel boxers and an absurd silk robe that hangs on him a little like a cape. He turns around to wave at Lucia and me as we get into the car to head to school.

"Ay," Lucia murmurs, "he doesn't believe in clothes?"

But she says it like she doesn't entirely mind.

Once, Jo and I saw the Katzes having sex in their pool, which was notable because later that same day they had a pool party, with little kids and everything. We both thought that was deeply unsanitary. That said, the Katzes are very nice perverts, and not racist at all—as far as we can tell, anyway. You never really know. They have not one but two Clinton-Gore signs on their lawn.

"You're still going to school today, in this?" Mr. Katz says.

"Unfortunately," I shout over.

"Well . . . good for you, I guess. Go get those As! Stay out of trouble!" Mr. Katz winks as we pull away.

The Parkers adjust themselves and wave at me as I stare out the car window. Their hard guns rest across their soft legs like a threat.

The sky is an orange haze, that eerie glow that creeps over the entire city whenever there's a big fire. Yesterday, some of the protestors even walked up on the 101 and set the palm trees that line the freeway on fire. Palm trees! That's like a declaration of war against Los Angeles itself. Anyway, LAX has temporarily suspended flights on account of all the smoke. For now, by plane anyway, nobody can come into Los Angeles International. Nobody can leave. Lucia isn't supposed to leave for another month or so; still, some small piece of me hopes the airport remains closed indefinitely so she can stay. Then I feel like shit, 'cause that's easy to say when it's not your neighborhood on fire.

LaShawn comes to school by bus. I know this because when he's late, he tells the teachers the bus was running behind schedule, and they eat that shit up and smile at him apologetically because he's poor, and this embarrasses them all a bit. Bus service has been suspended in large portions of the city; that's probably why he's late.

When LaShawn finally enters class, it's ten minutes before the end of first period. The first things I notice are his feet. LaShawn is rocking a pristine, fresh-out-the-box, newest-edition pair of Air Jordans. They're white, silver, red, and navy blue, with metallic gold accents in honor of the upcoming Olympics. Instead of having Jordan's usual number, 23, they feature his Olympic number, 9, on the triangle. The boys elbow each other.

"Daaaaaaamn, homie," they say.

All the sneakerheads at school try to outdo each other with who can get the newest ones the fastest.

Mrs. Brooks pauses her lesson as LaShawn walks down the aisle to his desk. We stop taking notes to look at him. She leans down to talk to him, and her freckled breasts spill over the top of her silk shirt. He whispers to her and she turns a little red. LaShawn has this effect on students and teachers alike. This isn't the first time we've watched grown women turn into schoolgirls in his presence.

"Are you okay?" she says as she returns to the chalkboard.

"Yeah," he says.

"Good. If there's anything you need, you let me know."

LaShawn is always getting away with things like this. It wouldn't be so bad if it weren't for the fact that he's in at Stanford, and I'm on the wait list. I know I shouldn't be jealous of him, but I am.

What must it be like to have the world in a leather ball at your fingertips? Despite what Kimberly said, LaShawn didn't get into Stanford just because he's poor. Everybody knows that. Academically, he's one of the top-ranked kids in our class. LaShawn is handsome and smart and talented and funny and will probably be worth millions one day. What must it be like to know at eighteen that, as long as you don't screw it up, everything is yours for the taking?

I stare down at LaShawn's new shoes and think about the crush of people moving from store to store, taking and playing with fire. Then I think about that looter on TV this morning, the sneaker boxes in his arms spilling over like a bouquet.

Mr. Holmes starts to work on our review of rotational kinematics formulas, then stops. He turns around slowly to face the class, and when he does, it's like the reveal in a comic book, his raw side turned to the light.

He hoists himself up onto his desk like a teacher in an inspirational movie about troubled youths. We're only mildly troubled at best, but I appreciate the effort.

"We had a store off Avalon. It was a small convenience store with a deli in the back. My mother was from Syria and a single mom. She had to work late at the store a lot, since it was just her, so the next-door neighbors would take me in and feed me dinner; I'm talking black-eyed peas, gumbo, greens. Catfish! Half the neighborhood was from the South. . . . I'm getting hungry just thinking about it. Anyway, our store didn't get looted during the riots in 1965, but my mom moved out of Watts after that, from a nice little two-bedroom house on a street where I could bike around to a cramped apartment in Sherman Oaks. I went from having lots of black neighbors to having none."

Mr. Holmes is lost in his own memories, like a person telling you about a really vivid dream.

"My best friend's name was Tanya Jefferson. Like the street. Or George, I guess. The other kids used to make fun of me because of my face, but not Tanya. Anyway, I never saw her after we moved to the Valley. I feel bad that I never called. I should've called. I tried looking her up in the phone book a few days ago, but she's probably gotten married and changed her name. That's the trouble with women."

He laughs and shifts his weight around the desk a bit more.

"Something's gotta give, you guys. I hope when you guys get to be my age, the world is better for you."

Mr. Holmes looks to be on the verge of tears. I can feel the room tense up; we aren't used to grown men's tears.

I look down at LaShawn's new Jordans. Two years ago, this high school kid in Philadelphia was killed over his Jordans. Two dudes tried to rob him and he struggled with them, and then they shot him in the heart.

"How did you get that way?" Steve Ruggles asks Mr. Holmes.

Joanie Wang gasps audibly.

Anuj Patel says to nobody in particular, "Oh shiiiiiit."

If it were anybody other than Steve Ruggles asking, on any other day, I don't think Mr. Holmes would answer. He pauses for a long while, deciding how much of himself to give to us today.

"My brother and his friend were playing with fireworks one Fourth of July. I think they meant to startle me. We don't talk anymore . . . but that's not why."

"Did it hurt really bad?" Steve says.

"It took several surgeries to put me back together again," Mr. Holmes says. He breathes in deeply and exhales. Then he turns back to the chalkboard.

"So . . . instead of displacement there's angular displacement . . ."

And just like that, we're back to physics. Physics isn't my favorite science, though Mr. Holmes is my favorite science teacher. I loved AP bio best because I loved reading about the secret worlds under our skin.

After class, I linger while Mr. Holmes stands at the chalkboard wiping everything away. The white of the erased chalk fills the board in little clouds.

"I'm sorry about your face, Mr. Holmes," I say.

Mr. Holmes turns to look at me. He closes one eye, then opens it and closes the other, like I've done to him so many times. Then he laughs.

"Did you hear they're thinking of canceling prom?" Courtney says as we cram into the restroom to look at Kimberly's new hoo-ha.

We peer down at it, raw and pink like uncooked chicken skin. "It doesn't even make sense. It's not like anybody's rioting here."

"I had to put ice on my vagina for hours last night. They are so not canceling this prom."

"You put ice on your vulva. Dude, we're practically grown-ups. You guys really need to stop being ashamed of your own bodies and start saying the right words for these things." Heather crunches her words. She's already started to snack on some baby carrots.

"Don't eat in the bathroom," Courtney says.

We sit at our usual lunch table. Kimberly and Courtney eat matching salads. Heather eats a cafeteria burger and fries. Lucia has packed me a sandwich. I almost always get sandwiches, except for when I get leftovers. I guess I'm old enough to pack my own lunches now, but Lucia usually draws little doodles on my napkins for me—like today, she's drawn a little cartoon puppy with his tongue hanging out and a speech bubble that says "*¡Comer!*"

I take the bread off my sandwich. It's messy, but at least it saves me some calories. Without its top, my sandwich is vulnerable and unsteady, guts exposed; kinda like our city right now.

"Seriously, Ash, you do that, like, every time. Why don't you just ask Lucia to skip the bread?" Kimberly asks. I never knew she noticed what I did and didn't eat.

"I nibble at it." I'm only a little bit defensive.

"You're such a weirdo sometimes," she says.

"Where's Michael?" Heather asks Kimberly.

"Speaking of weirdos . . ." She shrugs. "He's been weird as hell recently."

"Maybe he's just nervous about prom night." Heather humps the table next to Kimberly.

"Don't be gross," Courtney says. She reaches over to grab one of Heather's fries, then a few more, and Heather slaps her hand away.

"Mine!" Heather says.

"So if the world were ending and you had to choose between Sarah Connor and Ellen Ripley to protect you, who would you choose?" Courtney says.

"The world *is* ending." Kimberly sighs.

"Not everything's about your cooch!" Heather throws a carrot at Kimberly, who catches it and puts it in her mouth.

Alien 3 is coming out in several weeks. When we were going to see *Aliens*, Kimberly said it looked like a boy movie, so Heather, Courtney, and I went to the movies without her. Then after everyone at school was talking about it, she felt all dumb and left out. Now, every once in a while, she'll say she wants to see something and one of us will mock her and say, "I don't know. That looks like a boy movie."

"Ripley's more badass," I say.

"Sarah Connor's hotter," Courtney says.

"They're both kinda butch," Kimberly says.

"So?" Heather says.

I turn my attention to the black kids. There aren't as many of them at school today. Lil Ray Ray with the flattop is missing. So are old lady Mildred and one or two others. The rest of them huddle around a boom box, listening intently. *Where are the rest of them?* I wonder. The metallic parts of LaShawn's Jordans glimmer in the sunlight. On his big-ass feet, they look like astronaut boots.

"LaShawn's shoes are, like, really expensive for somebody who's supposed to be poor," I blurt out.

I know as soon as I say it that I shouldn't have.

Their eyes grow wide and they glance over at LaShawn. He sits on the ledge with the other black kids—the remaining ones, anyway.

Courtney and Kimberly continue to look over at LaShawn's Jordans, and I feel like I might vomit. During freshman year, Heather and Kimberly went through a shoplifting phase, which meant that Courtney and I went through an accomplice phase. Now we're older and wiser, and so we're mostly reformed teenage thieves.

"Omigod, what if he stole them?" Kimberly says. "Doesn't he live, like, right where all that shit's going down?"

Why did I just do that?

"He could go to jail," Courtney says.

"He'd lose his scholarship," Kimberly says.

"LaShawn wouldn't do that. He just wouldn't," Heather says.

I look over at her with relief. She returns to perusing the latest issue of *Sassy*. Heather speaks with more authority than any other teenager I know. She shuts things down.

She wasn't always that way, though.

The night she started to change, Heather called, and Jo drove me over to her house. I knocked softly on her door.

Mrs. Horowitz flung the door open wide and pressed me deep into her bosom. Mrs. Horowitz is short and sturdy—"peasant stock," Heather says. She's not beautiful like my mother, but she wears her hair curly and wild and bites her lip like a girl who's forgotten herself. Heather's *bubbe* rested on the couch in the background, her hair like a pink-tinted cotton ball that shook as she threw her head back and laughed at some kid running into something on *America's Funniest Home Videos*. Sometimes her *bubbe* refers to me as the *Schvartze*, even though I'm right there and she knows my name, but I try not to get too offended because of the numbers tattooed across her arm.

Mrs. Horowitz kept rocking me and cradling my head, but I think in that moment I was Heather for her, or maybe she was rocking herself.

"She's upstairs."

I walked up the staircase toward Heather's room and knocked on the door.

"Heather?"

"Come in!"

I walked into the room and looked around, but she wasn't there. She poked her head out from the bathroom. Heather's bathroom is covered in pink and black. It's from the 1950s and vintage and so ugly that it comes out the other side toward beauty. Heather stood in the center of the bathroom in her bra and orange granny panties, the wings of a thick pad peeking out from either side. This was back when she was still reading *Cosmo*, shaving her pits, and dyeing her hair blond and frying it to look like the Courtneys.

"I'm so sorry."

I went over to hug her, but before I could get there, she tossed the razor to me. It seemed like some shit people do in the movies, but I guess also in real life, because there we were.

When we were done, Heather looked at herself, newly bald, in the mirror.

"It's kinda punk rock, right?"

"Definitely."

Heather's grandfather owns a recording studio, and sometimes after school, instead of hanging out with us, she'll hang out with bony boys who think they'll be rock gods and leather men who already are. I think Heather sits around all those controls waiting for the rush of drum and bass, eager to listen and love. Anyway, she didn't want cancer to cramp her style.

"Why did you just call me?" I asked her. "Why not Courtney and Kimberly, too?"

"I wasn't ready for all that. Not yet. We Esses know what it's like to have people look at you like you're different," she said. "I'll tell them tomorrow."

The overhead light bounced off the top of her scalp. I brushed away the few remaining stray hairs.

"My head's not too lumpy, right?" she said.

I bent down and kissed the top of it, leaving a faint lipstick smudge in the middle of her pale scalp.

Heather reached up and grabbed me by the hand, and in the mirror we looked posed, like in an old-timey photograph. "Today, we are new people."

I didn't know what I'd done to be a new person, but maybe she was right. Like in *Star Trek* when they transport, maybe we assemble and dissemble particles and build ourselves anew in each place we travel, including right there in Heather's pink bathroom with the Barbie tiles.

Several weeks later, the two of us rode our bikes along the boardwalk, past the musclemen and the pockets of piss, past the dreadlocked vendors with their incense, past the airbrushed shirts hanging like flags, past the gangsters, past the tourists and the bikini butts. Heather pedaled faster and faster still.

"How do you feel?" I said, afraid she was going to make herself sick. She had just had her first round of chemo several days before, and for most of the last few days she'd been too weak to do anything at all.

"Aerodynamic." She laughed and threw her face into the wind.

They broke all her cells down, and Heather reassembled herself into some stronger, better version. This Heather says what she feels like saying. This Heather doesn't apologize for taking up space. This Heather wears her curls wild and dark and her pits hairy, and doesn't let Kimberly tell her who to be. When the boys call her Whorey Horowitz, this Heather flips them off and yells at them about the patriarchy. This Heather hears a rumor about LaShawn and says no.

By the time lunch ends, my friends are over talking about LaShawn, and we've decided by a vote of three to one that we'd rather be Ripley. Ripley kicks ass in space.

When Courtney reaches for the last of her fries, Heather says, "Stay away from her, you bitch!"

Sarah Connor doesn't say anything nearly that cool.

LaShawn moves through the stacks with a cart piled high with books. He's tall enough that the top of his head rises just above the labyrinth as he checks each spine. Normally, Michael has his free period when I have my free period, and usually that means we find each other and sit together somewhere and listen. Today, I don't feel much like listening, or being found, which is why I'm in the library with its faded leather, Dewey decimals, and ceiling spit wads. I watch LaShawn until I lose him, then return to Emily.

My English teacher said Emily Dickinson never left her house, and yet somehow she was crazy prolific. She wrote a lot about being lonely, which makes sense. Somebody probably should've tried harder to force her out of her house, though. Sometimes I think I could be a hermit.

"Whatcha reading?" LaShawn startles me half out of my skin.

I show him the book cover.

"'I'm Nobody! Who are you? Are you—Nobody—too?'" LaShawn recites, and laughs.

"You're a fan?"

"Remember when we had to memorize a poem for AP English? That's the one you chose."

"How do you remember that?"

He shrugs and blushes. "I have a good memory."

I look down at the cart.

"Do you work here?" I say.

He laughs. "Nah. Well . . . sorta. I took out this book last year and lost it. Now I got this crazy-ass fine, and I got a letter the other day that said I can't graduate until I pay it. But I talked to Ms. Hawley, and instead of making me pay, she's letting me work in the library for a week. Ms. Hawley cool as hell."

He throws up a peace sign to Ms. Hawley, who watches us from the front of the library hunched over a sad-looking ham-and-cheese sandwich. She's a very stolid woman with a stentorian voice who wouldn't be entirely out of place at a Russian work camp—certainly not anyone I would've thought of as "cool as hell."

She returns his peace sign with one of her own.

"Her husband's black," LaShawn whispers. "She don't look like she'd be down at all, but you never know, right?"

"Right," I say. "What's the book that got you here?"

"It was more of a graphic novel," he says, "*Watchmen*. You heard of it?"

"I think so," I say.

"It's good. You'd like it," he says. "I think. It's about Reagan, but not."

"I thought it was a comic book."

"Graphic novel. And comic books are political as hell."

"I always thought they were kinda like 'Oh no! It's a bad guy! BOOM! POW!'"

"Nah. You should read it for real."

"Except that you lost it."

He starts to laugh and fiddles with one of the books on his cart. He seems almost nervous, though I don't know why he would be. At least, not around me.

"Shit's crazy right now, isn't it?" I say.

I glance down at LaShawn's new shoes. His feet are huge; he's like a puppy when they're all paws and ears and the rest still has to catch up.

"Yeah. But shit's been crazy, too," he says softly.

Ms. Hawley continues to watch us from afar. She finishes her sandwich and wipes the remaining crumbs on her pants. Then down-ass Ms. Hawley wipes a spot of mustard from her chin.

"I should get back to work." LaShawn sighs.

"Hey, when you were little, did you go take pictures with Black Santa or White Santa?"

He starts to laugh. "That's hella random."

"I know."

"Neither. My mom told me Santa wasn't real. She didn't want me believing that no white man came into our house in the middle of the night and gave me things for no reason. 'Everything you got, I buy or you earn,' she said."

"I sat on Black Santa," I say awkwardly as he starts to roll away. LaShawn turns around to look at me but keeps pushing the book cart forward.

"Did he give you what you wanted?"

"Except the pony."

"How was the nigga supposed to fit that down the chimney, though?"

LaShawn disappears once more around the corner, still laughing. He's got a great laugh, a little high and a little low, with a hint of nerd snort thrown in.

I shouldn't have said what I did at lunch about him and the shoes. LaShawn has never once said or done anything unkind to me, or to anyone else for that matter, far as I know. It's not his fault everybody loves him and he's beautiful and he's in at my dream school while I wait. *Forgive me,* I think, even though he knows not what I've done.

CHAPTER 7

THROUGH THE GLASS window of the front office, I can see the school secretary watching the rioters run into and out of buildings on a little black-and-white portable television. They fuzz out of focus, and she bangs on them to make them clearer.

The school pay phone smells like spit and hormones. There are a lot of penises etched into it. Two boobs. One very detailed dragon. Many pronouncements of eternal love, like "LOY+KGF 4 ever" and "N+T BFFs!" I personally wouldn't declare myself anyone's soul mate next to a pay phone dick. But I guess love does make you do crazy things.

Sometimes I'll see kids sitting and eating lunch alone inside the phone booth, as though the act of being there renders them as invisible as they feel, until some asshole kicks the glass and yells at the poor loser, "I gotta call my mom, dipshit."

Jo actually picks up the phone. She sounds like a person underwater.

"Were you sleeping?"

"I was out late last night."

"What? Why? You said you were going to stay home."

"I never said that. We went out to hand out flyers and protest at the Parker Center."

I think back to last night, the images of the protestors turning over the parking kiosk in front of the Parker Center, standing on it, fists raised in the air, and lighting it on fire, like those photos you see of coups in faraway countries. The Parker Center isn't that far from Jo—less than ten miles—but it's not that close, either. Not when the city's hemorrhaging left and right.

"How did you even get there?"

"Our friend drove us. It was kinda crazy, but we made it."

"You guys could've been hurt, or killed, even."

"We were fine. Besides, you can't let fear keep you from doing what's right, what you believe in. Harrison and I are communists, Ashley. Communism gets a bad rap, but that's only because there's never been a truly communist state. This isn't just a race riot; it's also about class. It's a rebellion of the poor and disenfranchised. The communist party has a long history of supporting the rights of black people, you know? Langston Hughes, Richard Wright, Ralph Ellison, Chester Himes, and W. E. B. Du Bois were communists. Lena Horne was blacklisted. Angela Davis was a communist."

"The Afro lady?"

I don't know how to argue with my sister because I don't know much about communists other than that we're supposed to hate them, but honestly that never quite seemed right to me, either. The Wall's down. The USSR's dead. The Gulf War's done.

Several months ago, Bush said that we won the Cold War.

"What good are flyers gonna do in the middle of all of this, anyway? Everybody's gonna dump them in the trash," I say.

Jo ignores me and continues, "It's not just about Rodney. It's about all of us. About all our black and brown brothers and sisters struggling to make ends meet in a system set up for them to fail. We have to change the system."

Now she sounds awake, like she's revved up, a person about to start. Start what? I don't know.

"Our parents aren't failing." I know exactly what she's trying to say, but her dumb ass doesn't need to be out in the streets saying it. Not now. It's too dangerous.

"Don't be willfully obtuse, Ashley. I could've been Latasha. Or you. If there's not justice for one of us, there's no justice for any of us."

"Is that from one of your flyers?"

She grows silent on the line.

"Please, Jo . . ."

I let my sentence dangle. I don't know what to say or how to say it, exactly. *I hate you I love you I miss you come home everything's on fire and our parents are scared I'm scared*, but we aren't sisters like that. If we were brothers, instead of our silence, maybe we might punch each other in the teeth or in the gut. We would use our bodies to say what we couldn't. We would feel bone against bone and tendon against tendon, and, bruised, be reminded of the shared DNA in our black and her blue. Or perhaps we would be like Mr. Holmes's asshole brother and lob firecrackers at each other without any regard for where they might land. So maybe it's better that we're sisters after all. We hurt, but at least we still have our pretty faces.

"Do you have to go to work today?" I ask.

"The office is closed." Jo sighs.

"What about Harrison?"

"He's usually off today anyway."

"So why can't you just come home?"

"Ash, I gotta go," she says, and just like that she's off.

"But where?" I say to nobody at all.

I'm about to head back to AP statistics when I feel hot words brush against my left ear: "Run away with me."

My body shivers a bit.

"Where are we going? Paris, Bora Bora, the North Pole?" I say. I think actually traveling with Michael might drive me batshit crazy, but being anywhere but here sounds amazing right about now. Anywhere I could crawl out of my own head and skin and just be still. Honestly, I wouldn't mind being a sentient blob at the moment.

"We could chill with the polar bears and scientists," Michael says. He jumps up and grabs on to a wooden beam as we walk. He dangles from it by one arm before dropping back down again. Boys my age can't seem to get enough of climbing and jumping on and over things, like their testicles are propellers commanding them always "Up!"

Michael's skin is still red from the other day in the sun. It looks like it stings, and also like he might get cancer if he doesn't start putting on sunscreen.

Michael leans forward and fiddles with the voices until they're nothing.

I start to cry a bit. Michael wipes a tear away from under my eyelid and licks it off his finger.

"Weirdo," I say, and start to laugh.

"Guess Kimberly was right after all," he says.

I shouldn't be in this car alone with this boy.

I can't tell if loneliness is being black, or being young, or being a girl, or if Lucia's right and I need new friends. I don't know.

"It might be lonelier / Without the loneliness," Emily wrote.

And she was white as shit.

Lana Haskins sits down next to me again on the stairs at the front of the school where all of us losers without cars wait for our rides. Apparently, I've managed to make a new friend, four weeks before the end of our high school career. She pushes her hair back from around her face, pulls out a pack of American Spirits, and starts to light one. My world is doing that thing it does when you've smoked too much and it's so big and bright and brilliant and you could touch your fingertips to everything and not feel enough.

"Smoking's gonna fuck up your teeth," I say. I should probably not be talking right now.

"Yeah." She starts to laugh. "But my morning shits are beautiful."

I'm not sure whether to be grossed out or to laugh. Ladies don't talk about morning shits, but maybe we're not ladies. I like her.

She digs into her backpack for something. An orange, bright and round like a setting sun in her hands.

"You want a piece?" she says.

"What do you think the scientists do when they're not doing science shit?" I say.

"Hang out with Eskimos."

"You're not supposed to call them that."

"Did you know they kiss with their noses? 'Cause it's so cold up there," he says.

That's not true, actually. I know this because my mother said something about Eskimo kisses last year, and Jo had taken one of her anthropology or sociology or whatever classes where they'd deconstructed *Nanook of the North*, so she was militant about the Inuit for, like, two weeks.

Instead of the North Pole, we go to his car. The parking lot is full of empty cars waiting for their owners, most of whom are still in class where they belong. We are flesh in a sea of metal.

"Kimberly thinks you're being a weirdo," I say.

"I don't want to talk about her right now."

For the last few months or so, after he's done with homework or with talking to Kimberly, Michael usually calls me before bed, and we fall asleep unspooling our brains across the distance. Other times he'll call me up and press the phone to his stereo and whisper, "Listen."

He hasn't called since the thing that happened last week. I would say it hurt my feelings, but I really hate that it made me feel anything at all.

Today, we get into his car, light up, and lean the seats way back like we're looking up at stars and not shredded upholstery.

"We should talk about what happened," he says after a long pause.

"No. We shouldn't," I say.

Instead of talking or listening to music, we listen to the people on the radio talking about the riots. Callers are on the verge of tears or explosions. We hear the fire in their bellies and the pain on their tongues.

Michael draws a new alien along the frayed white of his Converse.

"I mean, I get racism, but also I don't. Like . . . it's just skin, right?" he says.

I raise my eyebrows but say nothing. Easy for him to say.

Why the hell am I in this boy's car again? I think.

I go back and forth on Michael's depth as a person. Sometimes I think he's a murky but sizable lake, and other times he's a front-yard Kmart kiddie pool. Last week he was an ocean. Atlantic, not Pacific, though.

"You know they're not really kisses. Eskimo kisses, I mean. It's a greeting, more so; not so much a romantic thing. White people made that part up," I say.

"Well . . . you know us white people." Michael laughs and trails off.

He takes another puff, then reaches over and brushes my hair out of my face. He pushes his forehead into mine, then takes his freckled nose and rubs it back and forth against my skin. We stop moving and let our foreheads and noses linger, pressed together. Our eyelashes flutter like so many butterflies.

"Hi," he says.

These are my high thoughts:

Everyone thinks the riots are only about Rodney, but they're

not. Jo was right about that. They're also about Latash

Latasha was a black girl my age in Los Angeles. Latasha

Latasha was a girl. Latasha was my age. She went into

store to buy orange juice, and the Korean woman at the

thought she was stealing. She wasn't. They got into a fight

Latasha tried to walk away, the woman at the counter shot

the back of the head.

Over orange juice.

Her killer got probation, community service, and a five

dred dollar fine. Five hundred dollars for a dead black girl.

mom's got shoes that cost more than that. The judge said the k

was really the victim.

Rodney got brutally beaten on videotape. Nothing.

A few weeks after Latasha's killer got nothing for her dead blac

body, a man got thirty days in jail for kicking and jumping on hi

puppy, felony animal cruelty.

No Justice. No Peace.

"I could've been Latasha. Or you," Jo said.

Nobodies.

"I'm Nobody! Who are you? Are you—Nobody—too?" Emily

Dickinson wrote.

There's too much pain in the voices on the airwaves. I don't

want to hear it anymore. Not here. Not now. *Make it stop*, I think.

Enough.

My heart is beating really fast. I tell Michael about my heart. I

think it's going to explode. He laughs and squeezes my hand and

says, "Just breathe."

"Turn off the radio," I say.

"Sure."

We eat together, the juice dripping down our chins. Each bite is a bitter, sweet, fleshy burst on my tongue. Each morsel is a forever. I've never chewed anything so long as I chew this orange. When we're done, Lana licks her fingers, so I lick mine too.

"So why don't you have a car?" she says.

"My parents are trying to teach me responsibility or some shit," I tell her.

"Is it working?"

"Definitely not," I say. "Why don't you have a car?"

"Because I'm poor," Lana says, and we both burst out laughing.

"*I wanna sex you up!*" a freshman boy sings as he walks past us with his friends. He's no taller than five-foot-two, with a face like the surface of the moon.

His friends elbow him like he's soooo badass.

"Which one of us?" Lana asks. "You gotta be more specific, little dude."

He shrugs, laughs, and, with a half skip, runs over to his mother's car.

Lana stretches her arms to her feet. Her entire body folds in half like a taco. I blurt out the next thing that comes into my head.

"What'd you do while you were expelled? Did you have to go to rehab?"

She looks over at me intently. Up close, her nose kinda looks like it was broken and never reset. It makes her face that much more interesting to look at, but maybe it's also a little sinister.

"You're the first person who's actually asked me about it."

"I'm sorry."

"It's okay. I don't mind. Usually I feel kinda invisible, even though I know people talk about me."

Like one of the phone-booth kids.

"So what'd you do?"

"I stayed at home, watched a lot of *Oprah*, and drank," she says.

We both start laughing. She even snorts a bit. Lana's super-duper tan with a big-ass mouth, lips like a life raft, and teeth that rise to the task of filling the whole thing up.

"I don't have a drinking problem. I just have problems," she says.

LaShawn passes by and waves.

Lana leans in closer until her breath is hot on my ear. "Did you hear the rumors that he stole those Jordans?"

"Who told you that?"

"Somebody said they heard him talking about going out looting last night," she says.

Lana's not a mean girl, as far as I can tell. She doesn't have a reputation for being a liar or a gossipmonger. If it's trickled down to her, then it means it's only a matter of time before my words make their way to LaShawn, or, worse yet, to any of the adults.

"He wouldn't do that, though." She exhales in a ring and with her fingertips whisks it away. "Right?"

My fingers smell like orange juice.

CHAPTER 8

THERE ARE LOOTERS in South Central and K-Town, in Hollywood and Mid-Wilshire, in Watts and Westwood, in Beverly Hills and Compton, in Culver City and Hawthorne, and even all the way out in Long Beach and Norwalk and Pomona. There are fires in rich areas and poor areas and the spaces between. For once it's not only those of us on uneasy hillsides who are afraid. Lucia and I pass a condemned home that's dangling by its fingertips on the hillside. The riot didn't get to it, just California itself.

"Don't push me 'cause I'm close to the eddddge, I'm trying not to lose my head," I rap to the house.

"What?" Lucia says.

"It's like a jungle sometimes, it makes me wonder how I keep from goin' under," I say.

"You better change clothes when we get home, before your parents smell that stuff on you," she says.

But before I can get respectable, we have to stop at the store.

The tiny corner store looks as though it's been cleared like in

Supermarket Sweep, except it's a really sad version where there's no prize at the end. Inside, it feels like one long blinking fluorescent bulb. The two sun-bleached cashiers, Brittany and Marla, are around my age and usually look a little high, but not today. Today, they dart their eyes at every customer who enters. They're either fearless, stupid, or just really need the money for a car, or prom, or new shoes.

"Welcome," Brittany says as we enter, and her greeting sounds like an SOS.

These are things that we need that are missing: milk, eggs, firewood, chicken, and paper towels. There are plenty of vegetables left. Lucia and I talk to each other in Spanish while we wait in the longer-than-usual line. The lady in front of us turns around to glare, and I think she's gonna tells us to speak English or something, or maybe she can smell the pot on my T-shirt, but I glare harder, so she goes back to minding her own business. Everyone around us has their shopping carts piled high with what remains. We look like people preparing for a war.

On the news this morning before I left for school, they showed how stores were running out of wood planks, so business owners were going to Home Depot and buying and using actual doors to board up windows and other doors.

"What is happening to us?" an older lady says to the cashier, and looks at her like she's actually expecting an answer.

"I don't get it." Brittany nervously flips her blond hair. She and Marla look exactly like the kind of California girls who wind up on the postcards tourists send back home—like, somewhere in Italy somebody's *nonno* is looking at a photo of Brittany's blissed-out butt cheeks on the beach.

"This country is going in the wrong direction." The older lady shakes her head mournfully.

When activists argued that choke holds were proving to be unnecessarily deadly force, Los Angeles police chief Daryl Gates actually said this about how blacks and Latinos responded to choke holds: "We may be finding that in some blacks when it is applied, the veins or arteries do not open up as fast as they do in normal people."

Normal people.

That was ten years ago, and he's still the police chief. Yesterday, when the verdicts were announced and the city was a powder keg, he left LAPD headquarters to go to a fund-raiser in Brentwood to fight police reform efforts.

The Beach Boys are famous Californian "normal people" from Hawthorne, which isn't really on the beach itself but is just a hop, skip, and a jump away from the water. They built the 105 through the area where their house used to be.

Jo made me listen to what she said is arguably their best album, *Pet Sounds*, a few years ago. We stretched out across the carpet in her bedroom and she turned the dial on her turquoise record player higher and higher so that we could feel those surfers' harmonies all the way in our eyeballs.

"Close your eyes," she said. "Hear all the layers."

Like every song was a really good lasagna.

Then she told me that back in the day, Hawthorne used to be a sundown town, which means that they didn't want black people around after the sun went down. There used to be an actual sign posted outside the city that said, NIGGER, DON'T LET THE SUN GO DOWN ON YOU IN HAWTHORNE.

So I guess there's always been good vibrations for some, but not all.

"I don't get it," the California girl said.

As we pull out of the parking lot, a middle-aged black man, his gray fuzz in a crown atop his head, crosses the street in front of us. His clothes are faded but proud.

"Lock your door, *mija*," Lucia reminds me.

I know the man hears the lock click into place, because afterward he looks over at me, puzzled, then saddened, and I feel ashamed of myself.

Lucia grew up in the middle of a civil war and carries that with her in her bones. She's always a little bit on edge in public places. Even when we're in an empty parking lot, she has me walk just a little bit behind her, her body as a shield.

"Just because you can't see the danger doesn't mean there isn't any," she says.

Sometimes it feels like Lucia is a single mother and I'm her child, and we're just two girls in the world trying to figure it out together. My parents are very busy, and so Lucia has taught me a great many things: how to ride a bike; how to tie my shoes; how to throw a punch (the latter of which she taught me when the boys at school took to calling me "Hooters!" because my chest had grown into two hard, painful knots under my skin seemingly overnight).

In her village, she said, the girls knew how to fight and the boys didn't mess with them, until eventually they got older and didn't want to fight and did want the boys to mess with them. There were other people to fight by then.

"Who got kidnapped and killed?" I ask her as we drive along PCH.

"What?"

"You were talking to Daddy about it the other day. You said, 'They kidnapped and killed all of them. The women and children, too.'"

"You're too nosy, babygirl," she says, and shakes her head at me. Even so, she tells me the story as we drive.

While Lucia was on bed rest waiting to have Umberto and Roberto, the people in the Mayan village a few miles from hers just vanished one day.

"They all just disappeared, *mija*. And for a minute we asked ourselves if they'd even been real. Then the boys were born, and they were so beautiful and perfect, and I felt guilty for feeling so happy."

"Who did it?"

"The military."

"Why? How could anybody do that?"

"They hated the *indios*. They wanted their land. They thought the *indios* were more likely to be guerillas, or at least to sympathize with them. All of these reasons. None of these reasons."

"What'd you guys do?"

"What do you mean?"

"When they disappeared, what did you guys do?"

"We didn't do anything. . . ."

"But, like, what happened after that?"

Lucia shakes her head and grows quiet. I'm used to it by now, these stories she starts but never finishes, like a bunch of half-woven blankets.

A lone seagull screams across the sky.

Somehow, Lucia is always both afraid and fearless. I wonder if growing up in a war zone disarms you so you can't even tell why your heart races, just the constant awareness that it does.

The radio station takes calls from around the city. If yesterday's calls were full of anger, today's are full of fear. The power is out in several areas. People are shooting guns into the air without regard for the fact that there are children around. The businesses on fire are dangerously close to family homes. There's too much danger in this anger now, people, they say. Stop.

As Lucia and I turn into the driveway, I watch in the rearview mirror as the simple Parker paces his front yard, a cigarette dangling from his mouth. His rifle is on the ground. He's definitely not staying vigilant. It's weird to see a gun out in broad daylight on our sleepy street, something that could tear right through you and turn your insides out. It never occurred to me that anyone here might own one. It's not that kind of neighborhood. But I guess now maybe it is.

"What did I tell you about smoking? Are you trying to light the whole neighborhood on fire?" his mother yells from inside the house. He extinguishes his cigarette in a nearby planter before picking up his rifle and heading back inside.

Fat squirrels chase each other in fat spirals around the trees outside. Normally, the pool guy would've come today; instead, the leaves float across the surface and collect in a pileup by the gutters.

Inside the house, our air tastes like artificial lemons. I set my back-pack down, take off my shoes, and *Risky Business*–slide across the newly waxed floors.

Onscreen, the looters run into and out of stores cradling televi-sions, their cords trailing behind them like tails.

"You'll split your head open." My dad peeks over from the couch. Nobody ever actually splits their head open. Jo fell off a roof and didn't even split her head open. Grown-ups act like we're all just walking watermelons.

Neither of my parents went to work today because the riots have everyone afraid to do everything, even make money. Even though they made me go to school. It's weird seeing my parents so undone at this hour. My father lounges in a pair of gray sweats and a faded white V-neck. His normally slicked-down hair is curly and wild like Einstein's. I ruffle my hands through it before plopping down on the leather next to him.

"Animals," my father says under his breath. "How was school?"

"It was . . . school." I lean over and give his belly a big slap like a drum.

My dad's clothes are usually tailored so you don't see the soft of his belly. That's a newer thing, like the grays. If before he was like a board, now you can grab a handful of him and give it a good shake. My mother does this to him a lot. Each time she giggles and giggles at my father's new pudge like it's a three-piece corduroy suit.

"Have the Parkers been out there all day?" I ask.

"Those idiots . . ." My father sighs.

"My physics teacher was telling us about Watts during the riots."

"I didn't know you had a black teacher."

"He's white. Or half-white, I guess. Syrian. He said his mother made them move afterward. Do you remember the Watts riots?"

"We didn't live in Watts," he says distractedly, watching the screen. "But your grandma Shirley was worried about the store. There was a curfew in place in the black areas. You couldn't go anywhere. Back then people wrote 'Blood Brother' on the walls to let people know that black folks owned it. Your grandma sprayed it around the building in deep red letters as a precaution. I remember that specifically, 'cause when she came home, she had red on her hands and smudges all on her face and her dress, and Ronnie and I rushed over to her hollering, thinking something awful had happened. But it was just paint. . . ."

On TV, a stubby black man staggers around on broken glass. He stands in front of his emptied business. BLACK-OWNED, the handwritten yellow placard says.

"I'm from here," he yells. "I tried to make it."

His pain is visceral as he yells at everyone around him. He is a grown man in the middle of a mob crying over his dreams. They back away slowly like he's an injured wild animal. He could almost be Uncle Ronnie, but without the good hair.

"How's Uncle Ronnie doing?" I say.

"He's all right . . . he's doing Ronnie." My father sighs. "You know how he is."

I don't, not really, but I nod anyway.

The fighting continues. President Bush comes on screen and tells everybody that anarchy will not be allowed.

Next, we watch footage of a bunch of Koreans firing guns at the looters.

"Good for them," my dad says. My dad is a man who values order. He and Lucia talk in rapid-fire Spanish about the rioting, and my mom stands there trying to figure out what the hell they're saying. I could translate for her, but I don't.

Latinos are out there rioting and looting, too—this is what Dad and Lucia are talking about. Her friend's son came back with a big television, and her friend beat the crap out of him for doing it but kept the new TV, Lucia tells my father, and they laugh.

On television, the people cluster in ant mounds around storefronts. There's almost a collaborative effort in it, the passing of goods between friends and neighbors, until the police come and everyone scatters. I look carefully at the screen for my sister.

"Have you spoken to Jo?" I ask.

"She's letting all my calls go to her answering machine." My mother's hand shakes a little as she sips from her wineglass.

"I spoke to her," I offer.

"What'd she say?"

That she's fomenting rebellion.

"She's okay," I say.

"Good," my mother says, and leaves it at that, even though I know she's worried sick.

Bill Cosby appears via a prerecorded PSA and tells the rioters to stop what they're doing and watch the final episode of the *Cosby Show* on NBC. And I know everybody loves Cosby because Dr. Huxtable and Jell-O or whatever, but it's condescending as hell. Even to me. And I'm not burning anything here in my living room overlooking the ocean.

On another channel, they show everyone in line at this gun store in the South Bay; people like us who don't live anywhere near South Central. California's gun rules mean that not any old person can go out and get a gun and ammunition whenever they feel like it, so some of the people on TV are mad. Besides, the only guns left are antiques, like World War II–surplus rifles.

I think about the Parkers on their lawn, lying in wait for something or someone that Mr. Katz says isn't coming. The only gun we have in our house is a pellet gun. My father said he bought it in case of mountain lions. Sometimes they crawl through the hills and into backyards, where they eat people's precious pets.

Once Jo had to take care of the class hamster, Giggles, and left her outside to get some fresh air.

"Be free!" Jo said, and left her to wander around the backyard, and Giggles got so free she disappeared. After Giggles may or may not have gotten eaten, my father decided to get the pellet gun. For our safety, he said, and he and my mother have been arguing over it ever since.

My mother and my father argued over the gun yet again last night. But this time it felt different.

"It's more dangerous to have that gun out to all of us than it is to anyone or anything that might be out there."

"It's a pellet gun," my father said.

"Somebody could lose an eye."

"The kids made it all the way to adulthood and didn't neither of them shoot the other one's eye out," he said.

"Technically I'm not an adult," I said. "It could still happen."

"Be quiet, Ashley."

"How many times have I told you I don't want that thing in my house?" my mother said.

This morning, my father took it out and placed it by the front door.

"Just in case," he said.

My mother said nothing and walked away.

I leave the television to go upstairs and call Jo from the roof. The air tastes faintly of char, even all the way over here. On the news, they were telling everyone to stay inside. The National Guard has even shut down the beaches as a precaution. The beaches!

I enter Jo's number into the pink phone.

"Hello, this is Jo . . . and Harrison! Leave a message . . . or don't."

"Yo. It's your sister. Pick up. I just want to know that you're safe. . . . Don't be an asshole," I say into the phone.

I linger, hoping that Jo will finally answer, but she doesn't.

Before I can crawl back inside, the phone rings.

"Jo?"

"What? No. It's me," Courtney says.

"I haven't done the homework yet," I say.

"I don't only call you for homework!"

"Yeah. Kinda. Now, anyways. Not before, maybe."

"I'm sorry. It's . . . this shit's, like, really hard for me," Courtney says. "Like, harder than I think it's supposed to be . . . I can barely make it through high school. If I'm this stupid, how the hell am I supposed to make it through college?"

She sounds genuinely afraid.

"You're not stupid, Court. Nobody's gonna ask you about trinomials after this."

"It's not just math. It's everything." She sighs.

"College is different. They'll let you major in watching and writing about movies and TV and shit if you want! Plus, there's more to life than being smart."

"It feels like school is this maze and they keep giving you cheese to help you find your way through it. But then they release you out into the world and you have to figure out how to be your own cheese. Do I want to be, like, brie or cheddar or mozzarella or that random fancy moldy shit my mom brings out for parties? I just want somebody to tell me what to do."

"When in doubt, get moldy," I say.

Our conversation is interrupted by yelling. From up on the roof, I can see the Parker boys across the street, their hunting rifles aimed at their prey.

My uncle Ronnie's silky braids fall down his back, and his hands stretch up to the sky as he yells, "Don't shoot!"

"I gotta go." I hang up on Courtney.

Mr. and Mrs. Katz run out into the cul-de-sac.

"This man was pounding on our door, trying to break into our house," the Parkers yell.

"Should I call the police?" Mrs. Katz says.

"My brother lives around here," my uncle says. "Craig. Craig Bennett."

The Parkers keep their rifles aimed steadily at Uncle Ronnie's head.

"I'm sure there's been a misunderstanding." Mr. Katz walks

very slowly toward them. The Katzes are wearing near-matching pastel-yellow polo shirts, like they just got back from a doubles match. But that's just their life.

"How come you don't know where your own brother lives?" the simple Parker says.

"That's my uncle!" I stand up and yell from the roof.

"I had the wrong house." Ronnie talks very, very calmly to the Parkers, like he's talking a man off a ledge. "It was a mistake. Please, my daughter is in the car."

Inside the truck, my cousin Morgan watches, paralyzed. It's been some time since I've seen her, and my first thought is, *Her arms have gotten kinda pudgy.*

I wiggle down off the roof so that I land in the bushes below. Barefoot, I run through the backyard toward the street. The bushes scratch along the length of my arm, and it starts to hurt as it hits the night air.

"Stop!" I pant.

Morgan starts to open the car door, and Uncle Ronnie yells at her to stay in the car.

"What's going on here?" My father stumbles out the front door of our house with the pellet gun.

"Craig!" my uncle says.

"Ronnie?" my father says.

"You know each other?" the Parkers say.

"He's my brother," my father says, gun still raised.

"See, he belongs to the Bennetts," Mr. Katz says, and exhales deeply. Like Uncle Ronnie is a pet or a slave, or, I guess, family.

"I said that already," my uncle snaps.

The Parkers lower their rifles and shrug. "Sorry, yo."

Mrs. Katz looks over at me. "You're bleeding, dear."

Morgan gets out of the car and walks toward us. Up close, her freckles make it look like she's been tanning through a screen door. Her hair color looks like it came out of a box—wine or dye—but that's from the shameful Scotsman buried deep under the family tree. When I go to hug her, you can still feel the fear in every freckle. Every inch of her trembles.

The last time my cousin Morgan came to stay with us was when Uncle Ronnie and Auntie Eudora went on their belated honeymoon. Morgan's older sister, Tanya, came too. Tanya and Morgan are light-skinned, with long curls like Jo's, and they always made it a point to remind us of how we were the darkest in the whole family, even though we really weren't that dark, comparatively. Anyway, my cousins weren't particularly pretty or smart or funny, just light-skinned. The world had already taught them that was enough, I guess. Ronnie and Auntie Eudora got divorced several years ago, and Eudora moved all the way to Las Vegas. Now Ronnie's a single dad trying to make it in the world, which I guess during the middle of a riot means making sure his livelihood doesn't burn down. Tanya's away at college, which is good, because I don't think I could handle both my cousins at once.

Whenever Jo and I would beat them at anything, Tanya and Morgan would start in:

"Whatever. You black as coal."

"You black as the La Brea Tar Pits."

They must've just gone on a field trip.

"Black as a butthole!"

"We are not black. We're brown!" I'd yell.

"Ignore them," Jo said.

Jo and I both somehow knew that whatever they said to us, we weren't allowed to respond with the obvious insult, which was that they were poor. So instead we refused to share our toys and got into a fistfight the last night before they left, which may have culminated in some biting, and Uncle Ronnie and Auntie Eudora never left them at our house again. Until now.

Morgan doesn't want to be at our house. I know this because she says very loudly over and over, "Do not leave me here."

Uncle Ronnie pretends not to hear her.

"'Sorry, yo'? *Yo?*" Uncle Ronnie says. "Seriously? Those mother-fuckers—"

"Don't start in front of the girls." My father sighs.

"Motherfuckers pulled a gun on me in front of the girls," Uncle Ronnie snaps. "I think I can call them motherfuckers, right, girls?"

"Two guns," Morgan says.

"Coulda lived in View Park, or Ladera Heights, or—" my uncle says to my father.

"Don't start," my father interrupts. "How's the store?"

"Still standing. Guadalupe and her husband have been helping me keep guard. You should be there, Craig. It's yours, too. It's Mama's. It's our blood."

"I gotta get stuff done here."

"Of course you do."

My father and my uncle stand around awkwardly facing each other.

"We have insurance, Ronnie. It's not worth risking your life over vacuums."

"Not enough for this. Besides, do you know I got that brand-new Dyson in the other day? The one that won the International Design Fair. Put me back a pretty penny, had to order it by catalog. Anyway, I'm gonna take it apart and figure out how they work so we can get a head start on being best in the neighborhood for Dyson repairs. They're gonna be huge soon, Craig."

"Fuck the Dyson, Ronnie," my dad says.

"Don't start in front of the girls, Craig." Ronnie smirks.

"Why don't you show your cousin your room?" my mother says.

Morgan and I don't say anything to each other as we dutifully climb the stairs up to the bedrooms.

"What happened in here?" Morgan says as we pass by Jo's room.

"They're converting it into a guest room."

"But you have a guest room already."

I shrug.

Inside, Jo's books are on the floor, their spines savagely splayed. Her tape tower has been felled. Her posters are torn under the weight of thrown clothing still on the hangers. Her trophies peek out golden from under the wreckage. She would be pissed about her records, which lie flat like tipped cows. It looks like a store in the process of being looted. Her room is painted like the inside of a pistachio and still smells faintly of boardwalk Rasta incense. I wonder what kind of cheese Jo is. I'd like to be a robust brie or Manchego, maybe, but I'm afraid I might actually be a sharp cheddar. It's better than being a Kraft Single, I suppose.

Morgan walks through the room, running her hand along Jo's former life.

"You guys got a lot of stuff," she says.

"Yeah, I guess," I say. We have about as much as everyone else I know, so I've never really given it much thought.

She picks a dress from out of the pile, looks at the label, raises her eyebrows, and places it back down on the bed without a word.

"How can you guys even breathe with people like that around you?"

"They're not all like that."

She gives me another eyebrow raise. Morgan's eyebrows are assholes. I want to shave that right one off in her sleep.

"I wanna stay in this room," she says. "We can be right next door to each other."

Morgan used to be afraid of our house, I remember. When we were little and my parents had her and Tanya staying in our guest room, Morgan would climb the stairs and hop into bed with my parents, or with Jo, or sometimes with me. There were too many noises, too many windows for burglars to climb through; everything echoed, and everyone was too far away, she said.

"Suit yourself." I shrug.

"Do you have a car?" Morgan says.

"Not yet. I'm saving for one."

"I thought your parents bought your sister her car."

"They did. But she crashed it, so now they're making me buy my own."

"That sucks." She makes a space for herself on the bed and plops down.

Before Morgan can get to it, I quickly snatch up Jo's diary from among her things.

It's puffy, plastic, and ink-stained, with blue lines across pink pages. A tiny lock secures the cover, to be opened by an even tinier key that I had to dig through the rubble to find. I used to read it sometimes when we were really little and I was feeling sneaky.

"It's kinda weird that I'm here and your sister's not," she says.

I shrug.

"She graduates this year, right?"

"Um . . . She's taking time off from school right now," I say.

"To do what?" Morgan says.

I'm not sure if my parents told Uncle Ronnie and Morgan about Jo's getting married, but I'm sure as hell not gonna be the one to say anything.

"I don't know," I say. "Live?"

Morgan once again raises her eyebrows but says nothing.

When Morgan leaves to use the restroom, the first thing I do is pry Jo's diary open, waiting for my sister to speak to me, only to find the pages torn from the spine. Her book of secrets is like an open mouth with all its teeth yanked.

Outside, my uncle and my father argue inside the orange halo of a streetlight.

"Dammit, just stay here, Ronnie!" my father says to his big brother. "Stay!"

"I ain't no damn dog," Ronnie says before he gets in his truck and heads away.

CHAPTER 9

Me and Kimberly: A Friendship in Three Parts
PART I: 1981

I didn't even know I was black until Kimberly's sixth birthday party, back when she was still Courtney Two. When I found out, I tried to drown her. The reason I did it was because she told me I couldn't be a mermaid, which is admittedly not the best reason to attempt murder. The sun was shining, and her birthday presents were piled up like a Christmas tree. Every once in a while, a newcomer would add another present to the pile, and one or two others would tumble onto the pool deck.

The concrete was hot and our fingertips Cheeto-stained when she announced, "Now, we're going to play mermaids. Except Ashley. Because black people can't be mermaids!"

Then she giggled.

It hadn't even occurred to me yet that there was anything I couldn't be, and the shame of the moment dug itself into my chest so deep that I couldn't breathe. And while I was standing there unable to breathe, all the other girls were doing cannonballs into the water. I don't remember how it happened exactly, but I know I grabbed her shoulders, wrapped my legs around her waist, and pulled us both down beneath the surface.

For a few seconds while I held us underwater, our bodies tangled up in each other, I could've sworn I saw the rainbow shimmer of scales and fins.

"Look!" I said to her in big bubbles.

"Help!" she bubbled back, unable to breathe.

I don't know why I did that. I'm not trying to excuse my behavior at all. But maybe I wanted her to know what it felt like.

When we got out and her mother started to yell at me, I looked down, and they weren't fins at all—just little brown legs with wet sunscreen leaking down.

Needless to say, they kicked me out of the party.

When we got home, my mother quietly walked inside the house to take an aspirin and lie down. Jo sat by our pool reading a tattered copy of *The Phantom Tollbooth*. I sat down on the broken pool chair next to her.

"Can black people be mermaids?" I asked.

She peered down from her book. "Why?"

"Courtney Two said no."

Jo placed her book on the chair next to her. She leaned toward me, stared into my face, and said very somberly, "Courtney Two is a Demon of Insincerity."

"Huh?" I said.

"Don't let her keep you from your castle."

"What are you even talking about?" Like I said, I was six.

Jo gestured with her index finger to come close, then even closer still. When I was good and close to her chair, she raised her foot and pushed it into my stomach, launching me into the water.

"Why'd you do that?" I sputtered when I popped up for air.

"Mermaids die if they're out of the water for too long." Jo looked at me over the top of her book. "You should say thank you. I just saved your life."

PART II: Earlier This Year

In January, Kimberly and I volunteered to deliver meals to the elderly as a service project. We would go to the volunteer center and pick up a bunch of meals to deliver to seniors after school. Kimberly is slightly afraid of old people, but I like them more than I like people my own age. Our favorite person was Doris. Her skin was delicate, like a butterfly's wing in my hand, and her hair was dyed a shade of blue like a cloud before the rain. She had a seemingly endless wardrobe of pastel tracksuits.

We were only supposed to be bringing her meals, but sometimes she insisted that we take her out into the world itself before she'd eat. This wasn't part of our duties, but Kimberly and I did it anyway.

We helped Miss Doris take out all her curlers, which weren't so much curlers as shredded bits of paper bag tied around her hair that did the trick. Then, Miss Doris had me pass her a lipstick that was coral and a shade too bright for her thin lips, but it made her happy, so even Kimberly didn't say anything.

Right before we headed outside, Miss Doris would say "Tweet, tweet" to a little bird about the size of a balled fist, before tapping its cage with her nails.

She turned her face toward the sky to drink it up.

"Any boyfriends?" she said.

"Not yet," I said.

"Same as before," Kimberly said.

"When I was your age, I was wild. I tarted it up all over town. Why, there was this boy who lived down by the marina who had the most beautiful car. He loved my ankles."

She lifted one of her ankles up out of the wheelchair for inspection.

"They're still beauties, aren't they, dolls? If you ignore all the spider veins."

Kimberly and I would take Miss Doris home, and Miss Doris would keep finding reasons for us to stay—something that needed to be fixed, or cookies she'd made that needed to be eaten. Finally, we'd have to pry ourselves away. Sometimes literally. Then afterward, Kimberly and I would talk about how getting old and being unable to do things for yourself must suck. Being an old person is a lot like being a kid, before you get your driver's license and the whole world splits wide open.

"You wanna drive us home?" she asked after one of these conversations.

"I don't have my license yet," I said.

"No shit, Sherlock. I know." She threw me the keys.

Kimberly started up where Jo left off. Jo taught me the basics, but Kimberly helped me practice each week as we drove back and forth to Miss Doris's and the others. She was a surprisingly patient teacher.

"Don't forget to use your blinker, Ash," she'd say through a mouthful of gum.

"You're jackrabbiting. Just slowly apply more pressure to the gas," she'd say as a light turned green.

Every so often, while driving from old person to old person, "I Touch Myself" came on the radio, and we would roll down the windows, all giddy and shit, and sing at the top of our lungs, *"I don't want anybody else, when I think about you, I touch myself,"* to random strangers on the street.

For a few years after the attempted drowning incident, before Michael, and after her dad left her mom and her mom was having a rough go of it, we were closer to each other than to the others. She would stay over at my house so often that my parents bought Kimberly her own toothbrush. She and Lucia and I would make those little pizzas out of English muffins and dance in my room to "Wake Me Up Before You Go-Go," and sometimes we would fall asleep in my bed whispering little secrets in elaborate pillow forts.

"I missed you," I told her once after I nearly drove us into a bus. I'm pretty certain I actually saw my life flash before my eyes and was feeling extra sentimental. "I miss us."

Kimberly looked over at me. "I'm right here."

Eventually, when we'd pick Miss Doris up, I would drive the three of us around for a bit. Miss Doris would stick her face out the window like a dog soaking up the world outside.

"Faster, child, faster!" she'd yell.

Kimberly was the one who took me to the DMV for my test. I was number sixty-nine, which we both thought was funny in a stupid way. The instructor was a permed she-devil who made me parallel park two separate times on a hill, and by some divine miracle, I pulled it off. When I passed the test on the first try, we jumped up and down and hugged and screamed in the middle of the DMV, while some girl in the corner across from me blubbered into her mother's shoulder.

"Freedom!" Kimberly said.

"I couldn't have done it without you," I said.

"No shit, Sherlock," she said.

Miss Doris fell down and broke her hip one afternoon, and her kids sold her house and placed her in a nursing home close to them in Florida. Kimberly and I stopped delivering meals after that. We'd already exceeded our required service hours, and I think both of us felt her absence like an ache. We stopped hanging out one-on-one again.

PART III: Today

The janitors are constantly cleaning, but somehow the girls' restroom always reeks of period blood. The left stall is flooded, which it does once a month. The toilet water starts to spread to the other stalls. I have to pee really bad, though, so I can't wait. The rising water barely misses my Keds.

I take a very funky piss. Cool funky, not smelly funky. I'm listening to the album *Maggot Brain* by Funkadelic, which is another of Jo's cassettes. The song I'm listening to is called "You and Your Folks, Me and My Folks," which seems like it was written for these times, except these times were decades ago. Eight years after John F. Kennedy was assassinated. Six years after the Watts Riots and Malcom X's assassination. Three years after Bobby Kennedy and MLK died. Bobby Kennedy was shot in Koreatown at the

Ambassador Hotel. If you drive down Wilshire, you can still see it, regal and crumbling. You wouldn't want to drive down there now, though, on account of the rioting.

"You know that hate is gonna keep on multiplying / And you know that man is gonna keep right on dying. . ."

On the cover is a black woman buried up to her neck in dirt, her Afro reaching toward the heavens, mouth open in a scream somewhere between agony and joy, while maggots squirm on the ground around her. All the songs make you feel like dancing, or like you're on drugs, or both. *"There won't be no peace . . ."*

This is what was on the news this morning:

Yesterday, Long Beach declared a state of emergency. In Riverside, there are fires. A security guard killed a seventeen-year-old when looters entered a discount store in San Bernardino. In San Francisco, young people smashed windows and set fires. In Atlanta, young people protested, while more than four hundred others gathered at a nonviolent rally in front of Martin Luther King Jr.'s crypt. They carried signs reading L.A. HAS NO JUSTICE; PUT JUSTICE IN THE JUSTICE SYSTEM; KING VERDICT WAS A WAKEUP CALL—STOP THE KILLING; and LIVE AS BROTHERS OR PERISH AS FOOLS. A peaceful protest against the verdict on the steps of Cleveland's City Hall almost turned violent when a thirty-one-year-old white man drove by in a van with both Nazi and Confederate flags flying from it. So far there have been twenty-five deaths, 572 injuries, hundreds of fires and arrests, and $200 million to $250 million in damages.

No peace.

. . .

In New York City, students at a private school in Queens walked out of their classes chanting, "Rodney, Rodney, Rodney."

Nobody is walking out of school here.

Walkman still on, I wash my hands. Somebody taps me on the back. I jump up, startled, and my sunshine player crashes to the floor.

"What are you listening to?" Kimberly says as I scramble to get to my Walkman before the flood does. She neatly applies two coats of mascara and flips her hair over one shoulder, smiles, then flips it over the other. For some reason she decides that shoulder's better.

"*Maggot Brain*. It's by Funkadelic. It's old."

I take the cassette cover out of my backpack and show it to her. She scrunches her mouth to the side and nods her head. I put the cassette back in the bag. She peers into my backpack. I've got a bunch of Jo's cassettes in there now. Sometimes when you want to disappear, it's easiest to hide in music.

"Since when do you listen to so much black shit?"

"I'm black," I say.

"Yeah, but you're not, like, blackity black," she says.

I don't know what to say to this, but Kimberly doesn't seem to expect an actual answer. She applies another layer of lipstick, gets a paper towel, and blots. We just got to school; I can't imagine she needs a touch-up already, but sometimes more lipstick is extra armor for the day ahead.

"You and Michael talk a lot, right?"

Her mouth is the color of guts. I can't tell if it's an accusation.

"I mean, not a lot," I say.

Anuj was right: They must've taken him aside to ask him about the shoes.

"Yo, I woulda been out there, too, if I could. Cop me some kicks. Fight the power and all that shit, right?" The white kids call Dustin Cavanaugh a wigger because he wears his clothes baggy and listens to gangsta rap and tries to talk like he came from the hood. He's like our school's very own version of Al Jolson. He doesn't actually talk to the black kids. Or, I guess, maybe it's more like they don't talk to him. If he's a wigger for "acting black," what does that make them? Or me?

"Yo, you're an asshole," LaShawn says.

"Me?" Dustin walks back toward him. He seems shocked that LaShawn didn't laugh or throw up signs in response.

"That shit ain't fucking funny," LaShawn yells.

Everyone around us grows silent. This is not the LaShawn to whom we're accustomed. The gentle boy who smiles at everyone and lets crickets out the window. The boy we watched scouts salivate over for several games in a row. The boy with the loud-ass mama who's never loud himself. The boy who always keeps his cool on the court, even during championship games when the referees are dead wrong. The boy our school paper actually described in earnest as "one of the brightest shining stars to ever grace these hallowed halls."

Our school paper is full of purple prose written by B-student drama queens. But they weren't wrong. Not about LaShawn.

We go quiet, and then we wait for Dustin's response.

"Yeah, well . . . Least I ain't no thief," he says.

This is the exact wrong thing to say at the exact wrong time,

She knows me well enough to know when I'm lying.

"What do you talk about?" she asks. "I feel like we've been together for years and we hang out and make out, but he doesn't, like, open up or whatever."

"Um . . . we talk about you," I say. "He's crazy about you."

She narrows her eyes. We stand awkwardly looking at each other in the mirror. What she says next is not what I expect from her at that moment.

"I miss us," she says finally.

"I'm right here," I say.

CHAPTER 10

LaSHAWN IS DRESSED in a Brooks Brothers polo and old-white-man khakis that crease in uncool places. He looks tired. He's on time for school because instead of taking the bus, he spent the night at White Brian's house, and now he's wearing White Brian's white dad's clothes. White Brian is Goofy come to life—long limbs, awkward gait, and a laugh that sounds like an infectious hiccup. They've been best friends since freshman year, when nobody knew how good LaShawn was, back when they both rocked anemic mustaches and video game T-shirts. They're an odd pairing, but somehow they make sense. Also, there's no Black Brian.

"I'm so sorry," I say to LaShawn as he takes his seat.

"What? You didn't do anything." He smiles wanly.

Mr. Holmes stands at the board, patchwork side of his face to us. He hasn't brought up any more about Watts or the riots. Instead, we came in and he got straight to work, like he was embarrassed that he'd shared so much of himself with us yesterday. The AC in the classroom isn't working, so sweat drips down our bodies in tiny rivers. Behind me, Phillip Murkowski is starting to smell. Teenage boys already smell bad enough without being slowly roasted in their own juices. While the city burns, even our rich-kid school is coming undone. Meanwhile, my cousin gets to stay at home. She's probably going through my stuff.

We're in the middle of reviewing gravitational orbit energy when the principal comes to the classroom door. Principal Jeffries looks like a former hippie who enjoys hiking and drinking on the weekends. She's got that leather to her skin, and even here at work, she wears Tevas as though at any time she might be called upon to climb a mountain of unruly teenagers.

"LaShawn, can you come with me, please?" she says.

LaShawn stands up, confused. White Brian's dad's khakis stop just above his ankles.

"I bet you it's about those shoes," Anuj Patel whispers behind me.

"Don't talk to me," I say.

When the bell rings, LaShawn still has not returned to class. White Brian places LaShawn's books, pens, and notebook into his abandoned backpack, zips it up, and carries it with his own out the door.

I see LaShawn between second and third periods. He kicks at his locker hard, scuffing his Jordans, leaving a dent like a metal wound.

As we pour out of our classrooms, LaShawn turns as if to address the entire student body. "Man, fuck this place. This is what y'all really think of me? This all I am to you?"

'cause this is what happens next: LaShawn, who never says any-thing mean to anyone; LaShawn, who remembers my Emily Dick-inson poem; LaShawn, who is Stanford-bound—LaShawn reaches back and punches him. Hard. Dude crumples to the ground.

I think of what Jo said once during one of her fights with our parents, right after they found out that she'd dropped out of school.

She said, "We have to walk around being perfect all the time just to be seen as human. Don't you ever get tired of being a sym-bol? Don't you ever just want to be human?"

I guess LaShawn finally had enough.

"Omigod. Omigod," some girl named Paula keeps repeating, even though, really, Dustin's pride is hurt way more than his nose, which is barely bleeding a little bit. He staggers up and looks around at the crowd that's gathered.

"You just got knocked the fuck out!" Anuj yells, and everyone starts to laugh.

LaShawn is frozen in place. He looks down at his fist as though it's a foreign object, as though the very body that moves so effort-lessly across the court, those very hands that almost never miss a shot, have now betrayed him. He looks up and out at the crowd, terrified, and over at Principal Jeffries as she hurries down the hall-way toward us.

The rumors were one thing—easy enough to ignore, even if some-thing happened, it wasn't on school grounds—but now there's been violence. Unsure of what to do with him, they park LaShawn in the front office near the school nurse. The front office is glass paneled so that you can see pretty clearly inside. The rest of us go from class to class and sneak quick peeks at the blackened golden boy behind the glass. At one point, he sips from a Styrofoam cup, and even this is news.

"I think he's drinking coffee in there," some girl says.

"I wish I were coffee," her friend replies.

If anything, this has now made LaShawn that much more attractive to a certain faction of the girls at school. Now he's even better than a golden boy—he's a bad boy.

Between periods, I hear the girls passing and joking: "I suddenly don't feel so well. I definitely need to go to the nurse."

Or, as one girl says more bluntly, "Let's punch each other so we get sent to the principal's office."

At lunch, the black kids huddle around. They're not as open with their bodies, as free with their laughter. They sit and whisper with one another. Them. Us. Our. They. My father gets mad when I refer to black people as "they."

"They are you. Those are your people."

"*I am he as you are he as you are me as we are all together,*" I say back.

"The classrooms smell like ball sweat," Heather says as we sit down to eat.

"God, I can't wait to get out of this place," Trevor says as he sits down at our table. "I mean, look at it right now."

"High school?" Courtney says.

"Dude, Los Angeles is in the middle of a damn riot, if you hadn't noticed."

"Don't be a dick. I thought you were talking about the broken air conditioners."

"'A riot is the language of the unheard,'" Trevor says. "Right, Ash?"

"That shit's real deep, Trev," Heather says before I can answer. "Where'd you steal it from?"

"Martin Luther King," Trevor says, all proud of himself.

"Junior," Heather says. "Martin Luther King, Junior."

"Whatever," he says. "Don't be pedantic; it's unattractive." She pushes him and he pinches her and she squeals, and all the rest of us raise our eyebrows 'cause they're definitely flirting, even if they'd never admit it.

Somehow, I've never noticed that Trevor has elf ears until now, or maybe they're more Spock ears? Trevor talks so much that those big-ass ears of his hardly get any use. I used to think it was because most white boys are taught that when they open their mouths to speak, the rest of us will shut up and listen, but when we went to get our corsages last week, Trevor told me he was the middle kid of five, which I somehow never knew about him. Now I think maybe this is why he's always so loud. He's just trying to hear his own voice. Although maybe it's a little bit of both. I'm beginning to think that's kind of what being an adult is—learning that sometimes people are a little bit wrong, but not for the reasons that you think they are, and also a little bit right, and you try to take the good with the bad. Right now, we're young and still figuring out how to be good.

"Did you know that in Manhattan alone—" Trevor starts.

"Shut the hell up about New York already," Heather says.

"You guys, my parents are talking about moving away if this continues," Courtney says. "They're really scared. They think Los Angeles is getting too dangerous."

"They're rich white people," I blurt out. "Who exactly do they think is coming after them?"

My friends all turn and look at me like I have five heads. Then Trevor bursts out laughing.

Before I have to answer for myself, Lana walks by and winks at me. Today she's wearing a baggy flannel shirt, her bra partially exposed above her tank top, combat boots unlaced. Her hair is in a greasy bun atop her head. She looks like spilled wine coolers.

"Omigod. What a lesbo!" Courtney says as Lana walks past.

"She probably had something in her eye," Heather says, and raises her eyebrows at me.

Heather has always thought Courtney is a little bit in love with Kimberly. Normally, I'd chalk it up to too much *Donahue*, but I think she might be onto something. At Jenny Liu's birthday party, we played Spin the Bottle, and Kimberly and Courtney wrapped their arms around each other's necks and kissed with tongue. Even when everybody'd stopped cheering and laughing, they kept kissing, until finally Kimberly pulled away and Courtney burned incandescently. But also, not two years ago, we blasted "Freedom! '90" and walked around in Kimberly's mom's clothes pretending to be supermodels, and Kimberly and Courtney got into an actual physical fight over who got to be Cindy Crawford, so who knows?

I want to follow Lana to wherever it is she eats, away from my friends. Maybe we could share cigarettes and oranges and talk about something that matters. Or even something that doesn't. Courtney could be right—it's possible that Lana is a lesbo. Or bisexual. I've never met any bisexuals that I know of; Lana would be my first. I know exactly three real-life lesbians.

The school loudspeaker comes on and the principal announces that the administration has decided to keep the prom on its scheduled date and time of tomorrow at 8:30 p.m. Everyone in the quad cheers. Courtney and Kimberly hug each other tight.

"Thank God!" Kimberly says.

Across the way, the black kids turn their attention only briefly to the loudspeaker, then return to their huddle. LaShawn is not among them.

Through the glass, I can see LaShawn's legs stretched out before him. I pull open the heavy glass door and LaShawn looks up. The student office assistant, a blond girl named Allison, sits next to him, her knees tucked under her butt and her hand awkwardly patting his back like she's trying to comfort him, but also like she's a little bit afraid of him, too. Allison's only a freshman, but the boys say she's got a pair of senior tits.

"Hey, Cricket." LaShawn looks up at me, and Allison glares at the intrusion.

Across the wall in the office are gold stars with everybody's names and where they're going to college. We're supposed to tell the school secretary as soon as we decide where we're going so our name can be displayed with the rest. "All our shining stars!" it says in gold glitter across the sheets of navy-blue bulletin-board paper meant to look like the night sky. People have been not-so-sneakily going into the office to check on where everybody else got in, to compare their good fortunes or to commiserate, but mostly to go back to their friends and say shit like, "How the hell did *she* get into Dartmouth?"

I pretend to scan the names.

"Got one to add to the wall?" LaShawn says.

"I'm not sure where I'm going yet."

I wait for him to say something in response, but he doesn't; he keeps staring out into the distance.

"So, what's the verdict?" I say, and nod in the direction of Principal Jeffries's office.

"They're still deciding," Allison chimes in, and LaShawn looks over at her like he'd forgotten she was even here.

"This school is fucking bullshit," he says. He looks like he's ready to burst out of himself, or out of the office, at least.

Once, freshman year, Lucia forgot to pick me up after cheer practice because she thought I was going to hang out with Kimberly afterward instead. I called the house and waited and waited for somebody to pick up, but nobody was around, so I left an appropriately pathetic message. It was in the fall, when the sun starts to go down entirely too early, and soon the lights came on in warm circles across the school grounds. All the other kids trickled out of their respective activities to their rides home as the air started to get nippy. Meanwhile, I was still in my short-ass cheer shorts and cold as hell. The wind began to lash at my skin, so I started to walk around the school while I waited, to keep warm. The basketball team finished practice and its little giants poured out of the gym and toward the parking lot, but LaShawn was still outside doing drills up and down the length of the court, even after spending all those hours at practice. Pivot. Pivot. Shoot. Fake. Two-pointer. Three-pointer. Layup. He wasn't as filled out as he is now, not as tall. Lankier. He still looked more like a little kid, with his ears all stuck out like the kid on the *MAD* magazine covers. It was just him on the court, under the orange glow of the lights. And me standing at the fence, fingers around the metal, silently watching.

"Hey," he said.

"Hi," I said.

"Why are you still here?" he said.

"My ride forgot me," I said. "Why are you still here?"

"I gotta stay here to stay here," he said, and laughed.

He stopped dribbling and walked over by the fence. It was like we were talking to each other through a cage.

"You think this school is worth it?"

I shrugged. "My parents seem to think so. I mean, I guess people get into good colleges from here."

"Mija," Lucia shouted at me from across the way. Her Corolla *put-put*-ed in the distance. I was briefly ashamed—not of Lucia or her car but of being the kind of person who had a Lucia to pick her up, who never even thought about the cost of the school I was in.

But also, I realized LaShawn must've also had a Grandma Opal to sit him down, look at him, and say, "You have to be better." And whatever it was, we both felt it in our bones and understood it to be in each other's heads, this metric of our worth. Pivot. Better. Layup. Better. Three-pointer. Better. Lift up, raise your arms, aim. Be more.

I wonder if LaShawn remembers that.

Across from us, the school secretary keeps her eyes glued to the portable television. She watches, her pretty face in her delicate hands, as the fires spread across the screen, eerie in black and white like an old rerun of *The Twilight Zone*.

"Are you here to add a college?" She briefly turns her attention to us, noticing me in the room for the first time.

"Nope. Not a shining star," I say.

She immediately goes back to the television.

"Look—you're right under your star," I say to LaShawn. His star is a little bigger than the others. I bet that's Allison's handiwork.

Allison looks like she's playing a game of double-dutch, waiting for the right time to get back into the conversation, to not get smacked in the head by the jump ropes.

LaShawn twists his head around to look at his name posted up on the bulletin board and rolls his eyes.

"I'm so sick of this place," he says. "I mean, I didn't even want to go here, you know? I wanted to go to high school around the corner like all my friends. My real friends. Not these goddamn phonies."

"Totally." Allison finally sees her opening. "Me too."

The secretary calls Allison away to stuff envelopes, and she reluctantly heads over.

"Sometimes I feel like I can't even breathe here," LaShawn says to me in a near whisper once she's gone.

"Me too," I say.

"It's a fucking black hole," he says.

I want to tell him that I started the rumor. That I'm sorry. That I didn't mean for everything to get out of control like this. That I don't even know why I did it. I want to sit next to him and lean my head back underneath these stars, to close my eyes for a minute and breathe.

"Well . . . I should probably get to class," I say.

As I get up to leave, I hear the reporter's high-pitched squeal as she thrusts her microphone into the face of a passing looter—same voice, same scene the channel keeps playing over and over: "Don't you know that it's wrong?"

Michael walks up behind me as I head toward my sixth-period class. He grabs me by the wrist and pulls me into the art room.

"What are you listening to?"

He leans in closer to my headphones, and we press our heads and arms and legs against each other. We lean into some poor freshman's oil painting. I can feel his breath across my collarbone.

Out of the itty-bitty speakers, Bono sings about all the things you say you want and you'll give. Jo used to love U2, but now she thinks Bono's a twat.

"How'd this happen?" He runs his finger along the length of my new scar.

"My neighbors were going to shoot my uncle, so I had to jump off the roof to stop them," I say.

"Fine, don't tell me," he says.

"Are you in love with Kimberly?" I ask.

"She's my girlfriend."

"That's not what I asked."

"I don't want to talk about her right now."

"You can't just pretend like she doesn't exist whenever it's convenient."

"Yeah, well, what about you?" he snaps.

"I'm leaving," I say.

"Don't go." He grabs me by the wrist and pulls me closer to him. "Please."

The lights go out. There have been large power outages throughout the city since the riots began.

"Everything's falling apart." He sighs. "What do you think is gonna happen to LaShawn?"

"I don't know."

"I kinda get what LaShawn did, you know?" He fiddles with the strap of my tank top.

"Because Dustin's an asshole?"

"Just, sometimes it feels like I got all this love about to burst out of me," Michael says. "But, like, also I hate everyone."

Inside my headphones, the violins swell and the guitars began to wail. Bono's voice pines and breaks at the crescendo. When the lights finally come back on, the back of my shirt is covered in damp bits of blue and pink and orange, like the sunset over the ocean on a clear day.

After school, the black kids stand in the quad, their fists raised, defiant like Tommie Smith and John Carlos at the '68 Olympics.

Lil Ray Ray's still absent. Mildred too. Fat Albert raises a pudgy brown fist to the sky. Candace too, though she temporarily brings her hand down to shift her pink backpack straps before raising her fist back up into the air. Her nails are like candy talons.

"What is that about?" I ask Heather.

"LaShawn's been temporarily suspended," she says gloomily.

"What? Whatshisface wasn't even really hurt."

"Zero tolerance." She sighs.

The black kids are resolute, all eight of them in the quad together. They look like a rainbow of Negro, from the pale of

Margie's freckled half-breed arm to Candace's blue-purple skin reflecting the sun.

"Like, honestly, if they hate us so much, they should go to their own school," some girl passing by us says to her friend.

"This *is* their own school, dipshit," Heather says to her.

The girl purses her lips and gives Heather the side-eye.

"Shit! I forgot something in my locker. I'll catch up with you in a bit," Heather says to me before jogging away.

Candace stares at me. It's either a challenge or an invitation. She can't possibly know that I'm the one who started the rumor, can she? Maybe she's imploring me to join them. I should join them. Jo would.

Instead, I sheepishly smile and walk past like everybody else.

CHAPTER 11

LANA DOESN'T SMELL like wine coolers after all, just cigarettes. I know because she sits next to me on the front steps while I'm waiting for my friends after school. Her flannel shirt rolls down her arm a bit, revealing a plum-colored circle of hurt.

"What happened to your arm?" I ask her.

She quickly buttons the sleeve so that it won't roll down again.

"You wanna come over?" Lana says.

I'm supposed to join Kimberly, Courtney, and Heather at Heather's house. It's a Friday, so we'll drink and smoke and float in her pool and watch television and invite the boys over. Courtney's mom will make us snacks and ignore the alcohol and the weed, because she says, "I'd rather you girls do that in front of me than out there in the world."

Lucia is always telling me I need to make new friends. A month before the end of high school seems a little late to heed her advice, but I guess better late than never. Also, I don't really want to go home to Morgan and her judgy eyebrows.

"Sure," I say.

"Cool," Lana says. "We have to walk a bit, if you don't mind. My mom has the car today."

Courtney, Kimberly, and Heather plop down around me, edging Lana out of the way.

"Hi," Lana says to them.

"Hey." Heather drapes an arm over my shoulder. Courtney and Kimberly kinda glance and nod at Lana.

"Let's go," Kimberly says.

"Actually, I think I'm going to go to Lana's tonight," I say.

"Wait, what?" Kimberly says. "Her?"

"Gee, thanks," Lana says, but she doesn't seem particularly bothered.

"It's the day before prom, Ashley," Kimberly says in that tone of voice she uses whenever somebody challenges the natural order of things, like when somebody thinks Coke is better than Pepsi.

"I'll see you guys tomorrow. Promise."

Kimberly rolls her eyes so far back that by the time they return, I think they've filled their passports.

"Suit yourself," she says.

"Let's go," Lana says.

Lana and I stand and start to walk across the street. While they're walking away, Courtney turns around, sticks her pointer and middle fingers up into a *V*, and darts her tongue back and forth between them.

Lana and I walk deeper into the hills along a tiny sidewalk. Every so often a car will drive by at twice the speed limit and Lana will protectively crowd me into somebody's hedges. We don't chat much, but it's a comfortable quiet.

"We're here." Lana stops in front of a carved wooden door amid yellowed hedges.

From the outside, the house itself is very California: mission architecture, big windows, Spanish tiled entrance. The yard is littered with multicolored pots containing various flowers and succulents. A fat orange tabby sprawls across the front steps. Lana scoops it up in her arms.

"This is She-Ra." She laughs. "Wanna pet her?"

"I'm allergic," I say.

She puts She-Ra back down, and She-Ra scurries off somewhere into the property.

"Your house is cute," I say.

"Oh, that's not my house. That's the owner's house," she says.

"Oh. Oops. I'm sorry," I say.

"Don't apologize. You didn't know," she says.

I follow her down a path of flat stones to a backyard. It's neatly manicured, and mostly empty save for a huge trampoline toward the edge of the yard. Next to the trampoline is a guest house. It's about a third the size of the front house, with similar architecture. Two Adirondack chairs stand guard at the entrance with a planter full of cigarette butts. One of the two orange trees drops its cargo, and the orange rolls in front of the chairs.

"Welcome to my humble abode," Lana says as we enter.

Usually when the people I know say this, it's ironically. In Lana's case, it really is quite humble. Everybody at school thinks Lana is richer than the rest of us, since her parents paid for a whole new library so the school would let her back in. This place makes it look like they blew their life savings on the library. The furniture is mismatched and faded, but all around there are interesting things to look at—carved wooden statues, a hanging tapestry. The wall is painted an uneven bright blue around a crumbling fireplace. I point to one of the statues.

"That's really pretty."

"My mother got it when she was in Nepal," Lana says.

"What does she do?"

"A little of everything. Never enough, though," Lana says.

"She must be pretty cool," I say.

Lana doesn't respond.

The small kitchen is visible from the living-room area. An old stove abuts the cabinetry like an afterthought. The kitchen table is a deep brown, its legs carved in ornate shapes, its top marked up from a child's carelessness with a pen. Matching bright-green cushions fight to unite cacophonous chairs.

"Who lives in the front house?"

"Two of my mom's friends from when she was with my dad. She got them in the divorce. They're fun. Artists. Brad and Pham. Brad owns a gallery in Mid-City. Pham is a tiny Cambodian refugee and used to be an artist. I'm not sure what he does these days. He's a great cook, though."

"When did your parents get divorced?"

"Technically, they were never married. Least not officially. We used to live in this huge house a few blocks over. But when they broke up, he kicked her out, and I went with her. He pays for my tuition and whatever, though."

He must've been the one who paid for the library.

Lana takes the scrunchie out of her hair and lets it fall down around her shoulders.

"Want something to drink?"

"Sure," I say.

"Red okay?"

I'm used to cheap beer and wine coolers and those little bottles of airplane alcohol Courtney sneaks from her dad's suitcases. I have no preference. Lana pours red wine into two blue crystal glasses that refract the light in geometry around the room. There's not enough for two full glasses of red, so she adds some white wine to the top. I don't know much, but I'm pretty certain that's not how wine is supposed to work.

"Cheers!" she says.

Lana's room is very small, and mostly sparse. Her bed is a low wooden thing, and instead of on a nightstand, her lamp rests on a pile of hardcover art books.

"Who are you going to prom with?" I ask.

"I can't go."

"Your mom won't let you?"

"Nah. It was a condition of the school's letting me back in. I can't do anything like prom and Grad Night and all that stuff."

"That sucks."

"That shit's lame, anyway," she says, but I'm not convinced she means it.

She pushes play on the stereo, a big silver monstrosity on the floor under her window. Atop the stereo is a burst of primary color in a series of toy figurines from McDonald's Happy Meals. A young woman screams out of the speakers, followed by a rush of angry guitars. Wine still in hand, Lana begins to flail with wanton disregard for the actual beat.

It sounds like some shit that Jo would like. I finish my wine in one great gulp, and then I too begin to move jerkily across Lana's floor. She jumps up onto her bed and reaches her hand out to me, and then we're both up on her bed flapping around. We dance in exorcism until the song ends and Lana jumps off the bed.

"Trampoline?"

"Fuck yeah!"

If with my friends there's stillness and talking, with Lana there's movement, across the room, up and down, and now we rush back outside. Lana doesn't sit still for very long. I like it for now, although I can see how it might get annoying.

We jump and jump, and then we collapse into the black and lift our faces to the sun as it descends. It's the happiest I've been in a long while, here on this trampoline with a girl I barely know.

"What would you be if you could be anything?" she says.

"A fish."

"If you could only wear one color for the rest of your life, what would it be?"

"Yellow."

"What's your favorite cheesy song?"

"'Home,' from *The Wiz*. That was my favorite movie as a little kid."

"Where would you live if the world was your oyster?"

"It isn't?"

When it's nearly dark, she turns her body to face me.

"My mother's the one who did it," she says.

"What?"

"The bruise." She pulls up her sleeve. "There are others, too."

I don't know what I'm supposed to do or say.

"I'm almost out of here; I can make it through a few more months." She rolls the sleeve back down. "I think . . . sometimes maybe she doesn't know how strong she is."

"But why?"

"It's complicated," she says. "Aren't all families? It's like, I hate her a little bit, but she's my mother and I love her. Anyway, don't tell anybody."

"What about moving in with your dad?"

"Fuck that guy," she says.

This girl has offered me so many bruised pieces of herself, and so finally I offer her something in return.

"I did something really bad the other day," I tell her. I can't quite bring myself to say what out loud. Actually, there are two things. But one is worse than the other.

"Did you kill somebody?"

"God, no."

"Maim somebody? Help dump a body? Sell yourself for money?"

"Jesus, Lana."

"All I'm saying is, I can't imagine anything you did could be that horrible. Just . . . make it right," she says. "That's all there is to it."

"You don't want to know what I did?"

"Only if you want to tell me."

A light floods the backyard, revealing a body in silhouette. Lana's whole being tenses up beside me.

"Lana, babycakes! I made your favorite!" The man's thick accent sounds like the swell and pop of blown bubbles. Upon hearing the sound, she relaxes, and with two bounces launches herself out of the trampoline.

"Ashley, this is Pham," Lana says.

"Lana never has people over. You must be special girl." Pham reaches for my hand. He's compact but strong. His face is big and broad, the color of toasted almonds. His eyes smile, a deep dark to them.

"You must have dinner with us, new friend," he says with a flourish. "I insist."

I should maybe call Lucia and tell her where I am, but usually I'm at Kimberly's on Fridays anyway. What difference does it make, really? Unless these people are murderers, but I doubt it. I watch too much *Dateline* with Lucia sometimes, so I know murderers are almost never who you'd expect, and somehow also exactly who you'd suspect. Even so, I'll take my chances. I'd much rather stay here than go home just yet.

Brad and Pham move through their space in tandem, Pham finishing with a cutting board, Brad placing the used knife in the sink, Pham taking the silverware out and putting it on the counter, Brad picking it up and setting the table. Brad is balding; his hair is a silver donut in need of a trim. He's got the body and carriage of a ballerina, gliding through space as though even setting the table is a reason to dance. His light balances Pham's heavy footsteps.

Brad and Pham and Lana are a force together. They discuss art and the presidential race and Arthur Ashe and Magic Johnson and

Chechnya. Brad and Pham ask what Lana and I think about all of it. It's intoxicating, being around people who see the whole damn world as something to inhale.

"It's very upsetting, what's going on now," Brad says, "but not unforeseen."

"How do you feel about it, Ashley?" Pham asks.

"I don't know how to feel," I say. It's the truth. How do I tell people I barely know that I'm angry and sad, but also embarrassed? That I feel that anger along my spine, holding up the very shape of me, and in my fingertips like a curled fist. That the sadness is like a dull ache, heavy in the muscles fighting to keep my head up. That I feel ashamed that black people are both the agents and the victims of this chaos, and I don't want to be thought of like that. But I'm also ashamed of myself for thinking I'm somehow better. The shame I feel in my guts, pulsing, spiraling; but also everything feels very far away. I'm black, but my black is different from that of those rioters on TV.

"How did you two meet each other?" I ask between careful bites.

Pham and Brad look at each other.

"My parents were professors. The Khmer Rouge, they didn't like anybody with education, you know? My mother very smart woman. My father too, though not like my mother. And we are Vietnamese in Cambodia, so even worse."

He drifts over somewhere else, the way Lucia does sometimes when she talks about home. Brad takes over for him.

"My wife and I sponsored Pham and his sister," Brad says. "My wife was very religious, and I was too, then. Or I tried to be, anyway."

"So you, like, adopted them?" I say.

"Not quite. We paid for them to come to the United States. For their schooling here. We were kinda like their American family. There were so many people in need. My wife said we had to do something."

"I had to lie about my age," Pham says, "so they would take us both."

"I just thought he was wise beyond his years," Brad says. "In that way some kids are when they've been through a lot. . . ."

"But I was twenty-year-old!" Pham laughs. "I'm just . . ." He holds out a flattened hand and lowers it to the floor. Short.

"We would talk to practice his English," Brad says. "Sometimes we would stay up for hours talking."

"Even though my English was very bad then," Pham says.

"And then Brad and Pham fell in love," Lana interjects. "Messy, messy love."

Messy, messy love. I think of Jo and Harrison singing their pretty song, and my mother's sheer stocking in a ladder running up her heel as she and Jo both push against the door between them.

Brad laughs. It's a forced laugh. He kisses Pham gently on his temple.

In middle school, I remember watching a TV movie on *Walt Disney's Wonderful World of Color* about a Cambodian refugee who won a spelling bee. I don't remember much about it other than that it was supposed to be inspirational, and also that they didn't know how to pee in American toilets. I'd never thought that maybe different people might pee differently before that. I wonder if this is something Pham and his sister had to relearn.

Pham looks up from his plate. "My sister doesn't remember how I held her on my back when we ran. She spit at me when she found out about the two of us."

Brad sighs and grabs his hand.

"She'll come around," Lana says, and pats Pham on the hand. "I mean, for god's sake, it's the nineties!"

After dinner, Brad and Pham retire into the house and Lana and I go back to jumping on the trampoline. I do a back tuck into a front tuck, and Lana claps and says, "Again!"

We tucker ourselves out and sit in the ratty chairs in front of her guest house. She offers me a cigarette, and I inhale and hold it in my lungs. This is apparently the exact wrong thing to do. I've never actually smoked a cigarette before, only pot, and so I cough and cough and cough.

Lana laughs. "This isn't an after-school special. You don't have to smoke, silly."

"Why don't you tell them?" I say. "About your mom?"

"It doesn't happen that often. She gets frustrated. She's lonely, I think."

She links her arm through mine.

"Are you lonely?" I say.

Instead of answering, she kisses my cheek.

"Who did you used to hang out with?" I ask.

"You remember Gloria Dowd?"

"Yeah . . . kinda," I say. "With the . . ."

I feel bad when I realize that I don't remember anything about Gloria Dowd at all.

"Her father got transferred and her parents moved to somewhere in Orange County."

"It's not like she moved to Colorado or somewhere."

"Fuck. It might as well be another country," she says, and we laugh.

The alcohol combined with the cigarette combined with the food is starting to catch up to me, I can feel it.

"Are you a bisexual?" I feel myself losing control of my words.

"Does that matter to you?" she says.

"No."

"Yes," she says. "I think so. Why?"

"Do you like me?" I slur, and pucker my lips in her general direction. I think I could fall in love with somebody like Lana, even if she is a girl. Girl parts are way better looking than boy parts, anyway.

"Not like that . . ." She laughs and dodges my mouth.

"Why not?" I'm a little indignant.

Before she can finish formulating her response to my stupidity, the world begins to spin, and I don't feel anything. Then I feel everything.

I run inside toward Lana's bathroom while she chases after me laughing. "In the toilet! In the toilet!"

While bent over the toilet, as Lana holds my hair away from my face, I tell her the second bad thing but not the first.

"I kinda started the shit with LaShawn and the shoes. My friends spread the rumor."

"Your friends are twats," she says. "Kimberly's the worst."

I laugh and puke some more.

"She's had a rough couple of years," I say.

"So have all of us. That's fucking high school, man," she scoffs.

I think of the girl Kimberly nicknamed Jabba, after Jabba the Hut, last year, and now nobody even knows the girl's name. Everybody calls her Jabba. Kimberly's bitchiness coils in words that she doesn't even give a thought to beyond her own personal amusement. To everyone else, they're a series of blows to the gut, even if Kimberly's never once balled a fist.

"Make it right," Lana says as she pats my back. She doesn't know how much of it is wrong.

Back in the living room, we sprawl out on the couch, and Lana makes me drink a glass of water. After I gulp down the first, she goes back into the kitchen to get me another one.

We don't hear the door when it opens. Lana's mother is feline and startled. Her green eyes flash with fear at the sight of me in her living room, alone. She looks like Lana, but pale and hard. She begins to reach for the nearest would-be weapon, which happens to be a copper Buddha statue. I think of poor Uncle Ronnie with his hands to the sky and two rifles pointed at his head.

I stand and raise my hands to the ceiling.

"Don't worry, I'm not here to rob your house. Mine's nicer," I'm drunk enough to say.

Behind me, Lana bursts out laughing.

Her mother does not.

Pham drives me home. Lana sits in the back seat behind me. We sit silently, but it's a comfortable silence. After a bit, Lana squeezes her head up front between the two seats. "I'm sorry my mom's an asshole."

Lana's mother tried to blame her response to me on the riots, like I was a single solitary teenage looter who decided to break in and chill on her couch.

"You know how everyone's so on edge right now." Lana's mother sighed.

"It's okay," I said.

Like I said before, I'm always saying things are okay when maybe they're not.

"Sometimes people, they see your skin, and all they know of you is war," Pham says to me as we round a corner.

"I hate it," I say.

"Me too," he says. "You must come visit us again."

We're almost to my house when Lana starts to sing, "'*When I think of home I think of a place where there's love overflowing . . .*'"

Her voice cracks a little. Pham and I join in for as long as we can remember the words.

CHAPTER 12

F I COULD preserve my friends, as we were, in amber, this is the yellow day I would choose. Maybe it's a specific day, or maybe it's a composite of days. Maybe my memory has taken the arms from one day and an eyebrow from another and a few strands of hair from yet another day still. But this is it.

Kimberly is the first to befriend me. She is small and blond and already imperious, with her natural curls and chocolate-covered fingers. She walks up to me on the playground, the new girl, and, with a compliment, anoints me: "I like the way your lips are two different colors."

I'd never thought about the color of my lips at all until that moment. But right then I thought they were beautiful. A little brown, a little pink, with white teeth, like Neapolitan ice cream. Heather was pudgier than the rest of us, and her shirt rode up when we ran over to the swings. Her legs were covered in dirt from digging in the sandbox. I don't remember if she built any castles. Courtney had a frizzy bowl cut and carried around a little

Ziploc baggie that had previously contained her peanut-butter-and-banana sandwich with the crusts cut off. She walked around gently plucking ladybugs from leaves and zipping them inside with the others. She didn't know that they'd die later.

"Look," she said, and held out her baggie to me.

"This is Courtney, we have the same name, and this is Heather," Kimberly said, and Heather and Courtney both waved at me. Courtney wiped her nose with her arm, and the spotted ladies fluttered.

"I'm Ashley."

"We're friends now," Kimberly said, and we all spit into our hands and shook on it.

First, we pretended to be unicorns. We stuck our hands on our heads and pointed our index fingers like magic.

We hung upside down on the monkey bars, not old enough to care that our days-of-the-week undies were showing, and the boys were too young to notice.

We agreed that Ms. Glasgow was the most beautiful teacher in the school, but maybe that's because she had a stash of dinosaur cookies that she handed out like gold stars when we were good. Ben Gordon tried to kick us off the swings because we were girls, but together we fought back, strong.

By the end of lunch, we had a favorite song, "Flashdance . . . What a Feeling" by Irene Cara. We skipped around the playground and swayed our hips to the beat, pretending to be welder-stripper-dancers with hearts of gold.

After school, we went to the auditorium for Brownies. Nobody joked about my being a brownie in Brownies. Not yet. We learned a song: *"Make new friends, but keep the old, one is silver, the other is gold. A circle's round, it has no end, that's how long I will be your friend."*

We sang it in a circle and held hands, and afterward we let go only for chocolate-chip cookies that didn't melt in our mouths and juice boxes we squeezed to their deaths.

Courtney, Kimberly, and Heather are my first friends, my gold. So maybe that's why I make excuses for them even when I know I shouldn't. Why I keep my real feelings just under my tongue. Even as we're starting to feel less like magic and more like four mismatched socks all rolled up in a single ball and stuck in the back of a drawer together. I felt more like myself with Lana tonight than I have with my friends in ages. I'm not sure what that means, exactly. What do you do when the people you love no longer feel like home?

I miss us.

CHAPTER 13

MORGAN SITS ON the front steps of my house talking on the cordless phone with Auntie Eudora in Vegas. I don't think I'd want to still talk to my mom if she left me to chase after her new lover, but the riot seems to be pushing people together and pulling them apart in funny ways, and maybe that's sort of what being a family's like, anyway.

"What am I supposed do, baby?" Auntie Eudora says to my cousin over the phone.

"He's not picking up the phone," Morgan whines.

I hear Auntie Eudora tell Morgan that Guadalupe and her husband have gone home, so it's just Uncle Ronnie trying to keep the looters and arsonists away.

"You gotta wait until this whole thing blows over," Auntie Eudora says. "Just be patient."

Morgan side-eyes me as I stumble past.

"You're drunk," she covers the phone and says to me.

I shrug.

"I don't care. Tell him I wanna come home," I hear her say as I enter mine.

On Friday nights, before I got old enough to make bad decisions at other people's houses, I used to sit with Lucia as she got ready to make hers. I would watch as she shimmied into tight dresses, spread glitter across her face, and used Aqua Net to make a fortress of her hair. On the edge of her bed, I'd play DJ and watch her transform. She would strap on her gold heels and twirl me around like a disco ball to "Quimbara." While Celia sang, we sparkled.

Lucia has the weekends off, which means that she's able to stay out as late as she wants on Fridays and Saturdays. On the nights when she didn't come home, I knew that she'd either decided to stay over at her friend Damarís's or she was with a man. Damarís had a European hatchback like a spoiling tangerine, with a bumper that was half peeled off. She and Lucia would peel out of our driveway like they were in a race against time, like they had to get to the clubs and back before her car rotted away for good.

The Wednesday before last, Lucia asked for the evening off to go visit Damarís, who was going back to Guatemala for good, and I did something very stupid. I can't tell you about it yet, but I will.

Now, instead of being out with Damarís, Lucia sits on the couch in the living room, watching television, alone. She has fewer weekends left here with me than I have fingers.

I drape myself over her and give her a kiss on the cheek. Morgan comes in from outside.

"You smell like a bar," Morgan says.

I ignore her and turn to Lucia.

"I made a new friend. Like you told me to."

"Does your new friend come in a bottle?" Morgan points to the television screen showing coverage of the riots. "You know, not all of us get to party and pretend like nothing's happening."

"I wasn't partying," I say. "I'm worried about Uncle Ronnie and the store and everything, same as you."

"No. Not same as me. He's my dad."

"You're right. I know," I say, before belching pink wine.

Morgan gives me a dirty look. I know that she resents me and resents being here. She thinks I don't care. But it's not that; it's that there's so very much to care about, so much to feel, and instead of trying to sort out what's in my head, sometimes I don't want to feel any of it at all.

I'm sorry, I want to tell my cousin. *It's not that I don't care, it's that I don't know where to begin.*

It feels like a lifetime of biting my tongue has left my words flattened across the tops of my teeth.

Onscreen, they're rebroadcasting bits and pieces of the peace rally that happened at Wilshire and Western earlier today. I pretend to focus very hard on peace.

"Do you miss Damarís?" I ask Lucia.

"It's hard making new friends as you get older." Lucia sighs.

"Who is Damarís?" Morgan asks.

"Her best friend," I say.

When I was really little, Lucia would take me over to Damarís's place and I would play with the neighbor girl in the building's courtyard while the two of them gossiped in Spanish and exchanged news from home. Damarís lived not far from where Jo lives now, a little closer to the freeway. The neighbor girl was Chinese; her parents were recent immigrants who worked at a store down the street from the apartment complex. She didn't speak much English, and I didn't speak any Chinese, but somehow that didn't stop us. Childhood is its own language, of sorts. The Chinese girl moved away years ago, somewhere off the 10. I bet her English is pretty good now. The only Chinese I remember is *Ni hao*, hello; *Wo ai ni*, I love you; and *Nèi ge*, that one or um in Mandarin. I remember it because it sounds like nigger.

Last year, there was that coup in Haiti, and now on the news they'll show those strangers in the ocean floating and clinging to one another to keep from drowning. Once, while we were watching a boat of refugees being rescued, Lucia leaned in and asked if I wanted to know a secret. Sure, I said. She told me that Damarís came from rich people back in Guatemala, and that if it hadn't been for the war and coming here, they would never have been friends, much less best friends. I think Lucia was trying to tell me that she knew what those black refugees felt like.

Morgan, our refugee, wanders around the room touching things.

"Why would your parents go out in this?" she says.

"They have date nights on Fridays," I say.

They were supposed to go see *Phantom of the Opera* downtown, but it was canceled on account of the rioting, so instead they're going out to dinner nearby. When I asked them this morning if they were still going out, my father looked at me and said, "Even when bad things are happening, we have to keep on living."

"Your dad should be out there with my dad protecting the store," Morgan says. "Not eating fucking fancy pasta or steak or whatever."

I don't know why she picked pasta and steak as the foods my parents might be eating. Given the area and their personal preferences, it's more likely seafood, but now isn't a good time to be too specific.

Later, when Lucia has fallen asleep in front of the television, Morgan turns to me and says, "How good are you at keeping secrets?"

I think about all the secrets I keep. I'm like a walking safe, my guts full of everybody else's hidden parts. My friends'. Jo's. My own, and now Lana's, too. So many secrets.

"The best," I say. "I'm the best at secrets."

"Good. Come with me," she says.

I follow her into our entryway, where she slides on her sneakers and nods at me to do the same. Then she grabs my father's pellet gun.

"What are you doing?"

"It's a secret," she says. "Duh."

Morgan raises the pellet gun at me like she kinda wants to shoot me.

"You'll shoot my eye out," I say.

"Good thing you've got two. Let's go," she says, and a gust of warm air hits us as we walk into the night.

The Parkers aren't in front of their house anymore; on this third day of the riot, with no action, they've retired. I guess they've gotten bored of waiting.

"What are we doing?" I whisper to Morgan.

"Shhh," she says. "You're the lookout. So . . . look."

She raises the gun like she's got experience shooting at things and actually hitting them. The shot cracks through the night as the first pellet goes into the first tire. Then the next pellet into the next tire. Apparently, her expert marksmanship isn't limited to pelting people with lemons.

"They're gonna come out any minute," I say.

"Your turn," she says.

"Me?" I say. "No!"

"Hurry up. Don't be a little bitch." She practically tosses the gun at me.

I feel the weight of it in my hands, against my shoulder. It's exhilarating. It's power. I reach back and cock it. My pellet hits one of their plotted plants and it shatters, the dirt tumbling out like entrails. It's no tire, but still I'm a little high on destruction.

"That's for my dad," Morgan says. "Assholes."

A light turns on in the Parkers' house.

"Oh shit!" Morgan says, and we run back quickly into my house. Out of breath and laughing, we collapse on the sofa next to Lucia, who startles and awakens with a *"¿Que?"*

We have to be better. We have to turn the other cheek. We have to counter hate with love. Except when we don't.

It's like my sister said: "We have to walk around being perfect all the time just to be seen as human. Don't you ever get tired of being a symbol? Don't you ever just want to be human?"

So how good am I at keeping secrets, really? The best. Or maybe, depending on your perspective, the worst.

The Wednesday before last, I should've gone with Lucia to say goodbye to Damarís. Damarís put Band-Aids on my boo-boos and fed me ice cream and let the Chinese girl and me make forts out of her couch cushions. Instead, I did something awful. Or, I guess, I did something human.

Okay. Here goes. Like I said earlier, I'm mostly a good person. Or I used to think so, but now I'm not so sure.

Kimberly thinks she and Michael are going to lose their virginity to each other, but that won't happen, because I had sex with Michael while Lucia sat in Damarís's tiny kitchen among the boxes, saying goodbye.

This is how it happened:

Courtney and Kimberly and Heather and I sat on the front steps. Trevor and Michael joined us. Trevor kept sliding down the banister and walking back up to the top and sliding down again. Heather drew stick figures across Courtney's thigh with a ballpoint pen. Kimberly rested her chin against Michael's knees while he stroked her hair, and I tried not to feel anything at all.

The rain started to fall in big fat droplets, and we were bored. Eventually, Courtney and Kimberly decided they'd rather be bored and dry at the mall. Heather left to check out this new band recording their demo at her grandfather's studio. Trevor lingered for a bit, until he too decided there was somewhere else he'd rather be. Then it was just the two of us.

"Wanna chill in my car?" Michael said.

"Okay."

Normally, we would've been listening to something. We're always listening to something. But that day there was only the drill of rain against Michael's tinny car roof, loud like we were inside a drum.

"Inhale," he said. I breathed in.

"You know my dad tried to kill himself when I was a kid?" he said.

"That's fucked up."

"I was the one who found him."

I wonder what it would be like to walk in on my dad, blue and belted around his neck. It's weird to think of a real body hanging right in front of you, like it does in one of those lynching photographs with the white kids eating cotton candy and pointing.

"What's he like?"

"I don't know him well. He works, and when he's not working, he's golfing or whatever. He embezzled from his old company. That's why he tried to kill himself."

My secrets came out in a rush through my guts. Jo's failure to fly, and a few others that had wrapped themselves around my organs and often tried to slither up my throat. I wanted to give them to Michael in his shit-green tin can of a car, but also I was a little afraid. Sometimes when we talk, I feel like he's just trying to stare right into my brain itself, but more often than that I get the impression he's not actually hearing me at all.

Then I thought, *Maybe it's okay to tell everything to somebody who doesn't really hear you. Your secrets still stay yours, somehow.*

"My sister fell off the roof when we were younger. I think she did it on purpose—like, to hurt herself. But after it happened, we all just pretended it was an accident. It feels like we're always pretending things are okay when they're not. Like we're the goddamn Huxtables or whatever. But we're not. Nobody is. It makes me feel like I'm the fucking crazy one, somehow."

Michael held my face in his hands. He didn't say anything, and I wasn't sure if he'd heard me at all, but I didn't care. Then he leaned in and kissed me, and I kissed him back. It was the first time we'd ever actually kissed, though a few weeks before we'd come dangerously close. The kissing would've been bad enough, but we didn't stop there.

I remember the way the leather of his varsity jacket squeaked as he moved. He grabbed me by my waist and pulled me in closer. The stick shift dug into my side as he tried to pull my leg over toward him. He placed his hand on my boob and moved it around like he was trying to open a doorknob.

"Do you wanna move to the back seat?" he whispered.

No scratched at the back of my throat, but he kissed it away before it could come out.

Anyway, neither of us knew what we were doing.

Now I think maybe we were holding on to each other to keep from drowning.

It hurt a little bit, but not as much as I thought it would, and afterward we laid back and held hands.

Morgan was the first person who taught me about sex. Well, technically, she taught me how to put my Barbies' perfect plastic bodies together, rub them a bit, and close the curtain to their canopy bed. A canopy bed would've been a much more romantic place to rub bodies than Michael's shitbox of a Chevy Nova.

"First, they kiss," Morgan said.

"And then?" I said.

Morgan didn't know the specifics, just the rubbing.

"Good girls keep their legs together," my mother told me offhandedly sophomore year as we were watching a talk-show special on teen moms. No specifics.

In the car with Michael, I thought of that parade of beleaguered teenage girls and their pudgy babies. Were they bad girls, then? Was I now a bad girl?

I thought I was going to vomit.

"Wait . . . ," he said as I climbed over him and pushed and pulled against the car door, willing it to open.

"You can't go out in that. It's pouring." He tried to pull my arm back. "You'll get sick."

"Rain doesn't make you sick."

We struggled in an awkward push and pull. Finally, he let me go.

It wasn't supposed to rain that day. The water soaked through my thin dress as I ran across the parking lot until I was some heavy, waterlogged version of myself.

"Ash!" Michael called after me, but only just the once.

CHAPTER 14

THE WORLD OUTSIDE is still. A singular insomniac bird chirps off and on. My head is pounding. I shouldn't have had so much to drink at Lana's. Sometimes when I drink too much, I wake up way earlier than I normally would and can't get back to sleep. Before I woke up, I was dreaming of falling, and when I opened my eyes, my stomach felt like it was in my throat. After staring at the ceiling for a while, thinking about all the things I shouldn't have done in the entirety of my seventeen years on earth and all the things I should do, I decide to call Jo.

"Hello?" Harrison says into the phone like he's still in the middle of a dream.

"Hi. May I speak to my sister?" I say. "It's Ashley. Ashley Bennett."

After some rustling and muttering, Jo answers, "What's wrong, Ash?"

"Nothing. Everything."

"Are you okay? Are Mom and Dad okay?"

"They're fine. It's not that. . . . Everyone's all right. I wanted to know you're all right. You haven't been answering any of their calls. . . . They're worried about you."

She sighs. "I'm as well as can be expected."

"What does that mean?"

"The rebellion. It's dying. They're militarizing the streets."

"Jo, this isn't something for you to take one of your stands on," I say.

"People have been dying," she says. "That's the whole reason for the rebellion. That's the whole reason for taking one of my stands. Protesting isn't supposed to be easy. Revolution isn't easy. Not when you're trying to dismantle an entire system."

"You're a revolutionary now?"

"You sound like Valerie," she exhales with a deep sigh.

"Mom just wants you to be safe."

"Worrying about being safe is what's dangerous, what deters progress. We get treated like some crazy fringe group—"

"Who's we?" I interrupt.

"The Revolutionary Communist Party, Ashley," Jo says, like I'm supposed to know who the hell she's talking about. "But what's so crazy about wanting people to be equal? Capitalism doesn't work, Ash. This country isn't taking care of all its people—just the ones with the right skin color, the right genitals, the highest bank accounts. You don't have to be crazy to acknowledge that. If we don't do something now, then when?" She pauses for a moment. "Can you keep a secret?"

Not this again.

"I thought about what you said. You're right. Flyers aren't enough. People throw them away. You gotta do something more permanent."

"I definitely didn't say that part," I say.

"I've been writing on the walls with spray paint. Slogans here and there."

"Why can't you collect clothes and cans of food or whatever like a normal person? They can arrest you for graffitiing. Doing graffiti? Whatever."

"It's not graffiti. It's a movement," she says defensively. "Hold on a second."

I hear soft static, then a bit of rustling and movement.

"Where are you?"

"I'm on the cordless. I stepped outside. Harrison's gotta be up for work in a few hours."

A fire destroyed an electronics store on Pico and Fairfax, and a Vons nearby was looted. This is super close to Jo's place.

I imagine Jo sitting on the steps in front of her house in this twilight, the two of us looking out at the sky at the same time, like little lost Fievel and his sister in *An American Tail*.

Years ago, when that wildfire burned down the hillside and Daddy refused to leave, Jo was the one who left first.

She was nine and had packed her own suitcase and mine with clothes and Handi-Snacks and Fruit Roll-Ups. Jo was a tiny kid, not much larger than me, even though we were years apart. The suitcases were as large as us both, and sometimes we would take turns hiding inside and zipping ourselves up so that all we could feel was dark; then we would roll each other along on the wheels and pretend to go to far-off places.

"We're in Paris!" the sister pushing the suitcase would narrate to the sister inside.

"We're in Istanbul!"

"Now we're in Djibouti!" and then we would laugh, because booty.

Until eventually it got to be too much, and the suitcase sister would scream to be let out: "I can't breathe!"

"We're going," Jo said to my dad.

She grabbed me by the hand, and we started walking down the hill. She'd brought her softball bat with her in case of coyotes, and she let it dangle from her small right hand like a warning. A family of squirrels ran past.

"Get back here," my mother shouted.

"Now," my father added.

My father and mother looked on incredulously as Jo and I kept walking.

Jo gripped my hand tighter still.

"I'm the parent; you do as I say," Daddy shouted.

We were halfway down the road by then, past the emptied driveways of our neighbors who'd already fled. In a few more steps, we'd turn the corner and disappear.

"Girls!" Lucia yelled, "*¡Eschuchen a sus padres!*"

I turned back to look at Lucia. Jo and I stood in the middle of the road. One of my hands held on to Jo's, and the other to my blond Skipper doll with all the hair cut off. Our adults were starting to look small.

"Maybe we should go back," I said.

"It'll be alright," Jo said.

That was all before.

"I don't want to lie to Mom and Dad for you anymore, Jo . . ."

"Then don't. Just don't tell them. It's not like they tell us anything about themselves. They're so damned secretive, even about the stuff we should know. It's like we materialized out of thin air, according to them."

"What's that supposed to mean?"

"Ask Dad about Grandma Shirley."

"What's Grandma Shirley got to do with anything?"

I hear her inhale and exhale deeply again.

"Forget it."

"The looters are fucking over people like Uncle Ronnie, too, you know? Not just bad people or corporations. You can't treat people like collateral damage . . . Just come home. It's safer here. . . . When are you gonna stop being mad?" I say.

A siren grows louder and louder in the background.

"Morgan's here while Uncle Ronnie guards the shop. She shot out the Parkers' tires with Daddy's gun. You would've loved it."

"Those assholes." She laughs.

"I miss you," I say.

"I miss you, too."

"Come home."

"This city is our home. All of it," Jo says as the one siren becomes a chorus screaming somewhere out there.

Home: A Personal History

This is where we're from, best as I can tell from the breadcrumbs that my parents and Grandma Opal and Uncle Ronnie have left that lead to the story of us. Our grandparents moved to Los Angeles from the South, all of them. They drove across the country carrying with them in their veins all that trauma and all that hope and used it to lay the bricks for lives brighter than the ones they left. Nobody's actually from Los Angeles, except for those of us who are.

The canals and the pier in Venice were dreamed up by a developer and tobacco mogul named Abbot Kinney, who envisioned it as kind of a Coney Island West. At least Coney Island was built by black people fleeing the South. Even though they built it, black people couldn't live near the boardwalk and canals, because racism, so instead they settled in Oakwood, which was a small community set aside for black folks. This is where my mother's mother, Grandma Opal, settled when she eventually moved here with her brother Wallace. She was the first of my grandparents to make their way west. My mother's father, Grandpa Moses, settled downtown in Little Tokyo, or, as it was known at the time, Bronzeville. Blacks were able to move in because the Japanese who'd previously lived there had been sent to internment camps. Grandpa Moses was an accountant, and my grandma was a trained actress and singer folks said would've been huge, if only she hadn't had the misfortune of looking too black.

"I could've been bigger than Dorothy Dandridge, or even Hazel Scott! I was lighter than Hazel, you know? My nose was keener . . . ," Grandma Opal would say on occasion, whenever somebody brought it up.

"What does that mean?" I asked, but before Grandma Opal could tell me what a keen nose was and what that had to do with anything, my mother shooed me into the next room. If you look closely at some of the films of the era, you can see Grandma Opal's beautiful smile and long legs dancing across the background.

Meanwhile, according to Uncle Ronnie, my dad's mother, Grandma Shirley, moved out here with her mother; her sister, Minnie; and two brothers, Gordon and Elijah, who would be lost during World War II. They crammed together into a house in what was then a working class but stable neighborhood that would eventually, after years of government neglect and discriminatory policies, become the hood. But before that, there were new trees and fresh lawns and neighbors who looked out for one another, the kind of neighbors who would stand next to you and tell you all their business and try to get into yours as you watered the lawn. All of them came to Los Angeles to be free from Jim Crow, to claim what they could of the orange groves and the ocean breeze and the sunshine. Even if they were a little disappointed, even if it wasn't exactly as advertised, still it was better than.

Grandma Shirley started Shirley's Vacuum Repair Spot a few blocks from that house sometime in the late fifties. Grandpa Charles ended up dying in the war, like her big brothers, and so she used her savings from working for years in factories plus what the country paid her for her husband's sacrifice to open the store. With the earnings from the store, she eventually bought a home of her own. There's a photo of my dad and Uncle Ronnie holding her hands at the store's grand opening, all of them beaming. My dad looks like a nerd in huge Coke-bottle glasses and, somehow, a black-boy cowlick. Uncle Ronnie is clearly feeling himself in a leather jacket that looks like he loved it so much he probably wore it to bed. It's the only photo of the three of them my dad has in the house.

This is how we came to be: Darla was my father's college girlfriend, a hairdresser. He would sit next to her doing homework, or studying, or just staring at her while she did her clients' hair. Darla wasn't in college, but they'd grown up with each other and started dating during their senior year of high school. My father would go over to her house and stay for days at a time. "Her parents took in strays" is how my dad phrased it. He liked her place because, unlike his, there was enough space to sit and think and write and be. Darla was quiet and very kind, according to both my parents. My parents met when my mother came in to get her hair done, and there was my father, next to Darla, watching. My mother said she stole glances at him in the mirror, and he at her, the entire time Darla straightened and curled the length of my mother's long hair.

"What are you studying?" my mother finally worked up the nerve to ask.

My father told her, and even though they weren't studying the same thing—they weren't even at the same school—my mother said, "We should study together sometime."

Right in front of Darla, he said, "Okay."

It wasn't very smart of my mother to do that while Darla still had a hot curling iron in her hand. If you look closely, you can still see the exact dark moment kind Darla lost my father and found my mother's right temple.

They never told me that story directly; I overheard it while they were hosting a dinner party and were feeling extra in love and extra social for a few months.

So you see, she wasn't wrong, my sister. Jo and me, we've got the hood in us as much as the beach, as much as Downtown, and even as much as Hollywood itself; the length of Los Angeles stretched in our veins like the crisp lines of a vacuum across carpet.

I don't know anything about before my grandparents got to California. I guess I never really thought to ask.

Home: 5:13 a.m. Today.

It's still late when I hang up with Jo and walk downstairs to grab a glass of water. Or, I guess I should say, early. My dad is up watching the news coverage of the riots on television, although I don't know how he can bear to keep the TV on anymore. He's sprawled out on the couch in his pajamas, a pillow tucked under his head and one under his arm like a teddy bear.

"Are you worried about the store?" I say.

I visited the store a few times as a little kid, back when my dad would still occasionally stop by to see how Uncle Ronnie and the store were doing. Mostly what I remember is swiveling on stools, waiting for something to happen. A customer would come in with a vacuum, and Uncle Ronnie and my father would rush over, lean over the thing, and inspect it like their mother had done so many years before. Vacuums take away the dirt and the ugly and make things look like new. But the dirt goes somewhere.

"What are you doing up?" my father says.

"Can't sleep."

"Join the club," he says.

When I was really little, right after Grandma Shirley died, my dad used to come into my room at night, lie down on the floor, and cry. I would pat him on the head and say, "Don't cry, Daddy," and sometimes he'd stop crying. I don't really remember her, but I remember that. He did it for a full week until my mother walked in, caught him crying, and told him to stop it; he was scaring me. I wasn't scared, though. I just wanted him to stop being sad. Sometimes when your grown-ups are sad, their sadness feels even heavier than your own.

Later, when I asked my mother how Grandma Shirley died, she froze and said, "Can you do Mommy a big favor, Ashley?"

"Okay!"

"Don't ask Daddy that."

"Why not?"

"You see how sad he is, right?"

"Yes."

"That'll make it worse."

"But why can't you tell me?"

"Just . . . Just let Daddy tell you when he's ready."

But I guess he's never been ready, and I've never worked up the balls to ask. Whatever it is, I know it isn't something like cancer or a heart attack, because people talk about people who die of those things. He and Uncle Ronnie don't talk about her much at all.

After a few too many beers one night, Uncle Ronnie told me that their mother used to close the shop and take them out of school and buy them ice cream and drive them up into the hills or along the coast for hours, talking to them about their friends at school or civil rights or their father who died in the war. Other times, he said she would lock herself in her bedroom for several days straight, and even if they pounded on the door and screamed "I'm hungry!" she wouldn't come out. They almost lost the store multiple times.

I imagine it would be hard to grow up with a mother like that—a mother who loved you hard and then retreated, like the flow and crash and ebb of a wave, so you never quite knew whether you were floating or drowning. My mother said that to cope with his mother, my father hid in himself; then for a while he hid at Darla's, until finally my mother met him and yelled at him to come out. But how do you take a turtle and tell it overnight to be a dolphin?

This is exactly what she screamed at my dad during one of their fights.

"You're being a turtle, but I need you to be a dolphin, Craig."

My father and I sit across the couch from each other, and I try to make sense of the man in front of me.

"You never tell me anything about before we were born," I say.

"Did I ever tell you that my mother used to take us fishing?" my dad says.

"No."

He tells me how his mother used to pile them into the truck when they should've been in school and drive them up or down the coast. There the three of them would sit, fishing lines in a row, until something bit and the others would whoop and holler, cheerleading as he or she reeled it in. Grandma Shirley had grown up in the South, with brothers, and had grown up fishing with her brothers until she moved far away, had my dad and Ronnie, and eventually picked up where she'd left off. They'd bring home the day's catch in a cooler, fish guts and scales stinking up the tiny kitchen with its homemade curtains, Grandma Shirley humming as she brined.

"I stopped wanting to go," he says.

"Why?"

"Wanted to be in school. I liked school."

Grandma Shirley taught both boys everything there was to know about vacuums. Ronnie took to it, but I guess my dad wanted more school, something different, somewhere away. Anyway, Grandma Shirley used that vacuum money to send my father to a fancy college and then to grad school, while Uncle Ronnie stayed home and worked on fixing what was broken.

Sometimes I think we gave my father a good excuse to run farther away from his bad memories. Maybe this is where Jo gets it from. Turtles have shells, which are these very complicated structures meant to protect them from the world around them, but shells also hide your heart. Shells can blind you to beauty, even when you're right in the middle of it.

"How did Grandma Shirley die?" I ask quietly.

My father pretends like he didn't hear me and turns up the volume. The distance between us is exactly one shell.

In the end, it's not fire that gets to Grandma Shirley's store but the looters.

This is what they take:

Broken Hoovers, Bissells, Sanitaires, and Mieles

Newly refurbished Hoovers, Bissells, Sanitaires, and Mieles

Ronnie's prized, brand-new, fancy Dyson that won the International Design Fair last year, bought special from the catalog

The cash register and the entire safe

The brand-new Apple computer Morgan used to do her homework after school

The toilet paper and paper towels from the small restroom?!

En masse, the looters push into the dream that my grandma built with her calloused brown hands in a city of angels. They pull these things out through the door and the broken window, stepping over all the broken glass.

This is what they leave:

The curtains that she sewed by hand in the waiting room
The baby pictures of me and Jo and Morgan and Tanya that
Grandma Shirley nailed, hands shaking, into the wall, and
Uncle Ronnie kept
The pictures of all the youth sports teams she'd sponsored
over the years, the boys and girls in them long grown—at
least one of whom tried to scream above the looters to
"Stop! Stop this now!"

My father's life was built in part on vacuums, but I've rarely seen my parents use one.

A few years ago, while Lucia was cleaning up, our old vacuum let out a loud, unsettling roar and then a series of death gasps. My mother argued that it was time to finally get a new one.

"No, not yet," my dad said.

What I remember most is the way my father bent over the vacuum for hours like he was doing open-heart surgery, or scaling a fish. Looking very much at home.

CHAPTER 15

ORGAN WAILS LIKE somebody's died, and I guess maybe she's kinda got a point, 'cause that store was an important part of all of us. Right now, I feel it a little more like a missing appendage, and she feels it like a ruptured spleen or a punctured lung. My dad walks around dazed, as though something pulsing and vital has been ripped from inside.

"Everyone's okay," my dad says, like he's trying to convince himself.

"Everyone's not okay!" Morgan screams.

"I'm gonna go pick Ronnie up." My father searches around for his keys.

"Lemme come with you," Morgan says.

"No. You stay here," he says, and heads out the door.

After days of burning, there's a heavy smoke cover that's descended upon the city. Outside feels like a heavy comforter I want to kick off. But inside feels oppressive in its own way too, with Morgan's sad wafting through and filling up every room.

Finally, in spite of the news warnings about the shitty air quality, I decide to go for a run, lungs be damned.

For the most part, ours is the kind of neighborhood where teenage girls feel safe running. Just a few weeks ago, I got sprayed by a skunk. My parents were out of town, and when I called her, Jo said to bathe in tomato sauce. It looked like a horror movie when I popped up out of the tub. It didn't work, though, because after that, instead of skunk, I smelled like SpaghettiOs. Skunks aside, there was a brief period of time before I was born when people were afraid of a band of crazy white people in quiet canyons, but I'm not a famous person, and those murders weren't in our canyons. Usually, I'm more afraid of the mountain lions or rabid coyotes than people. I don't expect to run into my mother, who maybe scares me a bit too.

My mother is in her jogging clothes and sweaty, but she's also having a secret cigarette. She took up smoking when she and my dad were having marital problems a few years back and quit when I guess they decided things weren't so bad after all. My mom and dad spent the better part of two years yelling nastiness at each other throughout the house, him cornering her, her cornering him, until I grew to hate angles and all the anger they could store. It's like for years at a time they barely talked to each other, or they talked only enough to fight. Whenever Jo and I would try to stop their fighting, they would tell us it was none of our business. But they were fighting so loud we couldn't sleep, so it kinda was. Jo said of their fights, "Different monsters, same shadows." And yet somehow they didn't give up on each other. Anyway, I didn't even know my mother still had cigarettes around. That's how I know she's really worried about Jo, even if she refuses to do anything about it.

"You're smoking," I say.

She takes a last drag and extinguishes it under her road-battered Nikes.

"Nasty habit," she says. "Don't let me catch you doing it."

"I hear it makes your morning shits great, though."

My mother looks at me quizzically. "What on earth . . . ?"

"Never mind," I say.

"The Parkers came over early this morning," she says slowly. "They were very angry. Somebody shot out their tires last night. Do you happen to know anything about that?"

It takes everything in me not to burst out laughing. I shake my head.

"That's what I thought. I told them my daughter would never do anything like that," she says, and then we both start to laugh.

We're almost to the house when we see the straggly coyote and her cubs walking across the street. They amble along, sniffing at trash cans. My neighbor's Pomeranian barks at them from the window and the mama coyote's ears perk up, but for the most part she seems unbothered.

My mother splays her arm protectively across my chest, like we're in a car coming to an abrupt halt. Coyotes don't bother you, mostly, but anybody with sense knows not to mess with a mother and her babies.

"Stop. Don't move," my mother says, and it's the closest I've felt to her in years.

. . .

Uncle Ronnie's only a little banged up. There's a cut across his forehead from the glass that shattered as the looters burst inside. As they surged forth, he tumbled backward over the window ledge and sprained his arm, which is in a sling. He rests his back across a giant heating pad but has a big bag of frozen peas folded across his shoulder. Morgan sits next to him on the couch, looking dutiful and forlorn.

My mother gently places her hand on Uncle Ronnie's shoulder as she walks by. "I'm glad you're okay, Ronnie."

"Thanks, Val." He places his hand on top of hers and pats it. Then my mother disappears into the house to shower.

"You're covered in sweat." Morgan crinkles up her nose at me, and I pretend to wring my shirt out on her.

"Come here, babygirl." Uncle Ronnie reaches out his arms and hugs me so that the bag of peas smashes into my face. "Let me hug my favorite niece."

"Am I really your favorite?" I say.

"You're the one who's here right now." He belly laughs, then grimaces. "So . . . yes."

"I'm glad you're okay," I say.

"Daddy, do you need new peas?" Morgan says, and I laugh 'cause it's kinda funny, but nobody else seems to think so.

"You know, if I was younger, I could've taken every last one of those punks," he says.

I imagine poor Ronnie sprawled out on the floor as the looters rushed past him, taking everything he'd worked so hard to get.

"I held on to that Dyson for as long as I could, though, I'll tell you that," Uncle Ronnie says. "I grabbed ahold of that motherfucker's leg and didn't let go . . . Well, at least not until he kicked me in the face."

"He could've killed you." My dad's voice wobbles like he could cry. I didn't even know he was in the room.

Uncle Ronnie looks as though he wants to argue with him, but maybe it's something about the way Daddy says it, like a declaration of love instead of a punch to the face, that makes Uncle Ronnie instead say softly, "I suppose he could've."

"I'ma get you new peas," Morgan says, and runs toward the kitchen.

On the news, the anchor announces that troops are coming into the city to help the National Guard—thousands of soldiers, army and Marines, with their armored vehicles that scream war. It's the first time the military's been sent to a city to quell disorder since the 1968 MLK assassination riots. The last time the military was in Los Angeles like this was in 1894 for the Pullman Strike, which started in Chicago and spread countrywide to involve almost a quarter of a million railway workers. For months, they shut down railroads across the country and crippled businesses, including the US Postal Service. Then the government sent in the army, and thirty people ended up getting killed.

The news shows the troops tumbling out of their Humvees, ready and green like plastic toy soldiers.

"Well, will you look at that," Uncle Ronnie scoffs.

While Morgan and Uncle Ronnie talk about the store, I feel guilty that my personal crisis is that it's a few hours before prom and there's nobody available to do my hair. Patrice, my hairdresser, is six feet tall and pecan-colored, with Flo-Jo nails that she'll dig into your scalp like a rake as she washes your hair. It hurts, but it also feels like she's scratching the bad away. There aren't many black hairdressers near us, so to find Patrice my mother and father went through the entire phone book calling places in the area and asking almost apologetically, "Do you do black hair?"

Patrice is always late and never apologizes for it, but she's very good at what she does, so I don't complain to her face. When the relaxer starts to burn away my kinks and I cry out, "It's burning!" Patrice screams like a coach, "Just hold on, we're almost there, girl!"

Earlier this morning, when I tried to call the shop to confirm the appointment, it went straight to voice mail. So I tried again, and again. There's a slight chance the store is gone, burned down, looted, and disappeared. I tried calling Patrice's home number, but I got the dull beep of a disconnected line. The power's out in large portions of South Central, according to the news.

My mother tries calling several other black hair salons in the phone book, but the story's the same: answering-machine messages saying they're closed until further notice.

"I'll do it," Morgan says.

She sits me down in the kitchen and parts my hair into thin lines with a rattail comb. Her hands are impatient, and I try not to scream as she jams the weight of the blow-dryer comb into my head like it's a dive bomber.

"You're hurting me," I say.

"Sorry," she says, and tugs a little softer.

She sticks the hot comb atop our kitchen stove. It's the only hot comb we have in the house, old and slightly rusted, with a green wooden handle that my dad recovered from his mother's stuff when she died. With the hum of the dryer gone, it's me and Morgan alone together.

"Pops used to say the store was my inheritance. And I was like, whatever, because vacuums are fucking vacuums, you know? They're not exactly glamorous. But I did love that store. I grew up in it."

"I'm really sorry," I say.

"Me too." She sighs.

"The Parkers asked my mom about the car," I say.

Morgan presses my head into her stomach. As she runs the comb over my edges, I can feel her stomach gurgle in my skull.

"What she say?" Morgan blows on the comb.

"I think she knew we did it," I say. "But she told them we would never do such a thing."

"Yo momma ain't no snitch!" Morgan says, and we laugh hard until she accidentally burns the top of my ear.

Lucia enters the kitchen and begins to straighten up to the beat of the yellow Walkman on her hip. She carries around a spray bottle of bleach like it's a six-shooter and this is the Old West.

"You smell like bleach," I say.

She points the bottle right at me, and I stagger back like I've been shot.

She sings a song by this Tejana and moves around the kitchen shaking her butt. Her date with Jose from Western Union is tonight.

"Maybe you two will get married after all," I say. If he marries her, maybe she'll stay nearby.

"I've already been married," Lucia says. "I don't need to get married again. But love? Love is good."

"If you stay here and move in with him, I can come visit you," I say.

She laughs. "Babygirl, let's see if I like him first."

"Well, then why are you going out with him if you're just gonna leave soon?"

"Can't I have a little fun before I leave, *mija*? Dating doesn't have to mean you get married. Sometimes it can just be to have a good time with a pretty face." She laughs again.

Umberto and Roberto have grown into men while their mother raised me. I've charted their growth alongside my own, something adult metastatic in us—the ripening of our bodies, the ever deepening of their voices when they call the house phone: "Hello, Miss Ashley. May I speak to Lucia, please?"

I wonder if they would trade their nice school and guitar lessons and textbooks for this moment in the kitchen with their mother, curls wild, dancing. Maybe by now she's an ache they've learned to live with.

She goes over to the radio on the wall and tunes it to the station she's listening to on the Walkman. The Tejana's voice bounces around our tiled kitchen.

"Lucia?" I want to tell her everything. I want so badly for her to tell me how to make everything better.

"*Baila esta cumbia,*" she sings. So I do.

My father enters the kitchen and we dance with each other. He laughs and twirls Lucia around.

My mother comes down the stairs, her Jheri curl in flat wet

rings around her face, and my father looks up, guilty, 'cause he's been caught being a dolphin with somebody else.

My mother looks askance at Lucia, and Lucia abruptly stops dancing. I feel a quiet nimbus beginning to swell in my mother. Best to provide a distraction before it rains, I decide.

"I spoke to Jo this morning," I blurt out.

My mother stops looking at Lucia and my father together and turns her attention to me. "You didn't think to tell us this earlier?" she says.

My father starts to scratch above his eyebrow. "How is she doing?"

"She's fine. She says she's a communist now," I say. I don't dare tell them that she's been out doing whatever the hell she's been doing in the middle of the riot. Jo would never forgive me if I did.

"That's what college kids do. They go to college. They try these things on," my dad says.

"But Jo's not in college," I say.

"I'm gonna call her," my mother says.

"I don't think that's a good idea," I say.

"Your sister's gonna be the death of me." My mother collapses into a nearby chair.

Lucia quietly leaves the room. I think my mother's afraid that my father's having an affair with Lucia. That's not it, though; I think Lucia and my father just understand something elemental about each other. I overhear him telling her things he's never told us, things I'm not sure he's ever told my mother. The less my parents talk to each other, the more he seems to talk to Lucia. Being an adult sometimes seems even lonelier than being a kid.

e thought, and not because she needs a response.

When we got back home, my mother poured a glass of wine for erself and sat down on the couch.

"Try it on for me again," she said.

I ran up to my room and pulled the dress over my shoulders.

Then I ran back down the spiral staircase to the living room. My mother and Lucia both sat on the couch. Lucia clapped when came in.

"*Que bonita,*" Lucia murmured.

I twirled around the living room feeling the tulle in my hands. Tulle is a wonder, scratchy and dense, yet somehow managing to ook like clouds.

Like the story he told her about his friend Quincy's Uncle Earl. He and Quincy used to shoot hoops in the park by their house, and Quincy was the happiest kid ever. Quincy had a momma and a daddy who were both teachers at the local high school and who seemed like the happiest teachers to ever teach, and even sat and laughed together during their lunch breaks like best friends instead of married people. Quincy's uncle had been Daddy's third-grade teacher and taught him about Frederick and Booker T. and how it was important to stand up straight and be a good man, even if nobody expected it of you. One day, while he and Quincy were shooting hoops, they found Quincy's uncle lying really still on a park bench. He could've been anyone, but they knew it was Earl because of the birthmark the shape of Texas on his cheek. After that, Quincy and Daddy didn't play ball at that park no more. Then, Quincy's parents didn't eat lunch together no more. Finally, Quincy moved with his momma back to Louisiana, where she was from, and Quincy's daddy ate lunch in his classroom in California all alone.

"That was the first person I knew who died of a drug overdose," he told Lucia. But not me; I'd just overheard because I'd been standing outside the kitchen the entire time listening. Lucia and my dad both feel slightly unknowable to me. Their lives before me are so foreign to mine and yet also somehow not so foreign to each other, some invisible bridge crossing the years and thousands of miles between them.

Sometimes my mother gets strangely competitive with Lucia over weird things, like she did with my prom dress. Lucia and I had already driven around together shopping for dresses, and

I was pretty certain I'd narrowed it down to the final two. She'd taken me to somebody's *abuela* on Santee Street who had gnarled hands that made exquisite things.

"None of your friends will have one of her dresses!" Lucia exclaimed.

I told my mother this, and she looked up over her reading glasses and narrowed her eyes like she was deciding something.

"We should pick out your dress together," she said. "The two of us."

"But Lucia and I already—"

"I'm your mother."

And that was it.

We went to the Neiman Marcus near Rodeo Drive, which was full of crusty old farts with big fat baubles dripping from their ears and necks and fingers like candy tumors. Many of the salespeople are up their own asses for having the good fortune to serve such wealthy, important people. I didn't want to be there.

The first dress my mother saw that she liked was the pale pink of a ballet slipper. She held it up to my body, and we both tried to ignore the women in black following us like shadows. The next dress she picked up was the bright yellow of a canary, or sunlight, and against the dark of my body it popped brighter still. The navy dress was too adult, but the gold beading across the top was exquisite, heavy and weighty, which made the dress feel too important to put back down. The women in black didn't say anything to us, even as they talked to the ladies around us: "What size?" or "What occasion are you looking for?" or "We just got that one in!" It was like that scene in *Pretty Woman*, except we weren't hookers in

thigh-highs and my mother didn't need some john's ch[...] afford anything in there. Being a rich black woman in [...] is like being a trashy white hooker in a fancy store, [...] you something about everyone in that fancy store. Th[...] mother settled on was red, like fire, and one of the mo[...] items in that section, which is exactly why I think she [...] down on the counter. I liked the dresses I'd picked out [...] better, but I didn't dare say so.

My mother walked over to a cash register in the [...] slightly removed from the section we'd been in before. [...] was young, with delicate features like a model, or a stat[...] walked over to him, he said, "Hellloo, ladies!" like we [...] friends who'd walked into a club.

"Did anybody help you gals today?" he said.

"No," my mother said firmly, and we heard the shad[...] per behind us.

"Omigod, I fucking love this dress." He ran his fingerti[...] like it was gold. In his voice, I heard a bit of the South, fro[...] I assume he'd fled.

In the car on the way home, my mother said, "Your si[...] her dress from a thrift store."

"I remember."

"She didn't even ask me if I wanted to come with her."

"Maybe she didn't think you'd want to go to a bunch [...] stores."

"I would've gone."

I wasn't sure if I should say anything, because sometim[...] mother says things out loud as though she simply wants t[...]

CHAPTER 16

MY FRIENDS ARE glitter bombs. Their hair is straightened and curled and teased and doused in sparkle. Their dresses dangle in garment bags like satin spooks. There are still things to be done—makeup, nail polish, a careful evaluation of the evening's expectations. They shriek as they stumble out of Courtney's car and into my driveway. Then, we shriek together.

Courtney bares her fangs as soon as she reaches me. "Look!"

"What are you doing?" I say.

"I bleached my teeth!" She smiles like a carnival clown and twirls, as though somehow that'll help showcase her mouth better.

"But your teeth weren't yellow," Heather says.

"I mean, they were a little, kinda," Kimberly says.

"Who's that?"

"My cousin."

"Since when do you have a cousin who lives with you?"

"Since there's a riot."

My friends peer in at Morgan's pain and recoil.

"What's wrong with her?"

"Her father's store got looted. They took everything."

I don't tell them that it's our store too, kinda sorta.

"Dude, that sucks."

"Yeah."

"Should we say something to her?"

"Like what?"

"Like . . . Sorry about your store?" Courtney declares.

"Yeah, let's do that."

My friends enter the room together. It's the first time I've ever seen Kimberly look almost timid.

"Sorry about your store," the three of them say in unison.

Morgan looks over at me and raises her eyebrow, and I shrug.

"Who are you?" Morgan says.

"I'm Courtney. This is Kimberly and Heather."

Morgan looks at my friends intently. Then she starts to laugh. "Didn't Ashley try to drown one of you guys when she was little?"

Kimberly widens her eyes and then narrows them. "That was, like, forever ago."

We run up the stairs and through my house in a pack.

Upstairs, we paint nails and pull on dresses and talk extensively about Kimberly's virginity. We paint one another's pouts the same shade of period red. Miraculously, the color works on all of us.

We blast 2 Live Crew's *As Nasty as They Wanna Be*. Our adults, Tipper Gore, and the courts hate it 'cause it's obscene, so we love it. Even feminist Heather. When we're just girls alone, we can gyrate on each other and yell filthy lyrics out of our pretty mouths without anybody thinking we're asking for it, whatever it is.

"I'm gonna miss you guys so much next year." Courtney sighs.

"We're not going anywhere. We're gonna get old and wrinkly together and be like the Golden Girls," Heather says.

"Courtney is Rose," Kimberly says. "You're Dorothy. Ashley's Sophia. And I'm Blanche. 'Cause she's the sexiest."

"Dorothy's the sexiest. Blanche is a ho. Besides, you can't be Blanche; you've never even had sex," Heather says.

"Why the hell am I the old lady?" I say.

"They're all old ladies." Kimberly shrugs.

"Sophia's the funniest, anyway," Heather offers.

"Wait. Am I Rose 'cause you think I'm dumb?" Courtney says.

Kimberly glues on our fake eyelashes; years of pageants have made her an expert. When she finishes, she blows across our eyelids like Tinkerbell. While Fresh Kid Ice raps, together we flutter our new lashes, revel in our new faces, and will tonight to be magical.

Trevor and Michael arrive in Trevor's dad's vintage Rolls-Royce. It's impeccable and sleek, a haughty glossy white with off-white tire rims. Courtney wanted to rent a limo, but limos are apparently on the list of things Kimberly finds tacky. There isn't enough room in the car for all of us, so Courtney and dateless Heather are going in Courtney's date's car.

Courtney met her date at a support group for adopted children. She started going to meetings earlier this year, and at lunch she sometimes tells us stories of international orphans rescued from abject misery and brought all the way across the world to live in, like, Chatsworth. Rusty's parents adopted him from Korea, but they're white. This is gonna be our first time meeting him. She's shown us pictures; he looks very handsome, lithe with thick, dark hair down to his shoulders. Heather spent weeks telling anybody who'd listen how lame prom was and how it was the ritualized subjugation of young American women. Then at the last minute, when she decided she wanted to be subjugated after all, there was nobody left to ask her. We watch Trevor and Michael pull up and get out. We shriek again and run back down the stairs to the front door, to our boys, transformed.

If Trevor's tuxedo is a joke, the powder blue of a lazy afternoon, Michael's is the sleek still of midnight. They hold our flowers in plastic boxes with pins topped by pearls.

Courtney's date, Rusty, is an hour late to meet up at my house. Together we sit around the living room, waiting to take pictures and raging against the melting of our faces. Uncle Ronnie sprawls out on the couch, so we position ourselves around his body, like we're at a wake.

"Don't mind me," Uncle Ronnie groans. He wasn't groaning before my friends came, so either his pain meds are wearing off or he's being theatrical. Knowing Uncle Ronnie, it's probably both. "Where's your date, Ashley?"

I point at Trevor, who goes over to shake Uncle Ronnie's hand, all formal-like.

"I remember my prom. Better not do none of what I did." He laughs and then moans.

"No sir," Trevor says. "Definitely not."

"Boy, I didn't even tell you what I did." Ronnie laughs again.

We sit there awkwardly for a few moments until Courtney opens her mouth to speak.

"So, did you get shot at? Did they beat you up? Were you scared? Did your life, like, flash before your eyes?"

"Jesus Christ, Courtney," Heather says.

"What?"

Uncle Ronnie struggles to sit up a little bit. "I was scared."

My friends stare at him expectantly.

"That was my mama's store. Ashley's grandmother. She started that store back in '51. Do you know how hard she had to fight to keep it? A woman by herself—and a black woman at that. She kept it running through the Watts riots and the recessions. People tried to buy her out twice, but she refused. I was scared, but only because I didn't want to see everything my mama worked for go up in flames on my watch. Those looters, though? I wasn't scared of them. Not physically. They weren't going to hurt me. Not much, anyway. They're angry as hell, but it ain't at me."

My friends sit there flabbergasted.

"Why don't you kids go ahead and put on some television," he says.

We can't decide between the news and MTV, but Courtney says, "I don't want to watch depressing shit right now, it's prom!" so MTV wins. My mother runs around the house looking for where she put the film for the camera.

I think Ronnie's fallen asleep—his eyes are closed, body still—when I hear him start to harmonize with Eddie Vedder as he sings, *"'Ohhhh, I'm still alive.'"*

"How do you even know this song?" Courtney asks, and Uncle Ronnie looks at her like he's trying to figure out if she's asking because he's black or old, but it's probably both.

"I know everything," Uncle Ronnie replies, and Courtney nods as though she believes it.

"You have a really good voice," Heather says. "You could be a singer. Like, professionally."

"And she should know; her grandfather owns a studio," Kimberly chimes in.

"I came close." Uncle Ronnie sighs. "You know, I almost went on tour with the Delfonics. . . . You kids too young to know who that is? But there was Mama to take care of . . . and the store." He drifts off.

I never knew this about Uncle Ronnie. How many other things don't I know? I realize I'd kinda rather stay here and find out. It feels wrong to leave my family right now, in our hour of need, or mourning, or whatever it is.

"Anyway, let me leave you kids to it." He starts to stand, and Michael and Trevor rush over to help him up.

Before he hobbles out of the room, Uncle Ronnie leans over to me and whispers, "They don't got any black kids at your school?"

I think of the black kids yesterday with their fists raised in protest and how I should've joined them. Or like how I shouldn't have even started this shit in the first place. And how, once it started, I should've done something to stop it. Last year, LaShawn was prom king. Today, I wonder if he'll even be allowed at prom. As if he can read my thoughts, before I can say anything, Uncle Ronnie shakes his head and walks away.

With the adult out of the way, Trevor and Michael start whipping their heads around to the block of Pearl Jam videos. When Pearl Jam stops jamming, Trevor loses control of his head banging and flails into the coffee table, sending Heather's glass of water flying in an ill-fated splash so it looks like she peed her pretty dress.

"Jackass!" Heather screams.

"Can we all just get along?" I hear Rodney King stammer on the MTV News bulletin as I walk down the hall toward the bathroom.

Rusty looks like a skater or a surfer, like even in his dressy tux, his body wants to be balanced on a board somewhere, moving. He greets everybody with, "Hey, dudes!"

His face seems to be built around his broad stoner smile, as though everything else is an afterthought. Yesterday, a Korean kid only a year older than us was shot to death in front of a pizza parlor in K-Town, his shirt so bloodstained that it looked like it had a big black hole in the middle, an empty space in the image where his heart and guts should've been. I wonder if Rusty saw that and thought, *Maybe, in some other version of my life, that could've been me.* I wonder if he looked at that kid laid out and saw himself with a bloom of blood across his chest, a victim, the way I look at dead black kids sometimes.

In Koreatown, seven thousand people attend a clean-up rally on a baseball field.

"We will not retaliate. We will wait with patience. We will forgive with love."

These are their prayers.

• • •

Outside, Morgan floats in the pool on a flamingo, tracing her finger along the surface of the water in lazy circles. She wears dark glasses and one of Jo's old bikinis like she thinks she's in a different movie from the one we're in.

Michael sits down next to her. He's rolled his pants up so that his bare feet dangle in the water. He leans over and says something to her and my cousin says something to him, throws back her head, and laughs so you can see her one gold crown.

"It's time for pictures, Michael!" Kimberly calls across the backyard. Michael scrambles to throw his shoes and socks back on before jogging over to the grass, where everyone is getting ready to pose.

I walk over to where Morgan floats, close to the pool's edge.

"I never knew your dad could sing like that," I say.

Morgan peers at me over Jo's sunglasses. "We're a family of many talents."

"Apparently."

I think of how easily Morgan hit the Parkers' tires last night. I'm afraid to ask her where she even learned to do a thing like that. "What were you and Michael talking about?" I say.

"A Tribe Called Quest," she says. "He was asking if I liked them. Then I was like, 'Why didn't you ask me if I liked R.E.M. or Nirvana or whatever? Is it 'cause I'm black?' and he got silent and awkward, and then I started laughing."

"But do you?"

"Hell yeah." She swirls her hand in the water around her. "But I also like R.E.M. and Nirvana. He was too easy to fuck with."

And we both laugh so hard that Morgan belly laughs herself right out the floatie and into the pool.

"Ashley, come on!" Kimberly yells over to me.

"You smoke with them?" Morgan says.

I shrug. "Sometimes."

"Just be careful. You think they'll have your back if y'all get caught?"

She lets the question hang in the air.

"I guess I should get over there," I say.

"Yeah . . . good luck with that." Morgan wipes her curls away from her face and rests her freckled elbows on the concrete.

On the lawn, Kimberly stabs Michael with the boutonniere pin, and a tiny pearl of blood erupts. She wipes it away with her finger and licks it like a teenage vampire.

"Ouch!" Michael says as she does it again.

Kimberly continues to prove herself untrustworthy around pointy things, so instead I take over.

"Here, I'll do it," I say.

I pin the cornflower-blue flowers onto his suit for him. For a minute, the two of us belong to each other, until Trevor throws his arm around Michael's shoulder.

We line up according to height. Lucia, my mother, and my father snap photos so that one day, years from now, we can look back and laugh at the heft of our dresses and the bright of our eyeshadow. First is Heather, then Michael and Kimberly. Courtney and Rusty line up next to me and Trevor. Trevor wraps his arms a little too comfortably around my lower waist, and my father stares him down until he moves his hands up a bit higher.

"Say cheese!" Lucia yells, and we smile.

My mother starts to tear up.

Before we get into the car, Lucia squeezes me tight.

"Don't have sex, *mija*," she whispers, and laughs.

On the car ride over, Trevor blabs about meditation and Cobain. I glance at Michael and Kimberly in the back seat. Every so often, they both drink out of a flask that Kimberly keeps in her pink satin purse. She rests her head on Michael's shoulder, which is entirely unlike her. Normally she'd be too concerned with messing up her hair to do a thing like that, but tonight, she's punch-drunk on love and vodka. Michael catches me looking at them in the mirror. I look away and stare at PCH as it unwinds, dangerous, before us.

When we first walk in, past the hotel lobby to the grand ballroom, Kris Kross is telling us to *"Jump! Jump!"*

Kimberly screams, "I love this song!" and does. For a moment, all I can see are blond curls and pink-and-purple taffeta.

The hotel is all marble and ornate columns. Old, rich Italians sit like sun-drenched leather on a velvet couch in the lobby. We shriek and rush past them to Heather and Courtney, even though we saw them not twenty minutes ago.

Heather and Courtney hug us and drag us by our wrists to the girls' bathroom, where I watch as they do E and pass around a bedazzled flask of vodka.

A woman wrapped in a mink stole, with wrinkles so deep you want to stick your fingers in, her gray strands in an elaborate updo, emerges from her bathroom stall. Courtney scrambles to hide the vodka behind the poof of her dress, but the lady definitely sees it. We think she's going to chastise us or drag us to our elders to face punishment, but instead she washes her hands and gives us a knowing wink in the mirror.

"Have fun, my pets!" She laughs and totters out the door.

I don't do drugs. Not the real ones, anyway. My friends all do, but if there's one thing my father has taught me, it's that black people do not get a pass with these things.

Last year, my cousin Reggie went to jail. Reggie's kind of a superior asshole; like at Thanksgiving the rest of us will be talking about some shit like *Coming to America* and he'll start in trying to compare grades and SAT scores while we're eating boring Great-Auntie Delilah's amazing mac and cheese. I think that's him trying to make his mom pay attention, though. Sometimes the right numbers are better than the right words when you're trying to get your parents to love you. Mostly he's a good kid. Anyway, he got caught with coke at some party the police busted in the Palisades. My aunt Carol is a judge and she pulled some strings to get her son out, but my father made it clear he will do no such thing.

"If you get arrested trying to keep up with the white kids, I will not bail you out. I will not pull any strings, you hear?"

I sip from Kimberly's flask and let the alcohol burn down my throat. That'll have to be enough for me.

Soon, I'll be the only one who isn't rolling.

Trevor holds me by the elbow, which is an awkward place to hold somebody, but it's better than holding hands, which I don't want to do. Trevor is actually a very considerate date. He holds doors and walks slowly to make sure I can keep up in my heels. He only talks a little bit about things I don't give a shit about.

Michael and Kimberly hold hands. She keeps kissing Michael's cheek. His parents have paid for a hotel suite for us tonight. Everybody knows what that means. Kimberly thinks something major is going to happen, something that will cement things and seal the distance between USC and Rutgers and keep them together forever, but she doesn't even know about Michael's finding his dad's near-lifeless body, or the fact that his mother gets drunk before ten every morning. I've held both their hands. I know where Michael's fingertips are guitar calloused, where the weird mole is on Kimberly's index finger. I've held both their secrets.

I'm not sure that I'm jealous, exactly, but maybe I am kinda sad. Even after all these years together, I'm not sure either of them really knows the other. Plus, Kimberly thinks something magical is about to happen, when as of last week Michael didn't even know how to properly fondle a boob.

We stand in line to get our pictures taken by a professional before our faces melt and we stink of questionable decisions. The photographer corrals each group and poses the girls with their right hands on their hips, heads tilted to the left, one leg ever so slightly extended forward. The boys are adjusted into and out of varying stages of doofy.

When the photographer gets to us, he starts to snap at me, "Where's your date?"

He repeats it again with increasing frustration. I'm confused until I realize that he thinks Heather is with Trevor and I'm the odd one out. I point at Trevor.

"Oh . . . ," he says, and moves over to Heather to physically adjust her.

• • •

They aren't allowing LaShawn into prom, on account of his suspension. Several of the chaperones stand around him and the other black kids like confused security guards.

"C'mon, it's prom," Tarrell says.

"You guys can go in," somebody's dad says. The sleeves of his once-crisp white shirt are already rolled up, and the sweat pools at his temples and under his armpits. "LaShawn's the only one who's been suspended."

Candace, Tarrell, Julia, and Fat Albert link arms with LaShawn, and the chaperone exhales a big-ass sigh, like *Why did I agree to do this?*

Wigger Dustin looks over from where he's doing the worm, or attempting to, anyway. His right eye is still swollen, a faded purple-maroon blend like the eyeshadow on a tacky off-brand doll.

A bunch of kids look in the direction of the black kids trying to see what the commotion is about. The entire dance floor presses in closer to them, like we're one big moving ear.

"I just wanna dance with my friends," LaShawn says quietly.

The chaperones look at each other, unsure of what to do.

"Let him in!" somebody screams over the music from the bowels of the dance floor.

Then another person joins in: "Let them in!"

The entire dance floor begins to rumble above the music like the roar of the bleachers during a game. The dance floor boos and jeers like Principal Jeffries and our adults are our rivals from across town.

Principal Jeffries looks ill at ease in a dress, like even though her dress is flowy, it's somehow more constricting. Her dress flats look like those old-lady mall shoes with the extra old-lady cushioning. She ushers Dustin and LaShawn off to the side.

After a lengthy discussion, closely monitored by a bunch of sixteen- and seventeen-year-olds, Principal Jeffries decides to let LaShawn in.

Fat Albert raises up LaShawn's arms in victory, and everybody on the dance floor loses their shit like he's scored the winning point in a championship game.

Schadenfreude. We learned it in English class: taking pleasure in others' misfortune. Now that LaShawn has fallen from being the golden boy, now that he's begging to be let into prom when last year he was prom king, our school has rallied around him once more. It's like they say: Everybody loves a comeback.

We do the Humpty Hump, then we drink punch, sip from Kimberly's flask, and mate the two in our mouths before we bob our heads and jump up and down while the Beastie Boys tell us about girls. We boo when the DJ puts on "Ice Ice Baby" and then dance to it anyway. With each sip, our bodies get more fluid, our vodka-soaked hands find their way to one another's shoulders and hips and butts. At one point, Courtney and Heather straight-up slap each other's asses to the music.

Mr. Holmes dances with Ms. Garcia. Trevor tells me somebody once saw them making out in the parking lot late one night after school. Mr. Holmes is a surprisingly good dancer; maybe he got that from being around all those black folks in Watts. Although I'm black, I live in a house full of black people, and I can't dance, so maybe not.

Heather, Trevor, and I start dancing in a circle. Then they start to dance up on each other, the E in full effect. I wish I were on what they're on. It's hard for me to let go.

Courtney and Rusty dance tentatively, an arm's length between them, the way people dance when they don't quite know each other's bodies yet.

Michael and Kimberly clumsily hump to "It Takes Two" together. Every so often, when he's not looking, she'll beam over at the rest of us and offer a thumbs-up, like every air thrust is a prelude to something more.

LaShawn and the other black kids dance in a circle together. A piece of me wants to join them, to raise my palms into the air and yell "Awwww yeah!" when "O.P.P." comes on, even though I'm only kind of down with O.P.P.

The DJ switches over to slow jams, the lights go down a little, and half of us find our way toward one another, while the other half awkwardly scurries to the punch bowl.

Trevor places his hands on my hips and guides me in a one-two to Boyz II Men's "End of the Road." We collectively decide that this DJ is on crack, because everybody knows this is an end-of-the-dance song and we're not even halfway through the night.

"'Although we've come to the end of the road, still I can't let go,'" our classmates shout at the ceiling.

I know the song's romantic or whatever, but I'm thinking about Lucia. About how she and Jose are off on their date somewhere. They're learning all about each other, and maybe by now she likes him even more. Maybe she's leaning in close to him and sharing noodles like in *Lady and the Tramp* and shit. Maybe she's planning for her life without us, without me. Why should Jo and I be the only ones to grow up and move on?

When Heather, Kimberly, and Courtney run off to go "powder their noses" with Georgia Franklin and Molly Schmitt, Michael cuts in on Trevor and asks, "May I have this dance?"

Trevor and Michael say something to each other, and then Trevor walks away.

He whispers something into my hair.

"What?" I can't hear him over the music.

"I'm sorry," he says as we dance under a gilded chandelier.

"For what?" I say.

"I don't know. I'm just sorry. It feels like we should be here together. You and me." He places his cheek closer to mine, and I can smell the alcohol on his breath, through his skin.

"You're drunk."

"That just means I'm telling the truth." He laughs. He pauses, and then his face grows drunk serious; you can almost see the boozy light bulb go off above his head. "I'm gonna tell Kimberly the truth. I'll tell her now, okay?"

"Michael, don't."

"Isn't that what you want?"

What do I want? To be understood. To be happy. For my sister to not be so sad. For my parents to not be so stressed, for them to get along. For Lucia to not leave me. To be loved. Real love that feels like feathers, like flight. Right now, I feel like I'm sinking.

"Please just let me be the one to tell her." I start to panic. "It should come from me."

Before he can respond, Courtney, Kimberly, and Heather return.

"Hey, bitches!" Heather wraps her arms around Trevor's neck, and the two of them fake romantically dance with each other, but honestly it seems pretty real to me. They look into each other's eyes, and the way they look at each other makes me sad that there's only a few more weeks to go before Trevor heads off to New York and Heather is in Ohio at Oberlin. Then there will be hundreds of songs between them instead of just their own pride.

"May I have my boyfriend back, Ashley?" Kimberly says.

We let go.

I will tell Kimberly everything when the night is done after the lights go bright and we all stumble toward our hotel rooms or after-parties or limos, before she and Michael make it up to their suite and she gives him even more of herself than she already has. It's not that I think she should avoid having sex itself; just not with him, not if she's only doing it to keep him hers. *Keep that part of yourself yours for just a little bit longer*, I want to tell her. My first friend. I'll come clean. But for now, I'll get punch.

At the punch bowl, LaShawn and Candace survey our peers.

"Hey, Cricket," he says. He places the ladle into the bowl and carefully pours into a red plastic cup before passing it over to me.

I extend my hand to Candace. "I'm Ashley."

She laughs. "Girl, I know who you are."

"Groove Is in the Heart" comes on, and Candace says, "That's my jam right there! C'mon."

"Be there in a minute," LaShawn says while Candace shrugs her shoulders and shimmy-shakes away.

"I'm glad they let you in," I say.

LaShawn shrugs. "I wasn't gonna come, but my mama told me I paid for my ticket same as everyone else, and I got a right to be here. Plus, between the tux and the flowers and everything, that shit wasn't cheap, and she work too damn hard to waste her money like that, she said. So . . . yeah."

He laughs and it's defiant, but also, there's a bit of sadness underneath.

"I'm happy you're here."

"You look really nice, Ashley." He blushes, then stutters, "I mean, you always do, but you look . . ."

"Nicer?"

"Right."

"You look nicer too," I say.

We both wait for the other to speak.

"Did you know female dragonflies fake their own deaths to get away from unwanted advances?" he blurts out. "Brian and I watched this documentary last night. . . ."

"So what you're saying is, I should fake my death to get away from guys' advances?"

"Only the unwanted ones," he says.

We both stand there, frozen still and blushing.

"Well . . . I guess I should go find my friends." I turn, take a few steps, and then the dance floor eats me right up.

I wander through the crowd looking for Courtney, Kimberly, and Heather. I'm surprised to see that even weirdo Steve Ruggles is at prom. With his hickey arms covered by tux sleeves, he almost looks normal. His date is kind of cute, even. I'm pretty certain she doesn't go to our school. Nobody cute who goes to our school would go out with Steve Ruggles.

"Hey, Steve, do you know where Kimberly and Heather and them are?"

"You know my name?"

"We've been in the same classes for six years."

"Eight."

"Right. Have you seen them?"

"This is my girlfriend, Becky."

"Nice to meet you, Becky."

Her hands are very cold and very small, and her eyes are reptilian, but in a pretty way. She must be a very strange girl herself to love a boy who kisses himself for entertainment. But I guess love works in strange ways. There's someone for everyone, as Grandma Opal used to say.

"Check outside." He shrugs. So I do.

The party has spilled out to the hotel pool, which the prom committee has decorated with tasteful little tea lights. When it gets too hot inside, I walk to the double doors and out into the night air.

This is a mistake.

Michael and Kimberly sit by the water talking. I'm paralyzed; too afraid to stay outside, too afraid to go back in. The decision is made for me when I turn to retreat and Kimberly yells across the pool, "Don't you dare move, Ashley!"

I stay right where I am as she bounds over to me. Everyone outside grows silent. And then Kimberly is up in my face, her blue eyes glowering.

"What is wrong with you?"

What is wrong with me? I think. The question plays in repeat on a turntable in my head as Kimberly yells. I don't actually hear most of what she says until the very end. She doesn't yell this. This she whispers.

What she whispers is: "You stupid nigger."

Then she pushes me into the pool.

My dress billows up around me as I sink to the bottom. It's red and looks like flames, or blood, and it's actually a really pretty disaster, like something that should be in *Vogue*. I'm so embarrassed that I don't want to get out. I want to stay here at the very bottom of the pool, next to these dead flies, thinking about how I got here.

Nigger: A Brief Personal History by Ashley Bennett

Age 6. Somebody scrawls it across our front gate in black spray paint. My mother refuses to tell me what it means, not yet.

Age 7. A woman lets it slip while she's complaining to her friend at the grocery store until she notices Jo and me standing behind her and turns bright red.

Age 9. Some boy says it to Jo at school, and she punches him in the gut. They both have to serve detention together, and my parents threaten to pull her out of the school but don't. Late that night, she comes into my room and tells me she wishes she'd punched him harder.

Age 10. Three men yell it at me from their peeling Nissan while I'm pumping my mom's gas in a gas station by the water on our way home from visiting Hearst Castle.

Age 11. There's the Special-Ed kid hiding in the clothing racks in the kids' section at the mall. He whispers it at me as I walk past and giggles when I turn my head. I'm too tall for most of the stuff in the kids' section but too skinny for most of the juniors' section. He keeps repeating it so that it's like a chant or a mantra.

Age 15. Boys like Michael and Trevor sing along with songs at house parties. All these white boys raise their pale hands in the air and shout it like it's theirs. I drink until everything, including their voices, is a dull blur.

Age 17. This.

Nèi-ge—Um . . .

Nigger. The word is like a stone I want to pin me down.

When I finally float back up to the surface, everyone is staring at me. Michael and Kimberly have gone who knows where. Nobody helps me as I struggle to hoist my body onto the deck. The hair Morgan spent hours doing has lost any pretense of straightness and is getting larger by the minute. My dress is heavy on me, and the weight of it pulls me down. My mascara stings my eyes; I'm not crying, but I might as well be.

As I begin to walk back toward the ballroom, this kid yells out, "Can't we all just get along?" and the entire yard erupts in laughter.

CHAPTER 17

LaSHAWN SITS BY the fire near the double doors, waiting. He looks angry, like something deep inside is waiting to burst out of his chest.

"Are you okay?" he says.

"What?"

"You're drenched! Come with me," he says.

I'm too tired not to. I walk with him silently through the ballroom.

"Yo, Brian, can I get the key?"

White Brian hands it over to him without question. The black kids look over at me. Candace says, "Damn, sweetie, you okay?"

I shake my head. The news hasn't yet made its way to them. It will eventually, as these things do.

I follow LaShawn through the hotel lobby. Everybody stares at us as we pass. He takes out a key card and swipes it, and soon we're on an elevator.

"That's messed up, what she did to you," he says. His voice is smooth like honey and comforting, and his fingers are long and thin and elegant. I've never noticed that about him before.

"I deserved it," I say.

"No, you didn't," he says.

We exit on the tenth floor. The suite is probably like the one Michael's family has rented for us. There's a sitting area, a dining area, and a separate bedroom. For a moment, it feels as though we're in our own little house, and I realize I don't know why he's brought me here.

"There's a robe inside the closet," he says. "Change in the bathroom, and we can try to use the blow-dryer on your dress."

When I walk out, LaShawn has the news on. It's the fourth night of rioting and things are crazy, but not as crazy as they were. He motions for me to sit down next to him.

"That's two blocks from my house right there." He points to a building in flames on the screen. "My sister, my mama, and my grandmama, they right there. And I'm here. Dancing. What kind of man does that make me?"

He looks at me as though expecting an answer. I wish I had one, but I don't. Nothing worth saying, anyway.

"Do you want me to fix your hair?" he says, and points to the bird's nest of shame atop my scalp.

"Okay."

I sit down between his legs. It's kind of sexual, being between a boy's legs like this, my head gently resting against his crotch, but also really comforting. It reminds me of when I was younger and Lucia used to French braid my hair before school.

"I do my sister's hair 'fore she goes to school," he says, as though he's in my head.

"You know how to braid?"

"Didn't I just tell you I do my sister's hair?" He laughs.

"Can you do two French braids for me and then pin them together in the back, please?"

"Just you wait, I'ma hook you up!"

His is an easy laugh, and it makes me wish we'd been close all these years. He takes off his tuxedo jacket and neatly drapes it across the chair. His cummerbund is the color of a robin's egg. He gets up and disappears into the bathroom. I hear him rustle through the drawers until he's located the dryer.

"Got it!" he shouts.

He starts to blow-dry my hair. I can't hear anything above the dryer, so for a while it's just flashes of fire and newscasters and shots of the soldiers in a line. It looks like Vietnam or something, but it's only the ghetto.

"You know, more black folks are out there right now helping and tryna do good than riot, but the media don't show none of that."

He turns the dryer off and begins to braid.

"I need to tell you something," I say to him. "Something important."

"Aight."

I turn around to face him. "I don't know how to say it."

I'm afraid that as soon as I say what needs to be said, he'll leave. I don't want to be left alone with my thoughts in this room, but it's time to do the right thing. I think about what Lana said yesterday: "Just make it right."

"I started the rumor about you looting. About the sneakers. I didn't mean to. It just happened. And I'm sorry. On Monday, I promise I'll go to Principal Jeffries and tell her everything. I would understand if you left right now."

He looks at me. "If I was you, I'd a waited until my hair was finished to tell me that."

We don't talk while he finishes the next braid and pins it down. Then he moves from his perch on the bed down to the floor. He sits with his knees tucked under his arms. We're almost close enough to kiss. *In a different world, he could be the Dwayne to my Whitley,* I think.

"Say something," I say. "Please."

"I honestly don't even know what to say to you right now, Ashley."

"Just . . . something."

"Okay . . . well . . . I thought you was better than them girls you hang around, but you're just like them. I thought maybe . . ." He trails off and stares at some point in the corner. "Anyway, you're an asshole like all the other kids in this stupid school."

I know I deserve it, but when it comes out of his mouth, it's like being pushed into the pool all over again. I hear myself whimper, "I'm sorry."

"You know I could lose my scholarship?"

"You won't."

"You don't know that!"

"What do you want me to do? How do I make things right? Tell me what to do and I'll do it."

This is not how this was supposed to go. Although I guess there's no other way it really could've gone, given the circumstances. He goes quiet for a long time, retreating somewhere into his head.

He places his chin atop his knees.

"I didn't steal those sneakers," he says finally. "My mama got them for me for getting into Stanford."

"I know you didn't steal them."

"But I ain't gon' pretend like I don't want to be at home tearing something up. So, I don't know, maybe I would've stolen them. We got a right to be angry. Our lives don't mean anything to them. Doesn't matter if Rodney was an ass; he didn't deserve to get beat like that. And Latasha Harlins didn't deserve to die over some damn juice. And nobody cares, 'cause we don't matter. They treat us like we're goddamned animals." His voice cracks like he's about to cry.

"Isn't it kinda stupid to steal and set your own neighborhood on fire?"

"Maybe. But maybe it's the right kind of stupid."

I think of my sister out there doing God knows what in the name of rebellion and progress, and Uncle Ronnie laid out on the couch, and Morgan and my father's sad filling the whole house today, along with the ghost of Grandma Shirley's American dream.

"I don't know. I just wanna be home," LaShawn says.

"I have an idea."

We're going to LaShawn's house. We're black kids in a car that isn't ours, and there's a riot going on, and this is reckless behavior on both our parts, but Trevor is rolling on E, and his car won't be reported. Plus, LaShawn wants to check on his family, and I kinda owe him big-time.

"Do you want to listen to the radio?" I say.

My dress drips on the seat all around me, still kinda wet from the pool. It's uncomfortable, but I figure it's better than running around the city half-naked in a bathrobe.

"No," LaShawn says.

"We could listen to the news, or KJLH. They've been—"

"I said I don't want to listen to anything."

"So you have a little sister?" I say after we've been driving in silence for what feels like forever.

"Yeah. Kaitlyn. She's fifteen," he says.

"Your mom didn't want to send you guys to the same school?"

"Only reason I'm going is 'cause of the scholarship. We couldn't afford this shit otherwise." He sighs.

I think I've seen Kaitlyn before in the stands at LaShawn's games. A husky girl with glasses and bright-red braids atop her head like a girl on fire.

"Do you guys get along?"

"We used to. She's really, really smart. Smarter than I am. And funny. And she's damn near as good as I am at basketball. But she stopped applying herself. She's starting to talk back to my mama and acting like she's grown. I think it's 'cause of the girls she's running around with at her school. She's pissed that my mama drags her to my games and spends all this money on me for basketball, and I get to go to this fancy-ass school. Meanwhile, she's at the school around the corner where they don't even got books half the time."

"I'd be mad too, I guess."

"Yeah. But my mama's trying her best."

"Maybe she feels like your mama doesn't care as much about her 'cause she's a girl."

"I don't think that's it. But what do I know? I've never been a girl."

LaShawn's sister is only two years younger than he is. I imagine what it must be like to grow up playing, wanting the same things. Her brother says I want the world, and her mother does everything in her power to give it to him. She says I want the world, and everyone—including her own mother—tells her that's too much.

Sometimes it's hard being a girl, and it's hard being black. Being both is like carrying a double load, but you're not supposed to complain about it. There are so many things you have to remember about how to be.

First things first: be pretty. Never take up too much space; your breasts, arms, lips, hips, thighs, and even your nose should always be just so. If your body should spill over just so or not quite fill it up, well, honestly, I don't know what to tell you. Just don't. Be a good girl, but not too good; nobody likes that girl. Laugh, but not too loud; you'll make them nervous. No, don't be sour, never that, even if you're having a bad day, month, year, life. They'll think you're angry. Make sure you smile so they can see your teeth. Be smart, but never smarter than; or they'll think you're uppity. Be more. Yes, that's it! Practice! Dream! Rise! Wait, not so high, girl! Those stars, they aren't meant for you.

I open my mouth to try to tell LaShawn what it feels like to move through the world with that in your head, all these things Kaitlyn and I have pinned to our thoughts like paperweights. At times, all those paperweights heavy in your head make it so you have trouble telling left from right—the right friends, the right people to give yourself to, the right thing.

"I'm sorry," I say to LaShawn.

"I know. . . . Ashley, I don't want to be an asshole or nothing, but, like, I still don't really want to talk to you right now," LaShawn says as he stares out the window. Then he adds, because he's polite, "No offense."

"Right. Okay . . . I'm sorry." I shut up and drive.

We follow several detours around road barriers and through emptying or emptied streets, before we end up in a part of town that scares me. At the nearest red light, I roll the windows up and lock the doors. LaShawn softens a little bit, then finally opens his mouth and says, "This was a bad idea. Let's go back."

So instead, I keep going.

There are a number of ways we could die right now, ways I've never even thought about. Here we are in our city, but we're also in a war zone. The smoke is already beginning to stick to my skin.

We park Trevor's dad's car near an empty squad car and start to walk.

LaShawn grabs my hand. "Stay close to me. Keep moving, okay?"

"Okay."

A man talks very animatedly to himself as he pushes a shopping cart across the street. I pause for a half second to take him in.

"Keep moving," LaShawn says.

LaShawn leads me through streets I've heard of but never been to. We keep pace with each other, our steps in sync over broken sidewalks.

In front of us, the firemen in their yellow unfurl their hoses and spray. Their smudged faces look like Ash Wednesday. They look weary. Firefighters have been getting shot at. One of the first few people to die in the riot was a firefighter.

It looks like an apocalypse, like we've found our way into some Arnold Schwarzenegger film, or a disaster movie where we need a hero in a helicopter to rescue us in the nick of time and carry us up and away. Papers blow down the street like urban tumbleweeds. There are lots of abandoned shoes.

A woman wanders past us, frail and glassy-eyed, her eyes ancient and her body almost childlike.

"Hello," she whispers.

We're only two blocks away from his grandmama's, but a huge National Guard tank and a line of guardsmen block the way. Most of them don't look too much older than we are. A National Guardsman's glasses slip down his freckled nose, and he pushes them back up again.

Here, it's so clearly us versus them. And, for once in my life, it doesn't seem so blurry who is the us and who is the them.

LaShawn pulls me around a corner and down an alleyway. He looks down the length of it, darting his head back and forth. Half-way down, a man is slumped over like a rag doll, and I think he might look over at us or head toward us, but it's as though we're not even there.

"Can you hop a fence in those?"

He points down at my heels.

"I'm not a comic-book character," I say. I expect him to chuckle, but I guess he's still kinda mad at me 'cause he doesn't.

"Okay, you'll have to take them off."

I nod.

"You first." I step my bare foot into his hand, and he lifts me and propels me into the sky. As I straddle the fence, I hear something in my dress rip; I think maybe the lining, but it's a layer of tulle. It hangs down behind me like a blood trail.

"Hurry up over," LaShawn says. It's a long way down, and I take the landing wrong. My ankle hurts as soon as it hits the concrete.

"Ouch," I say.

LaShawn's dress shoes slip-slide against the wall as he climbs. He launches himself over the wall quickly.

"Are you okay?" he says.

"Yeah."

I hobble down a quiet, tree-lined block. The street itself is dark. The streetlights are out.

"We're almost there."

LaShawn's house is small and gray, with white siding, a metal gate, metal on the windows, and a metal security door. It looks like a face with braces. He opens the front gate and we walk up the concrete steps to the front door, past the fat planters with roses in bloom. It doesn't look like anybody's there to me, but he rings the doorbell, then knocks on the metal door, which rattles with a *clang-a-lang*.

"Are you sure somebody's home?" I say.

"The power's out, remember? They're probably in the back of the house," he says.

He pounds on the door louder. *Clang-a-lang-a-lang.* No answer.

"The front door's lock is a little janky," he explains. "Follow me."

He heads toward the back, and I follow.

The back of LaShawn's house looks as though whatever used to be there has been paved over in favor of a mini makeshift basketball court. A partially deflated ball sits in a plastic lawn chair off to the side next to an old grill. More potted plants line the area.

LaShawn pounds on the back door. No answer.

Then he takes out his keys and opens the door.

Inside, the house feels like a cave. Moonlight streams in small slivers across the tile floor.

He grabs my hand. "Careful."

Along the wall, on the floor, there are candles melted down like in an abandoned haunted house.

"Mama!" he yells into the house. No response.

School photos of LaShawn, of his sister, Kaitlyn, with her hair like fire, and others line the wall. The photos fade as we go deeper into the house and farther into the past, like a photographic origin story that begins with what I assume are LaShawn's grandparents, posing in front of a house—this house, before the metal was added—looking like they're ready to start their young lives.

In the kitchen, LaShawn goes through a drawer looking for a flashlight, or matches. It smells ever so faintly like the trash that hasn't been collected this week. There are plants everywhere, some invisible tenderness making things grow beautiful in unassuming corners.

"Maybe they left you a letter."

There's an intimacy in being in somebody else's house. Sometimes when I'm in my friends' houses, I think, *Who would I be if I grew up here?* Would I be me, or someone very different if I'd grown up in LaShawn's neighborhood, and he mine?

There are so many sirens outside, coming, going. *Wee-oooh-wee-oooh* closer, *beeep boop beep beep*. And also there's the whir of helicopters. Voices on bullhorns. We're less than ten miles away from my house, but the sounds of this neighborhood are so different. The city vibrates around us. I close my eyes and hear the layers.

One of the windows in the living room is broken. A piece of cardboard covers it.

"What happened there?"

"Miss Violet's grandkids next door were playing catch. Mama hasn't been able to fix it yet."

The kitchen wall by the telephone is covered in phone numbers etched into the faded paint in pencil. Plumbers' numbers, handymen, friends, and relatives. Next to the numbers are childhood doodles, presumably made by LaShawn and his sister over the years. LaShawn runs his fingers along the wall like he's searching for braille secrets.

"What are you looking for?"

"My aunt's number. She'll know where they are."

My favorite of the drawings on the wall is of a princess wearing a poofy dress and a crown, holding a bloodied knife with somebody's phone number impaled on it. Little kids are so weird.

LaShawn raises the receiver and dials the number. It rings and rings, but nobody picks up. He places it back down in the cradle.

"Fuck."

He reaches into one of the drawers and takes out a pen, then snatches an envelope from the mail piled on the counter to write the number down. Then he opens the envelope, glances at its contents, and pins them to the refrigerator with a magnet. A slightly past-due electric bill. I look at the number on the bill. I never knew electricity costs so much. But I guess I've never had to know or worry about what anything costs, really.

Then LaShawn pockets the envelope with the scribbled number and walks toward the front of the house.

In the middle of their living room, a cardboard Nike shoebox sits, probably exactly where LaShawn left it. Partially open, tissue paper on the ground.

He picks it up off the floor, places it on the worn leather couch, and sits down next to it. I sit down on the other side of the shoebox.

Why did I say what I did about him and the shoes? Jealousy? Yes. I want to be this boy, but also, I think . . . I want this boy. To be in his skin, to wear my brown confident and easy, and to have the weight of his golden skin on mine.

He sinks his head into his hands and starts to cry. It's kind of like seeing Mr. Holmes tear up in front of the whole class, or my father sobbing after his mother died all those years ago. He tries to twist himself from me, hiding his tears, because boys don't cry—certainly not black boys. Except when they do. Then he does that awkward thing where your sad makes your whole body quake. I place my hand on his back, but he shrugs it away.

"I'm really sorry," I say.

The smell of him is so familiar, cocoa butter and something else I can't place, but he smells like home.

"We could stay here and wait for them," I whisper.

I don't know why I'm whispering all of a sudden.

He looks up at me from under his huge wet lashes.

"No." He awkwardly lifts his head up and wipes his eyes with the backs of his hands. "Maybe Miss Violet knows where they went."

· · ·

We exit out the front door. LaShawn has already pulled the door behind us, we've already walked through the metal gate, it has already clicked into place, when he realizes that he left his keys in the back door.

"Aww shit," he says. "Stay here."

He's about to hoist himself back over the metal gate to go get the keys when a flashlight shines on us.

"Are you trying to break into that house?" a female voice says.

Like we would say yes if we were?

The policewoman approaches us with her hand by her hip. She's smaller than we are, her dirty-blond hair tied back in a ponytail. Her eyes dart around as though at any moment more of us might come, a roving gang of wayward black kids in expensive formalwear.

"No ma'am . . . uh . . . officer. I live here," LaShawn says.

"We were trying to see if . . ." I walk toward her, but she draws her gun and I freeze.

"Don't come any closer!"

The barrel is the size of a girl's index finger.

I think of Uncle Ronnie and the Parkers. What he must have felt standing across from two barrels who saw only his black in the wrong place and not Ronnie, son of Shirley, brother of Craig, father of Tonya and Morgan, a good and fair store owner, an above-average ex-husband. I think about my friends and what they're doing right now, still bouncing around on hormones and expectations, awkwardly gyrating to "It Takes Two" or something like it. I wonder if they've noticed I've gone, or if they even care.

I think about my two mothers, Mom and Lucia, and how if this woman shoots me, the bullets would probably rip through the dress my mother chose, but not the one I liked best. I think about Daddy and Morgan floating around the house in mourning for Grandma Shirley's looted dream. Mostly, I think about Jo, somewhere out there. She needs me and I need her. If I die here, they'll probably all be wondering why I was so far from home.

"This city is our home. All of it," Jo said.

People will probably think LaShawn and I came here to bone. I imagine our bodies in awkward angles, bleeding out on a fading front lawn. I think of all the things I'd never get to do, the people I'd never get to meet, the places I'd never get to go, the things I'd never get to be. I've never been in love. I don't want to die, not yet. I'm think I'm only starting to figure out who I am.

Then I think of those three little black boys who belonged to each other, afraid outside the 7-Eleven near Jo's, that cop's knee in the baby's back. "But we didn't do nothing."

My mother and I should've done something.

"When I think of home, I think of a place . . . ," I think.

"Down! Now!" the cop screams.

We sink down to our knees. Chemical smoke from the burning insulation and rubber sticks to our lungs whenever we inhale. Our knees grind into the gravel.

Little bits of ash fall around us like snow and land on our clothes like polka dots. We're so close, we can almost feel the fire on our faces.

CHAPTER 18

ON THE NEWS, they showed the arrested rioters laid out across bits of lawn and parking lots with plastic zip ties around their wrists, their bodies lined up like one of those drawings of slaves crammed into slave ships.

LaShawn and I are down in the grass, spread like stars, the police officer's flashlight bright in our faces. To anyone walking by, we look like criminals.

I'm very afraid, and also very angry. Both of these feelings dig their knees into my heart and slam against my lungs so I can barely breathe. Whenever a black or brown person gets shot or hurt by police, people say, "Well, but what did they do to deserve it?" The assumption is that it's always deserved, somehow. Or "They should've listened." We don't get the benefit of the doubt—we, they, you, even me, with my fancy school and my fancy house and my fancy clothes.

Here I am, to quote Kimberly, "blackity black."

This is what Jo meant when she said, "It's not just about Rodney. It's about all of us."

I get it now. I get it.

I want to live. I'm not even a whole-ass person yet. I want to be.

If I get to be an adult, I already know that I will carry this with me, a barely scabbed-over wound of being facedown, black, and helpless at the hands of a white cop, my gray matter inches from the barrel of a gun.

"Where is your driver's license?" the woman asks LaShawn. He begins to reach toward his pocket to retrieve it when she yells at him not to move again.

LaShawn doesn't have a driver's license. Because he doesn't drive. Before he can finish telling her that he has his school ID on him, in his left front pocket, a very elderly woman in a faded yellow duster eases her way down her front steps. "What are you doing to them kids?"

The blue and red of the cop car's lights flash across the deep lines in her brown face.

The cop looks over at her. "Ma'am, I don't want any trouble."

The elderly lady keeps coming closer, unsteady in her steps but steady in her resolve. "I know that boy ain't done nothing wrong. He's a good kid."

"Ma'am," the cop says, "step back."

"She's hard of hearing," LaShawn says to the cop.

The cop looks around like she's trying to decide what to do.

"Miss Violet, you know where my family went?" LaShawn yells at Miss Violet, who cups her ear toward him.

Miss Violet yells, "What?"

Another neighbor, a middle-aged man in a white tank top and denim shorts down to his knees, walks to his front gate in his white s though she's trying to figure out her

 are bright across our faces now, blue

quick flashes, sad, then angry.

says finally as she gets into her car and

le bit. "Just doing my job."

my body. I can feel the goose bumps

der my skin.

 wouldn't be in the middle of all this

ters under his breath after the cop car

the night.

n," LaShawn says to Tank Top.

gment in our direction and heads back

e's about to topple over, and LaShawn

 her.

y family went?" he yells into her ear.

f his arm, and the two of them walk up

 behind. "To your auntie's, I think. She

wherever?"

says.

u want," Miss Violet says. "I can make

ing! You like hotcakes? Everybody likes

 of Miss Doris from the nursing home,

wonder what it must be like to get that

ly, everyone you care about pass away or

 take her up on the offer.

for a moment and then shakes his head

HRISTINA HAMMONDS REED

soc
at
"
"
"Ca
L
som
"1
"V
of a l
"Ai
says.
"G
Mis
ing. Tl
get up
The
ponyta
Tank
"You
We b
The o
We sa
"You'r
and wait
Lucky.
I think
getting in

The officer looks around
exit. The lights from her ca
and red, like two moods in

"Have a good night," she
rolls the window down a li

I wrap my arms around
along them, the fear still u

"If they did they job, w
right now," Tank Top mu
turns the corner back into

"Thank you, Mr. Freem

He grunts an acknowle
inside his house.

Miss Violet looks like s
rushes to her side to stead

"Do you know where n

Miss Violet grabs hold
her front steps while I tra
the one out in Covina or

"Yes ma'am," LaShawn

"Y'all can stay here if y
you hotcakes in the mor
hotcakes."

She reminds me a littl
eager for the company.
old and have friends, fan
move on. I kinda want t
LaShawn considers it

no. "Thank you, Miss Violet, but I gotta get her back home safe. Take you up on those hotcakes another day?"

"*Mi casa es su casa*, as they say," Miss Violet says before her security door slams shut with a loud metal clang.

Uneasy palm trees loom over us as we walk quietly back to Trevor's dad's car. Palm trees belong to the ghetto as much as anywhere else in the city, maybe more so. They peek their heads up over the top of the 110 same as they hover over the mansions on Rossmore. Everybody thinks they're native to LA, but they're not. Missionaries started putting them in around the same time they started taking out the natives. Then rich people got in on it. Then the city thought, *Well, hell, that looks good, why not?* and used palm-tree planting as a way of making work for the unemployed during the Great Depression and before the 1936 Olympics. We studied it in our section on California history last year. They're starting to die off now, those palm trees planted by that generation before the greatest one. Every so often you'll hear about a dead one falling onto a car, or a building, or a nice man out on his morning walk. I don't want to die by palm tree, but maybe I'd deserve it. LaShawn grabs my hand; both of us are still trembling.

"Breathe," LaShawn says.

I open my mouth in a wide O like a fish and swallow the night.

We don't talk the entire way back to Trevor's dad's car. When we finally get there, I look down to see that it's been keyed, like somebody ran their house keys along the length of it in a series of uneven stripes. I guess I'm lucky in the grand scheme of things. It could've been stolen.

"Fuck," I say.

LaShawn looks back in the direction of his grandmama's house, worry keyed across his face.

"I'm sure they're okay," I say. "We can try calling again in a little bit."

Above us helicopters whir, suspended in a cluster in the sky. Watchful floating eyes.

I get into Trevor's dad's car and start the engine. The car begins to move, but barely. It sounds kinda like a fork in a garbage disposal. I get out of the car again to inspect it. The front tire on the passenger side puckers with several deep, intentional gashes, wounds that can't be patched.

When I finally look up from inspecting the tire, I notice for the first time the fresh graffiti on the wall across from us, maybe even written by my sister or somebody like her, a call to revolution in big defiant loops across the brick.

LA REVOLUCION ES LA ESPERANZA DE LOS DESPERADOS.

Revolution is the hope of the hopeless.

And then I start to laugh.

CROSS THE PAY phone windows, letters are scratched and marked with intent and occasionally with flourish, letting people know somebody was here, that this place belongs to somebody or somebodies.

Nobody is home. Not Lucia, not my parents, not Jo. My friends are at prom, and, let's be honest, they'd probably leave me stranded here, anyway. I stand inside the phone booth and flip through the white pages while LaShawn stands outside, alert, watching.

Make new friends, but keep the old, one is silver, the other is gold. Except sometimes it's the new friends who are gold.

"What happened to you two?" Lana says.

I look down at my dress, slightly torn and covered in grass and mud. LaShawn's suit hasn't fared much better. We look like the kids who only barely survive a horror movie.

Pham flings open the car door, sparkling in a purple feather boa. He kisses me on both cheeks. His breath smells of whiskey.

"Little troublemaker," he says.

LaShawn steps forward to shake Pham's hand. "Hi, I'm LaShawn. I go to school with Ashley and Lana."

"So tall! Handsome boy!"

Pham throws the boa around LaShawn's neck. He kinda has to jump to do so, since he's so short and LaShawn is six-foot-three and still growing. LaShawn laughs. Then Pham goes to the back of his car and retrieves a donut tire.

"Where's Brad?" I ask.

"Brad can't fix shit." Pham laughs.

"I thought Trevor was your date," Lana whispers.

"It's been a very long night."

"Hold the flashlight," Pham says to whoever's listening. I walk over and shine the light on the slashed tire. He crouches down and removes the hubcap, then begins to crank the lug nuts loose. He tumbles back a little before righting himself.

"Is he sober?" I ask.

"Nope. Definitely not. But I drove," Lana says. "We just got back from a party when you called."

He places the jack under the car and raises the wheel up, up, up. He works quickly, like somebody who's done this many times before, like he could do it in his sleep, humming to himself as he removes and replaces and tweaks and lowers and replaces again before standing up and wiping his hands clean on his party pants.

"All done." Pham grabs his boa back from LaShawn's neck. *"Allons, les enfants! Aujourd'hui la vie est belle . . ."*

LaShawn and I get back into Trevor's car and follow them to Lana's house, driving slowly so we all stay together.

• • •

Pham tells us to sit down in their living room, so we do. He asks us if we want tea, then rushes to the kitchen to put a pot on the stove before we can answer.

"Get up, Brad, we've got company!" I hear him yell from the kitchen into the house.

"So you guys were at a party?" I say.

"Well . . . kinda," Lana says.

One of their friends is dying. An artist Brad's exhibited at the gallery. Not old—only thirty-one, which is a real grown-up, but not, like, grandpa age or anything.

I don't know anybody who's died of AIDS, but I've seen the AIDS quilt, with its patchwork of grief and love and protest. It came to town and they took us on a field trip to see it, but some of the parents protested and started a petition arguing that the school was encouraging deviant behavior.

Kimberly's mom tried to get my mom to sign the petition when she came to pick Kimberly up from my house one day. Lucia answered the door. My mother paused Jane Fonda mid leg-lift; walked over to our front door glistening in her pink leotard, purple leg warmers, and white Reeboks; and told Ms. McGregor to her face that the petition was "ludicrous and hateful." Then she turned around and went back to her video while Kimberly and I said a muted goodbye. I thought that was pretty ballsy of my mother. Every so often, I think maybe my parents are kinda cool.

Anyway, Brad and Pham's friend is dying, and instead of waiting until he's gone to have a funeral, he asked his friends to come to his home for a party. As Lana tells us about their friend, Brad stumbles out of the hallway smelling of wine and cigarettes, a streak of Pham's glitter across his cheek.

"He was in a lot of pain, but he looked happy, don't you think?" Brad plops down on the couch across from me.

"Yes." Pham nods. He places two teacups on coasters on their sculptural coffee table.

"So many of my friends died alone because everyone was so afraid." Brad sighs. He starts to tear up, and Pham grabs his hand.

"It was almost canceled because of the uprising. You know, a lot of our friends protested the verdict in West Hollywood. But we don't know how much longer Danny has," Brad says. "We didn't want him to feel like he'd been abandoned."

There's a riot going on, and it's consumed all of us for days, but you forget that in the middle of it there are people in other parts of the city just quietly living and dying, and other people who love them.

"The nurses wheeled his hospital bed out to the living room, and we sang his favorite songs and danced," Lana says. "It was sad, but also kinda fun in the saddest way, because . . . I don't really know how to explain it."

"Y'all had a homegoing, kinda," LaShawn says.

"What's this?" Pham says.

LaShawn explains that to our ancestors, death wasn't a thing to be feared. It was freedom—slaves no more, they would return to God, or Africa, or whatever. And funerals weren't somber affairs, they were celebrations of life.

"Yes!" Brad smiles and wipes his face with his boa. "A homegoing. He would've liked that."

. . .

We talk about everything and nothing, and the evening stretches into the hours when everything outside is still. Brad and Pham gather up pillows and blankets for us before excusing themselves to their chambers.

"This is the part of the evening when we old folks retire. Can't party like we used to," Brad says with a wink.

LaShawn sits in a pretzel on the living-room floor. Lana and I lean against each other on the couch.

"You know, you two are the first people I've had over in four years of high school," she says.

"How is that possible?" I say.

"I don't know. I didn't want anybody coming over and judging me. You guys live in these ridiculously fancy homes, and I live in a guest house on somebody else's property. I'm not embarrassed, I just . . ."

"I get it," LaShawn says.

"Nobody invites me over, either," she says.

"You can come over to mine," I say.

"I don't think your friends will like that much," she says.

"I don't know if they're my friends anymore," I say. "Not after tonight."

I run my hand along a crisp, yellowed houseplant. Part of it crumbles and falls. Sometimes awful things happen to you that you can't tell anybody about. Sometimes you're the awful thing.

"I don't know what's wrong with me," I say. "I think maybe I'm kinda this like really selfish, awful person."

Maybe Jo and I are more alike than not, just broken in different places. I miss my sister in the present tense. Lana takes my face into her hands and looks at me intently.

"You just want to be loved. That's what's wrong with most of us," she says.

The bruise her mother gave her has transitioned from angry plum to subdued mauve. It's faded, but it's still there. I lightly press my fingertips to it and feel the heat of her skin and the blood moving under her pain. It's the most intimate thing I've ever done with anyone. Lana exhales. I didn't even realize she was holding her breath.

We fall asleep together in Brad and Pham's living room, LaShawn buried in blankets on the floor, Lana and I curled up in each other and the couch cushions. Lana wraps her arms around my waist, and I can feel her heartbeat at my back as I start to dream.

Around four o'clock in the morning, I wake up, even though I've only been asleep for an hour. I open my eyes to see LaShawn sitting up, staring into the darkness.

"It's too quiet here," he whispers. "I'm not used to this."

"I don't sleep well in other people's houses," I say. Lana stirs, and I gently extricate myself from her grip.

"You wanna go outside?"

"Do they have a house alarm?"

"I don't think so."

We step barefoot onto the early morning dew. A few lonely birds chirp across the trees.

"Listen," LaShawn whispers.

Crickets.

We laugh. LaShawn laughs loudly, and I put my hand to LaShawn's mouth. His lips are soft under my fingertips.

He moves closer to me, and I lower my hand from his mouth.

"You're not an asshole," he says. "I'm sorry I said that earlier."

"Maybe I am a little bit. But I'm trying not to be . . ."

Instead of responding, he pulls me toward him, we lean in, our mouths press against each other, and my whole body feels in bloom. It's so stupid.

Before he can say it was a mistake, or anything at all, I quickly pull away and rush up onto the trampoline, bend my knees, and start to jump. He climbs up after me, and then we're both jumping.

Sometimes real assholes like to joke and say that in the dark the only thing you can see of a black person is eyes and teeth. It's meant to be an insult, but at the moment, with LaShawn smiling at me, I can think of no better thing to be distilled into. We're two smiles in the night, together.

Under the stars, in our fits of flight, we're astronauts, weightless. Then gravity yanks us by our legs back down, and we have to relaunch ourselves. It's exhilarating, though, the fight. We bend our knees and reach up our fingertips to get just a little bit more. We mean to fly, and for a time, we do.

 **FAMILY OF EARLY-RISER** lizards scurries across our path, and LaShawn bends down to let one of the babies crawl across his hand. The valet raises his eyebrows at the scratches along Trevor's dad's car as I hand him the keys.

Bleary-eyed girls in velvet and bare feet fill the hotel entrance. Their boys cluster in circles, tuxes askance. Everyone's a little hungover, drunk off alcohol or excitement. A maid in a rumpled white apron, a pretty girl who looks no older than fifteen, cracks a smile at Nicola Anderson with her arms around the planter like she's hugging a toilet bowl. I would feel bad for her, but Nicola acts like she's so much worldlier than the rest of us just because her parents are Australian and speak in drunk vowels. Anuj Patel walks by and yells right into Nicola's ear, all Crocodile Dundee–like, "G'day, mate!"

The thought of going into the hotel suite with Kimberly and Michael makes me feel nauseous, but it could also be the not-too-distant smell of Nicola's puke. As if he knows what I'm thinking, LaShawn grabs my hand.

Early this morning, we fell asleep on the trampoline looking at the stars, holding hands, and when the sun came up, Lana came outside and said woo-woo, and I told her to shut up.

Before we left the house, LaShawn called his aunt's number again and finally got through. From the living room, Lana and I could hear him whisper like a little boy, "I'm fine, Mommy . . . I love you guys."

"You can hang with us in Brian's suite until you can catch a ride home," LaShawn says. "I'll give Trevor his keys for you and explain everything."

Before I can respond, Heather bolts toward the two of us. "Ashley, we've been looking all over for you!"

She grabs me by the wrist and drags me toward the hotel lobby.

"Can we do this later?" I say.

"Dude, hurry up," she says.

I see Jose before I see Lucia. I'm so tired after last night and so I'm confused; at first I think maybe he's taken her to this exact same hotel for their date. He looks nice, but he also looks very tired.

I don't see Lucia until she's right in front of me.

"We have to go, *mija*," she says. "Now."

"What's wrong?"

Then Lucia tells me that my dumbass sister is in jail.

"Where are Mom and Dad? Why aren't they getting her? Do they know?"

"They went over to your uncle Ronnie's."

"To do what?"

"Help him with the store."

"And Morgan?"

"She's with them."

"What did they say?"

"I can't get ahold of them, *mija*."

Until now, to the best of my knowledge, nobody in our family has ever been arrested, unless you count Reggie getting busted at that party in the Palisades. We're not dealers, or pimps, or criminals, or even speeders. We're the "good kind" of black people. The best. We smile and pose slightly off to the side in the company photos, in the private-school brochures. We earn awards and own businesses and go to college and donate to our inner-city brethren and do our part to uplift the race. We definitely do not walk into riots with Molotov cocktails and get arrested for arson.

"What are we going to do about her bail?"

"That's why I came and got you, babygirl," Lucia says quietly. "I have some, but not all of it. It's better if we pay in cash. Speeds things up sometimes. Your sister said you'd have the rest."

I wonder how Lucia knows so much about these things, but then I remember Arturo.

Jo needs my car fund, my Grandma Opal money. Grandma Opal would be pissed at how we're about to use it. This is definitely not what she meant when she said, "You have to be better."

Grandma Opal might even haunt me; although, Grandma Opal was the kind of person other people call "a riot!" so I don't know that I'd mind being haunted by her, much. It'd be nice to see her again.

"Why don't we wait and let my parents take care of it?" I say, but then I remember what my dad said to me after Reggie's arrest last year: "If you get arrested trying to keep up with the white kids, I will not bail you out. I will not pull any strings, you hear?"

"*Mija*, sometimes when somebody goes to jail, they have a funny way of not coming back."

"It's not like that here," I say. But I'm not so sure.

The car fund is hidden inside my mattress, which makes me feel like a gangster, or somebody during the Great Depression. It isn't a really original place to put it, but the only person who ever looks under there is Lucia. Jose waits for us in the driveway, his car *put-put*ting, even though Lucia told him he didn't have to. I don't know if he's being macho or chivalrous, or maybe he likes her a whole lot and wants a little more time with her. So instead of leaving, he stays in his Hyundai, windows down, waiting and unabashedly humming along with "Achy Breaky Heart" on the radio.

We pull up to the detention center, which towers ten stories into the skyline like a big middle finger. The streets are a little less abandoned, though it's a Sunday and Downtown, so they're still abandoned enough. The riots have waxed and waned. A few loose newspaper pages blow down the street. Broken glass from blown-out windows is still underfoot. There are men in uniforms with long guns pacing, joking.

"Stay in the car, *mija*," Lucia says. "I don't want you going inside."

"I'm a grown-up," I say.

"No," she says. "You're not."

Jose and I park the car.

"You had breakfast yet?" he asks.

"No."

"You need breakfast."

We walk over to a nearby stand. The vendor hunches over her cart, swaddling the hot dogs quickly but tenderly in bacon and grilling a few onions and peppers on the side.

"*Buenos días,*" I say.

"*Buenos días.*" She smiles.

"You're out here today?" I say. Things are a little bit more under control now, but everyone is still walking around like flies that have been half-swatted: not dead, just too stunned to move. Still fearful.

"You gotta eat. I gotta eat." She smiles and slaps a hot dog into a bun.

These could definitely make us sick, but at least for a few bites it'll be heaven, before the bubbleguts.

"Breakfast of champions," Jose says after taking a bite. "Does your sister get into trouble a lot?"

"Not like this. This is different, even for her," I say.

"These are different times," he says.

"I don't understand what's wrong with her sometimes. It's like she does this stuff to herself on purpose," I say. Jo's own pain never seems to be enough for her. It's like she has to take on the weight of everyone hurting everywhere.

"For some people, a little bit of trouble makes life interesting," he says.

Jose and I stuff our faces together quietly on the sidewalk. When we're finished, we walk around, and he tells me a little about his days playing semipro baseball in Mexico before he came here. "Are you still good at baseball?" I ask.

"Nah. I got both my arms broken once, and after that I wasn't nearly as good as I used to be. But that's a whole other story."

How do you get both your arms broken? I'm afraid to ask.

Nearby, smoke rises above the city.

"How long do these things take?" I ask.

Jose shrugs.

We stand across from City Hall, which is historic and architecturally impressive, but also kinda looks like a penis made out of Lego pieces. There are a ton of police cars and police officers guarding it, watching. I feel my heart start to quicken at the sight of them, so I take a few deep breaths. There's a slight haze, but even so, I lift my face to the muted sun, close my eyes, and let it bear down in squiggles under my eyelids.

Before we head back over to the jail, Jose gets fruit from a cart near the hot dog vendor. Jose selects the fruit—watermelon, cantaloupe, pineapple—and the vendor chops it up right in front of us before he places the slices in two plastic baggies and douses them with a healthy sprinkle of Tajín.

"Here," Jose says, and passes me a fork.

The juice dribbles down my chin as the chili hits the roof of my mouth. Together we eat fruit out of a baggie on a dirty Downtown sidewalk while somebody's boom box blasts "No Vaseline." I marvel at the beauty of the city in my mouth, a little sweet, a little bitter.

Lucia and Jo emerge from the jail when the haze has burned off and our street fruit's well into our bellies. We've seen a number of people enter and leave the place by now, the world a blur of human law and disorder. Jose helps me to my feet. The tips of his fingers are guitar calloused. I add this to the list of qualities I like about him for Lucia. Lucia loves music. This is perfect. Unless, of course, he's shit at it; then she's gonna have to pretend to like a lot of bad guitar playing. When I finally get a good look at my sister, Jo looks a little feral. Her hair is mussed in escaped curls; the front teeth that were in braces up until two years ago are chipped into opposing triangles. When she sees me, she starts to cry.

Jo wraps her arms around mine and buries her face into my shoulder. She smells so bad that I nearly gag.

"Did they hurt you?" I say.

She shakes her head no. Then yes. Then no again.

"Where does it hurt?" I say.

"Everywhere," she whispers.

When I was little and we would join hands and sing "Ring around the rosie," Jo changed the lyrics so I thought the song was just for me: "Ashley, Ashley, we all fall down."

Jose pulls into our driveway, and Lucia grabs him by the face. She kisses his mouth like they've successfully robbed a bank or fled an assassin together. I wonder if this is how she used to kiss Arturo. For some people, a little bit of trouble makes life interesting, Jose said. But when does it become too much? When are you a good person who did a few bad things? When are you a bad person?

"Thank you," Lucia says. "Let's do this again sometime."

When we get inside the house, Jo runs upstairs to her room.

"Wait!" Lucia says, but it's too late.

Jo walks back down the stairs and sits on the top step. "They're getting rid of me?"

"Just your stuff," I say, and sit down next to her. "They want another guest room. They have Morgan in there now."

"We already have a guest room."

I shrug.

"I should call Harrison and tell him I'm safe. I'll have him come pick me up, I guess."

I grab her hand. "Please don't go, Jo. Stay. You owe me that much."

She squeezes my hand back and it's an answer, but I don't know which one. Then she disappears upstairs. I hear the shower turn on, then I hear her yelp, and I laugh, because that shit's always too cold until it's too hot. It takes forever to find normal.

While Jo is on the phone with Harrison, Lucia and I collapse onto the couch. I kick my shoes across the room, where they narrowly miss the TV stand. Lucia takes hers off and places her feet on my lap. I pick up a foot and begin to rub it for her, and she moans like people do in the movies when they're having sex; then I guess I hit a pocket of pain, because then she yelps like people do in the movies when they're being killed.

"I like Jose. You like him?" I say.

"Yes. A lot. He's a very nice man." She sighs. "Too nice."

"How can he be too nice?"

"When you get used to bad men, you start not believing in good men. Even when they're right in front of your face. You think maybe he's hiding the bad for later, like the last one."

"If he's too nice, why'd somebody wanna break both his arms?"

"People from complicated places sometimes have complicated pasts. Or maybe he was a little wicked then."

She laughs, and I switch feet. Then she leans back and closes her eyes like the day's finally caught up to her.

Lucia never talks to me like I'm just a dumb kid. My parents sometimes seem like they don't know what to say to me, like they think their words don't translate to teenager.

"I bet your sons are good men."

"I hope so," she says, eyes still closed. "Do you like that boy you were with? The basketball boy?"

"'Basketball boy'? Jesus, Lucia."

"You still didn't answer me."

"He's nice." My voice rises several octaves, and I feel the heat burning through my entire body.

"He's nice!" Lucia squeaks, and laughs. "Ay, babygirl . . ."

Jo comes down the stairs wearing a familiar dress that's as pale blue as a summer sky. Not the kind of thing I'd think she'd normally pick for herself, but I guess I'm not sure exactly who she is these days. Neither is she, it seems.

With her in the pale of her blue and me in my red, we look elemental, fire and air. In chemistry we learned that they need each other to thrive. They keep each other going.

"Thank you," Jo says, and kisses Lucia on the cheek. Then Jo pats me on my knee.

"That's my dress," I say, and she shrugs.

Jo sniffs at the air around me, then takes a piece of tulle and raises it to her nose.

"Why do you smell like smoke?"

Before I can answer, we're interrupted by the opening of the front door.

"Lucy, I'm home," Morgan shouts into the house like Ricky Ricardo.

She skips into the living room and freezes awkwardly when she sees Jo. My parents aren't too far behind her.

"You're here," my mother says. "You came home!"

She runs over to Jo and hugs her, and the force of her love takes them both by surprise, so much so that Jo loses her mind and chooses that exact moment to tell our mother that she's been arrested.

"Are you okay?" my father says, and Jo nods.

"It was totally not a big deal, really."

"What were you thinking?" My mother pulls away and looks at Jo like she has two heads.

"What the hell happened to your teeth?" Morgan says.

Before Jo can answer, my mother sighs. "I'll have to call your aunt."

Auntie Carol's a judge, which means she knows judge-y things and court things and law people, and maybe she can be Jo's ruby slippers and with a click of her heels keep her out of prison, bring her back home.

"I'm sorry," Jo says.

My mom and her sister aren't close, and when I was a kid, I didn't understand why. *How do you go from seeing each other every day for eighteen years to not even visiting each other when you live only a handful of miles away?* I thought. But now I understand it,

I think. Sometimes the act of growing up cleaves you apart, and even though you walk through the world made of the same stuff, you can't quite make your way back to the start. There's too much matter between you. I don't want Jo and me to be like Mom and Carol—only Thanksgiving, Christmas, and Easter siblings. Pass-the-turkey sisters. Somebody's died, let's reminisce and then go our separate ways family.

Or, in this case, my daughter committed a felony, can you help a sister out?

"What is it you're trying to prove?" my mother yells at Jo. "There are better ways to find yourself than getting married and setting things on fire."

"But I didn't even set anything on fire!"

"I mean, honestly, Josephine, we would've paid for you to study abroad!"

"Where is he?" my father says.

"On his way," Jo says quietly.

"He left you to get arrested by yourself?"

"He didn't come with me."

I sense that things are about to blow. As always, best to provide a distraction.

"I nearly got shot," I say.

"You?" Jo says.

"At prom?" my mother says. "How?"

"I left with a friend. . . . We didn't do anything wrong. I mean, he wanted to check on his family, and . . ."

"Jesus Christ. Have you girls gone mad?"

"The whole city is mad," Jo says.

"You don't go rushing into chaos. You're girls. Pretty girls. Spoiled girls. We made you that way. You act like you know everything, but you have zero street smarts. You could've been hurt, or killed."

"We're already hurt." Jo sighs.

People glorify protest when white kids do it, when it's chic, frustrated Parisian kids or British coal miners or suffragettes smashing windows and throwing firebombs at inequality. If white kids can run around wearing their bodies like they're invincible, what do the rest of us do? Those of us who are breakable? Those of us who feel hopeless and frustrated and tired and sick of feeling this way again and again? Sometimes, we just go ahead and break ourselves.

Morgan, who I've forgotten is in the room right now, speaks up slowly, measured, like she's pushing each word through a strainer: "My daddy just lost everything in his shop. Our shop. The shop our grandma worked really, really hard for. That y'all never even visit. And you go to some neighborhood that isn't even yours to set other people's shops on fire?"

"What are we supposed to do?" Jo whispers.

"Not that!" Morgan explodes. "What the hell is wrong with you? How could you even do that after what happened to Grandma Shirley?"

"Exactly because of what happened to Grandma Shirley! It's not right. They can't keep doing this to us. They can't. We can't forget, or pretend that stuff didn't happen. We have to do something!"

Jo starts to blubber hysterically, body shuddering, snot running down her face. She looks to be on the verge of a nervous breakdown.

"Did you tell her?" my father says to Uncle Ronnie.

"I didn't know you hadn't. How could you not tell the girls?"

"When did you tell her?"

"She came over to visit the store about a year ago. Said she was doing a class project about family or whatever. She said you were too busy, so she figured she'd ask me for help."

"Why didn't you tell me she'd been over there?"

"You don't talk to me, Craig! When's the last time we had a full-ass conversation before this whole thing went down? Besides, I figured she'd told you she was coming over."

"Jesus Christ, Ronnie. I didn't want the girls living with that. Not like we did. Not if they didn't have to. I wanted them to have a new start. To *be* the new start."

"Ain't no new starts, Craig. It's their history. It's in their bones."

"The hell with that!" my father yells. "I wanted a new start!"

Jo keeps repeating until she runs out of air, "We can't just do nothing. We can't just do nothing! We can't just do nothing?"

Then she turns around and goes up to her room, taking with her all of the air. Her crying is so loud that you can hear it downstairs. Nobody yells at her to stop crying, or that we don't have the blues in the house or whatever, because whatever it is she's feeling, we feel it too.

"Um . . . ," I say. "So, what happened to Grandma Shirley?"

Uncle Ronnie and my father look at each other.

"You might as well tell this one too," my father says to Uncle Ronnie. Uncle Ronnie walks over to the couch, looks at me, and pats the cushion next to him.

"Your great-grandfather was a lawyer. His mama had been born a slave, but he worked and he studied and he scratched his way through school, even when his mama could barely read herself. He made it all the way through college and law school to become a lawyer. In college, your great-grandfather Elroy met your great-grandmother Ida, who, according to your grandma Shirley, was even smarter than her husband. But they got married as soon as they graduated, and he went on to more school and she got started making a home for them. Blacks and Indians had got rich on oil land, this oil land that the white folks didn't know had oil, outside Tulsa in this place called Greenwood, which folks got to calling Black Wall Street. All these black folks up from nothing, not even sixty years after slavery ended. So Grandma Shirley's mama and daddy got it into their heads to go out west and open up a practice there. And it was good for a while. Real good."

Uncle Ronnie pauses and looks at my father, who nods at him to keep going.

"Anyway, the trouble started the way these things usually do—a white woman accused a black man, and the white folks got riled up. It was at the height of the lynching season between the world wars. A bunch of the black men, World War I vets, decided to go protect the black kid from being lynched, so instead of lynching the one boy, the white folks decided to lynch the entire goddamn city. They used planes—fucking warplanes—to fly over the neighborhood and drop bombs on all the black people and their houses and businesses, to burn those uppity black folks to the ground. You know they had a machine gun mounted on a truck to fire at people? A fucking machine gun. They did drive-bys through the neighborhood, even the church—the goddamned house of the Lord." Ronnie raises his voice and spits a little as he speaks.

My dad stands up from where he was sitting and starts to pace the living room. Then he stops abruptly and turns to face me, his voice cracking as he speaks. "When your grandmother described the machine gun, she shook and *rat-a-tat-tat-tat*-ed on the table. Told us about choking on the smoke in the air. Everything was black, she said, 'I couldn't breathe.' When she said it, even all those years later, it was like she was still choking."

My mother walks over to my father and wraps her arms around his waist, and even though he's way taller than her, in her arms he looks like a little boy.

"Your great-grandfather had a gun and tried to defend his family, but they shot him in his own entryway. They called it a riot, but it was more of a massacre. Or like what they did to one of those Jewish areas in the old country." Ronnie pauses for a moment, searching for the word.

"A pogrom," my father interjects.

"Yes. That! The whole neighborhood was gone. Bunch of black bodies dumped into a mass grave. Your grandma said it was even in the *New York Times*. And then everybody forgot about it, like it never happened." Ronnie pauses again.

Across the room, my mother keeps her arms around my father, closing her eyes and rocking him back and forth. Morgan has tears in her eyes.

"She only ever told us the once, and even then, not till we were teenagers. I think she was kinda like those Vietnam vets you hear about who aren't quite right afterwards, who still rattle the war in their heads years later. Except it was right here in the United States, and your grandmother wasn't nothing but a little-bitty girl carrying that in her heart her whole life." My father chokes on the words, like all that heavy's too much even for his vocal box. He turns around and buries himself in my mother's arms.

Lucia speaks quietly, almost as if to herself, "*Como los indios* in the village next door. The disappeared."

"Yes," my father says. "Very much so."

"You know your grandma Shirley's brothers died in World War II? Enlisted soon as they could. Never did understand how they could do that after what their country had done to them," Uncle Ronnie says.

I think whatever sadness I thought I knew, whatever I've felt before, hasn't fully prepared me for this. Uncle Ronnie was right—it's in my very marrow itself. It's like when we first really learned about slavery in history class. It's not that I hadn't known; my parents introduced the concept to us when we were very young, bought us age-appropriate books, and told us we were from Africa. For Country Day at school during Spirit Week, I'd even dressed in ankara bought from a boutique in Leimert Park. But this was different. Our teacher put a series of photos up on the projector. Men and women, dark, glistening, and folded over fields, the stooped body of a kid around our age in the foreground. A famous photo that I've seen many times since of a man with stripes of flesh carved out of his back, a topographical map of scars, of evil. A series of black male and female bodies strung by broken necks from southern trees. The white folds of the dangling woman's skirt reminded me of the black angel ornaments we stuck on our fir come Christmas. *Enough!* I wanted to scream. *Enough! This is not where I begin!* The classroom grew so quiet that not even the smart-asses said a word. I could feel several pairs of eyes on the back of my head. I bit my tongue hard to hold in the tears until I could feel the metallic taste of blood pooling in my mouth. I would not allow my classmates to see me cry, so I waited until lunchtime to hide and eat and process what I'd seen in the handicapped stall. There I gasped, struggling for air, feeling the ropes tight around my neck every time I tried to swallow.

Right now, I can feel the black smoke in seven-year-old Grandma Shirley's lungs, the ash, the unbearable sadness of breathing.

A knock on the door startles us. It's followed by the *ring-ding* of the doorbell.

Morgan runs to answer it.

"Who are you?" she says, holding the door open only a crack.

"I'm Jo's husband."

Morgan opens the door just a bit more, still uncertain.

"Are you a giant?" I hear her say.

Harrison looks around bleary-eyed, like he didn't sleep. Under this lighting, his hair looks more brown than red, his eyes more blue than green. His pimples are gone, and what's left is smooth and ruddy. He's barely even able to grow enough stubble for two days' stress. What must it be like to look at yourself in the mirror and see something a little different every time? To have such an indecisive head? It's startling to see his whiteness after a story like that, like a ghost at the door.

"Where is she?" he asks.

Jo rushes down the stairs and practically throws herself into Harrison's arms as though none of the rest of us are here, and even if nothing else makes sense right now, the two of them fit together in each other's arms like the halves of a locket. It seems to me that's love, but what the hell do I know?

"You were supposed to keep her safe," my father says to Harrison.

"I was sleeping, and when I woke up, she was just gone." Harrison looks to be almost on the verge of tears. He awkwardly holds out his hand to shake my father's and my father doesn't shake it back, but sighs and heads back to the living room, Jo and Harrison following behind.

After hearing about Grandma Shirley, we're drained and full of so much sad that we don't have the space to argue, so instead we order pizza. We eat on paper plates in front of the television, watching a helicopter fly over South Central. The fires are almost out. Now, instead of Vietnam, it looks a little like the pictures in the history books of London after the Blitz. The newscasters bemoan the fate of several architecturally significant buildings that perished or were damaged in the flames like the Bullocks Wilshire, which people care about 'cause it used to serve famous people back in the day and it's in movies and stuff, but honestly it's kinda ugly.

After dinner, Jo and Harrison perform one of their songs for us with a guitar that Jo had in the garage from exactly two years of lessons, and Uncle Ronnie finds the harmony and joins in. Morgan rests her heavy-ass head against me so that her stray curls tickle my cheek and go up my nose. Across the room, my dad reaches over to grab my mother's hand while they listen.

It's decided that Harrison will sleep in the actual guest room, which is way on the other side of the house. Uncle Ronnie's gonna sleep in Jo's room so he can call out to one of us for assistance if he needs it. Jo tries to argue that since they're married, she and Harrison should stay in the same bedroom, but my parents say that Jo and Harrison are very lucky that they even let Harrison in the house given the situation, much less stay the night, and it's their house, their rules, which is how they shut down anything and everything—including marital bed-sharing, apparently. It's also decided that Jo, Morgan, and I are gonna share my bed. I am not consulted on any of these decisions.

Morgan says, "But I'm a guest."

"You're not a guest, you're a cousin," Jo says with a pout, and it's settled.

While Jo brushes her teeth, Morgan and I tumble into my bed. My cousin and I haven't shared a bed in forever, not since that first time she and Tonya came to visit and we had the fight that resulted in the unfortunate biting. Her feet are freezing. I tell her so, and she places them on my calves until I yelp and she giggles.

"I'm sorry we're not close," I say. "I wish we were closer."

"It's not your fault," Morgan says. "It's just family history."

"How did our grandmother die?" I ask Morgan. "Nobody's ever told me that part."

So she does.

My father's mother killed herself on a Sunday several years after I was born. The day before, Uncle Ronnie and the family had been over to dinner. Morgan said that, according to her sister, Tanya, my grandmother hadn't seemed that different. She'd made Uncle Ronnie's favorite dinner—lamb chops with a peach glaze, black-eyed peas, and broccoli. She'd yelled at Tanya to eat her broccoli.

She seemed happy enough; the store was struggling, but wasn't it always? When they were getting ready to leave, she begged them to stay a bit later, Morgan remembers. Ronnie and the girls wanted to stay, but Auntie Eudora reminded him that the girls had to sing in church the next morning. Morgan remembers them arguing over it in the car on the way home. Eudora was defensive. Hadn't Grandma Shirley always been the push and pull of a wave? Ronnie was a grown man now. Time to think of his life, his happiness, his family. Besides, where was my father in all of this? We had the money to deal with this sort of thing, and we never came around. Why did Ronnie and Eudora always have to be the ones to deal with her? The next day my grandmother tidied up her entire house, put on her finest outfit, and pinned her hair into a chignon with her favorite hairpin. Then she shot herself with one of my late grandfather's old pistols.

Anyhow, as Morgan tells it, Ronnie kinda blamed my dad and my dad kinda blamed Ronnie, and that's how we fell apart.

I think of Jo, and how she seems to go back and forth like a seismograph, extreme in kinda the exact way everybody describes Grandma Shirley.

"We gotta be careful, you know," Morgan whispers, and taps on her head. "It might be in us, too."

Later, after our grown-ups have fallen asleep, Jo finally crawls into bed with Morgan and me, and the three of us gleam together under the moonlight.

"She kicks," I warn Morgan.

"Good thing she's next to you."

We laugh, and eventually the room goes quiet except for the faint howl of a coyote outside, followed a few seconds later by a whole chorus of them.

"Jo?" Morgan cuts through the silence.

"Yeah?"

"We're here. We're alive, and we got each other. We keep surviving. That's not nothing, right?" Morgan whispers.

"Not nothing," Jo whispers back.

CHAPTER 21

THE FIRES ARE out, but the city's suffering from third-degree burns, pink and raw and bubbled and exposed, which I guess is kinda exactly where I am with Kimberly and my friends.

On the outside of my locker, Kimberly has written WHORE in big black Sharpie. On the inside of my locker, Kimberly has written SLUT in red Sharpie—like it wasn't enough to write one or the other; she had to write both for emphasis. And in two different colors at that. Pictures I'd taped up of the four of us through the years have been torn into emphatically small pieces. An egg has been cracked over my textbooks, the pieces of shell left on either side of my calculus book. The whole thing already smells rotten, which I guess she means as a metaphor for our friendship. Kimberly's always had a flair for the dramatic.

Courtney appears at the locker next to mine. She rests her hand on my shoulder.

"I'm not supposed to be talking to you now." She sighs.

"Yeah. I figured."

"What Kimberly did wasn't right. . . ."

I use a napkin from my backpack to try to clean the egg off my calculus textbook.

"God, that smells." Courtney leans against the locker. She holds the book while I pick up the little bits of shell.

"So, Heather and Trevor hooked up."

"Seriously?"

"Yeah. But they're both trying to say it was the drugs. Everybody knows it wasn't the drugs."

She takes a pocket pack of Kleenex from her bag and passes several to me to use on my locker.

"Here. And did you hear I made prom queen?"

"I didn't."

"Yeah. It was cool . . . I got to wear one of those stupid tiaras and the sash and everything. Except I had to dance with Anuj, and he was so sweaty. Omigod, Ash, there were, like, buckets and buckets of sweat. Anyway . . . Kimberly kept venting about you and yelling at Michael. Heather and I had to keep calming her down, and she didn't even once say congratulations to me. The entire time, I kept thinking how nice it was to have something of my own, you know?"

"I get it," I say. And I do.

"Can I tell you a secret?" Courtney leans in closer. "I'm happy we're going to different schools. So much of my life has been in Kimberly's shadow. Soon I'm gonna get to be my own person and see what that feels like."

The bell rings, and Kimberly walks past. She and Courtney have homeroom together.

"Skank," Kimberly hisses under her breath at me. "You coming, Courtney?"

Courtney squeezes my hand twice before she joins her.

In physics, Mr. Holmes is happy as hell, which makes me wonder if he and Ms. Garcia hooked up on prom night. But then I get the image of the two of them slapping their middle-aged bodies against each other, which is gross and very distracting, so I miss what he's talking about when he calls my name to ask a question.

"What?"

"Fifteen kilograms!" Trevor yells from across the room. Michael's not in his usual seat next to him.

"I believe I asked Ms. Bennett the question. But yes, Trevor. Thank you for your contribution."

"Are you okay?" Mr. Holmes asks me as I'm packing up my stuff to go to the next class.

"It's been a shitty week," I say.

"I know," he says. "Things will get better, though. A change is gonna come, right?"

He smiles and squeezes my shoulder. He means well. He's a very kind man, I think. I hope he did get some on prom night.

Outside the classroom, Trevor waits for me atop his skateboard. He moves from side to side like a pendulum, his hair flopping this way and that.

"I'm sorry about your dad's car," I say.

"My parents are gonna call your parents today. I tried to cover for you, but they were gonna make me pay for it with my own money."

"I'm really sorry, Trevor."

"Don't worry about me. I had a great night."

"So I heard."

"I swear, people got some big-ass mouths at this school. It's too small," Trevor says. He keeps rolling his skateboard from side to side. "Michael's an idiot."

"Where is he?" I try to ask nonchalantly.

Trevor shrugs. "Fuck him."

"That's what got me into trouble in the first place," I say, and fake laugh.

"Don't do that. Whatever that is. That's not you," Trevor says, and places his hand on my shoulder.

Rumors have a funny way of taking on a life of their own. First I was the one starting one, and now I'm on the receiving end. Rumors are stories we tell one another at other people's expense. This is what I have to keep reminding myself. It's a story; it's not me. I'm not that story. That's just a little bit of poetic justice.

LaShawn was a thief, a looter, a thug, and now I'm a slut, a whore, a man-stealer.

I slept with Trevor.

I slept with Michael.

I slept with both of them at the same time.

I slept with Lana Haskins.

I left prom to sleep with LaShawn.

I slept with the entire basketball team, and the football team, too. But not the lacrosse team.

I slept with the water polo team, but not the basketball team.

I hear the whispers in class, the hallways, the bathroom; they follow me around like shadows that get larger or smaller depending on who's shining the light on them.

As always, Kimberly is the sun.

At lunch, I look for Lana. I walk around the back of the school, hoping to find her among the strange girls who blow dandelions across the field, or the boys who hide under the bleachers. The back of the school, with its half-burnt grass and white lines, is where the invisible kids eat.

Steve Ruggles sits in the sun with a bunch of boys I swear I've never seen before.

"Have you seen Lana Haskins?" I ask.

"You really should keep better track of your friends." Steve bites into a sandwich.

"Aren't you the black girl who got pushed into the pool?" one of his pasty friends asks.

"You must be thinking of another black girl," I say, and head back to the quad.

The chubby girl Kimberly named Jabba sits by herself, eating and reading *Dune*, which is a nerd book. She's only a sophomore, but she's unmistakable.

"Do you mind if I join you?"

She shrugs and moves her backpack off the table so I have somewhere to place my food. She returns to reading her book, and we eat together in silence for several minutes. Her face is framed by a pretty bob that swishes with the slightest movement. Her Tupperware is full of these itty-bitty pork sausages, fried rice, and slices of tomato. *Filipino food,* I think. Probably homemade. Jabba's Filipina, so that would make sense.

"That looks good," I say.

She shrugs.

I try again. "What's your name?"

"Jabba," she says.

Jesus, how messed up do things have to be for you to refer to yourself by the name others use to tear you down? Unless she's reclaiming it, like nigga, but not.

Jabba is bigger than any other girl in school, and even the adults. I understand wanting to shrink yourself until you're almost nothing; I've been there. Especially when everybody else looks one way and you look another.

"I mean, like, your real name. . . ."

"Does it matter?" she says. "You won't remember it. But you'll remember Jabba."

"I'll remember."

"Do you know the 'The Little Mermaid'?"

"The cartoon?"

"The real one. In the real one with the original ending, she cuts off her tongue to be with that dude, but then he doesn't choose her. And her heart's broken and shit, and she becomes sea foam and dies. But not really, 'cause then she becomes this, like, air particle who has to do good deeds to get a soul or whatever."

"That's dark."

"That's what happens when you don't want to be what you are," Jabba says. "I'm Jabba."

"I'm Ashley," I say.

"I know who you are." She returns to reading.

I sit there trying to think of something to say. It occurs to me that I've always had the security of eating lunch with girls I've known since I was a little kid. I've never had to really socialize with anybody else if I didn't want to. I've never even considered the act of eating alone. Jabba doesn't seem eager for my company either. She seems content.

"So you're into sci-fi? Do you like Ray Bradbury?"

"Shhh," she says.

LaShawn taps me on the shoulder. "Cricket! I was wondering where you were."

"Hey!" My voice is too eager. Too high. Too girlish. Too something.

"Hi, LaShawn!" Jabba brightens at the sight of him.

"Blessing! Watup, girl?"

Yes, this is Jabba's name. The first week of school it was, "Hey, bless you!" Then Kimberly said, "Blessing? More like curse. That poor girl looks like Jabba the Hutt."

"Which part you at?" LaShawn says to Jabba.

"Paul's just become the Kwisatz Haderach."

"Shit's about to go down!"

"Don't spoil anything!"

"Girl, you know I wouldn't spoil it for you!" He turns to me. "You wanna come eat with us?"

I should stay with Jabba. It's not fair of me to invade her lunch space and then leave as soon as I get a weird story and a better offer.

"Okay," I say to LaShawn.

"You wanna come with?" I say to Jabba.

"I'm fine. Thanks."

"See you in the library?" LaShawn says to Jabba.

She reaches up to fist-bump him, giggles when their knuckles touch, and then goes back to her book.

I walk with LaShawn over to the black kids. This is my first time by this ledge, with all of them at once. The kids who were out during the riots have returned. I'm introduced to them formally so that the black kids now have names.

There is Mildred and Lil Ray Ray and Nigerian Candace and Richard, who doesn't go by Ricky or Rick or Rich, he tells me without prompting. Richard's mom is now out of work because the place where she worked burned down.

Fat Albert's real name is Percy, but his middle name actually is Albert.

There is Coke-bottle-body Tisha and Guillaume, who is Haitian. Guillaume's family used to own a shop, and now they own a pile of rubble.

Margie is so light she could probably pass if she straightened her hair and were so inclined.

Jason is mostly nondescript, save for his crooked glasses. He apparently lives not too far from me and has seen me around with my parents or Lucia, even if I haven't seen him.

Winnie is very soft-spoken and meek, and in a great bit of irony was apparently named after Winnie Mandela.

Q introduces himself as Q and doesn't elaborate, so I don't actually know what his name is or much else about him.

Tarrell and Julia are cousins who are, like, super into church and

Jesus or whatever, but they're nice and they cuss a little, so they can't be that preachy, right?

Jo always says, "Black folks love them some Jesus."

"Our church youth group is organizing a bunch of us to go help clean up," Julia says. "You wanna come with? You don't gotta be religious or nothing."

"Sure!" I say, and mean it.

Brian isn't black at all, but they seem to love him like one of their own. *Our* own, I guess. As far as rich white boys go, he's respectfully down. Down enough that they call him nigga. Down enough that he knows not to call them that back.

I sit with the black kids on the ledge and wonder why I never made this short journey across the quad before. Nobody here seems to care about the rumors, or even acknowledge them. I want to ask them if they've ever heard of Greenwood, of what happened to my grandmother and her family, if any of their families carry those same scars. But, like, there's no easy way to casually incorporate a massacre into a conversation with new friends.

"So, has LaShawn told you about how we used to call you Lisa Turtle?" Fat Albert says between bites.

LaShawn blushes. "Why you bringing that up now?"

"Like from the kids' show?" I say.

"Girl, don't go acting like you ain't familiar with *Saved by the Bell*." Fat Albert carries his weight around like it's a joke he's made, or keeps making.

"How am I Lisa Turtle?" I ask.

"Leave her alone," LaShawn says.

"So, like, Lisa, right? We never see her with the black kids. Just like Slater doesn't hang with Latinos, he just goes around calling everybody 'Mama.'"

"Lisa grew up with all of them, so maybe that's just who she's most comfortable with," I say.

"Or maybe they didn't have no black folks in Bayside," Julia says.

"Look in the background. They got black folks."

"Percy, I'ma need you to watch *20/20* or CNN or, like, some adult shit," LaShawn says.

"For reals. Why y'all going in on a kids' show?" Tarrell says.

"Kids' shit is important. It's, like, shaping the future or whatever," Fat Albert says, and takes another bite.

"You're not no Lisa Turtle," LaShawn says, and pats my knee.

Out of the corner of my eye, I catch Fat Albert raising his eyebrows at Tarrell and Julia, and LaShawn quickly removes his hand.

"So, LaShawn finally got you over here," White Brian says in a singsong.

"What?" I say.

"Nothing," LaShawn says, but White Brian winks at him.

I run into Heather at my defaced locker.

"Missed you at lunch." She's got this nervous energy, fidgety and shit like she doesn't know what to do with her limbs. I haven't seen her act this awkward since junior high.

"Yeah . . . well . . . you know," I say, and nod at my locker.

"Right . . ." Heather traces the outline of the scribbled S with her fingertips. "Nobody calls boys sluts," she says. "At least, not in the same way."

"No," I say.

"'Woman is the nigger of the world.'" Heather sighs.

"Niggers are the nigger of the world," I say. "And stop saying 'nigger.' It's not cool."

LaShawn's mother wears pink scrubs and chunky orthopedic shoes. Her dark hair is slicked back in a greasy bun instead of one of the loud wigs she usually wears to LaShawn's games. She looks worn, like she's come off a long shift spent on her feet. She and Principal Jeffries stand in the middle of the office, a bulletin of stars beaming down on them. I pull open the heavy glass door and stand inside, but I don't dare step any farther.

"It was a bad judgment call to have him come into the office based on student rumors," Principal Jeffries says. "You're absolutely right about that. You have every right to be angry, Ms. Johnson."

"I'm not just angry," she says, "I'm hurt. It hurts that you would do this to my baby boy after everything he's done for this school. That this is how he's going to remember his last few weeks of high school. How people are gonna remember him. Can't you understand how much that hurts me as his mother?"

LaShawn's mother looks as though she's already teared up several times in the course of their discussion. The school secretary rises from her desk and passes Principal Jeffries a tissue box, from which she hands LaShawn's mother several tissues. Ms. Johnson pauses to look up at her before taking them. She wipes her eyes and blows her nose, then looks around for a trash can before Principal Jeffries says, "I'll take them for you," at which point LaShawn's mother drops her boogies into Principal Jeffries's hand like a small child.

"Make this right," LaShawn's mother says.

The two of them stare at each other for what feels like an eternity.

"Ms. Johnson." Principal Jeffries breaks the uncomfortable silence. "Unfortunately, regardless of the circumstance, he did hit another child . . . we can't not do anything about that."

"Would you say the same thing if he weren't a scholarship kid?" Ms. Johnson raises her voice a little, and the school secretary looks up from her computer monitor and over at Principal Jeffries expectantly. "What about if I could donate a new library?"

"We treat all our students equally," Principal Jeffries stammers. LaShawn's mother raises an eyebrow and says nothing as she heads toward the door.

"Ms. Johnson, wait!"

LaShawn's mother turns back to face Principal Jeffries, eyes wary, her hands gripping her purse tight to her body.

"How about LaShawn helps out around the school as his punishment? Like sweeping, picking up trash, scraping up gum, or whatever, only for this week? And we don't report any of this to Stanford?"

"So now you want my child to serve as a janitor for these white kids?" LaShawn's mother says.

"Or he can help out at the office, then. I'm sure we can find a project for him here."

"And you don't report the suspension to Stanford?"

"You have my word," Principal Jeffries says.

"Okay, then. That might work. I'll let him know." Ms. Johnson pauses. "I'm curious, Principal Jeffries; what would you have done if LaShawn wasn't LaShawn in this exact same situation? What if my baby wasn't your star athlete? If he was any other black kid at this school?"

Principal Jeffries looks at Ms. Johnson long and hard, and, after a moment, slumps her shoulders a bit. "I don't know, Ms. Johnson, I don't know. . . ."

Ms. Johnson seems satisfied with that bit of honesty and nods like they've come to some sort of understanding, then starts back toward the door. There she catches my eye, and for a moment I freeze; maybe she knows I'm the one who's responsible for all of this.

Instead she smiles at me and says, "You keep your head up, babygirl, okay?"

"Yes ma'am."

I feel awful. Just truly rotten to the core. Like the scum of the earth.

Principal Jeffries has turned and started back to her office when I call out to her. "Principal Jeffries? Um . . . I kinda have to talk to you about something."

She sighs before gesturing toward her open door. "I guess now's as good a time as any."

Principal Jeffries's office has been worn down by decades of teen angst. It's very sparsely decorated but cluttered with books about child development and understanding your teen and educational psychology. There are several photos of her smiling on mountains with a sturdy, busty woman with a gray pixie cut. They look sweaty and happy, in each photo climbing higher and higher still. A peeling birch obscures the view of the school grounds through the office window. Principal Jeffries taps her hiking shoes on the floor nervously as I speak. They squeak.

When I'm done explaining, she says, "Why would you do that?"

In the quad last semester, the theater kids performed this whole number from *West Side Story* about juvenile delinquents. It's pretty funny. Come to think of it, a lot of the songs the theater kids sing are pretty funny. Anyway, one of my favorite lyrics from the song went, *"Hey, I'm depraved on account a I'm deprived."*

I don't say this, though. Instead I say, "Honestly? I think I'm kind of an idiot, Principal Jeffries."

Principal Jeffries takes a moment to contemplate this. "Do you have any idea what kind of situation you've created?"

"I have a pretty good idea, yes."

"Your sister was . . . difficult too." She takes a sip of coffee.

"That's the consensus," I say. I should tell her about Jo, but I can't talk about Jo right now.

Principal Jeffries reaches her hand across her desk and places it on mine.

"In a just world, actions should have consequences." She looks into my eyes intently. I think this is also her nice, liberal, white-lady way of obliquely talking about everything going on in our city.

"I agree."

"You will apologize to LaShawn."

"Yes ma'am."

"In writing."

"Yes ma'am . . . Are you still gonna make him stay after school and do whatever around the office?"

"Unfortunately, he did hit somebody, Ashley."

"But you know he's not like that, normally . . . I want to take responsibility for my mistakes. They impacted him. And they shouldn't have. He doesn't deserve it," I say.

"Yes, well . . . if only more adults would do that, right?"

"So?"

"I'll think about it." She rubs her temples.

"Also, I think Lana Haskins might be in trouble."

"Is this like how you thought LaShawn was a thief?"

Lana trusted me with her secrets, and friends are the people who are supposed to swallow your secrets until they belong to you both. But certain secrets you have to tell. Maybe the whole reason Lana told me was so it wouldn't be a secret anymore. Sometimes you have to speak.

"No. Look at her arm. Her stomach, too." I tell Principal Jeffries what Lana said about her mother, about the bruises and the scars.

She nods her head solemnly. "Thank you for coming to me. I'll take care of it."

I don't know if I should believe her or not, but I guess I don't have much of a choice.

In that same song from *West Side Story* the choir kids sang, "*'There is good! There is untapped good! Like inside the worst of us is good!'*"

That's not how it ends, but that's the part I like best.

After talking with Principal Jeffries, I feel super nauseous, which I guess is the price my bowels pay for doing the right thing. I rush to the restroom. Once safely inside the stall, I hear a familiar *click click* across the bathroom tile, and I know she's right next to me. I know those footsteps almost as well as I know my own. The distance between us is a bathroom stall, which incidentally is entirely too close, given what I've done. Then we finish, and the distance between us is less than a foot, but it might as well be the whole wide world.

Kimberly and I stand at the sink washing our hands, side by side. She looks over at me once, when she thinks I'm not looking. For a moment, we catch each other's eyes, and then we both look down and get super into washing our hands. We don't speak. There are some things that, once said, you can't unsay. There are some things that, once done, you can't undo.

We let the weight of our history sit like so many rocks in our mouths, silencing us as we wash ourselves clean.

CHAPTER 22

THE ANCHORS POSE in rubble and talk about rebuilding. Some people are now saying that some of the fires have been set on purpose by greedy business owners looking to collect insurance money in the middle of the unrest.

Repeated like a chorus on every news channel: fire-gutted strip malls, debris-filled streets, emptied shelves, scored to the sound of politicians saying the things they think people want to hear and who or what they think people want to blame, ending with we will be stronger, we will be better. I'm not even a grown-up yet, but even I can see the truth is both swirling around in the middle of all those fancy speeches and somewhere just outside of them.

Anyway, since it's an election year, everybody's coming to see the damage for themselves, to walk their shiny leather shoes among the ruins and proclaim what's wrong with Los Angeles and how their party's gonna make it right, or how the other party made it wrong. Governor Bill Clinton is gonna come visit, which should make the Katzes happy.

The National Guard is withdrawing; the army and Marines,

too. It's like we were in a boxing match and got knocked out, only to come to and have to reorient ourselves. Everybody in the city is wondering how the hell we get back up.

Sometimes I have nightmares in which I'm looking down the barrel of a gun.

I ask LaShawn if he has nightmares too, after what happened to us, if he wakes up feeling that kind of fear again. He tells me that wasn't the first time he's had a cop pull a gun on him, and it probably won't be the last.

"You get used to it." He sighs. "Or maybe you don't . . . but it happens."

Jo sits across from a judge in a small, wood-paneled room. A janitor squeaks a cart along the linoleum floor outside. My pretty dress is itchy. Jo's shoes are a tad too big; her feet slide forward in them, and then she readjusts to press them against the heels. Her hair is straightened and pulled up into an elegant ballerina bun that gives her the appearance of having had a face-lift, not that she needed one. It makes her look that much more beautiful, but also more severe.

Going through security at the courthouse makes you feel a little like a criminal, even if you aren't one. The inside is various shades of dreary, and the harsh fluorescents make everybody look sallow and vaguely unsure of themselves. We walked through the metal detectors and gathered ourselves, dimmed lights all. I watched the people coming and going while my parents and Jo waited for her lawyer.

These are the kinds of people I saw: scary-looking. Wary-looking. Harried-looking. Trashy-looking. Douchey-looking. Bored-looking. Scared-looking. There were even a few children clinging to adults in Sunday-school dresses and little-man suits. I don't want to think about why they might be inside. I tried to picture my aunt Carol walking in and out every day, making decision after decision on some of the worst days of other people's lives.

My mother says Auntie Carol is always lording her power over my mother's head, but I don't know because we never see Auntie Carol, and I don't know how somebody can do all that lording if you're never around to see it. But what Carol said to Jo several days ago was that actually she doesn't have the power. Not this time.

Auntie Carol and my cousin Reggie stopped by for a bit to discuss what she called Jo's options, none of which were very good. Reggie's slimmed down since the last time I saw him and is now a good-looking boy who carries himself like a newly good-looking boy, preening and flexing while doing things that don't really require that much flexing. Even as we sat discussing Jo's fate, out of the corner of my eye I saw him, muscles flexed, glancing at his reflection in the table.

"This is a really serious offense," Auntie Carol said, and sighed.

"But what about what happened with Reggie?" my mother repeated like she was refusing to listen.

Reggie briefly glanced up from looking at himself at the sound of his name. "That was, like, barely an ounce of coke, and I really was holding it for a friend."

Reggie is the kind of boy who likes to brag about fucking up the curve in his classes. I honestly don't know how he gets invited to parties at all, much less has friends. Auntie Carol glared at him to shut up.

My aunt paced the room like somebody who didn't know its edges, only that she was taking tentative steps away and toward her sister, my sister.

"That was different. This is a big deal. I can't make this disappear." My aunt stood across from Jo. "I promise I've tried."

"So, what does that mean?" Jo said, and Auntie Carol looked away like she didn't want to be the one to tell her.

This is what happened, according to Jo:

When Harrison dozed off on the couch, tired from his long shift, Jo snuck out with her spray can. She started walking without knowing where it was she was heading, exactly—just that she was here and she needed to be there. As she walked, she saw a small crowd gathered in the distance in front of a run-down strip mall. An older man walked toward her, a little unsteady on his feet and weighed down by two small grocery bags. He looked her up and down and said, "You're walking the wrong way, girl. You don't want no part of that." But she could feel the crowd pulsing, feel their vibrations from blocks away. Her friends had stopped protesting. It wasn't productive, they said; it was madness. *Fuck that,* Jo thought. The rebellion was on its last legs, but it wasn't dead, not yet. That was exactly where she needed to be, she thought.

The crowd gathered like a bee swarm, swirling and concentrating, dissipating, and then gathering together again to sting. Jo stayed on the edges, not sure what to do. She suddenly felt very silly with her spray can in her hand, ineffectual. By contrast, several of the young men carried glass bottles. They had torn up an old T-shirt and distributed the strips among themselves, and somebody poured the kerosene. All that was needed was a match or a lighter. They searched between them, and a brown hand emerged victorious, holding a small flame up to the sky like at a concert, or a vigil. The first young man had long, sinewy arms and pants that fell in small puddles at his feet. He lurched forth and nearly tripped over his pants, messing up his momentum. He grabbed up his waistband in one hand while he tossed the bottle with the other. The bottle bounced and landed in a small fire on the concrete parking lot.

Several of the young men jumped back under a hail of expletives, and a few began to run away. Still others bounced on their toes with energy like Tigger from *Winnie-the-Pooh*, their sneakers like springs, their swooshes egging them on to Just Do It.

"Let me do it." The youngest was clearly somebody's kid brother, whom they'd barely let tag along.

"Yo, let him have it." The boy in charge, as far as Jo could tell, looked almost exactly like the youngest one, but a little lighter and older, with his hair in two French braids that hung to his shoulders, a small but noticeable scar across his left cheek.

She watched as the younger boy wound his arm back like he was on a baseball field and released, a winning pitch. The bottle burst right through the window, the shattered glass fell like rain, and then there was fire. Jo felt the flame grow warm as the summer sun across her face.

There were more of them than there were of the police, but it didn't matter. The police swept through the swarm of people, cracking across backs and limbs and heads with their batons, grabbing limbs, rifles pointed, yelling, "Get down, stay down."

Stay down.

The police dogs barked.

"But I didn't do anything," Jo said as she felt her body thud to the ground, felt the bitter of blood in her mouth, saw most of her front tooth fall onto the sidewalk.

In the courtroom, Lucia sits next to me, her legs crossed at her ankles, eyes closed like she's reliving something she's never told me about. Harrison wears a suit that my parents bought him, navy and tailored and court-respectable. Jo stares straight ahead for most of it.

My mother grips my hand so tight I think she might sprain a finger as my sister enters a plea: "Not guilty."

Then they usher us out and move on to the next case.

We twist and turn our way back home in relative silence, except when we have to pull over for Jo to throw up. When we get inside, Jo goes upstairs to lie down, Harrison has to head out to work, and my father retreats into his office. My parents asked Jo to stay at our house for the duration of the trial, and surprisingly enough, she agreed. Honestly, I think they're a little afraid of her hurting herself, of her ending up like Grandma Shirley. In any case, my father has now hidden his pellet gun. Harrison goes to his construction jobs, then comes to our house to visit his wife, smelling of sweat, covered in dirt, looking like he's ready to build or rebuild Jo as needed. Lucia disappears into the kitchen to make dinner, and then it's me and my mother walking around the living room, kicking off our heels and peeling off our stockings. My mother throws her fancy tweed suit jacket on the couch.

"Did you know about what happened to Grandma Shirley?"

My mother pauses for a second. "Not all of it, but some. I thought it was your dad's story to tell you when he was ready. Not mine."

I nod my head. She plops down on the couch next to me and starts to rub her feet. She's always wearing heels, so the sides of her pinkie toes have little bumps on them where the heels have created little hills. Her toenails are a dark magenta, which matches her fading lipstick. When I was little, I thought she was supertall, like a giant or a superhero; now I know she's only kinda tall, like a human.

"It's a lot to take in, isn't it?" she says.

"Yeah. I feel so sad for Grandma Shirley. And Daddy . . ."

"Your father's been through a lot . . ."

I bend down, take her foot into my hand, and start to rub it. She leans back against the couch and closes her eyes.

"You don't tell me anything about your friends or school anymore. You used to tell me all sorts of things . . . ," she says.

"I was little. Little kids talk a lot."

"Trevor's parents called the other day." My mom opens her eyes and looks at me. "They say you stole his car during prom."

"I didn't want to be there anymore," I say.

"Why?"

"It's complicated."

She stares at me intently, as though she's trying to figure me out.

I could tell her everything, but I don't think she'd understand, or maybe she would; I don't know.

As though she can hear my thoughts, my mother reaches over and brushes my hair out of my face before gently grabbing my face in her hands. "We're both secrets to each other. But maybe one day we don't have to be."

"Yeah . . . okay. . . ." I don't know quite what to say, but I don't pull away, and she doesn't let go.

"We worked so hard to give you girls everything . . . to protect you from everything . . . maybe too hard. I'm not sure. The world doesn't let black children be children for very long. We wanted you to have as long a childhood as possible. We only meant to protect you girls, never to lose you. Your father and I both grew up long before we should've had to. Both of us, in different ways. Do you get what I'm saying?"

She holds her hand to my cheek as though she's trying to give me her thoughts through her fingertips.

"I think so."

She pauses for a moment as though she's going to say more, but instead exhales deeply, like she's been holding that same breath ever since I was born.

My mother walks over to the bookshelf and pulls out a photo album. "Your father and I have been putting together your yearbook page. It's supposed to be a surprise, but I want you to see this one photo."

She pulls out a photo of the two of us in front of a sleek glass building that looks really familiar. In it, she cradles fat baby me in one arm and holds Jo's hand with the other. Jo looks up at her, and I drool all over myself toward the camera.

"This was the first building I was the lead architect on. I started it when I got pregnant with you, and I was so scared I wouldn't be able to finish it. It was already a huge deal that I was the first and only black woman at the firm, and young, and a lot of people thought I didn't deserve to be there. I thought that once I told them I was pregnant, they'd make me hand the project over to somebody else. And I kept being afraid the entire time. At one point I even wanted to quit, to spare myself the indignity of being taken off the project, which I just knew was coming. But you kept me going—because I wanted to prove something to myself, but also to show you girls that I could. That one day *you* could. That one day you can. We drove by it that one day; do you remember?"

When I was little, we went on a field trip to a place out in Riverside called Jurupa Mountains Discovery Center. I was very excited, because field trips meant that we got to go on school buses and eat junk food like Lunchables and Fruit Roll-Ups, chased by Hi-C that came in bright boxes, yellow as the buses themselves. Our school required that parents put in a certain number of volunteer hours every year, so my father and mother drew straws, and she either won or lost. When we all started to pile onto the bus, she wanted to sit next to me, but I wanted to sit with my friends. So instead she sat next to Nancy Chang's mother, who also worked for a living. When we got there, we ran around in the dust and touched dug-up dinosaur bones, and at the gift shop I bought shiny, colored crystals dug from deep in the earth.

On the bus on the way back home, Heather and I were chatting about horses when my mother walked up the aisle and knelt down beside me.

"Look, Ash!" she said, and excitedly pointed out the window at a building, tall, gleaming, and new. "I designed that. That one is one of mine!"

I glanced at it.

"Cool," I said.

My mother waited for a second for me to say something else,

but when I didn't, she walked back over to Nancy Chang's mother, and I turned back to Heather, held my Fruit Roll-Up with my mouth, and let it dangle out like a tongue.

I didn't know it had meant so much to her then. I wish I had.

"I remember," I say.

She grabs my hand and beams like Christmas.

"You can do anything, Ashley. Be anything . . . But first, you're gonna have to pay for Trevor's car yourself . . . get a summer job . . ." She laughs.

"I guess I'll see if Hot Dog on a Stick is hiring again. I still have my hat around here somewhere. I forgot to give it back."

"I forgot about your working there . . . Did I ever tell you my first job was at a diner?"

I shake my head.

"It was the summer Robert Kennedy died. A girl from work invited me to this party at her house. I didn't like her that much, I thought she was annoying, but there was a boy I liked who was going to be there. We got drunk, and she had a Ouija board and tried to talk to Robert Kennedy from the dead."

"What did he say?"

"'Hello.' That's it. Just hello." My mother starts to laugh.

Once we played with a Ouija board at Heather's to try to talk to her *bubbe* after she died, but we never found out what her *bubbe* was trying to say because as soon as the pointer moved, we screamed and ran out of the room.

"What happened to the boy you liked?"

"Nothing." My mother laughs again. "I was too shy . . . So what happened at prom?"

"Kimberly called me a nigger and pushed me into a pool in front of the whole school."

"What? Why?"

"Because of a boy." I pause before I continue. "I messed up. Really bad."

I hope she doesn't ask me more. Instead, she grows silent. My mother seems to be coming undone. If normally her curls are perfectly styled and gelled down, today they're frizzy and frayed. Her foundation has melted with worry. I notice a puckering of the lips I've never noticed before; age. It occurs to me that this is the first time in a long time I've told her something about myself without telling Lucia first.

"You remember what happened with her and the pool when you were little?"

"Yeah."

"Your father and I wondered if maybe we'd made a mistake then. Sending you to that school. Raising you where we were raising you. You want things to be better for your kids. I don't know which better would've been best. We always tried to do what we thought was best for you. Everything was always for you."

She says it like she's asking my forgiveness. But she's still a little defensive, kinda.

"Thank you," I say, and she nods. I start to walk up the stairs, but before I reach the top, I turn around. "You're not mad at me?"

"You're more than your mistakes," my mother says, and I know that in this particular moment, she's not really talking to me at all.

• • •

"Hey, Daddy."

In his office, my father sits surrounded by piles of paperwork and several leather-bound reference books. A few overstuffed file folders threaten to slide off the desk, and I quickly grab them before they can leap to their doom.

"I really do have to get more organized one of these days." He scratches himself right above his eyebrow.

"You really should let Lucia help you before she leaves."

"I'm afraid if she straightens up, I won't know where anything is." He laughs, and his drugstore reading glasses lift up and slide down his face a tad.

I run my hand along the books in his bookshelf, these giant tomes on international accounting and financial trade and global perspectives on economies in transition, blah blah, numbers numbers. *Numbers are easier for some people than people,* I think. And yet there are always people behind them.

"I'm sorry about Grandma Shirley," I say. "I wish you had told me before."

He peers up above his reading glasses before taking them off. "Every day of my life we lived with the awful things that happened to your grandmother, and then the awful stuff in the news. Right in the middle of my childhood, we're coming home to watch hoses being set on people our own age for wanting to be equal, and the aftermath of people bombing churches and killing little girls. Girls who were even younger than me then . . ."

His file folders finally fall onto the ground, but he doesn't rush to fix them.

"When your sister was born, I remember holding her in my

arms and thinking I would do anything I could to keep the world from hurting her. Same with you. I wanted to raise you guys without that stuff in your heads. Not that I was ashamed, or that I thought you should be ashamed. We aren't the ones who should carry that shame. Just not . . . weighed down by it, I guess."

He reaches out to hold my hand as he speaks, and I feel like a little kid again. I don't remember the last time I held on to him like this. He used to say that when I was first born, I was so small he could hold me in one hand.

"I wanted you guys to get to be happy, carefree, even," he says.

"We were, sometimes. We are . . ."

Even when we're sad or scared, somewhere around the corner there's a bit of joy.

"Hey, you remember me and Jo when we had to evacuate during the wildfires in that gym?"

He starts to laugh.

There were four deer that walked the school grounds back and forth, as though that same ruddy fireman had told even them this place was safe, but they weren't quite sure how to be there. Outside, the smoke was an orange screen door around the very sun itself. The deer didn't run through the grounds or cause any damage; instead, they kept to themselves in the farthest corner of the field, away from people, away from the fire, evacuees like us. A bunch of us kids tried to creep closer, but our adults pulled us by our collars, away.

"Leave them be," they said.

There were enough animals to bother inside the gym itself. Jo and I played with a skittish guinea pig named Rat, who belonged to a sickly girl who lived three blocks away from us. Maybe she wasn't sickly, just allergic, but my main memory of her is that she coughed and constantly wiped her nose so that there was a thick yellow smear across her pink sleeve. Every once in a while she'd bring out a blue inhaler and puff and suck like it was the source of life itself. Anyway, Jo and I begged and begged for a pet, but my parents said we weren't responsible enough for one, and it wouldn't be fair to Lucia to make her clean up after our pet. Rat the hamster had what the sickly girl told us was a show-length coat, which meant that Rat kinda looked like a shih tzu. While the sickly girl watched, we braided Rat's coat into two soft pigtails that unraveled quickly.

Jo gently lifted a squirming Rat up to the light and declared loudly in front of our parents, "We would take such good care of you."

I nodded enthusiastically.

Patsy Cline's "Crazy" wafted in all dreamy-like from a boom box. Us kids ran from pet to pet and climbed up and down the bleachers. Jo and I made friends with several kids we didn't know who lived nearby and their pet dogs, a few goats, and even a miniature pony named Astrid who pooped green hay bits on the squishy gym floor. We shrieked at the top of our lungs and ran around, excited by the adventure, like it was one big sleepover—entirely forgetting that our houses could be gone, and our toys with them.

At night we slept in rows of green cots, like preschoolers, or soldiers.

The next morning, the fireman stood up on the podium and announced on the loudspeaker, "Fire's out. You're okay to go back to your lives, good people."

And just like that, it was over. We stumbled into the light and went home to see how much of our lives remained.

Mostly, I remember the sounds of all those different people in one room together—taking care of one another, breathing, snoring, being. As though we were one big heart.

"But I don't want to go home!" Jo whined as she fed one last carrot to Astrid. "We're having so much fun!"

Daddy laughs at the memory and leans back in his office chair, his hands behind his head. Bleary-eyed from her nap, Jo appears in the doorway and peeks in at us. "What are you two laughing at in here?"

"Yo' face," I say.

"Shut up," she says.

Daddy looks over at the two of us and grins. "Oh, my beautiful daughters!"

The media and the politicians keep stereotyping everyone who was out during the riots as "savage" or "lawless" or "hooligans" or "thugs," an "underclass" not representative of the "real America."

But Jo was out there, and that's not true of her at all. And if it's not true of her, then it's probably not true of at least some of the other people who were out there too. My sister is gentle and kind and thoughtful and opinionated and delicate, and also impulsive and outraged and angry. If anything, Jo was out there because of her values, because she cares too much. I've been reading a lot of the books that Jo left behind, all these history and civil rights books, some of her old textbooks from school, trying to understand the world. Trying to understand her. She was in the wrong place at the wrong time doing the wrong thing, but maybe some of her reasons were the right ones. Because a bunch of dudes beating on one dude who was already on the ground until he's brain damaged and broken is wrong. Because prosecuting people differently for the same exact crimes because of skin color is wrong. Because some people being able to buy private islands while other people sleep outside on the ground is wrong. Because knowingly destroying poor communities with drugs let in to fund wars against foreign regimes is fundamentally wrong. Because even though you finally enact a Civil Rights Act not even thirty years ago, it doesn't erase centuries of unequal wealth, unequal access, unequal schooling, unequal living conditions, unequal policing. You can't tell people to pull up on bootstraps when half of them never had any boots to begin with, never even had the chance to get them. Or when you let people burn whole, thriving black communities to the ground and conveniently forget about it. Because maybe the problem isn't only with "bad" people; maybe the problem is with the whole system.

Because we're supposed to be better than that in this country. Whoever we are. Because we can be. Sometimes people do real stupid shit when they feel invisible or powerless. Doesn't make it right, but maybe at least we can try to understand a little?

It's like the riots pulled focus from one Los Angeles to the other, but it's all part of the same photo, if you're looking. Always has been. The palm trees and the pain, the triumph and the trauma— all of us, one big beating heart. The "real Los Angeles." The "real America."

It's like Uncle Ronnie said: it's our history, in our blood, in our bones.

"Ain't no new starts," he said.

CHAPTER 23

LANA SQUINTS AT me from an eye swollen the color of midnight. I feel a little dizzy when I see it, unsteadied by its violence. Unwittingly, I reach my hand out to touch it, and Lana quickly grabs me by the wrist, hard. She-Ra, the cat, looks up at us expectantly from her perch on the front steps, like we're on *Springer* and the tabby is urging us to "Fight! Fight!"

"You told," Lana says.

"I did."

"Asshole."

The cat slithers through the small space in the doorway. Her tail thwaps me as she passes, and I can't tell whether it's a deliberate hit. It could've been a friendly "hello," or an "ugh," or maybe She-Ra doesn't even care that I'm here at all. *Cats are a lot like teenage girls,* I think.

"I was afraid for you," I say.

"It was only a few more months."

"And then what?"

"I don't know. I would've moved out. Or away. Something."

"Can we talk? Please."

"I don't want to talk to you, Ashley."

"Please? I can't lose any more friends. Please."

I guess I must sound really pathetic, because Lana cracks the door open wider and looks me up and down.

"Who said we were friends?" she says as she lets me in. She wears a pair of ratty jeans and a men's V-neck undershirt, with a red handkerchief wrapped around her tousled hair so she looks a bit like Axl Rose. I follow her through Pham and Brad's house to the backyard. Outside, cardboard boxes strain to hold their Sharpie-designated loads.

"You're moving?"

"To my dad's." Lana explains that the court gave emergency temporary custody to her father.

"Isn't he down the street?"

"Might as well be another country," she says.

The trampoline lies in pieces in the grass. It strikes me how delicate it is, a bunch of metal poles and fabric stretched over a circle, like a little world. That's all it takes to make a person fly.

"My mother might go to jail," Lana says. "Maybe she deserves to, but she's still my mother, you know?"

"My sister might go to jail too." I bite my tongue to hold back my tears.

"For what?" she says.

The tears well up. I haven't had a full night's sleep since Jo's arrest.

"She's so stupid," I say as the tears come down. "I hate her."

"No, you don't," Lana says. "Just like I don't hate my mom. Even though maybe I should."

She pauses for a moment before she grabs me by the hand. Then she sits down on the ground beneath us.

"Sit," she says.

We stretch our bodies on the grass like stars. Little-bitty bugs crawl around on our fingertips. A roly-poly makes its way from Lana's hand to mine. I can feel the tiny green blades along my cheeks.

"You know how if you close your eyes, it feels like you can feel the earth spinning under you?" she says.

"Yeah."

"It startles you at first. And then you remember we're so little and the world is so big."

I'm not sure I 100 percent get what that has to do with Jo, but I also think I get it. We lie there quietly until the cat pounces on Lana and starts to hump her leg.

"Stop it, She-Ra." She pushes her off.

"Your cat's a real horndog." I laugh.

"That was so dumb," she says, but then she snorts.

"I'm going to help clean up South Central with Julia's church group later. Wanna come with?"

"Look at you, being civic-minded! Wish I could, but I gotta keep moving."

A man I assume must be Lana's father peers over the backyard fence. He's desert brown, with bright green eyes. His hair is closely cropped to his head in the beginnings of tight curls. If she mostly looks like her mother, her mouth is definitely his, big and warm with teeth like Chiclets. He calls out to her in a language that sounds like a million grains of sand. She stands up and responds to him in English.

"I thought you were white," I say.

She laughs and pulls me to my feet.

"It don't matter if you're black or white.'" She does her best Michael Jackson impression, which is really pretty terrible.

She-Ra purrs an assent.

The black kids are supernice to me, but they have years of history with one another, the kind I used to have with my friends, so I feel like an interloper. Kimberly and Courtney and Heather and I have years of inside jokes, years of knowing what the slightest eyebrow raise means, what a twitch of the face tells. I don't know any of this stuff about my new friends, or if they even consider me a new friend at all.

"Man, I need a motherfucking car," Fat Albert says. He wheezes as we walk. I really should be calling him Percy now.

"You and me both," Tarrell says.

Candace invited everybody to her house after we finished volunteering with Julia and Tarrell's youth group, because she lives just a few blocks away. Julia, Tarrell, Percy, LaShawn, and I walk toward Candace's house. Our hands are sweaty from plastic gloves and calloused from shovel handles. The Timberlands I borrowed from Jo are giving me nasty-ass blisters, so each step feels like a potential land mine of blood and gross. I've done more manual labor today than I think I've done in my entire life. Still, there's something about searching for the beauty under the wreckage that has me pumped—hopeful, even.

Or maybe it's because LaShawn and I kinda hang behind the rest of them with each other, and every so often our hands graze each other and we don't pull away. He should hate me; I honestly don't understand why he doesn't, but I'm grateful. Sometimes we love the people we should hate, and we hate the people we love, and we're topsy-turvy, but it's like the song my dad likes to put on the record player when he's had a little too much to drink: *"It's a thin line between love and hate."*

"Are you sure it's okay that I'm coming? I don't want to impose myself," I whisper to LaShawn. "What if they don't actually like me but they're being nice because of, like, racial solidarity or whatever?"

"Girl, what? Racial solidarity?"

"I don't know." I shrug my shoulders.

"Everybody likes you," he says.

"That's not even remotely true, and you know it," I say.

"Well . . . yeah." He laughs. "But I like you, and they're my friends. You're fine."

Ranchero music drifts in from another block as we walk.

"You know, they act like we don't belong here, like we're just a bunch of thugs or illegals and the city would be better off without us. But we helped build this shit. We're fucking genesis."

"Here he goes again," Candace says. "This nigga walk around talking about LA like it's a girl he got a crush on. 'Did you know LA this? Did you know LA that?'"

LaShawn ignores her and continues.

Of the forty-four original founders of LA, only two were white. Twenty-six had some African ancestry. Sixteen were Indians or Mestizos.

Some of the wealthiest of them were the brothers Andrés and Pío Pico—of mixed Native American, Black, and Mexican ancestry. Pío Pico would become governor of Alta California before it became part of the United States. Andrés eventually became a senator after statehood. His son's house is the second-oldest residence in Los Angeles.

Pico Boulevard runs the length of the city, from the ocean air in Santa Monica all the way to the smoggy history in Downtown. It passes by Santa Monica High School, Westside Pavilion, the Fox Studios, a snooty country club, the Museum of Tolerance, the National Academy of Recording Arts and Sciences, and Roscoe's Chicken and Waffles. It passes through poor areas and rich areas and areas in between, through famous people and nobodies, through Black people, Mexican people, Persian people, Greek people, Jewish people, and Korean people, and everyone in between. If you get on the 30 and settle in, there it is out a smudged bus window, behind a gang tag, a curse, or an etched declaration love; all of Los Angeles on just one boulevard named after a nigger.

And before us there were the Tongva.

On the corner of La Brea and Pico, next to where a shopping mall went up in flames, somebody spray-painted in black along a white brick wall, LOOK WHAT YOU CREATED.

"All I'm saying is, this shit is ours as much as anybody else's," LaShawn says.

"Don't need no history lesson to know all that. Look at us. We here." Candace gestures around the neighborhood and up at the sky, like not solely Los Angeles but the whole world is ours.

The front steps of Candace's house are lined in a Spanish-looking tile. The path is lined in bright-yellow flowers. It's a small home but pretty, minus the pointed metal gates on the windows. A big blue pit bull tumbles over itself as it rushes full speed from some hidey-hole. It barks at us from behind a metal fence.

"Don't mind Horace," Candace says.

"He gon' eat my face?" Fat Albert says.

"Horace is a girl." Candace laughs and starts to open the gate to her home.

"But you didn't say no, though," Fat Albert says, and backs away from the dog.

"Horace, sit. Stay," she says, and Horace does.

We walk through Candace's house to a wood-paneled den, where her little brother sits on a worn black leather sofa playing video games. A fan rotates its neck, blowing breath back and forth, but the room's still stuffy.

"Out!" she says.

"No," he says, and somersaults Sonic once more into Dr. Robotnik. Robotnik waddles toward his escape pod and Sonic chases after him, mere seconds from beating the evil scientist, when Candace pulls the power cord from the wall. Her brother starts yelling at her in Igbo, and I swear I see actual tears in his eyes.

Julia and Tarrell curl up on opposite ends of the couch. Fat Albert plugs the Genesis back into the wall; the controller looks tiny in his hands. He passes the other controller to Tarrell, but Julia snatches it from him.

"Let's give Lisa Turtle a makeover!" Candace squeals.

The black kids still call me Lisa Turtle, only now it's to my face, and I can't get too upset 'cause it's far better than being called Fat Albert.

"I don't know." I look over at LaShawn.

"C'mon, let us! Candace lives for makeovers." Julia claps her hands.

"Do I look that awful?" I say. The last time I had a makeover was when we were in fifth grade and Kimberly informed me that I should straighten my hair and start wearing mascara if I was ever gonna get boys to like me.

"Let me braid your hair for you, at least," Candace says. She opens a three-tiered caddy and wiggles out two bags of braid hair. She pats the floor by her.

"Sit."

Candace carries herself like a princess, like she could be anything at all. When she tells me to sit, it sounds like a royal edict. So I do.

She takes a rattail comb and rakes the metal tip across my scalp, parting my hair into several sections. LaShawn sits next to me on the floor, legs crossed.

"So, what's the deal with you two?" Fat Albert says. "Everybody in this room knows this boy been had a crush on you for years."

I look at LaShawn but he turns away, his face red as a Jordan jersey.

"You know, people think black folks don't blush, but we do," Julia says. "Like right now you're blushing like a motherfucker."

"I am not," LaShawn says.

"Boy, why you lying?"

"Put your head down," Candace says to me. There's such an intimacy in the feeling of another person's hands in your hair, greasing and parting across your bare scalp, your brain at their fingertips.

Julia and Fat Albert load Streets of Rage while Candace works her way through my head. Julia tries to play as Blaze, probably because she's the girl and arguably the fastest character, but Fat Albert selects her before Julia gets a chance.

"Too slow!"

Together, they walk as the girl and the black guy down the city street, beating people up. They're supposed to be working together, but Julia keeps snatching up the food and weapons and then "accidentally" attacking Percy, who keeps yelling, "Stop hitting me, fool!" while Tarrell alternately yells, "Yo, go get that dude over there!" and "Why y'all so sorry?"

Candace's parents come home together. They yell out greetings and look as though they're leaning on each other so as not to fall over. Her father is a security guard at the same hospital where her mother works as a nurse, and they spend all day on their feet. In Nigeria, they had servants, Candace says.

Candace's father has the biggest, warmest brown face I've ever seen, like a sculptor took those cheesy images of the sun smiling and made them into a real person. They talk to Candace for a bit in their language. Her parents have thick voices, their words like skipping stones. Then the house absorbs them into itself. Her father turns on a drumbeat from inside its bowels.

"What is that?"

"My daddy loves himself some Fela."

I make a mental note to find out what "Fela" is.

"Hey, did you guys know Lana Haskins isn't white?" I say.

"Girl, duh," Fat Albert says.

"She's half-Egyptian," Julia says, like this was somehow common knowledge.

"Her white ass is, like, literally African American," Tarrell says, and everybody laughs.

I am he as you are me as you are we as we are all together.

I like being part of this we. It's weird how sometimes you can be part of us and sometimes you can be part of them, and find a way to be at home in both.

"Done. Want beads?" Candace asks.

My mother thinks beads look tacky, but I like the little wooden balls Candace has in her box of hair goodies. They look like somebody tore apart a necklace and placed its pretty entrails in your hair.

"Sure!" I say.

"What you wanna bet them white girls at school will see you and be like, 'Omigod! You know, I got my hair braided in Mexico once,'" Julia says, and we start to laugh.

Candace hands me a mirror, and it's like I'm looking at myself but not. I run my hand down the length of my hair. The thin ropes are thicker than the ones I got when I was little, but just as pretty.

"You look incredible," LaShawn turns to me and says.

Then the whole room starts echoing his words as Tarrell, Julia, Percy, and Candace proceed to mock the shit out of him.

"He's right, though," Percy says. "Candace got Lisa Turtle looking like a goddamn Nubian princess."

Then he belly laughs like it's the funniest thing he's ever said and smiles at me. "You're all right after all, Lisa Turtle. You're all right."

LaShawn winks at me.

I flip my hair to the side and hear the *click-clack* of wooden beads like a drumbeat, my hair a kind of music drowning out everything else.

The world is so big and we're so little; still each bead announces, "I'm here!"

CHAPTER 24

THE COURTROOM SMELLS like the past. The shellacked court reporter clacks in shorthand the details of my sister's supposed crime. Sunspots dot the top of the judge's head like speckles on an egg. He looks to be shrinking into his robes. The arresting officer takes the stand, a man who seems to be on a collision course with every doorway he enters, and the doorway might actually lose. He's hard, hair shorn, militarily erect, a recent Gulf War vet. He tells his side of the story succinctly—an agitated crowd, a Molotov cocktail, a building on fire.

Jo purses her lips as he speaks; her whole body screams, but she doesn't interject. I don't know whether you'd know that if you didn't know her, but she's my sister, so I can tell the frustration in the twitch of her eyebrow, or in the way she scratches at the dry patch of stress behind her ear.

"This is your fault," my father said during a quick break to Harrison, who, for once, fought back.

"Have you met your daughter? Do you know her at all? Your daughter doesn't do anything she doesn't want to do," Harrison spat back.

Jo said calmly, "Auntie Carol says Grant's one of the best. It'll be okay. Everything will be fine."

Grant is Jo's lawyer. He fiddles with his watch occasionally while the prosecution speaks—not checking the time but checking to see if time is still there. He carries himself exactly like Mr. Katz, a man used to getting what he wants. A man for whom no danger is imminent. He's confident in his remarks to the jury, charming. His slicked hair has a bit of gray at the temples, and his eyes are a beachy blue. His suit is perfectly tailored to the body he clearly approaches like one of his legal briefs, sculpting, erasing, adding until it's perfect. He looks like he belongs to one of those corporate clusters you see out in the water on weekends, floating on uninitiated surfboards, waiting for the wave on which they can briefly be somebody else. When he speaks to us, he smiles when it's appropriate and looks serious while talking about serious things. He speaks down just a little, because that's how he speaks to everyone.

Jo thinks he's a twat. Still, she's grateful.

When the jury foreman eventually reads Jo's verdict, my father will grip the arm of his chair to steady himself. My mother will grip him, her mouth wrapped around a whispered "No!"

I'll surprise myself by crying out, and some of the jurors will look over at me with pity, but most will look down or away.

When the jury acquitted the officers, the man who struck Rodney King the most, Officer Laurence M. Powell, smiled and said, "I am very happy, very happy."

When asked what he would say to those upset by the verdicts, Powell said, "I don't think I have to respond to them. They have to respond to themselves and make their own decision. I don't think there's anything I can do to change their feelings."

Jo will be shaking when she rises to hear her sentence, her pale-pink nail polish already bitten down. Her future will look different than any of us thought it would. Sixteen months isn't all that long, and yet it might as well be forever. I try to picture us when we're both older and she's a former felon.

"We're gonna fight this," Grant says, without an ounce of condescension, to my parents, who stand there in shock, our worlds turned upside down.

Because she's not considered a flight risk, Jo will have several weeks before she has to self-surrender. Until then, she waits.

When LaShawn calls that night to ask me how things went, he will sit with me in silence while I try to remember how to breathe. But that is not yet. That's after.

Before:

The jacarandas are in bloom, and their pretty purple petals line whole blocks. The fires got some of them, but not all. We stand in the middle of burned-out buildings, graffiti on the sidewalk under our feet. Power lines stretch across the sky in messy stripes. It occurs to me halfway through the morning that the reason the sky looks weird is 'cause I don't see power lines like this in my neighborhood.

I watch the succession of planes, sometimes two or three at a time, into and out of Los Angeles; more people, less people.

Less people. Ronnie and Morgan are leaving Los Angeles as soon as Morgan graduates. Last week they went to Las Vegas to scope out new places to build old dreams.

Grandma Shirley's store is much smaller than I remember it—

not much larger than our living room, although I suppose our living room is pretty large, as far as these things go. The carpet is boring gray but freshly put in and still plush underfoot, perfect for demonstrating the workings of a freshly repaired vacuum. It was soiled by the looters, but an old family friend is gonna come by and steam it at a huge discount. A pity clean. I can't help thinking what it must be like knowing that your neighbors, maybe even some people you considered friends, were among those trying to take what little it took generations to build.

A few older folks stop by to reminisce and offer Ronnie their condolences. They look at my father as though trying to place him, until they do.

"Haven't seen you round these parts in years!" they say, or "You forgot all about us, Craig!" And even though he's a grown-ass man with a good-ass job and a large-ass house in a nice-ass neighborhood, my dad looks like a little-ass boy, reprimanded.

The big window in front is boarded up with plywood until Uncle Ronnie can have it replaced. Usually, that window is bordered with seasonal decorations that Ole Felix painstakingly paints every few months, more frequently if it's holiday season. Ole Felix isn't that old at all—only a handful of years older than my dad—but he has arthritis that makes him bend like a much older person. He lived on the block and used to help look after Ronnie and my dad when their mother was at her worst. According to Ronnie, his designs are getting less intricate as his arthritis advances.

When Ole Felix sees my dad, he just holds him, less like a peer and more like a father, and neither of them says a word for a really long time.

"These are my daughters, Ashley and Josephine," my dad says.

"I remember them when they were but so big." Ole Felix gestures down to knee-height and looks at us like he's proud of us for the act of growing. "You got a beautiful family now, Craig. Just beautiful."

Together we pick through the rubble and try to find things to keep.

I try to pretend like I'm Indiana Jones, but it feels like we're grave-robbing, except the grave is our grandma's, or maybe our whole family's. Every once in a while, my dad and Ronnie find something that makes them lean on each other, and you can tell what they found belonged to their mother.

They seem happy to be in the space together, joking and laughing about old times.

"Girls, come here . . . ," Daddy shouts from deep inside the store.

Jo and I follow his voice to the little cramped office in the back. He lifts up a heavy antique front-desk push bell, the kind of thing used to summon somebody from somewhere deep inside. And guess what shape it's in? It's a turtle! My father, the turtle, with his antique turtle bell.

I start to laugh. Jo and my father look at me quizzically.

"This was from your great-grandfather's office. It's one of the few things my grandmother took with her when they left Oklahoma."

First he passes it to Jo, who cradles it in her hand for a little while before passing it to me.

It's heavy in my palm. I run my hand along the ornate etching swirling this way and that across the bronze shell. The turtle pokes its head delicately out the front. I hold it in my hand and use my finger to press the shell, and it rings out loud and clear as day. I press it two more times. It's beautiful.

Jo walks over and puts her arms around my father, who has tears in his eyes. "Thank you, Daddy."

Afterward, we all go to Ronnie's house, my grandma's house, which still smells of lemons.

The mint-green paint I remember is faded and peeling in several places. The wood trim needs to be replaced. Still, the house is proud, the yard tidy, save for a few scattered fallen lemons. Uncle Ronnie's not like some people who, after their divorces, let their houses fall apart like their marriages.

"I'm gonna miss this place," Ronnie says.

Ronnie's decided he's going to rent the house out while he and Morgan figure things out in Vegas.

"You don't have to go," my father says. "This is your home. Here."

But I think maybe Ronnie's decided now it's his turn to run away.

Our grown-ups go over the insurance paperwork on a dining-room set that looks like it's been there since my father and uncle were boys kicking each other under the table while doing homework.

A big burn mark shaped like a lake mars the polished wood in the middle. Jo runs her fingers along its edges.

"That's from when your father was ten and he tried to make a tuna casserole for dinner, but he put it down on the table fresh out the oven without putting something under it," Morgan says.

She knows all the stories that Jo and I do not. Morgan's lived in our fathers' old memories her entire life. I wonder how cramped that must've been, growing up with ghosts.

I try to picture my father and uncle as they must've been, two little black boys who had to fend for themselves while their mother either worked too hard or lay up in her room, too depressed.

"It's too quiet in here," Ronnie says, as though he can hear my thoughts.

He walks over to the record player and puts something on; a swell of strings and wah-wahs before a familiar voice rings out high and clear even through the elderly speakers.

Ronnie and my father both start singing along, moving their bodies percussively and mumbling through the lyrics until they get to the chorus, which they sing loudly so that it echoes off the small walls in passable harmony. *"And we've got love / We've got love / We've got love (we've got love) / We've got love (we got love).'"*

"Shit, Craig, remember when Mama . . ."

The both of them start laughing superhard, even though it's an unfinished thought.

"Go outside," my father says.

"We're not ten," Morgan says.

"Don't matter," Ronnie says. "Here."

He reaches into a hidey-hole in the kitchen containing a seemingly endless supply of hoarded plastic bags, gives us each two, and tells us to pick all the lemons we can from the trees.

"Maybe in Vegas, your dad'll be able to sing for a living," I say to Morgan. "Plenty of places for him to audition there."

"I don't know," Morgan says. "He's kinda old for that now . . ."

"But maybe?" I say.

"Yeah. You never know . . ." Jo drifts off elsewhere.

"Do you remember Grandma Shirley at all?" I ask.

Jo surprises me by actually answering. "She was good at chess and smelled like baby powder and wasn't a good cook. I remember I didn't like her cooking when we would come over. Daddy said she was too impatient to be a good cook."

She laughs.

"I didn't know you remembered her at all."

"It's just small things. I was too little to remember that much . . . Oh! Once, I broke this fancy vase that had belonged to her mother, and Daddy started to yell at me about it, but I remember she didn't. Instead she held me in her arms while I cried and told me we could put it back together. The two of us."

"I see her walking around sometimes," Morgan says after a long pause. "Grandma Shirley, I mean."

"What? Like Casper?"

"I know what I see." Morgan pouts, and I think she may actually be serious.

"But does she look like Casper or like a person? Is she a good ghost or a scary ghost?"

Movies and television have taught me that ghosts are people with unfinished business, like in *Ghost*. Maybe we're Grandma Shirley's unfinished business. Maybe our family's a little like the vase Jo broke, and somehow all of us have to put it back together. From inside the house, I hear Uncle Ronnie and my father laughing together, deep brotherly belly laughs.

Instead of responding to me, Morgan hits me with a lemon,

and I duck and hit her right back. Then she, Jo, and I run around the yard pelting one another and laughing while the fruit cracks open on our bodies, flies buzzing around us, our clothes soaked in bittersweet.

When we get home from Uncle Ronnie's, Lucia tells me she's going back to Guatemala to visit Umberto and Roberto. She hasn't booked a return flight, hasn't figured out what happens after that.

Lucia has told me all about the beauty of Guatemala—the sun-soaked days spent searching for Mayan artifacts with her cousins; the colorful carpets made of sawdust and flowers and painstakingly worked on by artisans and families alike for the Holy Week processions through colonial ruins; nights spent camping out with her friends on actual volcanoes; standing on the roof of her house in the middle of a lightning storm and looking around in wonder—but all we ever hear about is the blood. Three years ago, an American nun was gang-raped and tortured. Two years ago, an American innkeeper there was beaten and all but decapitated. And this year, a guerrilla married to an American was tortured to death. The only reason it even made the news here is because there was some connection to the United States. Damarís used to squint her eyes at the television whenever these awful things would make their way to our newscasts and say to Lucia, "It's the Americans."

I guess that's exactly how you'd view black people if you were from elsewhere and all you knew of us came from the news, like the riots. Still, I'm afraid for her.

"What about Jose?" I ask.

"*Que sera, sera*. But first, it's time to see my boys." She reaches over next to her and passes me an envelope. "The mail came."

It's from Stanford. If this were a few days earlier, if this were a different story, I'd leap up at the sight of it. It's funny how a few days changes everything.

"I love you." I put the envelope down, walk over to her, and hug her.

"*Siempre,*" Lucia says.

The clouds in the sky are small and dense like babies. I look down at the envelope next to me. I've picked it up several times, started to open it, and then dropped it back on the roof. I don't care, but also I do. It starts to slide down, and I quickly grab it before it falls off. Jo crawls out to join me from her bedroom window.

"You're not supposed to be up here," she says.

"I'm not the one who fell off," I say.

"I didn't fall," she says quietly.

"I know," I say.

She pauses for a little bit.

"Guess I fucked that up." Her chipped teeth whistle the tiniest bit when she laughs. I look over at her incredulously, but she looks down at the envelope next to me.

"Small envelope," I say.

"Sometimes good things come in small packages."

Mrs. Katz waters the plants around their yard while Mr. Katz suns his pecs.

"Home from school?" Mrs. Katz shouts over at Jo as she bends a watering can over some succulents.

"For now." Jo smiles. It's not her real one, but they don't know that.

"Open it," she says to me. "Your future awaits! Something good's gotta happen to one of us, at least."

My future didn't get in off the wait-list at Stanford. And with the rejection letter goes some version of myself that I had imagined, but there are new versions to imagine. Other schools. I'm in at Occidental, all of the Claremont schools, USC, UCLA, and Cal. Each of them hold other future versions of me. Maybe better versions, even.

Jo frowns, then pats my thigh.

"You're gonna be okay, Ash," she says. I'm not sure whether we're still talking about college.

Still reclining on the lounge chair, Mr. Katz reaches out a hand and runs it up and down Mrs. Katz's leg while she tends to their plants, sliding his fingers under the edge of her shorts.

"Omigod, they're such horndogs," Jo whispers.

"I guess it's kinda nice that they still love each other that much," I say.

"Love is good," Jo murmurs.

"I wanna be good. I wanna be happy. Sometimes it feels like there's so much that I want," I tell my sister.

"Me too." Jo sighs.

"I'm afraid," I whisper. "Are you afraid?"

She doesn't answer. Instead she stands up on the roof and stretches her arms out to either side of her like she's a plane.

"Be careful," I say, but then I stand up too. She reaches her hand out to mine. I grab it and extend my right arm so that we are, the two of us, planes together. A slight breeze rustles through the trees, pressing against our skin. The sun runs down the length of our wings. The Pacific glitters; everything is a little sun-drenched and desaturated except for our brown fingertips against the blue.

"It's so beautiful, isn't it?" Jo says.

"We don't got a lot to compare it to," I say.

We've traveled, but not as much as some of my peers, and mostly to places where you could still pronounce the city names. I've already decided that when I get older, I'm going to have a passport full of stamps, so many that I'll have to keep getting new passport pages. Maybe when we're older and she's better and I'm whatever it is I turn out to be, we'll get to see the world together: Paris! Istanbul! Djibouti!

"Doesn't matter—just look at it. Look!"

Jo inhales it all in, content to be right here, right now. Home.

("You better get your little asses off that roof," my father yells.)

CHAPTER 25

THE NIGHT BEFORE, *you will climb into bed with me and will be more talkative than usual, even though all I'll want to do is sleep.*

"Ash?" you'll say.

"What?" I'll say.

"I'm sorry I'm not better," you'll say. "You deserve better."

"Better than what?" I'll say.

You'll scoot in closer so that your breath is hot on my face, and I'll be able to smell the night's Thai food from your favorite restaurant, sweet like curry but sour from the hours.

"You didn't brush your teeth," I'll say, and you'll open your mouth, blow on my face, and laugh.

"Tell me everything I don't know about you," you'll say.

I won't know what to tell you, how to give you all the things in my head. Somehow it's easier to tell these things to people who aren't blood, to share pieces of yourself with people who have no pieces of you in them.

"There's not that much to tell," I'll say. I'll want to say more, and

you'll look disappointed but nod like you understand.

"Will you visit me? During your breaks from school, I mean?"
you'll say.

*"Of course," I'll say. I'll mean it when I say it, but after that first
time I visit it'll get harder and harder. I'll tell you all about school and
how I'm not sure what I want to major in but I'm leaning toward
biochem, and how I'm thinking about rushing but I don't know how
I feel about sororities, even if they are the black ones. You'll sit there
and listen and nod and say, "Maybe I should've done that . . ." And
I'm not sure which part of that you're referring to, but maybe all of it.*

*That night you'll sleep soundly. You won't thrash at all. In the dark
of early dawn, I'll lean my ear to your mouth to make sure you're still
breathing. I'll feel your life in small gusts against my cheek.*

*The morning we take you in will be chillier than usual. The fog will
feel like it's suffocating everything. You'll sit between her legs as Mom
braids your hair into two French braids and fastens them with little
colored bands still hidden in the back of drawers from our childhood.
You'll pull on an old sweater and jeans with some sneakers.*

"You're wearing that?" I'll say.

*"It's not a fashion show, Ash." You laugh, although there's no real
joy behind it. "Besides, I'm not going to get to keep any of it with me."*

*Harrison will pace back and forth as we eat breakfast. He'll drive
everyone crazy by doting on you excessively—is your breakfast too hot,
too cold, does your coffee have enough creamer, enough sugar, do you
need anything else, anything at all—until you finally grab his hands,
lean your forehead against his, and say, "Enough, love."*

*All of us will pile into Mom's car except for Lucia, who will kiss
you on both your cheeks and hug you tight like someone who doesn't*

know when she might get to see you again. She will whisper something in your ear, but none of us will hear it. We'll just see you squeeze her harder and not let go, until Mom tells you, "It's time, Josephine."

"Escucha a tus padres," Lucia will say to you as she takes her thumbs and wipes away your tears.

"Let Ash drive," you'll say. "She needs the practice, right?"

"I have my license already, remember?"

"So what? Practice makes perfect."

I'll carefully take each curve down the hills and onto the freeway. I'll be so nervous I almost miss the entrance to the 10, and Daddy will yell, "No! Your left! Get to your left!" but you'll say, "Dad, she's got it."

Before that I'll have the radio on, KIIS, which you used to love to talk shit about, but today we'll both sing along to "Hold On" by Wilson Phillips until I almost hit somebody merging right and Dad turns it off and we both go, "Oh, come on!"

"Ashley needs to concentrate," he'll say. "She's about to get us all killed."

You'll stick your face out the window like a dog, feeling the wind on your skin, and your curls will bounce and stretch in the breeze into and out of your face and your mouth and plaster to your forehead.

Several times, I'll catch Harrison staring at you as if to memorize every pore on your face.

We'll have to circle the structure two times before we find a spot.

"Geez! Are this many people going to jail?" I'll say, and you'll start to laugh. It'll be obvious that I'm trying to make Mom laugh because her lip is quivering, because you can see the rainstorms brewing on her face and in her head, and I'll try to find the sunshine.

"Mom, don't," you'll say. "Don't. For me. Please."

"Look! I didn't get us all killed!" I'll say as I finally pull into the space.

We'll march in a solemn procession toward the building. You'll link arms with Mom and Harrison and Dad, and I'll straggle behind. Downtown, the sun will beam down on the tops of our heads. Dad will throw his arm over my shoulder and it'll feel a little comforting, but mostly I'll notice the weight of his sad bearing me down.

You'll stop steps away from the entrance. We'll see all kinds of people enter, but we'll notice how many of them are black, how many of them are brown. We'll feel it circle around us as a family, this shared, unspoken thing. A man will nod his head at Daddy, and they will understand each other for a moment, as the man walks inside with somebody he loves.

"I think maybe . . . I don't want you to come inside," you'll say to us, and our parents will stand there stunned.

"But, Josephine . . ." Mom trails off and doesn't fight it much, because I don't think she wants to go inside either. She doesn't want to see what happens next.

In the end, it's Harrison who will go inside with you to see you off. When he comes back outside to us, his red eyes puffy and his cheeks tearstained, he'll say, "She's all set."

And that's the last thing any of us will say for a while that day.

Inside, you will be stripped and searched and showered. You will be given a set of clothing, underwear, socks, white sneakers. You will be given an inmate number.

That first night, as you lie awake in the middle of all those unfamiliar sounds, you'll think of Harrison and Mom and Dad and Lucia; your thoughts will drift to Latasha, and to Grandma Shirley. In that *moment, the jail will briefly remind you of the gymnasium after the wildfire, all those people breathing, snoring, and being, all that life pumping all around you like an organ.*

One woman will cry and one woman will laugh, and their voices will echo off the walls so that you won't be sure which one of them is doing which. That's it right there, isn't it? you think.

Mostly, you'll stare out at the handful of stars that manage to shine through the smog and city lights, the ones that beg to be seen, that push their way through. You'll look at the brightest and think of me.

And across town, I will think of you.

CHAPTER 26

THE HOT SAND feels almost ancestral. There's a picture in our house of a very young Grandma Opal and a bunch of pretty black women in two-pieces, their arms wrapped around one another, their brown legs planted like flags in the sand.

"That was three months after I arrived in California," Grandma Opal said when I asked her about it. "Santa Monica was still segregated then."

"What?" Jo and I said in unison. "Here?"

"That doesn't make any sense," I said.

"None of it ever did," Grandma Opal said, and shooed us off so she could nap.

This land is your land. This land is my land. This beach is your beach. This beach is my beach. Today this beach is ours. For now, anyway.

LaShawn wears socks with Adidas slides, and I don't know why he's wearing socks to the beach, but I've noticed it's a thing a lot of black dudes do, like they're afraid of their toes.

The skateboarder's hair is sun-bleached, shaggy, and almost as long as Lana's. His lips look chapped. If we were in the Natural History Museum, this would be his natural habitat behind the glass.

"Sorry, dudes!" he says as he skates past an overflowing trash can.

Gutter punks lean against each other on a small grassy knoll, faces tattooed so that they look like lizards, with their one-legged pit bull and a sign that says, NEED FOOD FOR THE DOG . . . AND ALCOHOL.

I place a dollar in their empty open guitar case.

"Thanks, sis!" the scariest-looking one replies.

We march past the gutter punks with their mangy dog and the skateboarders who nearly run us over and the families with entirely too much shit to stake our claim. LaShawn's slides fling sand all over everything with each step until finally he takes them off, socks too, and I see his toes, which aren't scary at all.

When we decide on our spot, LaShawn plants the umbrella in the sand like he's Neil Armstrong or Buzz Aldrin.

Aldrin's first words on the moon were, "Beautiful view."

Then Armstrong replied, "Isn't that somethin'? Magnificent sight out here."

Which is exactly how I feel right now.

Lana and I drop our stuff in the sand, peel off our land selves, and trudge toward the water's edge. We squeal at the cold and push in farther, LaShawn tentative steps behind us.

"I . . . I can't swim, you guys," he says.

"We won't go too far," Lana says.

Lana and I close our eyes and dive into handstands, only to get pushed and pulled by the tide. LaShawn stands awkwardly at the water's edge.

"We won't let you drown," Lana says. "Promise."

LaShawn comes closer and closer to us until finally he submerges himself for a one-two count and then pops back up with a primal scream. The three of us splash around in the water until Lana leaves to go use the restroom—number two, so she can't just pee in the water, she makes sure to tell us. Then it's the two of us amid the seaweed and the salt. The waves push LaShawn farther out, until it's harder for our toes to reach the ocean floor.

"Maybe we should go back," he says.

"Not yet," I say. "Try this."

I show him a basic breaststroke. It's simple enough, I tell him, like making a heart with your arms and then breaking it, over and over, but the heart is what keeps you afloat, keeps you going. He starts to do it, his hearts getting stronger and stronger still, until he dips his head briefly underwater and comes back up sputtering, but with a big grin.

"I got you," I say.

"Yeah?"

"Yeah," I say.

He turns around and faces the city. "It's so different from here, isn't it? Somehow, out here, it's like nothing happened at all."

A big wave knocks against both of us, and we push our limbs and chests and hips against its force.

I think about the dried-out husks of buildings I saw when we were volunteering with Tarrell and Julia. What's gonna happen to all the vacant lots like weeping wounds when everybody's moved on to the next thing? What's gonna happen to the people who live among them? You can already feel it in the air—the rest of the city beginning to forget.

"It's kinda like the riptide or current or whatever they're always warning you about on the weather reports. Everyone around you can be playing, having fun, all oblivious and shit; meanwhile, you're getting swept out to sea," he says.

To our right, two little blond kids in bright-orange floaties swim by with their mother, who wears one of those water skirts that some women wear when they start being ashamed of the puckers and dimples like little hiding spots in their thighs. One of her kids splashes me in the face as he swims past, and the salt water burns up my nose.

"Sorry," she says. "Tommy, pay attention to other people."

Heather appears, and with her, Courtney. Apparently, Lana told them about our little gathering without me knowing.

"I thought you weren't supposed to talk to me," I say.

"I wouldn't miss your eighteenth birthday!" Courtney says. "Besides, I'm my own person."

There's a series of wriggles in her beach blanket, and then finally out pops a head, small and vaguely mangy.

"The shelter gave me a graduation puppy!" Courtney squeals. "I named her Pepper, 'cause she's a little spicy. Isn't she the cutest?"

"You better watch out. Bitch pees everywhere," Heather says, and kisses me on the top of my head.

"Don't talk about Pepper like that," Courtney says, and squeezes Pepper closer.

"It was a joke." Heather shakes her head at Courtney.

"Oh yeah. Duh." Courtney laughs.

Heather runs her hands along my braids. "You look so different. It suits you."

I'm about to tear up, but I push my tears back down. Heather, Courtney, Kimberly, and I have celebrated every birthday together since we were six.

Kimberly and I were girls together, but we won't be women together, and maybe that's okay. In a few weeks we'll graduate, and then we'll go to college and make new friends, and after that maybe grad school and then out into the world, where we'll accumulate more people to hold on to. We'll float into each other's heads and remember how we belonged to each other only once in a while, and eventually maybe not at all.

As we're hugging, Pepper pees across her tanned leg, and Courtney shrieks, "Bad girl!"

She only means it a little bit.

A helicopter flies by with a floating ad for beer.

"If you kiss me, then I'll kiss you back," plays on somebody's boom box. Heather puckers her lips in my direction and laughs. She's splayed out reading some sort of zine. I thought Lana and Heather would hit it off the fastest, but Lana and Courtney did, surprisingly enough. They giggle a lot, and Lana gives Courtney's mangy new puppy lots of kisses as naughty Pepper jumps around the beach blanket between them. You're not supposed to have dogs on the

beach, but if anybody notices, they don't say anything. At some point, Courtney laughs really heartily and puts her hand on Lana's arm. Then Lana says, "I need more sunblock; can you help me?" While Courtney massages it into Lana's shoulders, Heather looks up from her zine and raises an eyebrow my way. Heather has dyed her hair and armpit hair bright purple. It suits her, although apparently her mom's pissed that she didn't wait until after graduation. I wouldn't have even thought to dye my armpit hair, if I kept any.

There's not quite enough space on our beach blanket, so part of my body rests in the sand, which sticks to my wet skin, but I don't mind. LaShawn's hand brushes mine, and in his fingertips I can feel the entire summer before us. He turns to look at me and smiles, his skin golden in the sunlight. I'm pretty positive I see the faint outline of a boner in his swim trunks. As if he can read my mind, he flips over onto his stomach.

Candace and Julia trudge through the sand toward us.

"You made it!" I say.

My new friends awkwardly greet my old friends.

"Candace did my hair," I tell Heather and Courtney.

"Dude! How long did that take you to do?" Heather says.

"About four hours," Candace says, and plops down next to them in the sand.

"I got my hair braided when I went to Mexico once," Courtney says.

Candace, Julia, and I start to laugh. Courtney doesn't know why we're laughing, and I feel a little bad, but not really. Sometimes there is an us, sometimes there is a them, and sometimes it's okay to be a we.

We girls do lazy cartwheels in the sand. Maybe next year we'll be too old for these, but not now. Not yet.

I think outside of myself and look down at us in this moment—our skin browning in the sun, bodies leavening, planes flying overhead. What's next for all of us? It doesn't matter. In this moment, there's ocean in our hair, and we're awash in the glitter of possibility. We're girls in neon bikinis laughing. Soon, the world will crack wide open before us, and we will be women. Here we are.

Around us, seagulls squawk. Beach umbrellas sway. On the radio, the DJs are discussing how the cops in Rodney King's beating are getting a new federal trial. This new federal case will go the right way, though. Those cops will get convicted. The evidence is right there on video for anyone to see. Because things have to get better, don't they? Or maybe they don't. But we do.

The DJs banter for a bit, and then they open the lines to callers.

"What you think, fam?" the DJ says, like every one of us in this city is family.

LaShawn and I wring water from our hair and bathing suits into the sand, which we scoop into several dense mounds piled toward the sky that almost immediately start to crumble and slide. Then Heather and Lana run down to the water and come back giggling with handfuls that they pour over what we've started, while Courtney tries to keep Pepper from smashing it all. All of us work together, adding more water, more earth, digging our fingers in, building and rebuilding, until slowly it starts to look like something real.

ACKNOWLEDGMENTS

David Doerrer, my incredible agent, thank you for your tireless and painstaking work at getting this to be what it could be, and for seeing the potential in it and me. You are my favorite person that I never actually get to see in person. And thank you, Abrams Artists Agency, for having the good sense to employ him.

Zareen Jaffery, my story doula, I knew minutes into our first call that you got me and you got this. Thank you for your thoughtfulness and for pushing every single page of this to be better.

Adriana Bellet, thank you for the absolutely perfect piece of cover art. I shed the happiest of happy tears the first time I saw it.

To Justin Chanda, and everyone at Simon & Schuster, thank you for championing this story, I'm truly so lucky to have you. Dainese, Audrey, Shivani, Lisa, I appreciate you. Jane Griffiths at Simon & Schuster UK, thank you from the bottom of my heart for immediately recognizing the universality in Ashley's story. Anna Carmichael at Abner Stein, thank you for getting my words across the pond.

Lucy Ruth Cummins, many thanks for this bomb-ass super-dope totally tubular cover.

To my copyeditor, Benjamin Holmes, thank you for helping me not look like an idiot. For real.

To the late Adina Talve-Goodman, Patrick Ryan, and the team at One Teen Story—thank you for seeing the beauty in this story and being the first to put it out in the world. I'm so eternally grateful to you for starting me on this journey.

To the *Santa Monica Review*—thank you for being the first to give me a chance.

I would like to give a shout-out to all my English teachers, for the refuge and joy my awkward ass found in their classrooms—especially Mr. Einstein, Ms. Tracy, the late and lovely Mrs. Madrid, Ms. Cheney, Mr. Sawaya, and Mr. Platt (even if you weren't technically *my* English teacher).

Aimee Bender, thank you for your encouragement, for your recommendations, for being both an amazing writer and teacher, and for telling me not to go to law school if I was only going to do it because it was practical.

Mrs. View—to this day you are my favorite librarian.

Cal State Long Beach's Young Writers' Camp—you were my first little taste of heaven on earth.

Elizabeth, thank you for allowing me to foist my stories on you before I'd even figured out what to say or how, for being one of my first and most encouraging readers, and for being one of the bestest bffls a girl could ask for.

Hyemee, my cheerleader before you'd ever even read a word I'd written, my other bffl, I'm so grateful to you for your friendship. Should I ever have a guesthouse, it's yours. Don't tell Bizzle.

Justyn, my twinface, I'm so glad the universe threw the two of us kindred blerds in that dumb box together. This 100 percent wouldn't exist without you. Thank you to Mama Rose and Uncle E. and your mama for welcoming me into your home and your lives.

Liz, my oldest friend, I'm so grateful we're still in each other's lives.

Carmen Samayoa—for being an inspiration.

Jimmy Cabrera—for sharing the beauty of your homeland with me.

Derek, thank you for never letting me quit on myself, for holding me through my blue and basking with me in my yellow. There's no way I could even remotely communicate what you mean to me. May our future be full of dolphins.

To the Smiths and the Kings, thank you for your kindness and encouragement and for bringing him into being.

To my fellow Angelenos, I love you even when you suck.

To my fellow black kids, fragile and strong, nerdy and cool, weird and well-adjusted, ugly and beautiful, rich and poor, and everything in between—"we gon' be alright."

Daddy, Mommy, Alicia, and Reza—I love you. I love you. I love you. I love you. Everything I do is to make you proud. I hope you are.